## ALSO BY SILVANA G. SÁNCHEZ

*Be the first to know when Silvana's next book is available! Follow her on Bookbub to get an alert whenever she has a new release, preorder, or discount!*

# STEEL
## AND
# STONE

USA TODAY BESTSELLING AUTHOR
# SILVANA G. SÁNCHEZ

SECOND STAR PRESS

*To the brave ones who face their fears
and chase their dreams.
Steel and courage to the end.*

*It was many and many a year ago,*
*In a kingdom by the sea,*
*That a maiden there lived whom you may know*
*By the name of Annabel Lee;*
*And this maiden she lived with no other thought*
*Than to love and be loved by me.*

*I was a child and she was a child,*
*In this kingdom by the sea,*
*But we loved with a love that was more than*
        *love—*
*I and my Annabel Lee—*
*With a love that the winged seraphs of Heaven*
*Coveted her and me.*

*And this was the reason that, long ago,*
*In this kingdom by the sea,*
*A wind blew out of a cloud, chilling*
*My beautiful Annabel Lee;*
*So that her highborn kinsmen came*
*And bore her away from me,*
*To shut her up in a sepulcher*
*In this kingdom by the sea.*

The angels, not half so happy in Heaven,
Went envying her and me—
Yes!—that was the reason (as all men know,
In this kingdom by the sea)
That the wind came out of the cloud by night,
Chilling and killing my Annabel Lee.

But our love it was stronger by far than the love
Of those who were older than we—
Of many far wiser than we—
And neither the angels in Heaven above
Nor the demons down under the sea
Can ever dissever my soul from the soul
Of the beautiful Annabel Lee;

For the moon never beams, without bringing me
	dreams
Of the beautiful Annabel Lee;
And the stars never rise, but I feel the bright eyes
Of the beautiful Annabel Lee;
And so, all the night-tide, I lie down by the side
Of my darling—my darling—my life and my
	bride,
In her sepulcher there by the sea—
In her tomb by the sounding sea.

— ANNABEL LEE BY EDGAR
ALLAN POE

Iron Sea

TO THE
NETHERWORLD

Silvermoon
Ocean

STEELBORN
CASTLE

THE
STONE
KEEP

REALM OF MAN

# NETHERWORLD

MERMAID'S
CAPE

TEMPLE
OF NYX

CHARON'S
CAVE

TEMPLE
OF HECATE

The
Midnight Lake

WATCHTOWER
OF CHRONOS

Hecate's
Sanctuary

The Unlost
Forest

TEMPLE
OF HADES

Bridge
of Fate

River
Styx

WATCHTOWER
OF HYPNOS

Cape of
Despair

WATCHTOWER
OF THANATOS

Midnight
Sea

## AURORA STONEWALL

*I mustn't lose heart, even as I summon death itself.* Whisperings of courage linger in my mind, rippling through my being as the tempestuous sea lashes against the castle's ramparts, like an enraged beast, shaking the formidable Stone Keep to its foundations. The deafening roar of thunder gnaws at my resolve, but I hold the parchment tight in my trembling hands, looking past the abysmal fear that permeates my veins.

My kingdom's desolation demands the highest feat from their grieving princess. What few survived the sickness cling to life by the frailest thread of hope. For months, Stonewall has withered away, sustained solely by the Steelborn's coffers. A barren land might yet thrive, but a shattered heart cannot be as easily salvaged.

I've made my choice. And steeling my nerves, I read the final words: "Great and powerful Dark Lord of the Netherworld, I humbly call upon you!"

And so, my fate is sealed. May the gods help me.

The creased parchment slips from my fingers and drifts away, carried by a freezing draft that creeps inside the forlorn ballroom. Shrill terror skitters down my nape as I clench my jaw and brace myself for the unknown. One deep breath, heart racing, and my stomach clenched in anticipation.

"Aurora?" Maleath says, her voice a tremulous whisper. The burden of doubt and trepidation weighs heavily on her since she's handed me the spell.

I hush her softly. My gaze drifts to my bare feet and sweeps the gold veins that glitter against the pale moonlit marble. Seven candles burn brightly in their holders, dust motes fluttering above their flames like tiny gems. A handful of thorned roses lay beside a simple wooden bowl brimming with ripe pomegranates and a goblet of Bloodmoon Red—the finest wine known to the five realms.

My offering to Hades is complete.

My skin prickles in sacred fear as the first candle flickers. Its small flame wavers and quavers, as if dancing to an ancient melody. The second candle bursts into a resplendent glow, compelling me to stay rooted in place. I freeze, drawn to the silent spell, unable to move or speak, as one by one, each candle snuffs out its light and drags me into darkness.

I shudder as malefic oppression swells around me. How does a dark god make his presence known? The gods have their secrets, but I keep my own. Who will reveal theirs first?

"Aurora, I don't like this," Maleath breathes, clutching her arms as she recoils into a corner. "We should stop."

I stiffen at the suggestion. I've battled for so long to make peace with my decision. Surrendering my one chance of righting so many wrongs is not an option.

My lips part to speak, but the words dissolve at the sound of a third voice, deep and velvety like heated honey. "Oh, don't stop now," it purrs, a waft of cool air kissing my nape.

His presence fills the ballroom with an otherworldly sensation. I hold my breath, too frightened to move, too

2

charmed by his speech, when he adds with equal dark delight, "We're just getting started."

A searing bolt of electric blue light engulfs us in a flash, and I see Maleath's figure, stunned in terror. Her eyes widen in shock and confusion, angling upwards as they size the towering creature that stands behind me.

My heart lurches, the rawest dread flowing through my veins. I can't help a sly smile from curling the corner of my mouth, however. *It worked. At long last, I shall meet with the Prince of the Netherworld and persuade him to spare my people from the curse that dooms my kingdom.*

Cautiously, I spin around. My piercing gaze scours the depths of the dark room. A brief gasp sails through my lips when stray beams of silver moonlight stream inside, outlining the towering god, clad in shadow. His sole presence exudes power and authority.

Faint details subtly emerge in the soft light. He stands tall and proud, alluring with his chiseled jawline and striking hazel eyes, glittering amber in the night. A single pauldron and bracer compose his armor, its burnished steel gleaming with an ethereal luster. Cryptic symbols of the blackest ink pulse and writhe on his neck and chest.

This is Hades, ruler of the Netherworld. My life's story rests in his grasp.

I find myself drifting towards him inadvertently, and when scarce feet stand between us, I realize how small I am compared to him.

"My prince," I murmur, my eyes trained on the mysterious engravings of his steel footwear, symbols that match the brandings that adorn his sun-kissed skin.

After what seems like an eternity, he says, "A prince?" The words slide out on an icy breath. A mocking laughter follows. "Unlike *you*, my good fortune has spared me from the nuisance of a crown."

I start, my widened gaze cutting to his. With a frown, I ask, "Are you not Prince Hades, the ruler of the Netherworld?" My spirit wanes in dismay as the bleak thought crosses my mind—*I have failed.*

His feet spread firmly in a wide stance, hands resting on his slender hips. The god's darkened eyes bore into mine as an arrogant smirk tugs at his mouth. "Alas, I am not him," he replies, heaving a sigh. In silence, his interest shifts to my offering. Like a lion on the hunt, he prowls closer to the altar lying at his feet. Finally, he reaches out, and with deft fingers, he plucks a red rose from its bouquet. Rolling it between his digits, he inhales its sweetness and sneers. "Mm. A favorite of Hades." He pauses, deep in contemplation. "I prefer poppies and lavender myself." With contemptuous ease, the flower tumbles from his grip, falling onto the floor like an unwanted toy.

*Poppies and lavender.* "Then you must be..." I venture.

"I *am* his chosen emissary," he declares curtly as he rises, his gaze raking me with an icy glance. "Princess Aurora, Stonewall's sovereign... It's high time you presented your offering to the gods of the Netherworld." His spite resounds throughout the room with the weight of a funeral bell. "What do you want?" he utters in a low, menacing growl, looking down at me as he slowly folds his arms across his chest.

The challenge in his tone stings my pride, dispelling all my fears, and the words roll off my tongue with the conviction that comes with a royal upbringing, "I want to meet with Hades. Take me to the Realm of Death."

An unreadable expression crosses his face, surprise and suspicion vying for control.

"Aurora, no!" Maleath cries.

But the god pays no heed to the sound. His interest

clings solely to me. He tilts his head, fierce, as he inches closer. "Why?" he drawls.

My eyes brim with tears as I utter the words, "The sickness has spread through my kingdom, causing countless losses and pain." My body shudders as my own grief comes back to haunt me. "Only Hades can put an end to this devastation." I suck in a deep breath, struggling to quell my emotions.

Dark delight flickers across the god's visage, and the stillness breaks when a tremulous laugh erupts from his lips and echoes off the ballroom's bare walls. "Ah... grief," he says, stifling his amusement. The god circles around the room, still not deigning to spare Maleath a thought. "A curious thing, indeed. You do realize, no one who's crossed the River Stix has ever returned to tell the tale," he warns me, his dark brown eyebrows arching softly.

But my spirit is unconquered. I'm driven by a power no force can extinguish. I am the Princess of Stonewall, and I *will* save my kingdom. Raising my chin defiantly, I reply, "I am aware of this risk."

"Mm." He shrugs in nonchalance. "If it means that much to you..." he pensively says, sauntering towards me.

"Aurora!" Maleath implores, desperation straining her voice.

"Silence, girl!" the god roars, his eyes burning with the Netherworld's flames.

With feline stealth, he stalks closer. A shiver runs through me as the devious god stops, his wide-shouldered frame towering over me. When his eyes bore into mine, their fire dwindles into the pleasant warmth of summer. He slowly lifts his hand and reaches towards me in a gracious gesture of invitation, and his voice comes divinely sensuous when he says, "Come with me, my princess, and I shall whisk you away from these sorrows."

## PHILLIP STEELBORN

*T*he Stone Keep rises in the stormy night amid furious lightning. Despite the raging maelstrom, the fortress withstands; its thick grey stone walls and unshakeable turrets, everlasting, indomitable as the sea that swells against them.

Anticipation builds up in my chest as I ride into the citadel earlier than planned, a fortnight prior to the day when my beloved princess and I exchange our wedding vows. The celebrations will extend for weeks, providing much-needed respite to the townsfolk who've endured the sickness' retribution.

Eager to surprise my sweet Aurora, I sneaked out of Steelborn Castle and slipped into the retinue that travels to her kingdom each full moon, attending to the needs of its ailing people and stocking up Stonewall's provisions.

As the caravan takes shelter in the citadel, I hasten across the towering iron gates, into the stillness of the castle, where my betrothed surely sleeps. I long to wake her from a sound-less dream, stealing from her supple mouth a kiss, deeper than the ones we've shared in her bedchamber's secrecy.

I rid myself of the sodden cloak as I move across the desolated great hall, into the vast corridor that leads to the stairwell. The long gallery seems to stretch for an eternity. I march forth, but halt at the roar of boisterous laughter as it breaks into the hallway—a sound so foreign in these days of mourning.

My blood freezes as I veer, my steps chasing the faint clatter of steel armor. I stop at the ballroom doors, and taking a deep breath, I cool my racing thoughts, considering only what waits beyond the threshold. Tragedy has weakened Aurora's kingdom, making it perfect prey to scoundrels and raiders.

I slowly exhale as my hand folds on the door handle, preparing myself to face my enemy.

The door creaks open, and a chill drops down my spine when I find my sweetest love, standing in the middle of the murky ballroom. She's dressed in her white sleeping gown, a moonbeam in a sea of shadows.

She's not alone. Maleath Snow, Princess of Whitehaven, seconds her, although she cringes in the corner, her light blue eyes swiftly meeting mine in soundless despair.

Horror spears through my heart when I finally see. A creature, too vile to call human, despite his mortal guise of golden brown skin and sparkling hazel eyes. His presence grows towering in the dark, his burnished armor glinting with unholy light.

A god walks among us. Not one I would worship, but the most damnable. *A Guardian of the Netherworld.* None to roam this realm do so on a sinless whim. Has he come to claim my dearest love? The sole thought hollows my soul.

Stealthily, I step forward, the heel of my hand easing its way to the hilt of my sword, Dawnbreaker. "You are not welcome here, harbinger of darkness," I denounce as every inch of me goes taut in silent anger.

The creature eyes me with an indolent glare. "Harbinger of Darkness?" he echoes with no inclination. "Nice title, but I've been called better."

I stalk forward, my expression hardened with rampant fury. "This kingdom has seen enough death and desolation." I clench tight my weapon's grip, and as I stand scarce feet away from the vicious god, I roar, "Go back to the Netherworld and never return!"

My beloved gasps in dread behind me.

The god squares his shoulders, looking down at me with stirred interest. "Do you dare face me in battle," he challenges in a low voice, his gaze drifting to my sword's hilt, "or will you turn away from greatness?"

A shallow breath escapes my parted lips. My heart rattles in my chest, eager for the confrontation. Slowly, my sword glides free from its scabbard. "I've faced your kind before. Many times, in several wars," I murmur, locking an icy stare with his. "And from those encounters, I've always walked out the victor."

The malevolent creature lets out a sinister laugh. "You cannot defeat me, mortal," the god hisses, and wearing an unbearable sneer, he rubs a hand across his chin, musing on what my next step might be.

"I need only to dispel you from these grounds," I mutter, brandishing my weapon with unwavering conviction.

The god's smirk spreads into a grin. His fierce eyes twinkle with wickedness. "Very well," he rumbles, rage stealing all amusement from his features.

With no warning, a flaming sword materializes in his grip, swinging high as he explodes, "Show me the might of your blade, human!"

Our swords clash in a mighty clang that sets off sparks of silver sputtering in the dark. He snarls and grates away his blade, only to unleash a flurry of strikes and thrusts. But I meet each one with grace and unabated fierceness, unde-terred, as the dark god continues his onslaught.

He swings again in a vicious arc, yet I parry the creature's blow with a force that renders his attack useless. We face each other, locked steel against steel, and his strength is unre-lenting.

"Foolish mortal..." he growls, inching closer to my face. "I am a god!" He shoves forth with the might of a thousand storms.

I brace myself, holding my stance, and steeling my resolve, I utter through clenched teeth, "You're flesh and blood now." In a flash, my free hand seizes the dagger cinched to my leg, and in one quick thrust, I stab the knife into his face, leaving a burning line of rage on the dark god's cheek.

Bright crimson liquid smears the dagger's edge as lazy rivulets spill down his face. When the first drop splatters on the floor, the god wavers in astonishment. His sword's grip relaxes, and he recoils, appalled.

I seize the chance, and swing my blade in silver fury, thirsting for the monster's head. The glistening steel cuts through the air, veering firmly towards its target when a voice, brittle like crystal, speaks, "Phillip, don't!"

I start at the sound. "Aurora?" I utter in dismay.

"Put down your sword, please!" she begs, her voice quiv-ering as she moves towards us. "I summoned him." My sweetest love moves forward, extending an appeasing hand to the monster standing at the point of my blade.

I blink in disbelief, unable to make sense of the scene that plays before me. "My dearest, what have you done?" I manage, my brows tangled in a frown.

"I've had enough," the dark god says under his breath, his vicious eyes boring into my betrothed's. "Come with me, princess."

Stunned, I discover she does not protest.

"You may *not* have her!" I lash out, fury streaming through my veins like brushfire. "For all eternity or *any* other part of time. She is mine, and she will remain here until our days have passed!"

The god's interest shifts towards me, unearthly fire gleaming in his feral stare when a sudden chill races through the room, enclosing us in a hazy embrace. Icy air clings to my skin, as with each ragged breath to leave my parted lips, tendrils of white mist coil around my face.

Frost creeps up the walls and crackles on the ballroom's mirrors. Time slows down. The frigid stillness fills me, so deep and all-encompassing, that it feels as though my blood itself has frozen.

"Aurora," I speak softly, pleadingly, "don't leave me."

I read the struggle of battling emotions on her flawless face as she turns towards me. "Phillip," she entreats me, her voice laced with sweetness and dread, "I can't escape my fate."

For the first time in my life, true fear crawls into my soul. The thought of facing a dark god barely phases me, but standing on the brink of losing my beloved shatters my every certainty.

My pulse quickens as I fervently reply, "Your *fate* lies here!" Fathomless angst breaks my voice. "You belong with your people—*with me!*"

No response comes, save the glimmer of pain mirrored in her pale blue eyes, so I step closer.

Her hand trembles slightly as I take it, my thumb gently brushing over the ornate diamond ring adorning her finger. "You are my betrothed," I murmur, my voice low. "Let this ring be a reminder of your promise. Let it bind you to me now."

The glittering jewel in her hand holds her in a daze, as Aurora contemplates the whisperings of her heart.

"Ignore the fool." A raspy voice tears her from the trance. The dark god saunters closer, his wavy chestnut hair dancing with an otherworldly gleam and his face wrought with gloom.

"I am a *prince!*" I bellow, my voice reverberating in the vast chamber, its very walls shaking in fear of my wrath.

The beast raises a scornful eyebrow. "Let me rephrase," he snarls, standing tall behind my beloved. And inching close to her ear, he adds, "Ignore the *royal* fool, my princess. End this now, and I will take away your pain."

"Aurora…" Her name leaves my lips like a fervent prayer.

"Make your choice!" the deity roars, restless like an untamed beast.

My love's face swings towards me, sweet eyes boring into mine. "I must choose *you*," she breathes, and her delicate hand quivers as the golden ring glides off her finger. She steps away as it falls, a profound clank ringing when it hits the marble floor.

"Do it now!" Her voice resounds with power and conviction as she faces the loathsome creature.

The warmth of forthcoming tears gathers in my eyes as my heart shatters into a thousand shards. Painfully, I realize begging her to stay would never do, for all my efforts have been hopeless. I'm forced to admit it—her love for me was never true.

The god bows deeply before her, proffering his hand. "My princess," he whispers.

"Aurora, no!" Maleath utters, a cry that comes too late.

Aurora's pale hand reaches for the god's. No sooner have her fingertips grazed the creature's palm than a brief cry escapes her. Flustered in dismay, my beloved retrieves her hand, revealing the thorny prickle in the god's grasp that stabbed her skin. And as a single bead of crimson rolls down her finger, she staggers back, and just as fast, tumbles to the ground.

I swiftly catch her in my arms, easing her down as she drifts into unconsciousness. "My love," I manage hoarsely through labored breaths, praying to my long-forgotten gods that she might hear me. But Aurora does not stir, her features pale and still; her frail form lies motionless in the center of this darkened room.

My body quakes, as merciless agony builds up inside me until it bursts through my throat in a wild roar of grief. Glazed with rage, my stare cuts to the dark god, and finds him, melting back into the swirls of shadows whence he came.

Maleath's moan of anguish rings hard in my ears as she stumbles towards my fallen princess. Glistening streams of sorrow streak down her porcelain cheeks, dread hardening her sapphire gaze. "Dearest gods," Maleath whispers, taking a hand to her lips. "I never should have told her of the ritual!"

The words stab me like a thousand knives, and I call to mind the memory of my beautiful Aurora, asking me to trust in Maleath's friendship—a decision that now cost me my love's life.

My desperate eyes stumble on the lingering shadow portal where the god once stood, then drift to the items gathered at my beloved's feet. Seven candles, thorned roses, a lavish jug of Bloodmoon Red. "An offering to Hades..." I blink out of my stupor. "Maleath, what have you done?" My voice comes low, a tortured cry.

Stricken with sorrow, I find the will to lean closer to her, and all but hiss, "Why would you worship a dark god of the Netherworld?" Accusation and wretchedness lace my words.

Tears gather in the corners of her eyes. Her voice shudders as she says, "I thought his power could save us all. I never imagined... I only meant to ease Aurora's suffering."

My chest tightens as I listen. Finally, I lash out, "So you summoned *a monster to kill her?*" with all the righteousness of a grieving lover.

Stark silence falls upon us, prickled only by Maleath's sobs. I swallow hard against the raging sorrow clawing its way through my chest. Countless emotions overwhelm me—guilt for not arriving sooner, despair for losing the woman I've loved so dearly. Without her, I've lost everything. The blazing love we've shared has burned to ashes like the dream of the life we'd build together.

Tears pool in my eyes, threatening to spill down my cheeks. I suck in a deep breath, composing myself as my gaze wanders over Aurora's face, contemplating every inch of her features, branded in my heart since the first time we met.

"Phillip," Maleath gasps. "She's breathing!"

Hope blossoms in my heart as her words sink in. I stumble to her side, desperate to believe them. My fingers tremble as they brush Aurora's cold cheek, searching for the smallest response. But I find nothing.

"A sleeping curse," I whisper as the realization hits me.

"Hypnos, the Lord of Slumber..." Maleath's voice stretches into silence until her body starts quivering in fury. "It was him! He tricked her!" she hisses with aching indignation.

I sit on the marble floor, drained, knowing I can do nothing to wake Aurora from this curse. Slowly, I shake my head. "What am I to do now?" I whisper, almost to myself, frustration and gloom tangling in my throat.

"Go after him," Maleath says with rekindled spiritedness. "The portal is still open. Chase Hypnos to the Netherworld and claim back Aurora's soul!" She urges me, her eyes flaring with conviction.

"I can't do that," I say under my breath, my hands curling into tight fists.

"Only *you* can bring her back!" she insists. "No warrior in the five realms is more skilled or more valiant than you!" Maleath stops to catch her breath. "Phillip, *you wounded a dark god!*"

Throwing my head back, my gaze shoots to the ceiling, and I sigh heavily, the weight of my duties crushing me like a millstone. When I look down, I drag my fingers through my hair and say, "You don't understand, Maleath! I would give *my life* if it meant I might bring her back. But I simply cannot risk it. I cannot forsake my kingdom *and* hers. Stonewall is in ruins as it is! The people need me!" My voice trembles as heartbreak seizes my throat. "Fires of the Netherworld, this is all *your* fault!"

My stare flickers up, long enough to catch a glimpse of the portal to darkness as it gradually dissolves.

"No one can know I had *anything* to do with this!" Maleath implores, clutching a hand to her chest. "If my father finds out, he'll cast me away, just like his mistress threatened." Her head hangs low, tears trickling down her blushing cheeks. "I've already lost my dearest mother—the same as you did. My heart will never mend if I'm forced away from him."

"Go back to Whitehaven," I reply quietly, my empty gaze locked on my beloved's face. "Speak of this to no one."

"But what about—?"

"We'll figure it out, Mal. Now go!" I urge.

She nods and rises to her feet, easing a gentle hand on my shoulder. "Keep her safe, Phillip," she whispers, "for Stonewall *and* for us." A bitter smile curls the corner of her mouth. Maleath quickly whirls and hurries off, her white fur cloak billowing behind her like moonlight on a cloudless night.

My heart races, pounding hard against my chest as the ballroom doors snap shut and Aurora and I are left alone. In this bleak stillness, the pain of her betrayal clings to my bleeding heart. And as my first tears spill down my face, I mourn—not the curse of my beloved, but the death of what I thought was our truest love.

I clear the tears away with the back of my hand and prop myself on one knee when the diamond glints off the marble floor, beckoning me with its sparkling light. I slide towards it, the tip of my fingers brushing against its smoothness.

Taking one last look at my beloved's face, illuminated by the moonlight streaming through the windows, I gather her hand in mine, reflecting on the softness of her skin against my firmness.

"Know this, my love," I whisper, tears pooling in my eyes. "You will always have my heart, which you have broken beyond repair." Tenderly, I ease the ring onto her delicate finger. "From this day forth, I vow to protect you and all you hold dear, though I can never again breathe the same air as your kingdom."

I bow my head and press my lips to my beloved's hand, allowing my kiss to linger. "Until the fires of the Netherworld extinguish, and all debts have been repaid…" I achingly murmur. "Goodbye, my love. I will never forget you."

# PRESENT DAY

Seven Years Later

# 1

# PHILLIP

"*coup*?" I started, reluctant to believe Maleath could fathom the penalties of treason. Stunned, I stared at the woman before me who, but a few weeks ago, had been a graceful princess—comely and subdued in nature, dressed in the finest silk gowns and the most exquisite jewels. Now, her breeches clung to her like a second skin, a rogue brand marked her delicate wrist, and her ebony tresses hung down in wild fae-like braids. I struggled to recognize her beneath this new façade. The warrior queen before me was a far cry from who she'd once been.

"Look around the great hall," Maleath intoned. "Do you see the fae hovering around the musician's platform? They will be my sword and shield. See the men cloaked in black hoods? They are the most powerful mages known to man— The Seven."

"Mercenaries of magic," I muttered in stern disapproval. Legends spoke of them as the most brutal raiders, and I had no wish to join their undesirable fellowship.

"Stay close to your sword, Phillip," Maleath warned me,

her determined eyes burning into mine. "Battle and blood are coming."

Sheer black dread washed over me as I heard the words, not for my sake, but for what I knew would come of them. "Battle and…?" I managed, disbelief tinging my voice. "No…" I shook my head, the blood freezing in my veins as I stepped back, noticing the hooded figures hidden in the bustling horde gathered in Whitehaven Castle for the Fae King's coronation. An ambush was coming, and it would bring bloodshed and death to all in its wake. Innocent lives of both men and fae would be stolen by this cruel scheme. The gods knew I despised the fae, but I would not wish this grim fate upon my worst enemy.

I glanced at Maleath, knowing I alone could never stop the turning wheels of such a merciless strategy.

"Phillip," she whispered, leaning closer. "Will you fight with me?"

I clenched my jaw. "No," I replied firmly, taking one more step away from her, towards the great hall. "I will have no part in this."

Her expression faltered in shock, but I continued. "I certainly did not come here to start a war. Not when we've reached a brittle alliance with the fae." I paused, desperately reading Maleath's face, searching for the slightest shift in her conviction. But failing to discover it, I pressed on. "You've been away for too long. Have you not seen the bloodshed they brought on when they marched into this land?" Dread seeped from my heart and streamed through my veins as my thoughts turned away, to a helpless kingdom by the sea.

But Maleath's face froze into a cold mask of apathy. "I will have my crown," she stated, unwavering. "I will take back the White Throne… with or *without* you."

"I see how it is." I nodded, barely containing my outrage. "You will excuse me. I have my own kingdom to look after."

I turned to the threshold but stood still. As fury hardened my expression, I looked back and faced her one last time, and added, "May the gods help us all if your recklessness leads to ruin."

As I stormed out of the castle, my pulse quickened with rising apprehension. A shiver spread through my being as the first laced snowflakes danced in the icy wind.

"Captain!" I growled. Despair strained my voice as I darted to the stables. White mist fled my mouth with each panting breath. "Captain!"

I squinted through the mist, my gaze landing on Captain Moorskill, clad in burnished bronze armor. My captain stopped sharpening a dagger and swayed towards the sound, ice-blue eyes peering through the helm's slit. Recognizing my wariness, Captain Moorskill seized my steed's reins and mounted a cream-coated horse, spurring them forward and galloping to meet me.

"A rebellion against the Crown brews in Whitehaven as we speak," I said, breathless, as I bestrode my horse. "I fear the toll the fae's wrath might claim upon us. Steelborn Castle must prepare for an imminent siege." I seized the reins and tugged as my horse pawed at the ground, restless. "Send word to the king immediately."

"Your Highness?" my captain replied with a frown, confused. "I don't understand. Are you not coming?"

"No," I said firmly, gliding a hand along my ride's shining neck as I appeased his temper. "Easy there. Easy..." I whispered into his ear. My horse whinnied in response and settled. I did the same.

My captain gasped in exasperation. In one swift move, the helm came off, clattering beneath the shining vambrace, and heavy locks of pale blonde hair fell over both pauldrons. "*Where* are you going?" she almost demanded, her face hardened with tenacity.

I'd never allow such insolence from an ordinary soldier, but Captain Moorskill had fought many battles by my side. The strife of war had forged genuine kinship between us— but beyond that, my father had raised us as siblings, although no blood linked us.

"Stonewall," I replied. "I must warn them."

"To the Stone Keep? *I* can do that," she replied earnestly. "You should be with your father. His health has dwindled considerably since..."

"You know full well my unspoken reasons for leaving, Eloise," I argued, my stare burning into hers. "*Do not* make me state them."

"Phillip," she continued. Her chest heaved with fury, passion... I knew not which. "You cannot be serious. Not after what she did." Her voice dropped in discretion, as if in deference to the secret she and I withheld.

"*Aurora* did nothing wrong," I whispered, hurt and regret tangled in my voice as I lowered my gaze.

"She broke your heart!" Eloise exploded, a scowl twisting her mouth.

"I will *not* discuss this matter with you," I replied, my tone harsher than I would have wished. "Do not forget, you are my captain. Now, do as I ask." My horse strutted forward, finally crossing the gates.

The canter of Captain Moorskill's horse echoed mine until a furred cloak and a pair of leather gloves flew towards me. "A storm is coming," she muttered. "You'll freeze to death if you ride out of here dressed like *that*."

I slipped the gloves over my numbed fingers and fastened the cloak to my shoulders, hearing her say, "Your Highness." When I looked up, Captain Moorskill nodded, and yanking the reins, her stallion reared, snorting clouds of vapor into the frosty night. "*Steel and courage to the end,*" she declared and galloped into white planes of snowy fields.

"Steel and courage," I replied in a daze, my heart heavy with the prospect of the harshest times to come.

"Your Highness, is that you?" a melodic voice crooned, full of adoration.

My gaze snapped to the sound's source, stumbling on a group of high fae lords and ladies riding towards the castle. I'd seen too much of their kind these past few days—more than I would have wanted.

The fae. I loathed them with my every breath. I was but a child when they'd stolen my mother from me, their magic doing nothing for her health but hasten her death... But I was no fool, and knew that current events demanded dealing with the fae if one wished to live. And my head must remain in place if two kingdoms so dear to me were to stand a chance of surviving.

My lips curved into a tight smile and I replied, "Good evening, my lady."

"Prince Phillip Steelborn," another sneered, my name dripping from his tongue like honey laced with mockery. "I've heard the legends, but never thought I'd see you in the flesh. How fares your father, the king? I've heard it said, he's been quite ill."

Rage warmed my face as I forced myself to remain calm. "He fares well," I replied with feigned warmth.

His smile turned shark-like. "I'm glad to hear it. For the warlord Maegon is newly intrigued by the kingdoms of this realm. Especially those that suffer... *vulnerability* as of late." He paused, spearing me with a knowing look. "I believe Stonewall is high on the list. Is that kingdom not under your regency?"

My blood chilled at the unspoken threat. This fae snake not only knew of my father's illness but was fully informed about Stonewall's weakened state, which made it ripe for conquest by any warlord.

Forcing composure, I replied, "So it is. Give Maegon my regards, though I'm afraid neither Steelborn nor Stonewall's coffers are currently open to visitors." With that thinly veiled warning, I tugged at the reins, preparing to spur my mount away into the night.

The high fae lady smirked, a glint of cruelty in her gaze. "Are you leaving, my prince?" she purred. "So soon?"

I slightly bowed my head, refusing to meet her challenging gaze. "I'm afraid so, my lady." My voice came strong and unyielding.

The leader of the group strutted forward. "Such a pity. You will miss Raathiel Ivasaar's coronation," he declared, his amethyst eyes alight with amusement.

"Regretfully," I said with a simple nod, eager for this conversation to be at an end.

"Your Highness." The high fae bowed low from atop his horse.

My nod was curt as I spurred my horse towards the horizon, leaving behind the frost-blanketed grounds.

As I raced into the wintry night swathed in silver moonlight, I feared not for my kingdom. Steelborn Castle possessed a powerful army and more than enough supplies to outlast the longest siege. But Stonewall was not as fortunate and its rightful ruler had slumbered for the past seven years by the cruelest enchantment, unaware of the forthcoming danger.

## 2
## AURORA

*I dream of darkness.*

## 3
## PHILLIP

The sky blushed a deep red and orange as I came upon the kingdom by the sea. Once, these waters glimmered a brilliant azure, beckoning me to their shores. But now the sea had turned a bleak steel grey, as if stained by the sorrow that filled my heart ever since Aurora's curse had torn us apart.

The Stone Keep's towers loomed harsh and tall atop the highest cliff, their shadows stretching like grasping fingers across the steely waves. Even as the golden light of morning waged against the shadows of night, a darkness of its own encased this kingdom. The salty sea breeze stirred my hair and brought a chill to my skin, for it also carried with it the reminder of the death and decay of countless souls cast into the depths of the ocean.

I rode through the citadel, encountering many whose spirits had been stolen, replaced by maimed and scarred survivors. Everywhere I looked, I met suffering and pain. I saw empty homes that had once housed the wealthiest families, abandoned carriages stripped for wood and iron; stilled marketplaces and their storages, depleted.

As I approached the stronghold's gates, memories of the days that were to precede my wedding came back to haunt me. Aurora and I had been in a tangle of joy and fury back then, our affections clashing as loudly as the swords we'd trained with. We'd quarreled incessantly after her parents' demise, her attempts to reach me through any means, futile.

An echo of our last conversation washed over me like a flood. She pleaded with me, her voice trembling with desperation, *"I must speak to the gods to save my kingdom."*

But I opposed her request, implacable. My wrath, relentless. *"I will hear no more of this, Aurora. The gods have failed us. They have no interest in the fate of Man, other than satisfying their need for amusement."* I looked up, my face ashen with grief, and added in a hollow voice, *"My family's coffers provide us with enough food and healers."*

Gliding her hands over my shoulders, she reasoned in a whisper, *"It's not enough, and you know it,"* her breath brushing my lips.

*"Your people do not need the help of the gods,"* I countered softly. *"They need guidance and leadership. They need a beacon of hope."*

*"How can I be that shining beacon, Phillip?"* she asked, her bloodshot eyes brimming with tears. *"How, when I have no hope to spare?"*

The dreadful images washed away as I entered the courtyard, the weight of my burden, heavier than before. I would soon face my fairest one, knowing her blue eyes would never see me again. She would always lay trapped in an endless slumber, waiting for me on a bed carved in stone.

I cut through the solemn hall, my steps ringing out against the marble floor. Every fiber in my being warned me to look away, and yet, I could not stop myself from glancing into the forsaken ballroom. Pain lanced through my chest as I reluctantly looked back upon that fateful evening many years ago. My heart had long since accepted losing Aurora to this cruel curse, but it still grieved knowing that I'd lost her love. And even when long after, I'd sought solace in other women's arms, all that had done was reopen my wounds, reminding me of that fleeting chance at happiness that escaped my fingers.

Beams of morning crept through the windows as I ascended the stairs, my limbs weighted with exhaustion. My pulse quickened with each step as I moved along the corridor that led to her bedroom. Apprehension coursed through me —my fear greater than any fate I could ever face in battle.

My steps were heavy as I marched towards the grand chamber. At length, I stood before the threshold. I steeled my heart and took a deep breath, gritting my teeth against the swirl of emotions threatening to overcome me. My mission was clear—pay my respects to Aurora and then meet with her Privy Council to arrange for the citadel's defense.

But before I could take the first step, the door creaked open, letting in an icy breeze and a sorrowful sound with it. Heart-wrenching sobs escaped through the small crevice, chilling me to the bone.

My breath hitched as I cautiously pushed the door open. The room seemed to pause in a moment of stillness, the air laden with a foreboding sense of dread.

I glimpsed the three sisters, huddled together on the balcony floor, their cries the only sound that echoed in my ears. Glistening tears streamed down their faces.

My heart twisted, half in panic, half in confusion. I shifted my gaze to Aurora's bed, her curtains drawn, a palatial fortress against all my memories. My chest tightened, a million different feelings pleading to be recognized, yet I pushed them away, tucking them into the depths of my soul.

I crept closer to her bedside, my footsteps so quiet that I could barely sense them. Sucking in a deep, fortifying breath,

I stood there for what seemed like an eternity. In silence, I braced myself for what awaited me on the other side of the silken white drapes.

Ripping back the curtains with a force that shocked us all, my heart plunged into a fathomless sea of darkness.

"She's gone!" one of the sisters murmured—I cared not which.

My stare remained locked on the empty bed, the shape of Aurora's slender form still pressed into the snowy satin. "Where is she?" I mumbled, my expression slowly stiffening with ire.

Whirling on my feet, I unleashed a savage growl, drawing my blade with a chilling hiss. My shaking hand curled around the hilt, my wrath alive in its glow.

The sisters recoiled with terror, trembling before me.

"Where—is she?!" I roared, my voice sharp and unnatural as it filled the chamber. "Tell me now or I swear on my honor, you will pay for this!"

I glared at the eerily beautiful sisters—Alys, Elin, and Ceridwen—who had raised my love, Aurora, since she was a child. Their powerful glamour disguised them as ageless ladies in waiting... however old *and fae*.

The eldest sister, Alys, stammered wordlessly, her freckled cheeks and glistening maroon eyes alight with wariness. But Elin's response came hot with indignation. "It was fate's will," she spat. "We could do nothing!" Locks of dark green hair spilled over her shoulders as she leaned forward, like the fiercest tigress instants away from pouncing.

I stepped closer. My heart seething with hatred and venom, I leveled my sword at her chest. "Isn't that always the case?" I hissed. "Your kind's magic cursed my mother to a withered life of pain and suffering, yet here you skulk around this castle, coddled by the princess' grace. Know this now—I will *never* forgive your kind for what you've done."

Elin's emerald eyes burned with brazen magic as she held my stare. She had a chin of iron determination, which she slightly lifted as a scowl twisted her exquisite features.

"Where is Princess Aurora?" I snarled. "Tell me, now!"

The youngest sister—and by young, I estimated the life-span of a century—cautiously moved forward. Ceridwen's pale hand slowly lowered the tip of my blade. Her expression filled with sorrow as she murmured in a hushed tone, "*He* took her."

"Hypnos?" I blurted, my soul spiraling into fathomless darkness as the name pulled me back to that horrific evening. "Why would he...?"

"Not the Lord of Slumber," Alys whispered, her voice grave with worry.

"The Dark Prince," Elin continued, shedding her anger as her wide eyes filled with dread.

"Hades stormed in through those doors and took the princess to the Netherworld," Ceridwen murmured as her unsteady finger pointed at the balcony.

My sword clattered on the ground at my feet, its sharp-ness forgotten in the face of Ceridwen's revelation. "No..." I gasped, the air burning my throat like wildfire. Agony seared through me, and I staggered back, the weight of a thousand screaming emotions crashing down on me. "Have I lost her to the Realm of Death?"

"Yes, Your Highness," Ceridwen whispered with a heavy heart. "But there may yet be a way to bring her back."

My grief suddenly ceded to a ray of hope. I straightened, strength returning to my veins with each word she spoke. Warmer now, my broken heart started to mend at the thought of rescue and redemption.

"If the Dark Prince wants her, he will not give her up so easily," Elin retorted.

"I will claim her," I declared, my voice like steel. "I will face Hades himself and bear the weight of his wrath."

"But beware," Ceridwen warned, her rosy mouth twisted in wariness, "for the prince is not alone. Countless sentries protect his realm, and his guardians are more ruthless than any army from this world."

"Hypnos and Thanatos are worse than *that*," Elin murmured in a wary tone. "They're his loyal brothers."

"And in the Netherworld beyond," Alys continued in the same cautious tone, "unspeakable creatures lurk the land, vicious and cruel."

Their warnings meant nothing to me. My heart only ached as my past failure came to haunt me—the guilt of leaving my beloved Aurora to fend for herself was still a deep wound in my soul. But no more. In this moment, I swore that I would not turn away or abandon her. Whatever lay ahead, I pledged to protect her, no matter the cost or consequences.

I glanced about the room, desperate to find a trace of shadows, a remnant of the magic portal like the one used by the dark god Hypnos long ago. But I found nothing. Finally, my gaze cut to the faeries. "What must I do?" I solemnly inquired, my courage swelling with each passing second.

"You must reach the hidden palace at the heart of the Netherworld," Alys instructed, a flicker of hope brightening her pale features. "There, you must confront the Dark Prince and reclaim what has been stolen from you—your one true love, Aurora."

I clenched my jaw, my gaze hardening in determination. "I will journey to the Realm of Death and save her," I declared, grabbing my sword and stilling it in its sheath. "Tell me, how do I get there?"

Elin muttered something, barely loud enough for me to hear.

"Say it again," I demanded, my expression taut with disdain. "Speak up!" My voice was sharp, each word like spears of flame.

The fae's bloodshot eyes found mine. "I said I'd rather *die* than do your bidding," Elin muttered, her voice smoldering with defiance.

Alys reached out to her sister. Her slender fingers curled around Elin's shoulder, seeking to appease her temper. "If he can save our child, what does it matter?!" she implored. A sob caught in her throat.

Ceridwen stepped forward. "We'll show you the way, Your Grace," she said, her sweet voice subdued by the strain of grief.

## 4
## BEAUTY

"*Open your eyes,*" a honeyed voice whispered in my ear. "*The time has come to rise and behold the beauty that awaits you. Open your eyes for me and I will make you into a goddess. I will make you... wholly mine.*"

His words rippled through me, so dark and seductive. They shot a thrill through my being that thundered in my core.

My heavy lids fluttered open, my gaze bleary with the tug of sleep. Velvety twilight clung to the room like a loving embrace, one I was powerless to resist. I swept the chamber with a slow glance, my eyes alert and searching for the source of that voice, but found no one. I was completely alone.

The air was heavy, cloying, and warm, lacking a familiar salty tang. I sucked in a long breath, and a sweet perfume filled my lungs, rich and redolent of an offering to the gods. As I looked down, I grasped the source of this delightful fragrance—my own glistening skin, anointed with luxuriant almond blossom oil.

I sat up, and a single-shoulder gown rippled down my curves and into a pool of silk on the bed. As I rose, my fair tresses tumbled over my shoulders like a woven drape of silk. My bare feet tread softly against the icy marble floor as I wandered across the room, slowly taking in the daunting sight before me.

A thousand candles flickered against the pristine walls, illuminating every corner of the vast chamber. "What is this place?" I whispered, my voice small and faint in the silent space.

My steps led me to an imposing terrace, where a peaceful garden flourished with the vibrant life of abundant greenery and majestic stones carved from ages past. At the bottom of the stone-wrought stairs, a gentle pond trilled a soothing melody.

The crackling of torches filled the air, their amber light washing over me as I stepped into the courtyard. A flood of ease swelled in my being as I ambled across the white stones, smooth beneath my feet, like cool river pebbles polished by a million shooting stars.

As my head spun around in awe, a palace emerged from the shadows. Majestic marble columns towered above me, gleaming brightly against the warm torchlight like some dreamlike vision from another world.

My pulse pounded in my ears, a steady drum of disbelief. "Is this real... or a dream?" I whispered. A shiver rippled through me, an icy wave of creeping dread. My left hand curled into a tight fist, my thumb gently caressing the soft underside of my bare finger—a gesture of comfort, a reminder of something I had lost long ago.

I wavered at the edge of the garden, uncertain yet intrigued. The dense foliage of untamed wilderness called to me with an inexplicable draw, and I found myself inching closer. Before I knew it, I'd left the safe lights of the palace behind and plunged into the unknown.

My chest quivered with wild anticipation—what kind of

secrets lay buried beneath the emerald shadows? With a deep breath, I swept forward, my gown snagging on brambles that seemed eager to yank me back. But I kept going, undeterred by the darkness that swallowed me whole.

My stumbling feet had taken me to the brink of depletion when an enchanting sound enveloped me. Waves crashing against the shoreline promised a majestic castle perched atop a cliff overlooking an endless azure ocean. Tears brimmed my eyes—how beautiful it must have been.

"It's dangerous to wander in these woods," a velvety voice said from behind me.

Heart thundering in my chest, I whirled around.

## 5
## PHILLIP

*T*wilight slanted through the towering windows as I strode into the strategy room, boots ringing on the marble floors. Candlelight danced across the weathered maps and sea charts strewn across the table as the small council turned to greet me.

I surveyed the ring of weathered faces. Lady Rhian, Master of Ports and Harbors, whose naval strategies had decimated many a foe. Lord Morgan, a seasoned Master of War, renowned for never losing a skirmish. The shrewd Master of Coffers, Lord Cassius, whose thrift kept the royal purse full. And, of course, the reputable High Priest Emrys, spiritual advisor to five kings.

Together, they comprised a formidable team of my father's most trusted advisors, carefully chosen to lead the kingdom of Stonewall in its darkest hours. This evening, however, would prove to be the most trying of their service.

Approaching the ancient carved map table, I ran a hand over the worn stone contours, saddened to see borders erased, villages burned away, entire harbors sunken into the sea. This once breathtakingly detailed relic charted not just Stonewall's dominion, but her soul.

And both were fraying badly.

The council watched me grimly, sharing my unspoken thoughts. No one could deny the kingdom had lost its luster since Aurora's curse was cast upon it. But seeing the evidence so plainly etched in stone still shook me.

The heavy iron-bound doors suddenly groaned open. I turned to see the three fae sisters slip inside, their flawless faces sullen, paled by mourning.

Outside, the ocean churned and roiled, its furious waves crashing against the cliffs beneath us, as if fully aware of the tragedy that had transpired—the abduction of its ruling princess.

"Your Highness," the Master of Coffers said with a deep bow. His voice carried over the chaos, stern yet soft. "We were not expecting you until the new moon."

My hands traced a steady path over the marble edge of the table. "There's been a change of winds, Master Alwyn," I uttered, my tone somber as I spoke.

Lady Rhian shifted in distress. "Should we be concerned?" she asked, her voice almost a whisper, as if fearing the answer my words promised.

Taking a deep breath, I met each advisor's eyes in turn. "Dark days lie ahead, but this council has weathered count-less trials and prevailed," I murmured.

"Your Highness?" Father Emrys uttered, slightly tilting his head.

I nodded grimly. "I will be brief. Hours ago, the Princess of Whitehaven gave word that a coup would be staged against Queen Roslyn's regime tonight."

Wordless gasps echoed around the chamber, as if each breath had been snatched away.

"Princess Maleath stakes her claim to the White Throne?"

The Master of War bellowed. "It would be a declaration of war! It would give the fae the perfect excuse to cross the Iron Bridge in their thousands and invade our lands!"

"The fae are *already* here," I said, my voice like frost in winter. I shot a pointed glance at Aurora's ladies-in-waiting, cloaked as humans beneath their faery glamour. Not a single word of their deception passed my lips, for honoring my betrothed's request for secrecy was more important than revealing their truth.

My gaze roved away from them, and I continued, my words a solemn echo in the grand strategy room. "The day the fae first stepped into our realm, they brought their ancient civil war with them. Regardless of who ends up sitting on the White Throne, I'm certain Raathiel Ivasaar's coronation will not be ignored by the rival fae courts." Silence filled the air as I weighed my next words. "My lords and ladies, make no mistake—one way or another, war is coming." A pause to let the words sink in. "And it appears that Maegon, a notorious fae warlord, plans to invade Stonewall Kingdom."

Bleak silence descended upon the grand chamber.

"Time is no longer our ally," I added. "We must move swiftly to protect this kingdom."

The Master of Coffers bowed deeply, his gaze never leaving mine. "We serve at the pleasure of the Prince Regent, Your Highness," he said.

My heart twisted at the title I'd been given seven years ago upon Stonewall's fall into darkness. For too long, I'd stayed away from the Stone Keep, upholding my foolish vow, and delegated matters to this council instead. But tonight, the fate of the kingdom was mine to decide—and I had to make that decision knowing I must leave by morning.

"What are your orders?" the Master of Coffers implored

me, his aged eyes reflecting a desperate hope that I would bring us salvation.

The weight of sorrow and regret settled inside of me like an iron anchor as I glanced upon my beloved's kingdom, knowing I was the only one who could stand between it and ruin.

My jaw tightened, and my words came through gritted teeth. "Master Morgan," I said somberly. "Prepare our army for a siege. We may not have much time."

An unspoken understanding passed between us—he knew, and I knew, what this meant.

"With the last shipment of supplies, we should have enough resources to outlast a few months," he replied, his stark finality ringing heavy in the air.

A few months. I barely nodded. "Good," I croaked, dread and despair throbbing within me. "It should be enough time until I return."

Lady Rhian's face drained of color as she gasped aloud. "Return, Your Highness?" she asked sharply. "You're leaving?"

Rage and misery shook my very core as I forced out the words. "Princess Aurora, she's—" My throat felt tight and raw. "She's gone."

"And you've kept this kingdom strong in her stead, Your Majesty," interrupted Master Alwyn softly. "We must never lose hope that our princess will break free from the sleeping spell and reclaim the Stone Throne."

"My lords and ladies..." The room shuddered with my words, resounding off the gray walls and filling the chamber with a power I had not felt in years. I waved my hand in a subtle gesture towards the guards at the entrance. At once, steel blades hissed from their scabbards, creating an intimidating line of defense that sealed the room.

"For what I am about to speak," I continued, my gaze lingering on the doorway, "I will need your vow of silence and supreme loyalty. Should any of you consider yourself unable to meet these terms, you may walk freely from this room now."

An expectant silence fell upon us, the only sound being that of metal clanging against metal.

"However, if you decide to remain here, and at any moment break this vow of secrecy," I declared, my timbre suddenly alight with the sharpest wrath, "I will make sure to reward your treason as is due."

I scanned their stoic visages, unwavering in their loyalty to the sovereign. I inclined my head at their discipline, and declared, "Princess Aurora vanished from the Keep this morning."

A heavy pause filled the air as I spoke.

"Vanished? How can that be?" The Master of War voiced what all were thinking. "Her royal guard keeps watch day and night, as well as her ladies-in-waiting."

My head coolly swung towards the fae sisters. With a firm nod, I granted the eldest permission to speak.

Alys' quiet tone sounded subdued as she recounted the story. "The Dark Prince broke past our lady's protections in the dead of night and spirited her away to his kingdom in the Netherworld."

"Prince Hades!" Lady Rhian exclaimed.

Murmurs of disbelief arose from the council as they exchanged wary glances.

"This is a great tragedy!" Father Emrys paced the room, restless at the sudden news.

"The fate of Stonewall now lies in your hands," I said, a silent plea beneath my words. "Tomorrow, I shall leave for the Netherworld and rescue the princess. I will break this vile curse that has tormented us for years."

"It will be done," Master Alwyn declared solemnly,

knuckling his heart in traditional Stonewall fashion. *"Strong as stone. A wall against darkness."*

"A wall against darkness!" Lady Rhian proclaimed, her fist pressed against her chest.

The other masters followed suit, each intoning their allegiance.

Lady Rhian fixed me with an earnest gaze. "What would you have us do until you return?" she asked.

"Carry on as usual," I commanded them. "No one else in this castle can be trusted with this knowledge—dispersing suspicion is our only hope for success."

The Master of War stepped forward. "We shall not fail you," he firmly said.

"I've no doubt, Master Morgan," I intoned solemnly, my voice ringing with respect. "I must leave you now. I sail tomorrow at dawn…"

"And I'll be ready as always," a stalwart voice declared from the shadows of the doorway.

I pivoted to find my captain, towering and proud in her burnished armor. Her stern gaze assessed me behind the visor of her battle-worn helm, the glint of her eyes hinting at her sly nature. The guards behind her kept a respectful distance, wary of her fearsome reputation.

"Captain…" I exhaled, stunned.

"Your Highness," Captain Moorskill drawled, her lips twitching into something resembling amusement.

I jolted back in shock. "How did you…?" I began before regathering my wits enough to order, "That will be all here. Everyone leave us."

Gradually, the room cleared until there was just Eloise and me lingering in the strategy chamber. We stood there, suspended in a moment of uncomfortable silence, the only hint of movement coming from the dancing shadows on the walls.

She broke the hush with words like shards of glass, "You'd sail to the Netherworld without me?"

Something inside of me lit up like a flame.

I stepped closer to her, my muscles tensed as I seized her arm. My voice was thick with authority as I commanded, "It is not safe to speak here... Let us go somewhere else." Drawing in a deep breath of anticipation, I gazed upon the forlorn scene before leading her away.

# 6

# BEAUTY

*B*efore me stood a striking figure. Not a sound had left his lips, yet his very presence commanded respect, as if almighty and royal. His body was a sculpture of beauty, encased in polished silver armor that glinted in the fading light. A single pauldron adorned his broad shoulders, a stark contrast to the dark leather clinging to his powerful frame.

He advanced, and the faintest gleam of moonlight cast its glimmering ray on his handsome face. I could just make out a thin white scar slicing its way across his right cheek, a lasting reminder etched in skin.

I stumbled back, pulling in a sharp breath. "Who are you?" I stammered, my gaze flicking around the clearing in a desperate search for an escape.

His chestnut locks swayed in the warm breeze, like an amber sea that framed his fiery hazel eyes. "I am known by many names, yet you may address me simply as Hypnos," he rumbled in a voice that echoed like a tempest. He prowled towards me warily, his fierce gaze devouring me with insatiable curiosity.

"The Lord of Slumber," I mumbled, a frown settling on my brow. "Is this a dream?"

He shook his head incredulously. "It's *very* real." The deity strode closer with measured might, as though I were a frail bird that might bolt at the slightest wrong move. Tangible shock seeped through him. The sheer intensity of his scrutiny filled me with unease.

"Where am I?" I croaked out, my throat growing tight with a hundred unspoken questions.

He suddenly halted, the space between us becoming charged and tense. A wry smirk tugged at his lips. "I believe you're a guest of the Dark Prince," Hypnos said, his voice smooth and gentle as velvet.

I breathed the word, "Hades?" My hand glided to my chest as my heart constricted, dripping dread into my veins like poison. "If this is the Netherworld, then…"

"You're not dead yet," he murmured, the shadows of his face concealing all emotion. "But you *will* be if you remain in this forest much longer." With a swift hand wave, he beckoned me to follow him. "Come. I'll lead you back to the Midnight Palace, where it's safe." At once, he whirled on the heel of his boots and started walking.

Anger and confusion broiled within me, and my hands curled into tight fists at my sides. "If I'm not dead," I rasped as I stood still, "then why am I here?"

The god looked over his shoulder and threw me a candid stare. "I'm sure I do not know," he warmly said, astounded as I was. "You may want to ask *him* next time you meet."

A tendril of panic flickered through my being at the mere thought of laying eyes on the Lord of the Netherworld. "And when will that be?" I pushed myself to ask as I trudged behind him.

His massive shoulders shrugged, casting a ripple on the sweeping black wings inked on his back. "The Dark Prince

44

comes and goes at his leisure," he said noncommittally. "Don't worry. You'll find many ways to keep yourself busy while you wait."

We strolled in silence through the dark jungle—a forest, he'd called it, though savage vines covered our path as the first glimpse of the palace appeared before us. My heart thrummed wildly in my chest as we approached its imposing façade.

The palace gleamed an eerie hue of blue, its pristine columns reaching into a black velvet sky like spires of ivory. An unseen force seemed to beckon me from within its walls as we moved closer.

Hypnos walked steadily towards the imposing fortress, not sparing the lush courtyards surrounding it a single glance. I could only gape in awe at the countless statues that adorned the pathways and immaculate gardens—each one spoke to me in their own silent language, as though singing of ancient secrets and long-forgotten tales.

We arrived at the ornate entrance, bedecked with golden fixtures. I craned my neck to take in the palace's magnificence and couldn't help but marvel at its grandeur. "This…" I mused, my voice ringing in the vastness of the hallway. "Is this your home?"

His reply came out like a blade. "No." His reprimand echoed through the regal space. "Such questions are not to be asked. It is *too human* of you."

My throat constricted, a wave of humiliation washing over me as I remembered where I was—the Netherworld— and what I was—a mere mortal lost in a realm of gods and monsters that were far beyond my understanding or control.

So far, a perfect harmony of queries had tumbled from my lips. Yet one question still remained, burning on the tip of my tongue: *Who am I?* My fate, my identity, hung in the air... waiting to be answered.

# 7

# PHILLIP

The door slammed shut behind me, and my whole body immediately tensed. "What in the fires of the Netherworld are you doing here?" I spat, my voice burning with venom.

Eloise's lips curved in a smirk as she lazily peeled off her gloves and lifted her helm. Her eyes glinted with amusement when they met mine, goading me on. "It sounded like you might need a hand with that mission," she purred, each word dripping with sarcasm.

"How did you get here so quickly?" I lashed out, cold and lethal. "I distinctly recall sending you to Steelborn Castle with a task."

Untouched by my harshness, Eloise plopped onto the chair before the fireplace, her smugness oozing from her pores. "You didn't *actually* give me an order," she snorted, folding her arms across her chest and pushing back with her heels so that the chair tipped on its back two legs.

I gasped, my voice barely more than a whisper. "What?" My brow deeply furrowed. Only Eloise Moorskill could shake the ground beneath my feet like this.

A small smile tugged at her lips. "You *suggested* I return to Steelborn Castle," she explained in a mellow tone.

My mouth went dry. "I…"

My captain held out an appeasing hand. "No, no. I remember it perfectly. You said, 'I *think* it's best that you return.'" She cocked her head to the side, her bright blue eyes narrowing in a challenge. "And I did follow your orders." Satisfied with herself, Eloise nodded. "I've set up everything and spoken to your father. Now, about that journey…"

I wearily slumped down on the dressing table, my fingers absently grabbing a goblet brimming with wine. "Return to Steelborn Castle," I commanded in a soft whisper. "Take care of my father. He's old and reaching the end." Lowering my gaze, I took a slow swig.

"His countless healers and chamber maids can handle his needs much better than I can," she replied, staring at me with tenderness. "And when I informed him of the situation, King Herbert insisted I accompany you. So you see, you were over-ruled." Worry tainted her every word as she continued, "Though of course, he had no clue about our trip to the Netherworld…"

"Must you insist?" I mumbled in annoyance, swirling the ruby liquid in my goblet with a vehemence.

A heavy silence blanketed the room. Finally, she spoke. "I pledged my life to protect you and your family when I accepted the rank of captain of your royal guard, and I mean to honor it." The words tumbled out of her lips with unwavering conviction. And after a moment's pause, she added, "But tell me, Phillip, is she really worth sacrificing so much for?"

"Don't start this," I seethed, my jaw clenched with rage.

Eloise ripped off her vambraces. "It's been a while, you've probably forgotten. So allow me to remind you." Lazily, she undid the clasps of her pauldrons and breastplate, letting them drop to the ground. "Aurora Stonewall shamed you and thoughtlessly threw away your love. Is that not enough reason to leave her and her kingdom to their fate?" Her sun-kissed cheeks faintly glowed with an inner fire.

Instant rage stirred within me, dark and hungry. I took a deep, steadying breath and shuck off my royal jacket in a single movement, fury seeping through my veins like brush-fire. "Is this the conversation you're determined to have?" I growled, barely able to contain my wrath.

Eloise looked me dead in the eye. "Yes," she stated unyieldingly, unshaken at the force of my temper.

I straightened. "Then let us have it right now. Not as prince and captain, but as a man and a woman who were both raised under our father's roof," I demanded with fervor.

"Very well." She agreed, her gaze unwavering as we locked stares.

My fury simmered as I spat out, "You don't know the *full truth* of what happened in that room seven years ago."

She gasped in shock, slowly rising from the seat. "Phillip, you..." As the news settled in, her expression slipped into a frown.

My hands curled into tight fists. "You *think* you know, because that's what I told you," I continued, my anger rising. "But the truth is... I wronged her." Tears misted in my eyes. "Yes, I did wound a god—yes, that gave legend to my name —but when I had the chance to chase him to the Nether-world and reclaim my lost love, I refused!" My emotions pummeled against me as I forced myself to stop.

"Phillip, she ended your engagement," Eloise murmured with caution. "And with such cruelty, choosing a dark god over you... Of course, you'd resist saving her! How could you ever forgive her?"

I clenched my jaw. "We were too young back then, too innocent to understand what we had in front of us," I whispered with an empty stare. "I cannot blame Aurora for walking away from our love when I was guilty of the same." My throat tightened. "Regardless of what lies between us now, I will do whatever it takes to get her back." I released a ragged breath, fury and determination coursing through me. "I have failed her once. I *will not* fail her again."

A spark of emotion lit up her gaze. "Very well," Eloise breathed, vulnerable as I'd never seen her. Firming her stance, she declared, "My blade is yours to command."

A chill ran down my spine, and I snapped, "This isn't a walk in the Red Forest, Eloise. It's the Realm of Death!"

But she only grinned wider, that mischievous glint still in her eyes. "Sounds like an adventure," she replied, shooting up a blonde eyebrow. "The kind to go down in legends…" And tipping her head to the side, she added with a smirk, "Now, stop being such a greedy hero, and give me the chance to be one too."

My heart sank. I forced myself not to respond, to keep my mouth shut. She was too brave for her own good. "This isn't a vanity affair and you know it." I gritted my teeth. "Stop pretending that you're in it for the honors."

She seized the decanter of wine and filled our goblets. "You know I hate it when you're mad," she purred, pushing a goblet towards me. "I know the risks, Your Highness." My captain swigged from her cup and settled back onto the chair. "But if it makes it any easier for you to swallow, hear me say you've *not* commanded me. I *volunteer* to the task." She threw her feet atop the stool by the fire, grinning triumphantly.

Anger bubbled up inside me and I faced her, aghast. "Eloise, have you gone utterly mad? You cannot—you *will not*—come with me to the Netherworld tomorrow!" I barked. My stance was resolute, unyielding. "I will not take you aboard. And I won't be swayed, no matter what you say!"

# 8

# BEAUTY

The Lord of Slumber stood before a grand staircase, his tall and well-built silhouette engulfed in shadows. He gestured gracefully with a slender hand, inviting me to ascend. Our steps echoed on the marble floor, resounding around us like an orchestra of whispers.

As we moved down the hallway, he stopped short and lifted his gaze towards mine. His expression was hard to read, but it seemed like he was trying to see if I could handle this. He bowed his head slightly in recognition of me before stepping aside and waving towards an intricately carved door at the end of the corridor. My pulse spiked. This was it. I swallowed hard and took a deep breath. Time to make this move.

I hesitated in front of the hardwood door; its panels, smooth beneath my fingertips, soothed my trepidations. I sucked in a breath and pushed it open, only to be taken aback by an even greater spectacle than anything I'd witnessed so far. The room was richly decorated—red and gold tapestries gleaming with threads of silver hung around the walls, while the glittering glass of the chandeliers sparkled above me. Everywhere I looked were lavish carpets and ornate furniture, each piece encrusted with precious jewels. A deep chill permeated the air, bringing with it a fear that seemed too strange for this opulent place. It was as if I'd stumbled upon ancient secrets, so powerful even these walls couldn't contain them.

We stepped through what I now remembered as my chambers, walls that seemed to faintly echo past glories. When we reached the bed, a gown worthy of a queen was spread across it—a midnight blue that seemed to coalesce with the darkness of the room, lavishly adorned in sparkling silver. Diamonds sewn into the bodice glimmered in the faint light, each reflecting it like a million twinkling stars set amidst the Netherworld's eternal night sky. Matching slippers, fit for the grandest ball, shone brightly atop a majestic marble vanity draped in graceful moonlight.

Hypnos gawked at the regal garments as if he had never seen anything so resplendent. "What wonders are these?" he murmured to himself as he gingerly picked up the gown's intricate layers and studied them with childlike curiosity.

I closed in on him, all the while tracing my fingers along the delicate embroidery. "This is a bodice," I said when a sudden wave of apprehension washed over me. Did I own such ornate dresses before? A nagging thought gnawed at my memory. *Who am I? Where do I come from?* I searched deep within my memory for a name, an origin, a home... But no answers emerged. Nothing, save sheer emptiness that left me feeling desolate and alone.

Nibbling my lower lip, I stepped back, and the supple silk slipped from my grasp.

"My lady." He beckoned me away, sliding the doors open to a chamber that looked like something out of a dream. "It seems you have a secret garden," he said, gesturing at the lush vines and blooming crimson roses coating the surrounding marble pillars. The walls were painted with intricate frescoes of mythical creatures and ancient trees. The stars shone through tall stained glass windows and shimmered down on us.

I crossed the threshold and beheld an emerald pond, its surface decorated with countless rose petals and illuminated by soft candlelight. A crystalline waterfall cascaded down one wall into the pond, creating a pleasant gurgling sound that filled the air. My breath caught in my throat as I admired this breathtaking view.

"This isn't a garden," I murmured in awe. "It's a washroom... a magical one."

Hypnos pushed away from the doorframe and stepped into the room, his brows rising as he took in its extravagance. "This is a bit much for a washroom," he breathed out, laughing in amusement. His eyes twinkled with admiration as he looked around the chamber. "But I have a feeling this is merely the beginning..."

I lingered by the door, unable to grasp his meaning. Before I could ask him, he turned to me. His lips tugged upward at the corners as he said, "How about you bathe away the dirt of your journey and meet me for dinner when you're ready?" A pleasant smile tugged at his lips.

A thrill raced through my veins. I glanced down at my crumpled dress, grimacing at the streak of grime that soiled the hem. A growl from my stomach broke through the quiet of the room and I couldn't deny it any longer; my body ached for food and rest. The thought of a hot bath and a hearty meal was inviting. Taking one last look at Hypnos, I smiled and nodded in approval.

"Good," he said, pleased as he walked outside. "I'll leave you to it, then."

The second the god vanished, I reached out, my fingers grasping at the tattered remains of what had once been a beautiful gown. With one last tug, the fabric peeled away and fluttered to the ground like dead snowflakes. I stepped forward into the warm embrace of the steaming bathwater, my limbs shaking in anticipation as each step brought me closer.

The warmth of the water wrapped around me like an inviting embrace, providing both comfort and solace for my weary soul. It bubbled and gurgled pleasantly around me as if to welcome me home. A tremulous sigh of bliss left my lips and I submerged myself completely into its depths, feeling the weight of my worries and anxieties floating away while I stayed below the surface. Finally, when my lungs burned with a desperate need for air, I broke through again into the blessed atmosphere, a new calm washing over me with every breath. With newfound energy, I repeated this process until I was fully renewed, just as the god who had granted me this gift knew I would be.

I took one final plunge, and that's when I felt it. A force like that of a charging horde of wild unicorns. The burden of a memory. The world around me vanished, and as I emerged again, I found myself adrift in a murky sea.

Mighty currents raged around me, threatening to drag me down into the abyss. Yet I refused to sink. I swam against the tide with all my might, screaming for help, but my voice was lost and swallowed by the ocean. Tears threatened to emerge as fear clawed at my throat, squeezing tighter with every stroke I took. Was this really how my story would end?

Then I saw a figure in the distance. Hope surged within me and I paddled desperately towards them, eager for a miracle. "Help! Someone! I'm here!" I shouted, a cry of hope as I inched closer and closer.

At last, my fingers grasped their shoulder and I twisted to see who it was. Shock coursed through me. Fear tugged at my chest like an icy hand. For in front of me lay a corpse— dead eyes staring blindly towards the clouds above us. My breath choked in my throat. A shiver went through me as realization dawned; this was not a savior but an omen of death—warning me that there would be no escape from this grim sea unless I acted quickly.

Determination burning in my heart, I once again began to swim against the powerful current, searching for a life raft amongst the raging waves. But then, an angry tide struck with force and terror seized my body as I plummeted beneath the surface, my mind spinning from the devastating sight of the dead body I'd encountered. My eyes fluttered open underwater, forcing upon me the sickening realization that a thousand corpses more just like it drifted in the depths of the ocean.

The sheer agony of it unleashed an uncontrollable scream from my lungs as I fought to stay afloat against the waves that buffeted me from all sides. It seemed an eternity until I managed to rise to the surface, my dreams of escape now a terrifying memory, and found my hands clawing at the wash-room pond's rim.

I quickly looked upon the pool, my chest heaving in horror at the vision I'd been given.

Tears stung my cheeks, and my throat tightened with a looming fear. A voice whispered in the back of my mind that perhaps I may not want to know the truth of my past, after all. I shuddered in unspeakable fright, more fearful of my story than of the fate that awaited me in the Dark Prince's Midnight Palace.

# 9

# PHILLIP

*I* stood alone atop the jagged cliffs of the Royal Harbor, my body rigid as an icy breeze cut through my clothes like a thousand knives. My gaze focused on the horizon, where the sky glowed red like molten iron, as if smeared with the blood of a hundred battles. The Silvermoon Ocean churned below, its steely gray waters both inviting and menacing in the same breath... Before me, lay a journey that would forever alter my future, and its outcome was a mystery.

"The winds favor you now, but the sea is no man's mistress. She could take you into her fathomless depths in an instant." The voice rumbled behind me like gathering thunder, laden with menace.

Unaffected by the harshness of the words, I did not move and waited until she drew near. My stare drifted to the docks below, where my most trusted men prepared my vessel for a harrowing voyage.

"I suggest you seize this chance and step down while you can," she continued. "The games of gods are not kind to mortal meddlers."

I forced myself to look back at Elin, knowing full well she held no love for me. Her emerald eyes shone like embers as they pierced me with a glare, their fierceness enhanced only by the stark contrast of her bronzed skin.

"I am not one to retreat in the face of darkness," I responded coldly, my voice clashing with the roar of the ocean.

The fae maiden clutched her gown tightly around her as she moved closer, the green satin skirt fluttering in the salty wind like worn leaves on a tree. Her lips parted, revealing a soft utterance that seemed to dance in the air. "Brave words," came her reply, each syllable grazing as it sailed through her lips. "Let us see if courage alone is enough to survive what comes next."

Dryly, I murmured my reply: "You deem me incapable of succeeding."

She shook her head gracefully, her gaze solemnly meeting mine. "It's not my place to pass such judgments," she replied, her voice soft but firm.

The corner of my mouth curled into a smug smirk as I stared at her, unblinking. "Yet you do it anyway," I uttered, each word laced with more harshness than I would have wanted.

Her mouth opened for a moment as if to speak in protest, but instead, she declared in a tone that carried a thousand years of unspoken wisdom: "I have served Aurora's lineage long before you were born, and I know what awaits us if you choose this path." A flash of ardency lit her countenance as she added, "Her fate will change our worlds forever."

Courage surged through my veins as I stood tall with unbreakable conviction. "She will not perish," I assured her. "I shall not allow it."

Elin's expression shifted, her iron-clad resolve finally

weakened. Her voice quivered as she spoke with a hesitance I'd never heard before. "Tread carefully as you venture into the Midnight Sea," she warned me. "Its waters are dark, impenetrable, and soundless. The Netherworld harbors perils beyond your darkest imaginings."

Releasing a determined breath, I answered, "Whatever they are, I'll be ready to face them."

Her gaze roved over me, assessing and unyielding. "They say you've wounded a dark god," she murmured.

"I have," I said curtly.

Elin's heavy lashes fluttered up. "You, a mere mortal, dared to harm a deity?" she asked, disbelief lacing her voice.

I nodded grimly, my mind flashing back to the moment when I plunged my dagger into the dark god's face, watching his eyes widen with shock before they turned cold and menacing. "I had to protect Aurora," I explained, my voice hollowed out by grief as I remembered how futile those efforts had been in the end.

Elin placed a gentle hand on my arm, her expression softening and compassion radiating from her fingers. "You are truly brave, Prince Phillip," she said quietly. "But do not underestimate the power of what you have done. The gods will seek revenge."

I stiffened and shrugged off Elin's touch, the thrill of anticipation coursing through my veins numbing any fear. "Let them come," I said with a confidence that could have rivaled Poseidon's rage. "I'll face them all."

Elin studied me for a moment longer. Dread flashed in her eyes, and swallowing hard, she looked away. "I worry," she admitted softly.

I startled. "My lady?" I said, tilting my head. My brow furrowed, confusion and surprise tangling inside me. "Do you find flaw in my skill with a sword?" I held her gaze, daring her to answer truthfully—if such a thing could be expected from her kind.

"I find *flaw* in your character," Elin declared, not cowed by my boldness. "You are a warrior without equal, Prince Phillip. But that same pride may be the downfall of you... and of us all."

I shifted on my feet, my gaze never leaving hers. "For seven years, I have waged war for the honor of Stonewall and Steelborn. I assure you, my lady, I've endured these battles, not for glory, but to prove myself worthy of my beloved Aurora." My tone was low and vehement, conveying the truth behind my words.

Elin exhaled, her hand trembling as she offered me a golden satchel. "Take this with you," she said. "In the darkness ahead, it may be your only guide."

I pried open the satchel and gasped at the sight of an ancient amulet with an emerald light that pulsed in time with my very heartbeats. Its warmth engulfed me, pushing away every fear until nothing remained but a sea of strength that flooded through me. Awe shivered down my spine as I stared up at Elin. "What is this?" I asked, deeply wary of anything fae-made.

"It is called the Blushing Star, Prince Phillip," Elin said, her emerald eyes searching mine. "A relic of my family, passed down from generation to generation, waiting and hoping for a champion to bring balance to our world. A great war is upon us, so I must pass it on. The burden—and strength—of the Star is now yours."

The wind howled around us as I clutched the amulet tight, warmth spreading through me with its touch. "What does it do?" I asked.

Elin's lips quirked into a small smile, and she lifted her chin proudly. "This amulet will grant you the power to wield fae magic against the darkness that lies ahead. But be warned,

Prince Phillip—it can be both a blessing and a curse. Use it wisely."

Grimly, I nodded. With each passing second, my hesitation towards the fae reluctantly faded, eclipsed by the pressing need to save Aurora. At once, I fixed the amulet around my neck, instantly aware of its power as it surged through me. I closed my eyes and breathed deeply as it filled me.

"I will," I murmured.

Her features hardened with unbridled resolve. "Go out there and prove your strength, Prince Phillip Steelborn," Elin said. "Go out there and be the hero that our realms desperately need."

I silently accepted the challenge. Whatever hardships lay in my path, I would overcome them with every ounce of bravery at my disposal. I had no choice but to prevail.

"Your Highness."

We turned and faced the formidable Master of Seas as she approached us. "Your ship is ready," Lady Rhian said dryly, slipping her hands into her black brocade coat's pockets. Her hair was pulled back into a tight bun that accentuated the Master's high cheekbones and tanned skin.

I adjusted my coat. "Shall we?" I asked.

Lady Rhian silently agreed. She led the way to the dock, where my ship waited. Its wooded hull was painted black, with simple sapphire sails embroidered in gold. It bore no sigil of either Stonewall or Steelborn houses. An ordinary trading vessel, just as I'd requested.

A small group waited for our arrival—the business of the day kept in ultimate secrecy. Master Alwyn and Master Morgan were at my side within moments after my feet touched the quay.

"Your Highness, are you sure about this?" Master Alwyn asked, his voice riddled with doubt as he eyed the vessel bobbing on the waves before us. It was a modest sight to behold, with its sails unfurled and prow roughly shaped like a dragon's head. There hadn't been a dragon sighting in all five realms in decades. Not since the great firebreather had taken Queen Laeessa's life—monarch of Whitehaven and Maleath's mother.

Master Morgan spoke up then, his pale cheeks flushed with apprehension. "We could provide you a royal brigantine and at least twice the men—"

"No need," I cut him off quickly as I marched to the boarding plank. "This ship is small enough to sail undetected and requires no additional hands but ours."

The Master harrumphed. "Very well." He bowed his head reluctantly.

Lady Rhian sidled up next to me and placed a comforting hand on my arm. "You were born for this, Prince Phillip," she spoke in my ear. "I'm confident you will prevail."

I could only offer a weak smile in response, although her encouraging words filled me with gratitude. Our enemies were shrewd and relentless, their tactics designed to be unforgiving. They would stop at nothing to see our realm crumble. This battle would not be easy to win, but I was determined to do whatever it took.

I boarded the ship with a firm stride, Lady Rhian at my heels. "This is the Dragon's Breath," she said with a hint of unmistakable pride. "She's more resourceful than she seems, with all the might of a large seafaring vessel encased in a small and fast craft."

"It's everything I hoped for and more," I uttered, pleased. The Dragon's Breath was a symbol of hope even in the darkest of times—and I couldn't help but smile.

"Allow me to introduce you to our captain," she added, gesturing towards a figure at the helm of the ship. "I know him and his crew well, Your Highness. They're some of the bravest and most skilled sailors in all the realm."

As we approached, I could make out the details of the captain's features. He was a tall man in his prime, with a muscular build and scars crisscrossing his body. His eyes were a bright blue, and they met mine with a stern gaze that did not falter even when he realized who I was.

"Captain Grey," Lady Rhian said, her voice strong and firm. "Meet His Royal Highness, Prince Phillip Steelborn. He will be the leader of this expedition."

The sailors cast their eyes down, no doubt recognizing the secret they were now privy to. It was imperative that they understood the risks before committing to this mission.

"It's my honor, Your Highness," Captain Grey said, inclining his head in a respectful bow. "My crew and I are grateful for your support these past years."

"The honor is mine, Captain," I replied. "I understand that we're sailing into dangerous waters, but I have faith in you and your crew."

Captain Grey offered a small smile at my words, showing his approval. "We've faced our fair share of battles on the high seas, Your Highness. I assure you, we'll handle anything that comes our way."

"May your fate be one of victory, Prince Phillip," Lady Rhian said, curling a hand around my arm, "and may you return to us with the light of triumph shining in your eyes."

A response came to mind but the words felt heavy on my tongue. I failed to speak them, offering a tight nod of acceptance to Lady Rhian's good wishes instead.

I escorted the Master of Seas on her way back to the dock, the air laden with emotion as the other masters gathered below, along with the fae sisters, to bid their farewell. As we drew nearer, I scanned the crowd hopefully, but failed to find the one face I longed to see. Eloise, my fierce captain.

Our parting had been bittersweet as much was left unsaid. Still, I had dared to hope she might come to see me off. But the quay stood empty, void of her ever-assuring presence. My heart sank with disappointment.

With one last look at the receding shore, I turned my focus towards the open sea. Before I knew it, we were off into the horizon—ready to meet whatever destiny awaited us on our journey ahead, and hoping I'd be able to return soon... with Aurora by my side.

"I trust you'll find your quarters to your liking, Your Highness," Captain Grey said, leading me down a narrow flight of stairs.

I took in the surroundings as we walked. The cabin was small but well-equipped, with maps and charts lining the walls, and a desk in the corner with several stacks of paper. Countless books were scattered around the space, evidence of the Captain's love for the written word.

"I'm sure I will," I replied, eyeing the books with interest. "I see you have quite the collection."

Captain Grey smiled. "I've always found solace in a good book, Your Highness. They remind me of the world I'm trying to protect."

His words struck a chord within me, and I couldn't help but feel a sense of camaraderie towards the man. He was a warrior, a protector, and a lover of literature—qualities that I admired greatly.

Suddenly the ship rocked with a violent jolt, and I stumbled against the wall. Captain Grey righted himself quickly and made his way to the door, calling out orders to the crew above deck.

"Your Highness," he said, his voice tense. "Please make yourself comfortable. Join me on the deck when you're ready."

# 10

# BEAUTY

*I* gazed into the shimmering golden mirror, barely recognizing the woman who looked back at me. The ghost of my former self hung around her, hovering like a dark cloud. Her blue eyes were haunted by the silent sorrow that seemed to seep from every inch of her body. The luxurious fabric of the gown clung to her curves, creating an elegant illusion that was undermined by the brokenness within me.

I felt cold in spite of such beauty.

Still, I could not turn away. The uneasy knot in my stomach urged me on; I had to know what lay beyond the door. A single step was all it took. A deep breath, and I stepped out of the chamber, like a knight into a battle, and allowed the unknown to swallow me up.

My skirts rustled against the smooth marble floors as I walked along the path that led to the dining hall. I followed the intoxicating aroma of roasted meats and rich sauces, the very smell of decadence, floating in the air. The bustle and chatter of servants were a distant echo, their satisfied sighs and light-hearted laughter reverberating down the hallway.

Eventually, I stumbled into a chamber overflowing with opulent charm. Intricate gold-embroidered tapestries hung from the walls, and flickering gold-encrusted chandeliers cast a luminous glow throughout a vast dining room. A grand banquet table stood in the center, topped with ornate silverware and dishes.

A wealth of crimson roses adorned the room, their perfume tangling with the inviting aroma of the feast served before us.

"My lady." Standing in the middle of the hall, Hypnos bowed low. His voice was deep and melodic, resounding through the airy room with its high ceilings and expensive rugs. His presence was regal, clad in a lavish sapphire and gold embroidered tunic paired with form-fitting brown trousers. As his gaze settled on me, his expression brightened with delight. "That gown suits you exquisitely." His lips quirked into a mischievous smirk. "I like the er... *bodice,* in particular."

I sauntered towards him, unable to stop a smile from easing on my mouth. When I stood inches apart from the handsome deity, he presented me with his arm. My hand glided over it, slipping on the satined sleeve, and he led me to the table.

My eyes widened in awe at the sight of the magnificent banquet awaiting us. The extravagance of it was almost too much. With a table that could seat at least twenty people, I couldn't help but voice my curiosity. "Are we expecting company?" I asked, hardly believing something so generous could be meant just for us.

"I don't think so," he murmured.

"It's a magnificent feast," I uttered as my fingers glided on the exquisite tablecloth embroidered in gold.

"One fit for the gods." Hypnos nodded proudly, hazel eyes twinkling in the candlelight.

His words echoed in my head, taunting me with my own inadequacy. I was a mere mortal amongst the gods, an ant scurrying in the shadow of a giant. What could the Dark Prince possibly want from me? I whispered a desperate plea into the night air, "I still cannot fathom why I'm here."

Hypnos snatched a glass brimming with wine from the table. "We'll discover the reason, by and by," he dismissed, and holding up the glass he added, "In the meantime, enjoy *this*, my lady."

"What is it?" I breathed, my fingers curling around the stem.

"Ambrosia," Hypnos replied with silent satisfaction. He swept a second glass off the table, and lifting it to eye level, he added, "Drink, and tonight, let us make pleasurable memories that will echo through eternity."

A thrill raced through me at that thought. "I'm sure we will," I said. "Your company makes everything more enjoyable." Bringing the drink to my lips, I took a swig.

The liquid was silk against my tongue, and its sweetness demolished all my worries. A sudden wave of comfort swept through my veins, and time seemed to stand still in bliss as the enchanting night embraced me. Tears of joy prickled in my eyes. I wished this moment would never end—this newfound sensation so overwhelming that it took my breath away.

Exquisite warmth rushed to my face, and stunned, I lowered my glass, my widened eyes locked in his.

"*That*, my dear, was your first taste of divine ecstasy," he purred, extending his arm with a grin. I hesitantly accepted and moved with him around the table. "Mind you, it is a taste only."

"I don't think I could handle more than that," I replied, unable to hide my astonishment.

Hypnos halted. He cracked a smile, considerably amused.

"Let's find out, shall we?" he tempted me, sweeping the decanter off the table as we sauntered to our seats.

We talked and drank, and laughed for hours, each sip of wine like a lick of flame on our tongues. I could feel my courage rising with every swig and his with every word. I studied him from the corner of my eye, his face illuminated in the flickering firelight. The thought of getting him drunk enough to answer my questions was tantalizingly close.

I sipped my drink a little slower, encouraging him to raise his glass a little higher each time. Until he was too liquored to know better. Until his drunkenness surpassed my own. I could feel my heart thumping beneath my chest as the moment came, and I whispered, "Do you know my name?"

"Your... *name?*" He cocked his head to the side, a strange light glinting in his eye. "Names have no power here in the Netherworld."

"I don't understand," I replied, my frustration rising.

Hypnos leaned in. *"All who enter the Netherworld abandon their names at the gates,"* he somberly declared, as if quoting from a long-forgotten scripture. "Only Prince Hades holds that knowledge."

My answer was within reach. At last, I understood the makings of my riddle.

I bit the inside of my cheek, determined not to delay. "What lies beyond this palace?" I questioned, pressing my advantage while the god's mood was still light.

The merry glint in his eye dulled, and he regarded me with a sober intensity. "You must not ask these questions," he responded with undeniable authority. "And never venture beyond the courtyard again." His icy words left no room for further inquiry.

"Are we in danger?" I whispered, desperate for a scrap of knowledge that might ignite my memories.

The edges of his lips curled up in a sly smirk. "I can

assure you, *I* am in no danger," he replied condescendingly, and upon meeting my gaze, he added, "As long as you abide by the rules of this palace, you have nothing to fear."

"What is there to fear?" I shot back, my voice laced with subtle defiance.

"Shades." His voice dropped to a hush as if he'd revealed too much.

"Shades?" I echoed. Fear began to prickle along my skin like thorns. "What are they?" My fingers curled around the edge of the table.

"Roaming spirits of the Netherworld," he replied darkly, and his gaze hardened as he realized my tone's authority. "They prowl and hunt in the Veiled Forest, and will not hesitate to lead you to your death if you're not mindful."

A shiver skittered down my nape. "How would I recognize a shade?" I pressed anxiously, countless scenarios dancing in my mind.

"That is rather difficult since they are crafted to appear human, like you and me," he clarified in a dismissive tone. "Although they're silent creatures. They keep mostly to themselves." Hypnos held my stare for a beat too long before he grinned wickedly and extended his arm. "But enough of this inquiry. Care for a dance?"

I scoffed disbelievingly as I shook my head. "There is no music..." I murmured.

He flashed me a wolfish smile, shifting his gaze from mine to the doorway. "*Music*," he commanded, and a low melody instantly filled the room.

I jumped, startled by the sudden sound, and opened my mouth to protest. But before I could utter a single word, Hypnos rose to his feet and outstretched his hand. "May I?" His voice held a note of mischief that made me hesitant yet oddly intrigued.

Against all better judgment, I accepted his gesture, and

together we glided across the room, towards the neighboring courtyard.

# 11

# PHILLIP

The hours dragged on as the Dragon's Breath sailed further and further away from home. Every breath was a step closer to our enemy's stronghold. Restlessness filled me like an angry beast prowling across the deck, eager for our confrontation.

My heart raced as we sailed towards the Realm of Death, but what unsettled me the most was the prospect of facing Aurora again. We'd been lovers once upon a time, tenderly embracing in a heartfelt kiss that seemed to have happened a lifetime ago. Now, we were strangers, with no connection except for a shared past and a last painful memory.

I clutched the wooden railing tight, watching impatiently as the churning sea took us closer to the Realm of Fae, and sighed heavily.

"Be at ease, Your Highness. The tides are in our favor," Captain Grey said, catching my fretful disposition.

I turned to him, meeting his aged gaze. "Are you certain?" I asked. "It feels too slow."

A small smile tugged at his lips. "It's all part of our plan," he reminded me. "We need the shadow of evening to shield us as we enter the Fae Realm's waters."

"Yes, of course," I said finally, my discomfort restrained. "We wouldn't want to alert the fae posts of our presence."

We had no choice but to brave the Iron Sea—a sea of legend, whispered about in dark corners of taverns and forgotten ships. Tales told of a gateway to the Netherworld hidden within its depths, and so we set course to discover it for ourselves.

As twilight cast sinister red and orange hues across the horizon, my apprehension built like a storm beneath my skin. With each passing moment, I grew more certain that Aurora was waiting for us on the other side. But what would that encounter bring? Would it be a clash of tempers reminiscent of our last few weeks together? Or would she be ready for battle, like so many times before? Uncertainty burned inside me, refusing to let go.

A deafening clap of thunder shattered the heavens, and a sudden blinding flash of lightning cracked across the blackening sky, brightening the tumultuous waters. Within instants, the peaceful sea took on a threatening turn, becoming restless as the turmoil brewing inside me. With each cruel wave that crashed against the hull, the ship rocked, its sails snapping in the fierce wind.

Abruptly, Captain Grey shouted orders from the helm, urging us onward. All around us, men on board scrambled to fulfill their tasks and braced for the forthcoming storm.

"The tempest brews ahead," bellowed the captain, his countenance hardening. "We have no choice but to plunge straight into the heart of it." His eyes bore into mine, a flicker of apprehension in their depths. "Your Highness, I humbly suggest you take refuge in your quarters."

I strode forward, emboldened. "No," I declared, shaking

my head. "I will stand with you and face whatever comes our way."

We stood face to face, a silent stalemate. I refused to back down; he forced himself not to smile in admiration. With one nod, the captain declared his ruling. "When we touch land, your part will come. Until then, I must ask you to take shelter. And although I say it gently, please understand this is *not* a request." The captain's stern demeanor left no room for discussion.

I ground my teeth, holding back unpleasant words that would only add to our present troubles. Reluctantly, I headed to my quarters, my heart heavy with frustration. I clenched my fists tight on the way and trudged along the steps that led to the cabin. A thousand worries swirled in my head, and the only way to shake them off was to step into the Netherworld and face the greatest challenge of my life once and for all.

I threw the door open with a bang and entered the cabin, stumbling back against the wall as the ship lurched beneath me. The hull creaked in protest, battered in the brutal tides.

A heavy sigh escaped me when I slumped onto the bed, dragging my fingers through my hair. I could do nothing now but wait—wait for the storm to cease, wait for the journey to end, wait for that first step into the Netherworld. Wait. Wait. Wait... Nothing could be more agonizing than this moment.

As those thoughts consumed me, a loud thud echoed off the wall, startling me into alertness. I straightened. My brows furrowed in confusion when another thump resounded, and my heart jolted into a gallop. Slowly, I rose to my feet, my hand gliding on the wall until I found what had made the noise. A secret door. It creaked open with a single push, followed by more thumping noises... and a *giggle*.

I grabbed the candlestick off the bedside table and thrust it into the hidden room. "Who's in there? Show yourself!" I demanded, my voice echoing off the walls. The light from the candle gradually illuminated a figure crouched in the corner, and my jaw slackened in shock.

I stopped short as I inched closer, my breath hitching. I hadn't recognized her at first. She looked so different—a striking figure in a white lace-trimmed gown, pale blonde tresses cascading down her delicate shoulders and rosy lips curled into an enigmatic smile.

She hadn't noticed me yet, too enraptured by the firkin in her hold while murmuring happily to herself. "Eloise?" I flinched as I stepped into the doorway, my tall frame barely fitting through as I crouched low. "What are you doing here? I *explicitly* forbade you from coming on this dangerous journey."

Eloise looked up at me defiantly, the small cask cradled in her lap. "Oh, don't pretend you're not happy to see me, Phillip," she replied with a coy smile. "You know you need me for this mission to succeed."

I shook my head in exasperation, though I had to admit she had a point. As infuriating as her disobedience was, her cunning and resourcefulness would be invaluable on the quest ahead.

"Lace, taffeta, and… wine," I said in a calmer tone. "Care to explain?" Firkin or gown, whichever she chose would be fine by me.

Eloise rolled her eyes dramatically. "Please—do I look like the type to pack ballgowns for a perilous quest?" she replied with a smirk. "That silly faery Ceridwen messed with my traveling satchel. She tossed in a bunch of airy dresses like this one, and got rid of most of my clothes."

I'd taken an oath to never reveal the identities of the three fae sisters, but Eloise kept my secret as if it were her own. Not in vain was she my Captain, whom I trusted with my life.

I managed a tight smile, trying not to laugh out loud. "How do you know it was her?"

"Mm... I don't know," Eloise drawled sarcastically, rolling her eyes. She nudged the bag on the floor with her foot. "Maybe because of the *good luck* note she left in my satchel, *with her signature?*"

My smile eased into a smirk. "You really shouldn't be here. But since you are..." I crouched beside her, gripping a stack of crates for balance as the vessel continued to creak and sway across the rough sea. "What's in the barrel?" I asked, genuinely curious as I leaned closer.

Eloise grinned mischievously, hoisting the firkin up higher. Her eyes glimmered with excitement. "Just wait until you see..." With a theatrical gesture, she popped off the cork and a heady aroma of fruit instantly filled the room.

"Is that...?" I started in disbelief.

A sly smirk tugged at Eloise's lips. "Bloodmoon Red. The finest wine in all the realms," she said. "Looks like this ship has seen more *action* than its crew would let on." She shot up an eyebrow, hinting at her meaning with a slight nod.

I stared at her, dumbfounded.

"Look around you, Phillip!" Eloise snapped, waving her arm at the chamber.

I raised the candle and peered through the shadows; countless wooden barrels lined the walls of the secret store-room. A realization dawned on me. "Pirates?" I uttered incredulously.

"*And* our new crewmates." She wrapped her arms protectively around the barrel. "Come on. Let's take this with us," Eloise commanded, rising gracefully from the floor.

I followed her into my bedroom, my eyes lingering on the way her gown moved like a cloud around her. I'd never imagined Eloise dressed so elegantly, but it certainly suited her. She set about pouring our drinks, then thrust a glass of Bloodmoon Red into my hands with a devilish smirk.

I took a hesitant sip, and the warm, spicy notes burst through my palate. "This is incredible," I marveled.

Eloise smiled before tipping her glass to her lips. "Who would have thought Lady Rhian was smuggling such deliciousness?"

I laughed, astonished at the scandalous thought that the proper court lady had been involved in piracy. "What are we going to do with these barrels? We can't take them back to court with us."

Eloise shrugged. "We'll figure something out. For now, let's just enjoy it." She raised her glass in a toast. "To new adventures."

I clinked my glass against hers. "To new adventures."

We drank and talked, and I found myself feeling more alive than I had in ages. The thrill of discovery, the danger of secret rooms and pirate crews—it was all so different from the stifling routine of court life.

The next drink led to another, and another, until we'd emptied almost the entire cask, and the sky outside our small window was dark, flickering flashes of lightning that lit up the room like firemagic.

Cold ale sloshed around the inside of my stomach as I laughed with Eloise. Our secret meeting had quickly become a bit of a wild night, and I embraced it eagerly.

Eloise tumbled onto the bed with a groan. "Seriously, for gods' sake, come sit!" she exclaimed, trying to peer up at me from her prone position. "I'm getting veritably ill just by looking at you in all this turbulence."

"Ah, I've finally found your one flaw," I quipped with a smirk, stepping closer despite the ship rocking beneath us. "You can't handle a bit of sea sickness, it would seem." With that, I tried to join her on the bed—only to slip and stumble as the waves caused an unexpected jolt.

"Oh… Look at you," she crooned, barely stifling back a giggle.

I groaned and lay there, helplessly staring up at the ceiling, while Eloise's laughter filled the room. We laughed for far too long before I gave up and ended up sitting on the floor instead.

"This was… a horrible idea," I stammered. "Drinking in the middle of a sea storm…" I leaned my back against the bed, carelessly dropping my empty glass and watching it roll along the floorboards until it clinked against the wall with a hollow sound. "What were we thinking?"

Eloise's hot breath tickled my neck as she leaned in. I quivered with anticipation, mesmerized by her smoldering eyes.

"You know," she said, her luscious lips curving into a mischievous smirk. "There's something I've been wanting to do for a long time."

I raised an eyebrow. "And what might that be?"

Her eyes sparkled like a glint of starlight, and she reached into the depths of her leather satchel. When she pulled out her hand again, a small object dangled from it on a delicate chain.

"A lyre?" I said in wonderment.

"A fae one, I think," Eloise replied with a hint of wonder. "Another *lovely gift* from Ceridwen!" She laughed, and so did I.

Suddenly, Eloise's mirth died away and her cheeks reddened in a shy flush. She looked up into my eyes sincerely, and said: "I want to sing you a song,"

I leaned back against the wall, resting my hand on my knee and nodding encouragingly at her. "Well, then… Let's hear it."

Eloise snorted derisively, her fingers plucking at the strings in a casual manner. But as her lips parted to sing, her countenance transformed into one of intense concentration. Her melodious voice was like honey in my ears, and I felt all my worries dissipating, leaving behind just me and her music. It was as if we were the only two people left on Earth.

*"Once upon a time, in a land far away*
*A love story began, it was fate, so they say*
*Two hearts entwined, in a bond so true*
*Together they lived, in a world bright and new*

*But as fate would have it, their love would*
*    not last*
*A storm blew in, and the die was cast*
*Broken hearts and tears filled the night*
*A love once so bright, is now lost in sight*

*But even in heartbreak, there is beauty to find*
*For the love they shared, will forever shine*
*In the stars above, and the depths of the sea*
*Their love will live on, through eternity..."*

My throat seized as I listened to Eloise's beautiful rendition of the timeless ballad. When she finished, I barely managed to whisper, "Your voice is... truly remarkable."

Eloise blushed at my compliment and murmured a quiet, "Thank you." She wasn't teasing or playful like usual. The sparkle in her eye was gone, replaced with a brooding sadness. Something seemed to be weighing on her mind.

I couldn't stay silent any longer, so I blurted out, "I don't know *why* you'd venture on this journey..."

Eloise didn't answer right away. Instead, she turned to meet my gaze with an intensity that stole my breath away.

She then said quietly, "It's simple. I care for you."

I shifted in place, my next words tumbling out, "I feel the same way."

Her expression softened as her eyes bore into mine. She then shook her head slightly. "No, Phillip," she said with conviction. "You don't."

Confused and conflicted, all I could do was whisper, "Eloise?"

She sighed. Unflinching, she said, "I don't think there's ever been a time when I haven't loved you."

The whole world shook beneath me as those words sunk in. My mouth hung open but no sound came out until Eloise suddenly interrupted my thoughts by saying hastily, "We're sailing to the Netherworld. If the worst should happen, I don't want to end up in the Fields of Mourning—where unrequited lovers go."

Panic rising within me, I shot to my knees and begged fervently, "Don't say that, please!"

An unspoken emotion hung in the air, so tangible it was painful. Eloise's love had been a constant presence even if her words were few. I looked back on moments both bright and dark, blessed but bittersweet. In hindsight, I could see how she'd revealed her feelings all along, yet I'd been too oblivious to notice.

Finding the courage to move, I shuffled over to sit beside her on the bed. My mind whirled with a million things I longed to say. But my following words I considered carefully, fearing they might cause her any pain.

All my efforts amounted to nothing as I stammered out falteringly, "Eloise... I..." My mouth went dry, and I found myself unable to finish the thought.

She swallowed hard, and a rueful smile tugged up the corners of her lips. "It's all right," she murmured. "I've learned to acccpt things as they are... Although, one thing must be said: you've got *lousy* taste in women."

I forced a bitter grin as her shoulder shoved mine, her voice rising on a chuckle that was anything but joyful. "Oh, for gods' sake. Wipe that fake grin off your face already." She sniffed. "And *please* don't let it get up to your head."

Her fingers clawed at her chipped nails, her gaze firmly on the ground.

"Eloise," I breathed, my thumb tracing the line of her jaw, bringing her face around. Our eyes met and I spoke earnestly, each word more heartfelt than the last, "I've always cared for you."

Her blush deepened and she pulled back, pressing a hand to my chest. "Oh, fuck off!" she scoffed with a teasing lilt in her voice that vanished before the words had even finished. Eloise started, and realizing her words, she amended with a grave, "Your Highness." Her gaze strayed from mine fast.

A smirk tugged at my lips. "It's all right, Captain," I assured her, doing my best to disguise the slur in my voice. "I think you might be drunk."

"So are you!" she retorted quickly with a laugh.

I paused, sobering. "Maybe," I replied more seriously. "You know, I've often thought of Elysium—the place in the Netherworld where legendary warriors dwell..."

Her expression wiped clean in an instant. "Hush!" she hissed, her gaze darting to the door.

I froze, straining my ears for whatever sound had made her go still like that. And then it came—the distant clamber of voices and feet, echoing through the corridors outside our cabin.

"Do you hear that?" she asked, her voice barely above a whisper.

I did hear it.

It was the sound of mutiny.

## 12

## BEAUTY

*I* stood on the threshold to the terrace. Crackling torches scattered golden light against the marble pillars, luring me into a world that defied reality, one that promised to fulfill my wildest dreams.

As I stepped through, the lingering warmth in the evening air kissed my bare shoulders, sending ripples of delight down my body. I sauntered closer to the edge, astounded, as my gaze swept along descending marble steps that led to a sweeping jade pond, its surface an undulating sea of lilies dotted with a thousand twinkling fireflies.

I glanced behind me, where Hypnos stood impassive and still. "Go on," he said. He spoke in a gentle tone, his voice ringing with assurance.

I walked down the steps. Upon venturing closer, the pond revealed itself as a sweeping lake with peaceful streams that weaved through a vibrant garden. Rosebushes curled around majestic marble statues, while lush trees blossomed with crimson pomegranates, alight beneath the flickering flames. Beads of ruby red peeked through the fruit's tough rind, tempting any who passed by to pluck one and sample the succulent seeds hidden within; their sweetness wafted through the air, blending with the gentle sound of water lapping at the shore and the distant thrum of strings.

Spellbound, I meandered through the starry night, lured by the music that whispered beyond. I stumbled upon an ancient stone bridge arching above the water. This beckoning path led to a solitary island of untouched marble, glimmering in the dusky moonlight, a pristine pavilion that stood as if it were its own kingdom.

I stopped dead in my tracks, the lush garden and grand palace forgotten. A ripple in the lake froze me in place, the faint glimmer of *something* beneath its depths trapping my attention.

Breathless, I leaned closer as I glimpsed the glint of silver scales... An icy chill skittered down my nape. My heart raced, willing me to jump into the frigid waters and uncover what lay hidden. Against every cautionary thought in my head, my body leaned forward, toes tingling as they edged closer to the bridge rail.

"Ah-ah. Tread lightly here," Hypnos warned me in a mellow voice, his strong arms snaking around my waist, firm and unyielding. "The water is alive with the promise of nereids emerging from its depths."

My eyes narrowed as I faced him. "Nereids?" I echoed.

He nodded gravely, his gaze like steel upon the rippling jade surface. "You might know them as *mermaids*. Moonlight reveals them to those willing to find them," he explained, his hand beckoning for mine to take hold. I did as he asked. "But they're not as kind as human tales would have you believe."

A chill prickled down my spine, my glance angling to the water once more.

"Come away, my lady," Hypnos warmly said, guiding me towards the pavilion.

"What do they want?" I asked, my voice barely above a whisper as my mind reeled with the fathomless marvels of this strange new realm.

"Mermaids are curious creatures," he mumbled, his thumb lightly tracing a spiral on the back of my hand. "They're drawn to the music that fills the palace in the evenings." He paused thoughtfully. "Some come to observe. Others, play tricks on unsuspecting guests... like you."

My heart clenched with unease. "What kind of tricks?" I asked cautiously.

Hypnos laughed, the sound like silk against my skin. "Oh, nothing too dangerous. Harmless pranks, like stealing jewelry or causing mischief. Nevertheless, it's best to steer clear of them. Nereids are great collectors—their ambition knows no bounds. Once that greedy *want* has settled in their hearts, they will do anything to claim what they desire." As we reached the pavilion's entrance, he pivoted, his voice a low warning. "*Anything.*"

I shivered, imagining myself the target of a mermaid's obsession. By the time I crossed the threshold into the island, I was relieved to have left the long bridge behind. But all my concerns washed away as the sweet melody grew louder, enveloping me in waves of tranquility.

"Where does it come from?" I breathed, glancing up at the night sky.

Hypnos stood beside me. "The music, do you mean?" He sniffed the air and answered, "Sacrifices from the realms. A symphony of prayers from devoted worshipers..."

Was he joking or telling the truth? It was too hard to tell, not with that cunning smirk twisting his lips. His expression left me in a swirl of uncertainty.

His minty breath tickled my ear as he murmured huskily, "Dance with me." His warm hand settled on my lower back while his other traced a line down my arm, leaving a trail of golden sparks in its wake.

My brow furrowed as I looked down at the scintillating line that snaked through my skin and coiled around a golden spiral in the back of my hand, the same place where the dark god's thumb had been tracing an unceasing pattern. My gaze cut to his, quizzical.

"An enchantment, my lady," he explained matter-of-factly, "to soothe your worries away."

The realization flooded me. The notes hadn't been a balm for my troubles; it had been his sorcery, his spell, that had allowed me to find peace.

A thrill coursed through me as Hypnos called me near with a curled finger. He stood in silence, poised and graceful, his sapphire and gold embroidered tunic shimmering under the starry sky, painting a divine figure amongst the ruins of the roofless pavilion.

When he clasped my hand, a wave of warmth surged through me. Hypnos grinned, his eyes alight with some inner joke. "Nothing I enjoy more than dancing," he said.

My face flushed at the self-assurance in his voice. I tilted my head, and batted my eyelashes playfully as I asked, "What about ambrosia?"

He cracked a handsome smile. "You once asked if this was a dream, didn't you?" he purred, then dragged his tongue lazily across his lower lip. "Let me show you where we truly are."

His hands were hot around mine as he pulled me towards him, twirling us through the dark night. I could almost feel our hearts beat in tandem as the torches flickered and grew dim, joining us in an ethereal dance. Suddenly, the music shifted to a low melody, an ancient chant that raised goose-flesh up my arms with every beat of the drums.

My gaze met his—eyes twinkling like precious amber

gems and skin shimmering like starlight on a midnight sea. He was breathtakingly beautiful, and looking away, revealed a transformed world. Instead of a lake lay a pool of liquid silver, lilies made of iridescent light swaying to the music, and fireflies that had grown into orbs of vibrant color floating about us.

Hypnos' strong arms engulfed me as the music swelled to a delightful crescendo. The sensation made my whole body tingle, every nerve alive and buzzing at his touch. I was completely consumed by him, by the burning fire that grew between us.

The notes grew louder and more powerful, gradually reaching a deafening pitch. Hypnos clutched me closer, spinning us faster until our joyous laughter filled the air and echoed throughout the night. In that moment, I felt more alive than ever before.

When he set me back down, he leaned close and whispered in my ear, "Are you ready for the next part of our adventure?" His words were like honeyed lightning, sparking promises of unimaginable delight.

My heart thumped wildly in response, anticipation flooding my veins. With Hypnos by my side, I had never felt so daring and prepared for everything.

He cupped his hand over my eyes, and I shut them without hesitation, waiting for the night to weave its spell. When he removed his hand, I gasped in wonderment. Hypnos had changed—gorgeous wings of ebony and onyx sprouted from his back, almost grazing the pavilion columns.

"Don't look so stunned," he purred with a hint of smugness. "I am a god after all." His arm tightened around my waist as he lifted us into the air. With a single flap of his wings, we rose higher, spinning gracefully in the sky together, weightless as the vaporous clouds that skimmed past us.

The cold wind nipped against my skin. But I felt safe in

his embrace, steady and sure, never wavering as we took one daring turn after another.

The landscape below became a blur of colors until Hypnos halted our ascent, and we were left suspended in midair, gazing into each other's eyes. His enigmatic stare held many secrets... I could see the words on his tongue, burning to be released, but he kept them contained in a prison of silence.

As Hypnos' stare broke from mine, we began soaring towards the ground.

Our flight had been too brief.

Soon, my feet touched a thin layer of grass. As far as I could see stretched an ocean of lavender, its heady perfume swirling around me in the breeze.

"You were right," I breathed out into the stillness.

"Mm?"

"I could never tire of this place," I replied, gaze drinking in the richness of the emerald grass, and the cerulean blue sky, blending into the crimsons of the horizon.

The wind stirred around me then, its chill prickling my arms like tiny needles. But something was different. It felt too perfect, too pristine. And then, I heard it—a rumble like thunder, reverberating through my bones. The sound stirred something within me, something forgotten and long lost...

"Can you hear it?" I asked Hypnos, my heart quickening with hope.

He gawped at me, failing to grasp what I could so clearly perceive. The crashing of the waves grew louder and more forceful until it tugged at my being's very core, urging me to move. I knew I must take my chance and go for it, or else accept that I would never face the truth about myself and my past.

Before he could protest, I sprinted up the valley. Hypnos yelled after me, but I didn't look back. I pushed forward, until the verdant landscape gave way to a shadowy wood shrouded in fog and heavy silence. Tall sycamore trees loomed over me as if guarding ancient secrets within the misty darkness.

Out of breath, I halted. I'd lost the sound of the waves again, and my heart sunk lower than ever before. But then a rustle stirred in the nearby shrubs, and fear displaced all heartbreak.

I spun around, my heart pounding in my chest, eyes frantically searching for the God of Sleep. But instead of his figure shrouded in mist, I found a woman standing before me. Her beauty was a thing unearthly, like midnight spilled on snow. A gown of leaves and vines clung to her curves. Her eyes burned like stars, and she met my gaze with an intense ferocity.

"You…" she hissed, drawing out the word like a snake. "You are… mortal."

Without warning, the woods around us shifted into something unrecognizable—twisted trees and howling winds that seemed to be coming from everywhere at once. Panic surged through me as I whipped my head frantically in search of escape, only to come face-to-face with figures of grace and power, glowing beneath the haze. But I knew, deep within my chest, these creatures would bring me no mercy.

I whirled around as my captors closed in, their menacing shadows engulfing me. Their long and bony fingers pulled at my skin, teasing and taunting until I could hardly breathe. Panic filled my veins and I squeezed my eyes shut, desperate for an escape.

"Let me go!" I pleaded, but no reply came, save their hollow laughter ringing in my ears like chimes in the wind.

"Away with you, shades!" a voice commanded, carrying a power so strong it shook the very air around us.

Suddenly, Hypnos appeared in a flash of light—his wingspan nearly obscuring my view. "She's under my protection, and no harm will come to her!"

The creatures backed away, dragging their claws through the dirt with hunger. Hypnos' gaze narrowed and his words became sharp as ice. "They've strayed too close to the palace this time," he muttered and his eyes flickered to me. "We should go back."

A gust of air caught my breath and lifted us into the sky. I clung to him, trusting in him alone in a world that changed faster than I could keep up with. My stomach lurched as we flew higher, faster, not stopping until we were safe again in the clouds. He then looked down at me with a certainty that comforted me like nothing else in this ever-changing realm.

## 13
## PHILLIP

*I* stood at the helm, aghast at the ceaseless bedlam of clashing swords and swinging fists flying in the air. The storm lashed hard against the Dragon's Breath, with daunting waves that crashed against the hull and the fiercest winds, dragging us into the depths of the Iron Sea. Ocean and sky blurred into impenetrable darkness, cracked only by the flash of jagged lightning.

Captain Moorskill rushed to join me, ready for battle. "What in the fires of the Netherworld is going on?" she all but hissed.

"I don't know," I mumbled sternly, and steeling my gaze on the figure standing by the wheel, I added, "but I mean to find out."

My heart thudded in my chest as I recognized his silhouette from a distance. His tall frame was eerily still while he held onto the ship's wheel with a white-knuckled grip.

"Captain Grey!" I called, hope rising in my throat even though the man's stillness unnerved me. "Captain!" But as I reached for his shoulder, a chill swept over me. The captain had shifted ever so slightly at the sound of my voice. In the silver lightning, his face was sallow and gaunt, marked with a vacant stare that held no recognition. Nothing like the man I'd spoken to earlier today.

The tilt of his head was both unnatural and precise. He stepped closer with a slow, hesitant gait. His dark eyes locked onto mine, unsettling, as they anchored me before him. His jaw dropped open but no words sailed through, only a broken sigh that seemed to drag on forever.

Icy dread clung to me so firmly that I couldn't tell where it ended and I began.

"Look out!" Eloise shouted, her voice high-pitched and urgent. I whipped around with a start, my eyes finding the long sword held aloft in a sailor's hand just before my body dodged the slicing metal by mere inches.

The man's steps were heavy and clumsy, his face an eerie mask with a black sheath that veiled his eyes. Again, he lunged forward and attempted to attack, but then I understood it was not me that he wanted—Captain Grey had drawn his own sword in defense. The clash of steel against steel filled the air as they sparred.

I scrambled back, feeling the hard wall of the helm behind me as I pushed to my feet. "What magic is this?" I breathed, barely able to believe what I was seeing.

"I have no idea," Eloise said in a ragged voice, standing just ahead of me. Her eyes sparkled in the dark, heavy with caution. "I've never seen anything like it."

A towering figure loomed behind her and a glint of steel glowed from its clutched hands. In an instant, he'd moved closer, ready to slit Captain Moorskill's throat.

"Behind you!" I roared, grabbing her shoulder and pushing her away from danger as my sword sliced through the air and crashed against his weapon, obstructing the attack.

The man came even closer and a grin lifted the corners of

his crooked mouth. A deep growl rumbled from his throat—wilder than any barghest's roar—and I knew then, nothing about this man was human.

The creature's sword ripped free from mine and he instantly directed his attention elsewhere. His blade flew towards Captain Moorskill, who had already pulled her sword in anticipation. "So you want my head, huh?" she spat as her silver flashed through the air. In a single strike, she beheaded him with an almighty thud. "Not today, demon."

Demons? Was that what these creatures were? I shivered at the thought.

"It's the seasickness," she told me, her voice a steady rumble over the mad chorus of screams from the deck. I glanced down and saw the headless body lying like a silent warning at my feet. "The fae waters," she continued. "Legends say they're poisonous for humans. They must have drank from them."

Shock coursed through my veins as I stared down at the raging horde below. "I don't know about fae curses, Captain," I murmured, gripping the shroud to keep my balance as a harsh wave crashed against us, setting off the helm's bell that chimed in a haunting song. "We might be getting closer to the Netherworld than we think."

At the clang of steel, my head snapped up, to discover Captain Moorskill sparring against another monstrous creature. Two more lumbered up the stairs, their eyes dead and unseeing—snared by some hidden force that controlled them. But again, their interest locked solely on her. As I stood there, swept in horror and confusion, I felt as if indeed I were a ghost, invisible to all save my captain.

Bolstered by an unstoppable urge, I darted towards them, fending them off their lethal course. With each swing, I struck true. And although they fought back ferociously, I finished both in streaks of red ruin. "I can't understand, why won't they come for *me*?" I yelled in a hoarse voice that sailed across the icy wind.

"I'd like to know that as well," Moorskill replied in a snarky tone, as her sword flashed in the pitch darkness, swinging in a vicious arc against the enemy. "Maybe your good looks are just too much for them."

My stomach churned in unease, even as I snorted at her words. "Nobody's *that* good-looking!" I took one down with a single slash and yet another monster appeared, pulling me back into battle.

Captain Moorskill delivered the final strike with a mighty roar, and her opponent hit the ground with a deafening thud. She stepped away from the body as I raced onto the deck, where I grabbed hold of the shrouds just as she stumbled against me, held up by my strength.

The crewmates had been engaged in their own battle, ripping at each other's throats with sharpened claws and blades. But suddenly, all sound ceased, and a mantle of dread descended upon us when everyone's gazes turned our way—pitch-black eyes that shone with something foreign and menacing.

A creature lunged towards Eloise, but I blocked the blow. My sword cut true through the demon's chest. I seized his arm with my free hand and pulled him to me, then hauled the fiend over my shoulder and tossed him overboard.

"Nice move," she praised me.

I cracked a smile. "I thought you'd appreciate it," I replied.

Captain Moorskill and I fought back to back atop the blood-slicked deck, desperately trying to hold off the horde of shambling, cursed sailors surrounding us. But it was no use. For each one I managed to cut down, two more lurched forward to take their place, hellish black eyes glowing with otherworldly malice.

My sword arm burned with exhaustion as I parried their jagged blades and clawed hands. Beside me, Moorskill panted raggedly between swings of her sword, hair plastered to her sweat-sheened face. I could see the growing despair in her eyes as we were forced to give ground under the onslaught.

These were sailors I had once laughed and caroused with, men who had sworn oaths of loyalty in fair winds and foul. Now their faces were twisted masks of rage and hunger as they came for our flesh. Whatever dark forces had claimed them, they were wholly lost to them.

Our backs hit the foremast, cutting off any path of retreat. This was it. Against these impossible odds, our struggle could only end one way. I let my sword tip sink towards the planks, no energy left to lift it.

Moorskill's fierce eyes darted about for some last gambit, some way out. But there was none. Fate had lured us into its jaws, and they were about to snap shut.

As the wall of cursed sailors tightened the noose, I gave Moorskill a solemn nod. "You have fought valiantly," I managed, winded and exhausted. But we were finally defeated. The horrors of the Iron Sea had proven too great.

With leaden arms, I raised my blade, determined to give my final breath in defiance. The possessed crew converged, ragged lips peeled back in gruesome smiles.

This was the end. We had lost.

"Phillip!" Eloise cried out in alarm. "The pendant around your neck—it's glowing!"

Panic surged through my veins as I stared down at the fae trinket, still swinging from my neck—and then it happened. The world burst around us in a brilliant white light that swallowed us entirely.

When the flash slowly faded into the horizon, Eloise and I were all that was left standing on the deck. Not a single noise split the silence, apart from the relentless pelting of rain and the sails flapping wildly in the wailing wind.

"Where are they?" she whispered, her sword shuddering with the thrill still rushing through her veins.

I replied in disbelief. "They're... gone."

14

BEAUTY

*T*he Realm of Death had instilled in me a morbid understanding—nightfall cloaked the Netherworld in a mantle of gloom, with no dawn or daylight.

My eyes flickered open to my luxurious chamber, swathed in golden twilight. The gleam of emeralds and rubies danced across my vision as I groggily turned my head to find a smooth black sword nestled atop the bedside table.

I sat up in bed, heart pounding. My hands quivered slightly as I slid the sword from its sheath. Intricate designs were carved into the hilt, and gems of every color glittered against the gold setting. The guard gleamed in the dim light, shaped like a pair of wings and crafted from pure gold. Despite its beauty, it felt surprisingly light in my hand. Yet somehow, I could feel fathomless power radiating from within.

A rush of energy surged through me, a feeling so strange and exciting that it sent shivers down my spine. This was no ordinary blade, but something more alive than I could have imagined—whispering dark secrets into my ear. *"Take this sword, Mortal,"* it said. *"Use it to face your enemies and claim your rightful place among the gods."*

I shook my head, desperately trying to ignore the sinister croon as I returned the sword to its scabbard. It had been nothing more than my own imaginings, I told myself.

As I ambled around the room, there it was—the precious evening gown laid out on the dresser night after night since my arrival. Always a different dress, more exquisite than the one before it. I trailed my fingers along the fabric, feeling its silvery luminescence beneath the vibrant purple shade. The cloth shimmered like stars on a summer night, making my heart ache with something almost forgotten.

I hastened to get ready for dinner with Hypnos, my curiosity mounting. Why had he gifted me the sword? Was he warning me of danger? I couldn't forget my close call with the shades in the Veiled Forest.

A shiver raced through me as the icy fabric of the gown wrapped around my body, shimmering in the waning sunlight. The sword's presence weighed heavy in the air, almost as if it could sense the fear that plagued my every step, a portent of what would be. With one last glance at the ruins below, I collected the sword and left to dine with Hypnos, apprehension lingering in my wake.

The palace was deathly still as I ventured to the dining hall. No laughter from mysterious guests, no whispers from servants. Just me and the oppressive silence. The only sound, my footfalls echoing off the travertine floors. Though I was surrounded by towering walls and magnificent statues, icy wariness seeped through me, making every step harder than the last.

I arrived in the grand dining hall, empty and hauntingly silent. Only the soft flicker of dozens of candles illuminated the somber atmosphere. Hypnos was seated at the far end of the table, his arms resting on either side of a plate, his gaze fixed on me upon my entrance. He rose when I approached, a hint of a smile playing on his lips.

"Good evening, my lady," he said gallantly, gesturing for me to take the seat across from him. I slid into it hesitantly, laying the sword next to my place setting with an echoing clang that seemed to hang in the air.

Hypnos scrutinized the weapon with a raised brow. "Interesting choice of accessory," he murmured over the rim of his wine glass. His gaze smoldered as he waited for an explanation. "Is there something you wish to tell me?"

My heart raced and my cheeks burned under the pressure of his appraisal. "Thank you?" I ventured, confused by the question.

His eyes narrowed into slits and he slowly leaned back in his chair, taking a thoughtful sip of wine. I took a few deep breaths to calm my racing heart before finding the courage to speak again.

"I can't shake this feeling that something isn't right," I mused, sweeping my arm across the soundless room. "It's too... still."

Hypnos threw his head back in a gleeful laugh, and my heart skipped a beat at the golden beauty of it. "Ah, so perceptive," he rumbled. His eyes flickered with delight as he examined me. He reclined in his chair, shaking his head ever-so-slightly. "I assure you, there is nothing to fear." However, I couldn't shake the feeling that there was something more beneath his words.

"Isn't there?" I challenged, holding the sword between us, my gaze boring into his. "Then why give me this sword with no explanation? It doesn't make any sense."

He paused, eyes flickering to the blade resting on the table so innocently. "That sword makes a formidable gift. But it was no gift from me," he said, his voice laden with caution.

A deep sorrow crossed his features as he added softly, "Though I wish it had been."

I frowned in confusion, my doubts growing like weeds inside.

"Let me see it." Hypnos stood, gesturing for me to join him, and I did, offering up the blade without hesitation.

His features drained of color as he stared at it in disbelief. "Is this really…?" he whispered in amazement.

"What is it?" I asked, perplexed by his reaction. Then I looked down at the blade in my hand. "Is something wrong with it?"

"*Is something wrong,* you say!" Hypnos echoed. He let out a laugh, shaking his head in disbelief. "My lady, what you hold is none other than Voidbringer—legendary sword of the gods!"

*Voidbringer.* The name stirred something deep within my soul.

Hypnos edged closer to the sword but dared not touch it. "This blade is a weapon of the Realm of Death, made to strike down the restless spirits that haunt its cursed lands," he explained in a foreboding voice. "The blade is forged from blackened steel, tempered by the flames of the Netherworld itself. Its hilt is encrusted with precious gems, each one glistens with the colors of the souls it has taken."

I shuddered as I saw the countless jewels that adorned the handle. But the god continued, "The guard is shaped like a pair of wings, crafted from the purest gold, a symbol of freedom for one who seeks to bring balance to the Netherworld." He paused, fierce gaze cutting to mine. "Only a true champion of fate can wield its power."

My mouth went dry as his words settled in. "Then you must have it," I said, lifting the sword and extending it towards him.

He bolted back, eyes widening with dread and disbelief.

"No!" he forced out like a warning, almost a plea. His stare then fixed on the sword. "Don't you understand? Voidbringer is only Hades' to grant. If he deemed you worthy enough to carry it, no one can take it from your hands—not if they want to survive it."

A chill settled deep in my bones when he said it. "Worthy?" I started. I couldn't even bear my own reflection half the time. "Hypnos, I don't even know who I am," I murmured, turning away from the table. "But surely, I am not *worthy* of a god-made weapon."

"Let's find out," he stated, walking in the same direction.

I froze, my heart thumping painfully.

"Draw the sword," he commanded, shutting the door to any further discussion.

Begrudgingly, I did as he asked.

"So, can you handle a blade?" he challenged with an arched brow. Before I could protest, Hypnos tore his sword free from its sheath and lunged at me with divine ferocity.

My body moved before I could process it, blocking his attack with an agility that astounded us both.

"Aha!" he exclaimed, pleasantly surprised. He then threw himself forward, his blade swinging again, and I blocked it with ease; this time, attacking him instead. He stumbled back, clearly stunned at my skill.

"Impressive," he said, slipping his sword into its scabbard. "You *definitely* know your way around a sword." He moved closer to me, eyes glinting. "I didn't know you were so skilled at it."

"Neither did I..." I shrugged, trying not to cringe away from the look of awe in his gaze.

My stare angled down to the burnished black steel, my own eyes trapped in its reflection, when a sudden image flooded my mind—a younger version of myself standing in a magnificent courtyard by the sea, battling with a handsome man with unfathomable grace and skill.

I shut my eyes tightly and shook off the image, burying the strange emotions it stirred.

"You are a mortal in a realm of gods and monsters, my lady," Hypnos continued, as he escorted me to the sideboard. "I strongly suggest you keep this with you at all times, especially now that the shades have drawn so close to the palace."

Averting my gaze, I nodded earnestly. Worthy or not, I wholeheartedly agreed.

# 15

# PHILLIP

*T*he storm raged, the wind howling like a thousand hungry wolves and the waves battering against us, as if our vessel were nothing more than a toy. I clutched the ship's wheel for dear life, struggling to keep us on course, but it was fruitless.

And then I saw it. Rising from the blackness of the horizon—a vast, gaping vortex of dark water. A vision of utter terror, dragging us closer and closer.

A paralyzing wave of dread crashed over me. "Captain!" I cried hoarsely over the rising wind. "Dead ahead! It's a whirlpool!"

Raging sea foam churned around us, drawing us further into its murky depths. The Dragon's Breath creaked and groaned beneath our feet, her hull shaking and shuddering as if it were about to shatter into a million pieces.

Moorskill's cry of alarm rang through the air, mingled with the deafening roar of crashing waves. The raging vortex spun round and round, a roiling abyss that seemed to stretch on forever. Its power overwhelming, its depths unfathomable.

We were mere specks in its grasp, headed for a doom we could not possibly escape.

Overwhelmed by terror and awe alike, I clenched the railing, unable to turn away from our inescapable fate. Wood shrieked as if in pain; ropes snapped under the strain of the current. But even these signs of resistance paled in comparison to the maelstrom's fury. We were helplessly being pulled into its clutches, spiraling towards oblivion.

This was no natural phenomenon—it reeked of dark and treacherous magic as renowned as the Iron Sea itself.

I sprinted to Captain Moorskill's side and grasped her by the waist, shouting over the roar of the storm. "We must secure ourselves to the ship before the currents drag us under!"

She nodded silently, and I pulled her towards the mast, where the thick halyard was coiled up. My hands were shaking as I hastily tied one end of the rope to the mast and circled it tightly around Captain Moorskill's waist—if she fell overboard now, it would be certain death.

"Good work," she bawled above the wind. "Now see to yourself!"

The gusts of wind whipped my hair into my face as I fumbled with the knots, securing the rope tight enough so that I wouldn't be washed overboard either. But before I had properly coiled my side of the halyard, a massive wave hit us from starboard. The ship lurched violently, stumbling me off balance for just a moment—then lunged me forward to cling desperately to the rope as I saw the raging foam of the whirlpool spraying across my face.

Captain Moorskill kept her usual cool composure despite the perilous situation, but my heart was racing faster than ever before. For now, our lives depended solely on clinging onto this rope.

"Hold on!" I screamed over the thunderous roar of the

ocean. "It's going to be a rough one!" Steeling my courage, I fought against the weight of the whirlpool with every fiber of my being, hoping beyond hope that we might still escape its deadly clutches.

But I knew it was a useless battle. As I saw the yawning maw of death open before us, I could feel despair settle like an icy blanket upon my soul. The Dragon's Breath would soon join the graveyard of ships at the bottom of this dark abyss, and there was nothing I could do to save us. Still, I refused to back down. Though darkness threatened to swallow us whole, we wouldn't cower in fear. Our courage was our own to keep until the very end.

This was our fate—but we would meet it standing tall.

## 16
# BEAUTY

*I* slipped out of the Midnight Palace as soon as the first rays of dusk stained the sky in fiery hues. I skulked through its desolate long halls, not a peep from the usual guests or servants who since last evening seemed to have vanished without a trace. Even Hypnos was nowhere to be found.

The air had shifted in the last few hours, a sign of greater events to come. But I could not afford to entertain those concerns now. Not when I had one which was far more pressing—uncovering my identity.

With my sword in hand, and my recently discovered fighting skills untested, I seized the chance to delve into the fathomless Veiled Forest. No sooner had I left behind the exotic courtyard and plunged deeper into the woods, than the whisper of the ocean reached my ears. It called me with its siren song, tugging at my soul.

My heart hammered in my chest as the sound echoed through the dense forest. A cold sweat trickled down my back and my muscles ached with exertion, but I couldn't stop running. The unknown loomed before me, and I pressed on until I stumbled into a clearing. As the noise grew louder, an unexpected warmth enveloped me, and for a fleeting moment, I felt oddly at peace.

My mind's eye conjured an image of a foaming azure sea, with peaceful shorelines, where cherished dawn doused the salty air in pale amber light. Sunlight danced across the sea's restless surface, reflecting off its depths in golden glints.

A vision of grandeur rose in the distance—a soaring white cliff, crowned with a greystone fortress that cut through the clear morning sky. Its splendor filled me with awe and wonder. It woke a strange sense of upliftment in my being and quelled all my fears. A smile lit up my lips, only to be abruptly extinguished when the ground beneath me shook with the might of a powerful earthquake.

My eyes snapped open, anxiety surging through my veins. The gentle sound of the ocean faded away in a heartbeat, replaced with an ominous noise of crunching leaves and snapping twigs steadily drawing closer.

I whirled around in panic, my heart thumping wildly, as the forest seemed to come alive around me. Something was coming my way. Something *huge*.

The foliage thrashed and shuddered before me. I swallowed hard, and squinted through the darkness, desperate for a glimpse. And then it burst into view—a resplendent stag, breaking through the wall of trees. It was larger than any other I'd seen, and had antlers that seemed to have been crafted from the stars themselves, glinting with an ethereal light.

The beast furiously charged towards me, its coat shimmering and pulsating with wondrous power. Fear and awe ran through my veins, each pulse of my heart heavy and loud within my ears. I froze, rooted in place like a weed. The stag's feral beauty held me captive in a trance, helplessly still.

Suddenly, my stare flitted away from the stag, caught by

the striking creature running alongside it. The black leathers he wore molded to his sculpted body like a second skin, and his raven hair flew wildly in the breeze. His gaze burned with a deep maroon hue, so bright and intense that it rivaled the stag's fierceness.

His beauty was a thing of legend, his presence a force that radiated through the woods and reached straight into my soul.

I started, as in one astounding move, he seized the stag's antlers and flung himself atop its back, gripping the fur with masterful prowess. In a blur, his arm lashed up, the long sword strapped to his back suddenly visible. Steel glinted in the deepening twilight like lightning as the blade swept down, its razor-sharp edge plunging deep into the stag's spine. A wild roar made my skin prickle as the beast dropped to its forelegs, skidding across the grass before coming to a shuddering halt scarce paces away from where I stood, anchored to the ground.

Tears welled up in my eyes, threatening to spill over. I choked back a sob as the hunter dismounted the beast, blade dripping with fresh blood. No remorse or mercy crossed his features as he shook the gore from his blade and returned it to its sheath.

My stare followed him intently, hatred taking hold of me with a relentless grip. "What have you done?" I finally spat out, the words more of a shriek than a question.

He glared in my direction, fiery maroon eyes enhanced by the gruesome mess that adorned his face. Not a flicker of emotion escaped him.

When his deep-set eyes found mine for the first time, my lungs seized. Fear and loathing entwined, twisting my insides into knots, and yet, I remained helpless to resist his magnetic pull. My body refused to take me far away as I took in the sight of his handsome face, chiseled and angular, with sun-kissed skin pulled taut over sharp cheekbones. His smooth brow with arched eyebrows, and nose, straight and slightly narrow, startingly added to the stern depth of his expression.

"Who are you?" I asked, my voice barely more than a whisper. My feet carried me closer to him, despite all warnings in my head.

He tightened his gaze, rage and despair smoldering in his depths. The stag's blood still coated his features, red as rust dripping down his skin like ceaseless tears. He stood there before me for an eternity of moments, until a chill swathed my heart like icy fingers. Then slowly, he turned away and strolled back into the misty woods, fading like a ghost into the endless night.

The truth hit me like a shot of lightning. I had been foolish enough to draw the attention of the shades. This was yet another warning from fate to stay away from these woods. But it was too late—I had to move fast. Surely, more shades were on their way.

My heart pounded as I ran, pushing through the thick underbrush of the eerie woods. Every rustle of a leaf, every snap of a twig sounded like an attack in the stillness. The wind seemed to whisper warnings, and the shadows shifted and grew darker with every step.

My mind raced, searching for a way out before it was too late. I stumbled over a root, falling to my knees and quickly scrambling back to my feet. The sound of someone pursuing me crashed through the forest like thunder.

As I charged on, the forest distorted around me—the trees taking on grotesque shapes and the shadows deepening to form leering faces. I could hear my heart pounding in my ears and feel my breath coming in short, labored gasps.

Hope surged through me as the forest began to thin. The

stars twinkled in a blanket of fathomless night and lit the palace courtyard with silver-streaked radiance. Glistening marble columns rose up before me, a glittering beacon in the darkness.

I had finally arrived.

# PHILLIP

*I* opened my eyes to a tranquil sea, the stars sparkling in silent celebration. Somehow, we'd made it through the storm and outside the daunting whirlpool—but *had she*?

The blood chilled in my veins. I jostled free from my binds, my frantic gaze searching for a trace of her on deck. Eloise was lying unconscious at the bottom of the mast, the loose ropes still wrapped around her slender frame.

Panic rising in my chest, I staggered on my way towards her. "Eloise," I breathed as I freed her from the tangle of ropes. "Eloise, can you hear me?" I inched closer, and although she gave no answer, the warmth of her breath against my cheek came as a sweet relief.

"Come on," I murmured, my voice heavy with grief as I scooped her up into my arms. "Just a bit of rest and you'll be all right." Cradling her limp body, I trudged to my cabin—a chaotic disaster of overturned furniture and scattered crumpled parchment.

Carefully, I settled Eloise on the bed, making sure I tucked the covers up around her. I stayed by her side longer than necessary, my soul weighed with unease and my mind frenzied with unanswered questions.

By the time I walked out of the cabin, a cloak of confusion enveloped me. What had happened to our crew? How could they simply *vanish* into the burst of light? Where had they gone? What power had Elin granted me? I looked down at the emerald pendant. No magic remained in the Blushing Star—a lifeless gem. My heart hammered in my chest with merciless uncertainty.

I hurried back on deck, scanning the soundless sea for any sign of our crew. Nothing, just endless darkness and an overwhelming silence that sent chills down my spine.

I stood at the helm, my body aching from the fight and the fierce tempest we had barely survived.

The Dragon's Breath serenely drifted in the stark sea, its depths an abyss of ink as I had never seen.

"The Midnight Sea," I whispered, and the fae sisters' warnings resounded in my mind.

A heavy sigh escaped me as I perched on the edge of the deck, my gaze scanning the high night sky. I started as it became clear to me: the stars had shifted, jumbled into disarray. I couldn't make out a single constellation. This meant one thing—we were far from land, and there was no way to read our true position at sea.

Sleep pulled at me, a heavy weight dragging me down into a welcome stupor. I gave in with grateful abandon, melting into the depths of an exhausted slumber.

In my dream, I saw her. Aurora. A starlit goddess, shrouded in shadows. She glided through an ethereal pavilion, a pristine white gown gracefully billowing around her as she hovered over the pond of darkness.

*"My dearest..."* My entire being burned with the need to rescue her and make amends. But my voice was but a whisper in the wind and never reached her ears.

A sudden force ripped me away, and though I fought its power with all I had, a mist of shadows quickly swarmed over Aurora, blocking out my view until no trace of her remained.

Even though I was a godless man, I prayed for help to Poseidon and Proteus, the mightiest gods of the seas, begging for a way to reach Aurora and save her from the Prince of the Netherworld's claws.

Soon, I drifted into a deeper sleep, but before it swept away my full awareness, I swore that no matter what happened, I would never give up on Aurora until she was safe in my arms once again.

# BEAUTY

*I* staggered into the palace, my body aching with throbbing hunger. But curiosity swiftly squelched my weakness. As I navigated the palace halls, I noticed an unprecedented number of servants in attendance. Everywhere I looked—in the corridors and the chambers, in the gardens and on the grounds—they hurried about with a strange sense of urgency. They no longer carried themselves with their usual subtlety; rather, they bustled through the halls like a flock of sparrows, squawking announcements left and right as if issuing orders from an unseen authority.

It wasn't just their behavior that shocked me either; it was their attire. Most wore long black hooded cloaks made out of a rich material, unlike anything I'd ever seen. What was once heavy twill was now replaced with solid velvet that draped richly. Even more puzzling were their faces: every one of them wore identical golden masks that covered their eyes and nose while leaving their lips visible.

I found this strange behavior even stranger when I arrived at my bedroom and spotted the evening gown laid out for me on the bed. The dress was made from a rich, silky black fabric that shimmered under the light, embroidered in gold—more lavish than any I'd worn so far. This time, matching jewelry displayed inside a box rested next to the dress... Hypnos must have planned a very special evening.

My bare feet pounded against the pristine marble floors as I hastened to the washroom, desperate to rinse away the dirt and dried blood from my skin. The long walk to the palace had been exhausting, and the stag's brutal slaughter weighed upon my spirit like a millstone—its once-radiant life extinguished before my eyes. Grief swelled within me, an aching tide threatening to breach the crumbling dam of composure I clung to. That beautiful creature's final agonized roar would haunt the corners of my mind long after this blood-soaked night surrendered to twilight.

As I let the warm water rinse over me, I couldn't shake off the feeling that something was off. The servants' strange behavior and exquisite attire made me uneasy, and I couldn't help but wonder what was going on behind closed doors. Was there some sort of secret event happening?

My thoughts were interrupted by a soft knock on the bathroom door, and I quickly wrapped myself in a silken robe before opening it.

When I emerged from the washroom, a silent figure came into view. Her face was obscured by a golden mask, but her eyes were luminous. She seemed to be studying me, watching my every move as if she could see through the veil of my skin.

As my gaze drifted downward, I noticed my gown, resting neatly over her arms. "Are you here to help me dress?" I asked quietly.

She didn't speak, but simply outstretched her hands in reply. Hesitantly, I stepped forward and placed myself into her care, feeling her silent warmth spilling over me. Everything else fell away as I gazed into her emerald eyes, wondering what it was that she saw in me.

She carefully draped the fabric of my gown around my figure, pinning it up with fasteners made of gold-set stones. She adorned me from neck to wrists to ears with shining gems, her movements a precise yet hasty rhythm—like an ancient ritual prelude to something magical about to occur.

A deep neckline and delicate straps crisscrossed my collarbones, descending in a low-cut back. The skirt cascaded from the waist in voluminous folds that swirled when I moved. Slit at the thigh, only a tantalizing hint of my leg was revealed as the black fabric shimmered beneath a sheer tulle overlay, its ethereal quality lending a dreamy air.

She toiled with meticulous precision, adorning me with rings and earrings, a golden headpiece that beamed like the light of royalty. "Do you have a name?" I dared to ask as I gazed at her, my voice barely audible. "Will you not speak to me?"

Her gold-flecked green eyes sparkled in the moonlight as she smiled, then lovingly arranged my blonde tresses into a familiar hairstyle. She stepped back, bowed her head in reverence, and then melted away into the night.

I stood there for what felt like an eternity, taking it all in, and held my breath, feeling like the world had come to a standstill, while I was trapped in a spiral of uncertainty. How much longer could I remain hidden amongst these shadows before my identity was revealed?

I finally exhaled, my gaze drawn to the idyllic silver-streaked night beyond the terrace. The courtyard below had been transformed into a breathtaking haven, with lounges scattered around the garden and magnificent stone fire bowls flickering amid the greenery.

The night was alive with merriment and the air was heavy with the scent of exotic perfumes. I watched as elaborate dresses glittered on swaying ladies, their laughter echoing in the garden. Masked servants moved swiftly among them, ever ready to meet their needs. Musicians played joyous tunes and dancers moved around the fires, spinning with delight. Everyone spoke of distant lands and wild adventures, and for a fleeting moment, all my woes seemed to be forgotten as I was swept into the night's embrace.

Darkness and moonlight entwined in harmony, like a symphony of hope. Drawing courage from that promise, I sauntered to the door.

With each step I took down the seemingly endless hallway, the voices echoing around me faded until I found myself standing in the entranceway of the dining hall. I stood there, mesmerized by the beauty of the room before me.

The room where Hypnos and I had spent many hours in conversation had transformed—its domed ceiling, a vault of midnight marble, glittering with shimmering silver stars that glowed softly like a night sky. The walls were now adorned with intricate carvings of mythological creatures, their shapes flickering in the undulating light of the candles that lined the room.

At the center of the space loomed an immense ebony table, its polished surface reflecting the quivering flames. The chairs that surrounded it were crafted of dark wood, carved with twisted vines and thorny brambles. Place settings at each chair were decorated with gleaming silverware, delicate black crystal goblets, and sumptuous purple napkins that seemed to shimmer in the candlelight.

On one side of the chamber, a massive stone fireplace crackled and blazed with golden flames, casting a warm and inviting light over the entire room. The walls on either side were lined with shelves filled with ancient tomes and mysterious artifacts, giving the impression that this palace had been here for eons.

I stepped inside, my heart already pounding. As I beheld this place of secrets and enchantment, I knew I had walked into something far more than a room. But for all my expectations, nothing could have prepared me for what now lay before me.

At the head of the empty table sat a man cloaked in night, his hand tracing lazy circles in a bowl of pomegranate seeds. Firelight flickered off his sharp eyes, and I knew right away who he was. It was *him*. The shade who'd callously killed that beautiful stag in the forest. The same one who had broken my heart with his cruel disregard for life.

He sat there, transformed by his attire. He wore lush black leather pants and a midnight linen tunic, but none of it changed what he'd done or how I felt about him—wrathful and disgusted until my last breath.

The shade's dark locks were tightly bound in a sleek bun, raven feathers adorning its tips. His boots were pure black leather, shining in the muted candlelight.

"You shouldn't be here," I whispered in disbelief, my heart running wild in my ribcage.

He stared me down with deep maroon eyes, their intensity drilling straight into my core. The world stood still until his lips parted.

"I see a feast fit for more than one appetite," he said, his voice as deep and dark as a moonless night.

I flinched, almost cowering beneath the oppressive atmosphere. "This palace belongs to the Dark Prince Hades," I choked out. "If he finds you…"

His lips curved in a sardonic smile. "I hear he's quite lenient when he wants to be," he drawled, slouching into the chair as if it were his right. Each word came out like a sharpened blade, cold and deadly. His ferocity could not but remind me of the wild stag, and I sensed its primal energy surrounding him—an untamed storm that was both terrifying and beautiful. The strength that surged through his veins left a tingle across my skin.

My jaw tightened as I hissed, "You're so sure of yourself."

He snickered, a smug smile on his lips. "He took *you* in, didn't he?" His words were drenched in irony as his dark eyebrow arched higher.

Heat flooded my face as my mind fumbled for words. Panic raced through me, my identity unknown, even to me. A mere human, standing in the fortress of the formidable Prince of the Netherworld—what could I possibly offer him? Nothing, and yet here I was: safe within his kingdom.

"You have a choice," he crooned. His eyes seemed to flicker as if evaluating my reaction. "You can either join me or walk away... Although—" He paused. "Although, I'm sure the trek from the Veiled Forest is strenuous on an empty stomach."

My stomach rumbled in protest and I knew I'd lost this battle before it began. I stood straighter, fighting the urge to scream and pound my fists against the table. He was right, of course—pride was my armor, but it did little to satisfy the hollow hunger that plagued me.

At my slightest sign of surrender, the corner of his lips curled up in quiet satisfaction. He pointed to the newly formed dishes: roasted birds glimmering from their basting of honey, succulent fruits that promised to taste like the sweetest nectar.

I dragged the chair out and sat, breathing in the aroma of food so different from what I was used to. My mouth watered.

Silence stretched between us like a lonely desert. All the while, he toyed with the pomegranates, splitting them expertly with his fingers, pouring the seeds into a golden bowl. Then, at last, he looked up at me, eyes shining with secret knowledge. "Pomegranates," he said, a wistfulness in his voice. He ran his finger over the smooth surface of one, then looked up at me with a sad smile. "My favorite food—can only be found in Hades' courtyard."

I nodded, finally understanding why he'd chosen to come here tonight, against all odds—not just for the sweet taste of pomegranates, but searching for a reminder of home, as I did when I thought of the sea. He and I were not so different, after all. Both of us stranded souls in the Netherworld, searching for a shred of our identity.

The aching longing in his gaze pierced my heart like an arrow. He must have missed home more than I could ever know to risk trespassing into the Dark Prince's domain.

He offered me the golden bowl, filled with ruby-red seeds. I bowed my head in gracious acceptance and he rose from the seat, carrying the dish with him until it rested before me. I took it, and he silently asked to join me in this brief respite from our tumultuous meeting. I agreed, and he took the chair beside me, glittering dark eyes resting on mine as my fingers dug into the small morsels. After what felt like an eternity of waiting, he finally picked up one himself—his hands closing around it like a precious gift.

The more time we spent together, the more his previous behavior confused me. My patience finally ran out as I cradled a wineglass in my hands. "Why do you do it?" I blurted.

"Do... *what?*" he responded darkly, a frown on his lips.

I swallowed back my fear and spoke boldly. "Why do you hunt them? The stags." I paused. "Is that what shades do?"

He stared at me for a moment before replying, holding an unreadable expression.

I took a swig, my gaze trained on him. "Is it a sport?" I pressed on, unable to soften the derision in my voice. "Do you find it *amusing* to take their lives?"

He flushed. His chest rose with a sharp breath and a

muscle twitched along his strong jawline. "One can only do *so many things* in the Netherworld," he said through gritted teeth.

My lips parted, ready to stab back with my reply when he dropped his napkin onto the table with a harsh slap and rose to his feet. "Enjoy your dinner," he spat, turning away.

And then, he was gone.

# 19

# PHILLIP

*A*t first, there was silence. Nothing stirred in the dark, save for the distant melody carried on a sorrowful breeze. Like an invisible tether, it called to me, and I drifted towards the sound until I lay suspended between sleep and wakefulness.

> *"Arise, arise, my dear prince fair,*
> *Behold the magic in the air.*
> *The Midnight Sea, a mystic sight,*
> *Unveils its splendor in the night."*

The enchanting song compelled me to open my eyes. I rose from the deck, drawn forward by its charm, until I was standing at the ship's taffrail. My hands folded on the railing as I watched a million stars blanketing the inky sea beneath me, twinkling and waltzing across the crests of its rolling waves.

*"Come, open up your eyes and see,*
*The wonders that await thee,*
*Beneath the stars, so bright and true,*
*A world of treasure... just for you."*

My breathing hitched. I'd thought I was dreaming, but there it was—the source of the voice. In awe, I watched as the night's obsidian canvas split open, revealing a breathtaking sight before me. An ageless shipwreck had been thrown onto a rocky island, its worn timbers a reminder of the courage and loss it had seen throughout its long travels.

Lightning thrummed through my veins, a mix of thrill and terror. What darkness had swallowed the crew once sailing these capricious waters? Had they suffered the same fate as the Dragon's Breath?

I rushed to the wheel and steered the ship with unwavering resolve towards the island. Riches had no bearing on my mission, but I sensed my answers rested in the depths of this ghostly vessel.

As I sailed closer, the cliffs of this strange island rose like sharp fangs from the sea. A chill crept up my spine—it was as if all my darkest fears were gathering there, waiting for me. My heart beat heavily in my chest with strange anticipation, and yet, I knew I must keep going.

Garnering my resolve, I steered the ship towards a hidden cove, its waters dark and still.

I readied the longboat to take me across the treacherous waters. My gaze remained locked on its spectral shape as I paddled closer to the brig. The ship loomed huge before me, larger than any I had ever seen before. Its wood was tarnished by time and sea salt and its rigging hung like tattered ribbons from its masts. Yet despite the deteriorated state, it held a certain majesty that stirred something inside me, promising danger and adventure beyond measure.

The song echoed on, a hauntingly beautiful melody that grew louder as I ventured closer to the ruins. It seemed to come from everywhere and nowhere all at once, a mysterious sound that captivated me with its strange beauty.

*"Oh sailor, hear my woeful croon*
*Of hearts that break and dreams that swoon.*
*When love is lost, what's left to do?*
*But sing this song of loveless doom."*

An epiphany crashed into me like a wave. "A castaway," I gasped, my senses on high alert. "Someone's on that boat!" Somewhere, out there in the turbulent sea, a woman was adrift.

My heart raced as I rowed closer, each pull of my oar rippling through the dusky night. Again and again, the woman's voice shattered the stillness, her song a painful lament that clung to my soul—I knew that ache, the loss of youthful dreams. Years ago, when Aurora had chosen a dark god over me, it had crushed my spirit, and I'd vowed then never to love again.

Pushing those memories aside, I scrambled on board, finding the ship deeply lodged into a bed of rocks. My hands were shaking with restless valor as I tied the rope around the splintered debris, and I watched as what little remained was immovable in its grasp.

I hurried off the boat. She was waiting for me to arrive, waiting for someone to hear her sorrow and rescue her from the clutches of the sea.

*"The waves they crash, the winds they howl*
*And tears are shed like falling fowl*
*For love is gone, and hope is frail*
*But still, I sing this mournful tale."*

The planks creaked with each step as I moved towards the helm's remains, following the sound. My gaze slowly swept the desolate landscape of splintered deck boards and fraying oars, flapping against the wind's bitter chill.

With my heart hammering against my rib cage, I finally reached the dilapidated cabin. Ancient swords hung from the walls, their edges gleaming in the dim light, while harpoons leaned against the doorframe like forgotten sentinels. Fine beads of perspiration dripped down my forehead as my hand folded on the grimy iron door handle. I took a deep breath and thrust open the door. The stench of mold and rot instantly assaulted me, but I pressed on, plunging further into the void. With each step taken, my torchlight illuminated more of the decayed interior, highlighting cobwebbed walls that hadn't seen the light of day in centuries.

The deep rumble of thunder suddenly shook the wreckage, rattling everything around me. My torch bounced and swayed as it clattered from my grip. It rolled down the floor and, stricken with horror, I watched it stop at a pile of human bones. Time had picked them clean, but their meaning was clear. This crew would never again make port.

But then, something glinted in the corner of my eye—a small, ornate treasure chest tucked away from the pile of bones, almost forgotten by fate. Drawn to it, I took one step closer... only to be startled by a splash nearby.

> *"The sea it swells, the tides they turn*
> *And still, our hearts do yearn and yearn*
> *For love is gone, but hope remains*
> *And in this song, we ease our pains."*

I heard the voice, closer now. Determination clawed up my throat. I had to get her out of there. My feet shifted cautiously on the moldy floorboards and clumps of dust rose around me. But the pull of her presence lured me ever closer, more powerful than before. One foot in front of the other, I moved towards a gaping hole in the wall—towards the figure that waited beyond it.

And then, I saw.

My breath hitched at the sight of her—floating in the night like an ethereal goddess, arms folded calmly against her chest. Her soaked chemise was tattered and billowed around her slender body, clinging to curves that seemed too perfect for this world. A soft halo of red floated around her head, crowned with a wraith of dark blue flowers, and her skin glinted in the moonlight like pristine porcelain. Clear blue gems sparkled in the darkness, her eyes, wide and brimming with tears, each one a reflection of my own pain.

A heavy mist descended between us, stinging my skin with its chill. I looked into her sorrowful eyes and spoke softly, though I knew it wouldn't be enough to bring her towards me. "My lady, you can't remain here in the water," I said, stretching out a hand as far as I could reach. "It must be freezing. Please, come out."

The woman watched me from beneath the surface, unmoved. I shifted closer to the edge, tempted to dive in and rescue her myself. But I could only wait—for an answer or a miracle—hanging onto my hope that she'd find her way back soon.

Her silence was tangible and thrummed like a living thing between us. I looked into her eyes, now wide, spellbound by the fragile beauty before me.

At last, the woman emerged, her lips parting to speak, "I've barely any clothes, my lord." Her pale lips glistened as the tip of her tongue ran over them, shifting their petal-pink hue into a deep, plum-violet.

My throat bobbed as I swallowed hard past the emotion that welled up in me, and I was suddenly aware of every beat of my heart. With great effort, I quashed the desire swirling through my veins. "You can wear mine," I offered softly.

Delight twinkled in her eyes and the corner of her lips tilted upward in a secretive smile. She gracefully swam closer until she stopped near me, delicate arms folded over the ledge. I sank to my knees, meeting her gaze with relief bubbling up inside me.

"Did you like it?" she suddenly asked, her voice ringing out in the stillness of the cabin.

I flinched at the sound, confusion clear on my face.

"My song," she explained, her voice trembling. She held my gaze for a moment, desperate anticipation clouding the fear in her eyes. "Did you find it pleasing?" The brokenness of her heart painfully lingered in the air between us.

"Your song touches me even as its sorrow aches," I whispered, my gaze settling on the hands that rested so close to mine atop the ledge. I leaned closer, daring to draw nearer to appreciate her beauty.

Her soft brows knitted into a frown. "Do you... despise my song, then?" The most delightful pout graced her lips, but the gloom in her eyes kept me from smiling in response.

"No," I answered gently. "No, I do not despise your song. On the contrary, my lady. It speaks to me on a deeper level. Your pain resonates with my own, you see. And I find solace in knowing that I am not alone in my heartbreak." My hand trembled as I reached for hers, until our fingertips finally touched. "Your song may be sad, but it is also beautiful, and it reminds us that even in our darkest moments, there is still beauty to be found."

A hint of surprise lit up her face. "You are both handsome and wise," she said in silent admiration. "You understand my pain in ways not many do, my lord."

I gave a slow nod. "I've lived it," I said gruffly. "I'm afraid I know heartache through and through."

In an act of boldness, the warmth of my hand clashed against the iciness of hers. My heart beat wildly as I felt a spark when she pressed her palm against mine. Her delicate fingers trekked up my arm, the heat of her touch spreading through my veins like wildfire.

"Your eyes are like the sea, my lord—one moment green, the next blue." She tilted her chin up, a slight plea in her voice. "Come closer so I can tell for sure."

"Only if you promise to come out of the water…" I looked away from her lips and into her eyes, beseeching her with my own. "My lady."

A ghost of a smile curved on her lips. "Princess Iseult is my name, my lord."

The words stunned me for a moment. A Princess? Here? Before I could recover enough to speak again, she continued.

Her gaze bore deeply into mine, searching for something only she knew. "I sense the power of royalty within you as well," she said softly. "Is this also true?"

"It is," I replied proudly. "I am Prince Phillip Steelborn, Ruler of…"

"The Iron-hearted Steel Lion," she said knowingly. Awe filled her expression as she took in my figure.

Instant warmth spread through me at her words. "You've heard of the battles I've won—the kingdoms I've seized?" I asked in undiluted wonder.

Her features softened as if a memory had flashed through her mind, though her gaze remained steeled. "Of the hearts you've taken," came her flat and cold reply. "Tales of your conquests have traveled far and wide, Your Highness."

As I looked upon her, I couldn't help but be drawn to the subtle movement on her neck. My pulse raced as I drew near, carefully brushing away a lock of damp red hair from her shoulder. At first, I thought it was a trick of the light, but upon closer inspection, I saw two delicate, yet intricate gills on the side of her neck. Exquisite, like small, translucent wings fluttering beneath her skin, undulating in a graceful dance as she breathed.

I couldn't believe what I was seeing, she was beautiful beyond compare.

"Tell me," the princess whispered, moving even closer to me. "Where do your travels take you now? Are you seeking more adventures?"

My unfocused mind could think of nothing more than her stunning presence. "I... I cross the Midnight Sea to... That is to say, I..." My voice failed me as my tongue became twisted with words that wouldn't come out right.

She smiled before continuing in a whisper. "Perhaps if I sing for you…"

An indescribable emotion filled me. Nothing else in this world mattered more than the heat radiating from her body and the sweet smell of flowers that emanated from her skin. "Perhaps then..." I breathed, my words dying on my lips as her delicate hand glided along my jawline, sending sparks of electricity down my spine.

A beautiful melody left her lips, and I was lost, enthralled by her nearness.

> *"So listen well, oh sailor dear...*
> *And let this song draw ever near*
> *For love is lost, but hope remains*
> *And in this song, we ease our pains."*

As her song faded, I felt an invisible force tugging me closer. Her words were a whisper in the stillness, and I barely even noticed her icy breath on my skin.

"My fair prince," she whispered, her enchanting voice holding me in her thrall. "Only *you* can break my curse."

My heart raced with anticipation as I realized what she asked of me.

"A single kiss is all it takes," she added, tilting her head ever so slightly.

I swallowed hard, trying and failing to move away from her. *No,* I wanted to say. From the depths of my soul, that was my answer. But soon, I realized no sound would come through. Again, I tried to move, to no avail. My knees were rooted to the spot, anchored by some mysterious enchantment.

In that fleeting moment when our eyes locked and her mouth opened in a desperate attempt to taste life, I saw the sharp glint of her ivory fangs reflecting off the flickering torchlight.

*No!* I tried to scream as horror struck me, frozen in place, yet unable to tear my gaze away. I wanted to fight, but no inch of my body answered to my will—it was as if everything in me lay at her command. And when her fangs drew closer, when death opened its arms to drag me under in one last vicious kiss, I found myself unable to resist it any longer.

## 20

## BEAUTY

*I* blinked. Had I dreamed it? Had I really just dined with the shade from the forest? My gaze trailed to the bowl overflowing with pomegranate seeds, and my doubts disappeared.

"Where have you been?" Hypnos barged into the dining room, startling me out of my trance. "It's a beautiful night! Everyone is here! I've been waiting for you outside for ages."

He dragged up a chair and seated himself right beside me. "Trust me, you won't want to miss the Midnight Ball," he added with gentle warmth.

I turned to meet his gaze, hazel eyes that shone like sunlight through the clouds. "What are we celebrating?" I whispered, my thoughts paralyzed by his mesmerizing stare.

A sigh escaped him. "My lady, this is the Netherworld!" he exclaimed, astonished. "We dance and feast and drink for no reason at all!" His hands flew in the air in a grand gesture.

I stared at the ruby-red spheres, reminded of my own desire, my craving to chase the sound of the waves and discover what lay beyond them. More than ever, I wanted my name. And as my insatiable longing grew, a dangerous fear settled in my heart. What if I never found it? What if I was doomed to wander the Netherworld, nameless for eternity? Prince Hades be damned.

"What if I don't feel like dancing and celebrating?" I murmured ruefully.

"Then I'd forbid it," he purred into my ear. His breath was warm against my skin and his fingers gentle as they touched my arm. "I want nothing but joy and delight for you, my darling." He lifted a glass from the table and pressed it into my hand. "Drink, my lady—drink and fill your heart with hope."

Persuaded by the god's divine power, I grabbed the glass and downed the drink in one greedy gulp. If one more night was to be spent in this palace with no recollection of who I was, then I would make it count.

The first sip of ambrosia was enough to make me feel something again. Grief and despair washed away with each steady swallow, and hope pulsed through my veins like a faint drumbeat. A smile crept across my mouth, barely noticeable but there.

A wicked smirk curled on Hypnos' lips as he pulled me to my feet. "That's more like it. Now, shall we?"

I pressed my lips together, took a deep breath in, and nodded. Without a second thought, I carelessly tossed the glass onto the table and followed him out of the room. Our footsteps were swallowed by the shadows of the palace hallway, which seemed strangely quiet compared to the music that echoed from outside. The fire bowls in the courtyard cast an eerie glow across our path, and the pleasant melody continued to grow louder as we drew closer to the gateway.

The garden glowed in the firelight, a captivating spectacle of beauty. Every man and woman was a vision, the ethereal gleam of their eyes reflecting the warm flames like Hypnos' spell on me. They were scattered into small groups, all equal parts breathtaking.

Awe cascaded over me as I took in the sight of the gods, each glowing brilliantly in their detailed garments. The flickering light of torches danced off the gold and silver threads that ran through the fabric like rivers of molten metal, with precious gems complementing each stitch. It was almost too beautiful to bear; it seemed like all the beauty of creation had been pooled together in this one place to be shared by these divine beings.

My eyes moved from deity to deity, and I couldn't help but feel a sense of insignificance in their presence. But at the same time, I felt inexplicably drawn to them, as if I belonged here among them in this enchanted world.

As we walked through the lively pathway, three figures cut through the commotion. They stood as stark contrasts against the celebration, wearing deep red and black cloaks that spread beyond their shoulders and cascaded down their backs. Black feathered wings peeked out from beneath them, and bejeweled swords hung from their waists, glinting against the golden armor they wore.

The scarlet glint of their gaze cut through me like a blade, and I shuddered as our paths crossed—their eyes glowing, just slightly, as though lit from within by some inner ember.

"*Don't* stare," Hypnos spoke quietly, his voice laced with caution. "The Keres don't appreciate it."

I shivered at the name. "The Keres?" I whispered in a fearful voice.

"Mm," he replied. "The hounds of Hades—bringers of violent death." Hypnos' fingers closed around my arm in an iron grip, dragging me away from the haunting creatures I could feel watching me.

We sauntered back into the courtyard, and as soon as we stepped through the threshold, I noticed a tall figure that invariably drew all eyes. He wore deep green robes that hugged his broad shoulders and swept the floor. A flash of gold illuminated his hair—slicked back from his strong jawline and rippling in waves to the base of his neck. His face was angular, with sharp cheekbones and a gaze that held both wisdom and power.

Green eyes like molten emeralds seemed to pulse with energy as he stepped forward and said, "Who is this lovely creature that accompanies you tonight, Hypnos? I do not recall having seen her in our realm before."

Hypnos responded with a chuckle, "Ah, this is my dearest friend, a mortal from the world above. A guest of our host, Hades."

Chronos' eyes widened in surprise at the revelation, and a smile played at the corners of his lips. "A mortal in the Netherworld? How curious." He swept me with an appraising stare. "I must say, she is quite enchanting. I am delighted to have made her acquaintance."

He bowed gracefully to Hypnos before turning towards me. "We must dance," Chronos declared, resolved. "You will bewitch all who behold you, and I shall be the most envied among gods." A flash of a handsome smile sealed the deal.

Hypnos folded his arms across his chest, and delighted, he gave me a swift nod of encouragement. So, I took the hand Chronos offered with a trembling heart and followed him into the center of the courtyard.

The music dwindled away to nothing, leaving us in the stillness. Just as the Lord of Time had expected, every pair of eyes was fixed on me and him. His hand rested firmly on the small of my back as a new melody began, leading me effort-lessly through the steps.

"I have a confession to make," he said sternly.

"Oh?" I uttered as he spun me in time with the melody.

When the music reached its crescendo, Chronos pulled

me close to his chest. "I am not just a god of time." His breath tickled my ear as he whispered, "I am *also* a god of dance."

I couldn't help the laugh that spilled from my lips at his silly admission. "Is that so?" I said. "Well then, I'd say you have quite a way with both."

Chronos chuckled. "Why, thank you for the compliment," he said with a hint of arrogance. "But I must warn you, my dance moves are not to be trifled with. You may find yourself under my spell before the night is through."

I raised an eyebrow teasingly. "Is that a challenge, Lord Chronos?" Another laugh escaped me.

He grinned mischievously. "It most certainly is, my dear." He paused. "I must say, you have a lovely laugh," Chronos remarked, his eyes crinkling at the corners as I chuckled in response.

"Thank you," I replied, feeling a blush rising to my cheeks. "This is a beautiful place, surrounded by such wonderful company."

Chronos nodded in agreement. "Indeed, it is a rare occasion for mortals to be invited to the Netherworld. You are fortunate to have the favor of our host, Prince Hades."

"Where *is* the host of this event, who hasn't even deigned to grace us with his presence?" I murmured sarcastically.

He cocked an eyebrow, but said nothing.

I decided to amend my words before he could question me further. "What I meant was that I am especially grateful for our kind host's hospitality—it has been an incredible opportunity to meet so many fascinating people. Like you."

Chronos grinned, a mischievous glint in his eye. "Well, I am certainly flattered. Perhaps I can even convince you to stay with me a while longer, and we can dance the night away?"

My laughter rang out and I felt a thrill in my heart as I

thought of all the moments to come. "I would like that very much," I declared, feeling braver than before.

The music grew louder and enveloped us in its beautiful embrace. I allowed the beat to flow through me, spinning dizzying circles until I felt as though I was soaring—forgetting everything but this moment in his arms.

The flurry of the dance floor seemed to explode around us as he twirled me with an intensity that left my heart pounding. His gaze burned into mine, and it was like we were dancing our own private ballet. I felt the electricity between us, raw and untamed, and my body moved without thought, without hesitation.

When the music faded away, the trance dissipated and he grinned at me. "What a pleasure it is, to dance with you..." There was a hint of something else in his words, something that reached out and pulled me closer. "Come, let us go for a walk so that everyone may see us."

My voice caught in my throat as I agreed, feeling like I was walking straight into danger.

We strolled outside the central courtyard, into the winding paths of the garden. The walkways were paved with smooth crystals that sparkled in the night light, reflecting waves of rainbows across this tranquil paradise. A strange sensation embraced me as I gazed at this wondrous garden— it felt like stepping into another realm entirely.

The fire blossoms that lined the pathway glowed with a fierce intensity, casting an otherworldly light on everything around them. Their petals were a vibrant red and orange, and their centers blazed like tiny suns. Alongside them, the blood roses added a touch of dark elegance to the garden. Their dark petals seemed to absorb the light from the fire blossoms, creating a stark contrast between the two. The scent of their blooms was heady and intoxicating, and I found myself drawn to them despite their ominous appearance. But my steps stopped altogether as I stumbled upon the strangest of blooms, large and bell-shaped, with petals of a deep shade of purple-black. The sweetest fragrance seeped from them into the warm evening air, delightful and quietening.

"I've not seen these before," I mumbled in sheer awe.

"Shadow Lilies," Chronos said from beside me, his voice cold and disinterested. "They're quite poisonous... and ghastly too."

My fingers lingered on the petals, delighting in their softness. "I think they're beautiful," I whispered, a smile tugging at my lips. Suddenly, the petals shifted from dark to bright crimson and gleamed as though lit from within.

I spun to face Chronos, eager to hear what he had to say next. But his expression morphed into something unreadable, and he took a step forward. His fingers curled around my arm, warm and strong as he steered me away.

"We need to go back now." There was an urgency to his voice that hadn't been there before. "This way."

My head dipped in a stunned nod. What had I done to provoke this? His steel gaze seemed to strip away my courage and I fought the urge to back away, or worse—ask questions that would only stir trouble. Silence seemed to be the safest path.

No words sailed between us as we moved, his hand still tight around my arm. I stopped walking as we reached the courtyard, and he did too, his piercing gaze meeting mine with an agonized look.

"Do you know?" he murmured, his eyes shining in the moonlight. His voice was soft and it cracked as he spoke. "You remind me so much of someone I used to cherish."

I couldn't tear my eyes away from him, even as a swarm of servants bustled around us. Draped in black and veiled with golden masks, they carried bouquets of vibrant flowers, heavy jugs full of wine, and baskets brimming with fruits and seeds.

My voice was almost too quiet when I asked, "What happened to her?"

Chronos shook his head as if he didn't have the answer. "One day, she simply... disappeared." His voice dropped to a whisper as his eyes glazed with nostalgia.

He swallowed hard. "We need more wine," he mumbled with a hint of annoyance. Swiftly, Chronos waved a hand at one of the servants and shouted with renewed vigor. "Wine!"

The servant obediently offered us a pair of glasses filled with ambrosia, and Chronos snatched his up immediately. He took a large swig before handing me mine.

I furrowed my brow. "Why cover their faces?" I asked as soon as the servant walked away.

Chronos didn't meet my eyes. "It keeps them safe," he said gruffly.

"Safe?" My expression shifted to a frown as I thought of what they could possibly need protection from. But before I could ask, a flock of ravens flew overhead, dazzling me with their luminescent feathers gleaming in a rainbow of hues.

The god's gaze followed them for a moment before angling back to me. He hesitated, his face taut with something too dark to speak aloud. "From Death's eyes," he whispered, then downed the wine in a single swig and tossed it away, carelessly discarding the precious gold-rimmed glass.

"Hades?" I mumbled with a frown.

"No. Not Hades," Chronos whispered. "His sentry, Thanatos." His tone was laced with derision. "Hades rules the Netherworld, but Thanatos is death itself, and he's as vile as they come."

Gooseflesh shot up my arms.

Chronos harrumphed. He then clapped his hands together with an abruptness that made me flinch. "Come now!" He turned a pleasant face towards the gathering of gods and goddesses. "Everyone must meet you!"

A strange mix of trepidation and wonderment filled me as I surveyed the gods and goddesses before us. The faces of the people around me were so singularly unique that they revealed their place within this magical realm without words. Although they were clearly from a different realm, I sensed an inexplicable connection to them—as if somehow, this was exactly where I belonged.

A regal figure caught my attention, standing at the edge of the courtyard. She stood tall and proud in a flowing gown of deep purples and her hair pulled back in a crown of twisted braids. She watched the revelers with a critical eye, her dress fluttering around her like a cloak.

Chronos noticed my gaze and followed it to the goddess. "Ah, there is the mistress of magic herself," he said. "Shall I introduce you?"

My heart beat faster as I nodded eagerly. Wasting no time, Chronos took my hand and led me across the courtyard to where Hecate was waiting for us, her single raised eyebrow conveying both curiosity and suspicion.

"Hecate," he said with a bow, "allow me to introduce this beautiful lady, a mortal guest of our host, Prince Hades." Chronos turned, gesturing towards me.

I felt like a mouse facing a cat as I stood before her.

Hecate's gaze pinned me in place, a spark of surprise flickering in her amethyst eyes. She exchanged a swift look with Chronos which was almost imperceptible. The god of time gave her a knowing nod, and she quickly recovered her composure.

"Welcome to the Netherworld," Hecate said with a smoothness that belied the underlying tension. "I trust you are enjoying our little gathering?"

I couldn't help being in awe of Hecate's presence. "Yes,

very much so," I replied weakly, trying to wrap my mind around the power and mystery swirling around her. "It's all so... magical."

Hecate gave a small smile that seemed to be hiding something. "Indeed it is. And tell me, have you any interest in the art of sorcery?"

I stumbled over my words, not quite sure how to answer. "I-I've never really thought about it, to be honest."

Hecate's smile widened in warm understanding. "Perhaps it is time you did. Magic can be a powerful tool, if used wisely." She reached out and held my hands with undiluted tenderness, her gaze intense and almost knowing as her eyes bore into mine. "If you're ever interested in learning more, come find me. I will be happy to teach you."

My heart lurched in my chest, and I could feel the intrusive eyes of Chronos trained on me to gauge my reaction.

"Careful, dear Hecate," he said, his voice lowered almost to a whisper. And looking at me, he added, "Our guest *truly* is bewitching."

Hecate said nothing, her expression offering little insight as to her thoughts. She turned gracefully to greet another guest who had just arrived, leaving me alone with Chronos.

I was both intrigued and a little intimidated by the comment. "What did you mean by that?" I asked.

Chronos grinned, pleased with himself as he held my hand and pulled me closer. "Ah, that is for me to know and for *you* to wonder," he teased, twirling me in a playful dance move.

He smelled like spice and leather, a heady combination that set my heart racing. I felt powerless in his presence, his charm and intensity too much to bear or be angry at. "But let us enjoy this divine evening," he added in a husky voice. "Who knows what other surprises the night may hold?"

## 21
## PHILLIP

*a* sharp whoosh cut through the thick, salty air. My heart leapt into my throat, pounding like a drum as a harpoon shot past me, barely missing my shoulder. It plunged into the murky depths of the sea, slicing through the water like a brilliant silver sword, headed straight for its target—the wicked creature that lurked beneath the waves.

The mermaid reeled back on her tail, hissing a ferocious challenge with each air-splitting screech that exposed razor-sharp fangs. The hideous sound echoed off the rocks jutting out of the water, which in the sudden play of light and shadows struck me as shapeless menacing skulls. Their grey, mossy surfaces turned slick with bloodred grime splattered by the furious tide.

"Leave him be, you wretch," the mermaid boomed in a voice not her own. "He's mine! I've claimed him!"

My body tumbled to the ground with a heavy thud. Stunned and dumbfounded, I could do nothing but lay there, a prisoner of the mermaid's paralyzing spell. My eyes darted from one end of the den to another, desperate to regain my strength and become free from this sorcery.

"He's *already* been claimed, Sea Witch." Eloise stepped up beside me, brandishing yet another harpoon above her shoulder. The torchlight flickered on her face, casting shadows across her deep-set eye sockets and supple lips. She looked like an avenging goddess. "Now swim away or this time, I'll aim."

Princess Iseult boldly drifted closer to the ledge. "*Please!*" she begged, her chest heaving with passion. "Please, I must have him! I am no Sea Witch, but the victim of the vilest monster who's cursed me." Her body trembled as she spoke, anguish and fury radiating from her. "I'm forced into this quest of blood and death, and cannot stop until *he* frees me!" A delicate finger pointed my way.

"I've no sympathy for your troubles," Eloise spat, undeterred. Never once did she lower her guard. "We're on a quest of our own, heading to the Netherworld to rescue his true love... You will *not* get in our way."

Iseult's lazuline lips parted in shock as her bright blue eyes widened in the depths of her tangled fiery hair. "To save his true love from the... Netherworld?" she stammered, confusion and concern creasing her forehead.

"Yes," Eloise affirmed firmly, her gaze unwavering.

With fathomless boldness, the sea nymph drifted closer to me, her movements graceful and elegant even as Eloise hefted the harpoon a little bit higher. "I'm warning you," she said sternly.

"I mean no harm," the mermaid replied undisturbed. Her long fingers extended like tendrils of seaweed, pleading for mercy. "I will spare him from the spell of my song."

Eloise nodded reluctantly. My gaze shifted to the creature. Iseult's glimmering eyes were filled with grief, yet they also held a hint of understanding. I could feel my heart soften slightly as her gills fluttered gently in the moonlight, while her tail swayed like a lost pendulum beneath the waning tide.

The warmth of her hand sent tingles up my arms. Everywhere she touched, my body came alive, the numbness fading away with each caress.

"My brave prince," she breathed, her voice raspy and laced with a sorrow that had taken root in her very bones. Her slender hand, drizzled with silver rings, trailed up my cheek, and the chill of her touch made me quiver with fear. "I have misjudged you. Your heart is true... Sail into the Netherworld, but be careful. I couldn't bear to lose you."

Bitterness coursed through me as the numbness faded, leaving behind a dull burn in every single muscle. My gaze lifted from my pain to Eloise standing beside me, her spear held steady and pointed at the sea monster mere yards away. Iseult's pale blue eyes stared at us in horror. But I couldn't look away, unearthly fear and fascination tangled in my core.

I dragged my weakened body over the slippery ground beneath me, my skin brushing jagged pieces of wood as I made my way towards the edge, seaweed clinging to my clothes and hair. My breath grew shallow in anticipation. There she was—the sea princess, her expression solemn but patient.

"That is enough," Eloise said with finality, her voice heavy with emotion. "Now, paddle away, mermaid!"

"Take heed of my warning," the princess declared, her voice ringing with authority and an urgency that sent a chill skittering down my spine. "All who enter the Netherworld abandon their names at the gates."

She gently removed the wreath of flowers coiled around her head and slowly pinched and unpinned each blossom until it was loose and dissolving in her hands. The damp petals were curled at the edges and shining, as though a dewdrop had been captured in the center of every bloom. Her hands trembled as she held out the wilting bouquet towards me, her voice low and stern when she said, "Eat these when you reach the Realm of Death's obsidian shores, so that you may remember."

The moon shone brighter as I watched the mermaid's flowery crown nestle itself into my open palm.

"Phillip!" Eloise hissed in anxious warning.

"It will be fine," I told her with a steady exhale.

Iseult's fierce eyes cut from Eloise to me. "Hold on to your fated love, my prince," she said. "For true love is the rarest of lights, and the world is ever darkening." Tears sparkled on her cheeks like stars. "A bleak time is coming for us all; but you can fight it, if only you remember who you are and what you stand for." Having said that, she whirled back, swimming away from me under the deep shimmering waters.

"I will," I whispered into the night, watching her luminous form fade away until it was lost among an infinite dark sea.

As the moon dipped on the horizon, a bleeding sun barely kissed the surface with the promise of a dawn that would never come. I remained on my knees on the shipwreck's ledge, stunned in sheer wonder. We'd truly left behind the world as we had known it and now journeyed into a realm of legend.

A loud clang rang out and reverberated through the water. I looked back, but there was no trace of Eloise. She had dropped the harpoon and was now pacing in the mermaid's dismal lair. Her steps echoed against the metal chains that wound around a ripped-open, overturned lifeboat. Clucking her tongue and shaking her head, she moved deeper into the cave of copper-linked metal shards, searching for something—anything—of value.

With trembling hands, she tugged at the tarnished chains around the chest, barely managing to loosen the lock enough for a glimpse within. A low groan of frustration escaped her as Eloise dropped her hands to her hips. "Too miserable for a treasure cove," she muttered under her breath. Then, glancing in my direction, she held out a hand and I took it. Her skin was warm from the strive to heave the chains. It smelled delightful, like seawater and lilacs.

Awe rooted me to the ledge as I looked back on that brief encounter with the sea princess. She had risen from the depths of the ocean, a vision of beauty and terror, so grand and mighty that my heart still raced with disbelief. I stood bemused by her memory, unable to comprehend her power.

"Phillip, are you all right?" Eloise asked, her voice surprisingly gentle as her hand folded around my arm.

My gaze remained fixed on the crimson horizon. It took a moment for me to respond. "I'd never seen a creature like her before," I managed with a frown. "Such extraordinary—"

"Gills?" Eloise cut in with a caustic edge, her blonde brow lifting in a challenge. "And a tail strong as an iron paddle." She gave me a wry smile while I glared at her interruption.

I drew in a deep breath, then released it slowly, the word, "Yes" echoing out into the stillness. Carefully, I slipped Iseult's gift into my satchel, then brushed away the sand sticking to my hands. "I guess so…"

Eloise chuckled, the sound of it tinkling like bells in the salty air. "You *guess* so? That's the understatement of the century." She shook her head, her long hair tickling my cheek. "What did you think she was, a pretty fish?"

I bristled at her teasing tone but couldn't deny the truth in her words. The sea princess had been more than just a sea monster, something beyond human comprehension. "She was… remarkable," I said at last, my voice low. "And terrifying." A bright bolt of lightning snaked around me, as if responding to my words.

Eloise's grip on my arm loosened as she stepped back, studying me with sudden intensity. "Did you feel it too?" she breathed.

I frowned, confused by the sudden shift in conversation. "Feel what?" I asked.

But Eloise just smiled enigmatically and turned back to the overturned lifeboat. "Never mind, Phillip," she said, her voice distant now. "Let's find something worth salvaging."

I watched her search through the twisted metal and seaweed, feeling a strange mix of fascination and unease. There was something about Eloise, something wild and unpredictable, that drew me in despite my better judgment. I wondered if it was the same quality that had captivated me in the sea princess, and whether it would lead me to a similar danger.

"We should head back," I muttered as I trudged through the wreckage. "These are treacherous waters."

"Mm… I agree." Eloise nodded solemnly before her lips twitched into a smile. "We wouldn't want to be caught up in a *fishy* situation, now would we?"

I stabbed her with a glare. "That's not funny at all," I retorted, and combed my hair back with a swift pass of my hand.

She shrugged without an ounce of guilt as she followed me outside. "I believe it is—the gods know what could have happened had I not snagged you *fin-handed*."

I gritted my teeth and steered her off the boat, towards the cove where our ship was anchored. "Enough with the fishy jokes. They're not cutting it today."

The corners of her mouth rose in challenge. "I've got loads more bad puns where that came from."

My lips quirked into a disbelieving smirk. "Somehow, I don't doubt it. But they're not going to cut it on that boat either." We shared a quiet laugh, and throwing an arm over her shoulders, I tugged her aboard the Dragon's Breath.

## 22
## BEAUTY

*I* jolted awake, and confusion crashed in like a rogue wave. From the night before came a flood of memories that left me rooted to the spot, uncertain and afraid. An evening with the gods had been a perplexing experience—dizzyingly gorgeous, yet daunting. Despite their amusement, I couldn't but wonder how they truly felt about having a mortal within their midst. Surely, it far from pleased them.

The gold of twilight suffused the room with a strange, surreal glow. Something had changed. I could feel it in the warm air. Gradually, my eyes adjusted to the light. That's when I saw her. A dark figure standing just beyond my bed. She was cloaked in shadow, but I knew her all the same. The servant who had gowned me the night prior, wearing the same golden mask as the rest—the mask that safeguarded them from the prying eyes of Lord Thanatos, Guardian of the Dead. Our paths had not crossed last evening, and I hoped they never did.

I warily shifted on the bed and peered up at her, my voice soft as I spoke. "Who are you?"

"We must hurry," she hissed urgently. I barely had time to rub the sleep away from my eyes before she dashed forward. "I've been sent by his divine grace, Lord Chronos, to offer you a way out of this cursed palace."

My heart clenched as a frown tugged at my expression. "Chronos?" I asked, my voice barely a whisper. I thought back on the fleeting moments we had shared, moments that had felt like an eternity then. Could it have made such an impact on him, in so short a time? "Are you sure?"

The woman nodded, her voice low and serious. "He also sends these," she said, laying a fresh set of clothes on the bed —an ivory linen shirt, worn leather trousers, a gleaming gold chestplate and bracers, and sturdy leather boots. She stepped back and clasped her hands together, her gaze fixed on mine as she added in a rush, "Below these walls lies the way to a secret labyrinth leading to freedom. You must go quickly before the gods awaken!"

The words rattled my heart like thunder. This was the chance I'd been waiting for, the only chance to return to the Realm of Man and discover who I truly was.

Not allowing myself a second to hesitate, I scooped up the clothes and unraveled the ivory shirt. A path to freedom, she said. But what lay ahead? It didn't matter, though. I had no choice but to flee or risk being stuck here for eternity.

Squaring my shoulders, I steeled my resolve.

My throat went dry as I slowly turned to face the servant. Could I trust her? Doubt gnawed at me, but when she spoke, her words were strong and determined. It was like time had been bent and Chronos himself whispered his instructions into my ear.

"Why is Chronos helping me?" I finally asked, tying the laces on my shirt.

The servant hesitated before turning to me with solemn understanding. "One does not question the gods, my lady."

The corners of her mouth turned down into a grimace and she shook her head slowly. "You must have faith that he has a reason. You *must* trust him." The intensity in her gaze broke through any doubt lingering in my mind.

I moved as stealthily as I could, hastily donning my armor and strapping Voidbringer to my waist. Then, her somber words pierced the stillness, carrying a weight of warning that electrified me. "Listen to me carefully," she said, and thus shared with me the secrets of the labyrinth. And a surge of hope swelled inside me, as I envisioned at last the path to freedom.

She held out her hand, offering a cold iron key in the shape of a bull's head—cold and heavy. I reached out to take it, my fingers closing around the metal, but before I could draw it away she stopped me. "Be brave," she breathed, like a prayer. Her gold-flecked emerald eyes never leaving mine, she stepped back into the darkness, until I was left alone with only the key in my fist. A promise of what could be.

Pushed by a force unknown to me, I rushed out of my chambers into a dark and winding corridor. My breaths quickened as I moved through the twisting passageways, fearing I might stumble upon Hypnos and lose this precious opportunity.

My chest cinched tight, every beat of my heart pounding against my ribcage. I stepped closer, following the servant's directions until I found the hidden door. The entrance was narrow and cast a deep shadow into the darkness beyond. With a trembling hand, I pushed it open, revealing a spiral staircase that descended into the unknown. A shiver ran down my spine as I stared into the abyss, and all my courage seemed to vanish in an instant.

I paused at the top of the stairs, bracing myself to descend. The door behind me closed with an ominous click, leaving me alone in the chill air. I forced one foot in front of the other without looking back, my hands trailing along the cold stone walls for guidance.

On my descent, I counted the steps, desperate to free my mind from the dread of wondering what lay below. At one hundred, I stopped counting and instead focused on memories of a world with soothing sunshine and the dawns I so desperately missed.

My boots crunched through the dust as I descended what felt like an endless staircase. Shafts of light reached me only rarely, and I had almost given up when a golden glint caught my eye. My pulse raced with possibility as the familiar sound of crackling fire reached my ears. The torch ahead burned fiercely, painting the chamber walls in its amber glow. Lifting my eyes to the final step, I was at last free from the darkness.

I carefully approached the concealed doorway and spotted two bright torches burning on either side. The tapestry before me depicted a formidable monster; with the head of a bull and the body of a warrior, it warned, "Enter with valor, or not at all" in shining golden script.

Terror laced through my veins as I considered my next move. All the same, my determination refused to falter. I had come too far to turn back now. Gritting my teeth, I crossed the threshold of the secret passageway, marching towards my inevitable destiny.

At the heart of the chthonic chamber, a colossal statue of a minotaur towered. Its eyes blazed like fiery rubies in the sputtering flame of the torches that lined the walls. A shiver ran up my spine as my instincts screamed at me to flee from this monstrous apparition. But then, I spotted it—a glint of a gold necklace looped around its neck, and suddenly, I knew what I had come here for.

My fingers traced the ridged surface of the medallion, revealing a winding map that seemed to offer me an escape from this disorienting labyrinth. I muttered a quiet prayer, my voice ringing off the granite walls. Taking a deep breath, I tugged firmly on the necklace, and it came apart in my hands. At once, I draped it around my throat with a sense of purpose, letting it become my guiding beacon as I ventured forward.

The minotaur that loomed over me guarded a secret. Behind it, a spiral staircase had been carved into the stone. I descended with heavy steps, listening to my echoing footsteps drown out all else. I finally arrived in an obsidian chamber with nothing but an iron door in the corner. It was locked tight, a bull's head-shaped keyhole taunting me like it knew I could never unlock it.

"The key..." I whispered, feeling fate on my back as I stepped forward.

My hands trembled as I reached for the key, slipping it into the keyhole. A perfect fit. I held my breath and turned it, a deafening click echoing through the space. Freedom or destruction lay beyond this door, and only time would tell what lay within.

The labyrinth stretched out for miles, the towering walls on either side of me like a great beast that had swallowed me up whole. My steps echoed against the marble floors, my progress marked by the intricate carvings that adorned every inch of stone—scenes of battle, gods long forgotten, and offerings to those who had gone before me.

Soft torchlight illuminated my way, and each breath brought with it a thick sweetness from the incense that clung to the air. An icy chill spread through me, like a whisper in my ear. I could feel eyes upon my back, but could not tell if they were worldly or otherworldly. All I knew was that something—or someone—was following me as I wound my way deeper into the maze.

After hours of navigating the perilous paths of the labyrinth, I stumbled into a grand chamber. A chill rippled across my skin as I stared in shock at the tall black mirrors that surrounded me. This strange structure seemed to resist my presence, yet I refused to turn away before uncovering its secrets.

Trembling, I stepped closer and what I saw there made me stop cold. The figure before the mirrors was unmistakable —the hunter who had killed the beautiful stag in the Veiled Forest. He stood there, his features shrouded in shadows of determination and icy certainty. No pomegranates for him this time. But what had drawn him here?

# 23

# PHILLIP

The fire burned bright in the hearth, the only source of warmth in the chilled galley. We huddled around it, my unease growing with each minute that passed. The night seemed to be eternal; time had crawled to a standstill. I peered out a porthole for a sign of dawn on the horizon, only to see dusky skies stretching endlessly across the sea.

Eloise emerged from the pantry, arms laden with her spoils. The loaf of bread was hard and stale, but we were too grateful for it to care. With an apple apiece, our mouths watered at the sight of something sweet. The warmth spread through my body as I watched the flames dance, and I breathed in the scent of baked bread with a growl rumbling deep in my stomach.

But my hunger was not just for food. It was a hunger that gnawed at me to no end, a hunger that left me restless and on edge. For some time now, I couldn't shake the feeling that something was deeply wrong, that the world had shifted beneath my feet and I was struggling to keep my balance.

As we gathered around the crackling flames, the rickety

vessel swayed back and forth on the tumultuous sea. The sound of the waves crashing against the hull was calming, hypnotic even. We chewed on stale bread and bruised apples in somber silence, our tired minds consumed with thoughts of what lay ahead. Would we survive another day? Or would the merciless ocean claim us before our journey was through? For now, all we could do was relish the small comforts we had, and pray to whatever god may be listening that it would be enough... Those merciless gods.

The silence thickened, and when she finally spoke, her voice was barely more than a whisper. "If I had known how scarce the food would be aboard this ship," Eloise sighed, "I would have captured that mermaid as soon as I saw it." She let out a low chuckle, then bit into the piece of fruit in her hands.

MY GAZE SLOWLY DRIFTED TO THE SMALL SATCHEL ON the table. I steeled myself as I reached in, my fingers trembling upon contact with the strange bouquet of icy blue wildflowers. As they nestled in my grasp, a grim sensation crawled across my skin. The beauty of these flowers seemed to swell my chest with hope and dread, all at once.

"Do you think we'll ever make it to land?" Eloise suddenly asked, all mirth fleeing from her expression.

I shrugged, not trusting myself to speak. The truth was, I didn't know. We'd been adrift for days, the winds and currents unwilling to carry us towards safety. I'd never felt so utterly helpless in my life.

But Eloise wasn't finished. "And if we do make it to land, what then? Do you really think everything will be all right? That we can just rescue Aurora and then move on like nothing happened?"

In silence, my gaze cut to hers. I pursed my lips. My

heart clenched at her words, the fear and uncertainty we both carried weighing heavy on my chest. I wanted to reassure her, to tell her that everything would be fine, but I couldn't find the words. Because I didn't believe them myself.

Because the truth was, everything had already changed. We were no longer who we once were. The shipwreck had taken something precious from us, something we couldn't get back. And no matter how hard we tried, we could never be the same again. Whatever lay ahead for us would only carve a deeper groove into our souls.

I snatched the hardened bread, ripping off chunks with my teeth. The taste was dull and flavorless, but it was a distraction from our greater worries. We were doomed, aimlessly drifting through a world we no longer recognized. How could I ever lead us back to a path that felt more like *home*? We were lost in more ways than one.

"I wish I had magic," Eloise mumbled, her voice almost too low for me to hear. I glanced up from the fistful of wildflowers in my grip, my gaze landing on her.

She stared out at the horizon with a faraway look in her blue eyes. "I'd get us out of here, for sure. Wouldn't that make me bloody perfect?" she continued, not noticing my stare. She sighed wistfully, then bit into her apple.

My eyes narrowed in a warning. "No." The pang of sorrow reverberated through me like an avalanche, ripping my heart to shreds. I wanted to tell her that she already had a magic of her own; that no wand or book of spells was needed to bring it forth.

With a start, she faced me as she frowned. "What do you mean?"

"You're perfect just as you are," I whispered closely, pressing our foreheads together. "Magic is not something we need. It is vile and deceitful—a tool of destruction."

Eloise shifted away, her lips curled as if in doubt. "Is this about the fae?" she asked with caution.

"The fae, the gods... they can't save us now," I answered. "Only our own wit and grit can get us out of this mess."

She was silent for a moment before giving a slow nod, her eyes searching mine. "You're right. We have each other, and we've been through worse," she spoke up, determination strengthening her voice. "We can do this."

Eloise always seemed to know what to say; how to make things feel better even when it all seemed so bleak.

A small smile tugged at my lips despite the tension knotting my shoulders. "I see no reason why that shouldn't be the case." I reached out and twined my fingers through hers, lacing our hands like a lifeline. "Together, we can make it through Tartarus itself," I said firmly.

Eloise's cheeks tinged pink, likely from the sweltering heat of the room. Her hand slid away from mine and my heart stuttered, stunned by the impulse to pull her back, to feel her warmth again. But I stayed still, as the realization dawned on me—more danger dwelled inside this room than outside in the Netherworld.

Her lips grazed a brief smile before turning to the window. She stared out at the world beyond with a strange mixture of sorrow and hope in her eyes.

I opened my mouth to call her name, only a dry, strained rasp coming out.

"I do wonder. About those mermaids..." she continued, speaking as if she hadn't heard me at all. "What do you think they taste like? It's either fish or chicken."

"Eloise." The word ripped out of me, harsher than necessary to catch her attention.

She stopped abruptly, all sounds replaced by a strangled gasp. "What?" she managed with a scowl.

"You told the mermaid I'd already been claimed," I reminded her gruffly, my pulse throbbing hard in my throat.

"I did." Her tone was even, but there was something in her expression that made me think a shorter answer wasn't forthcoming.

My stomach twisted as we remained in tense silence until I finally asked the question burning inside me. "By whom?"

Eloise's lashes fluttered rapidly before she answered in a whisper barely more than a breath. "Not by me," she said firmly, an edge to her voice that hadn't been present before. "Your princess... Aurora."

I couldn't bring myself to look Eloise in the eye, knowing she could sense my shame. Perhaps, I secretly wished for a different answer—one that would set me free from the chains of the past. "You lied then," I accused her fiercely. "She gave up any hold on my heart ages ago."

"That may well be," Eloise replied, her voice still heavy with judgment, despite its softness. "But you've not forgotten about her." She paused. "Have you?" She eyed me shrewdly, as if she could tell how much pain this conversation was causing me.

A bitter laugh escaped me. "I thought you knew me better than this..."

Eloise's expression tightened. "Then tell me," she said, taking a step closer towards me in a challenge. "Where is it?"

"Where's what?" I choked out, my throat tightening painfully.

"Where is the ring?" Eloise repeated slowly, her gaze sharp and darting like merciless blades. "The one she discarded when you were shamed?"

My jaw tensed and my blood ran cold at the reminder. "Must you speak of it like that?" I hissed through gritted teeth.

"Yes. I really must." Her words almost seemed to hang in

the air as they echoed off the walls. She raised an eyebrow boldly. "The truth is never kind, I'm afraid. But do tell me— where is it now?"

"On her finger," I bit out gruffly, humiliation rising in my chest.

"How'd that happen? You said she threw it away like it meant nothing." Eloise gestured with a wave of her hand.

"I put it back on after she—"

"Exactly," Eloise interrupted brusquely, no trace of sympathy left in her expression or tone of voice. She pinned me down with an icy stare and I felt the full weight of her disapproval pressing against my chest.

A second later, she marched out the galley, leaving me alone with the strain of my emotions, conflicting thoughts of fate and duty that seemed to stretch endlessly between me and the love I'd once proclaimed for Aurora.

"That was seven years ago..." I mused and hugged myself against the chill seeping in from the open doors, watching as the flames leapt in the hearth. "A lot has changed since."

# 24

# BEAUTY

*M*y heart raced with anticipation, my thumb absentmindedly running over my bare ring finger. And all the while, I drank in the sight of him, standing tall and proud with an aura of unapproachable beauty. He was a glittering mystery to me, shrouded in a veil of secrecy and forbidden intrigue. Mesmerized by his presence, I felt drawn to him, like a moth to a flame. Yet, as much as I wanted to unravel the layers that made up this man, I feared that if I ever got too close, his secrets would be lost forever.

A broken whisper sailed from his lips. "I've tried," he said, a hand running nervously through midnight strands, desperately searching for answers that weren't there. "Time and time again, I've tried and failed." His gaze lowered to the ground briefly before rising to meet the obsidian mirror before him. He looked into the dark depths of glass, struggling with something deeply hidden in the impenetrable surface. His expression was pensive and knowingly sad, his heart heavy with regret.

I couldn't look away. He was beautiful and captivating,

and my feet moved without conscious thought, leading me stealthily across the chamber until I stood behind him.

Shock widened his eyes as he caught sight of my reflection in the mirror. Recognition flooded his expression later. "You..." His voice was low and sweet. "What are you doing here?"

I swallowed hard, my eyes locked onto his as my hands shook slightly. "Why are *you* here?" I managed.

The air grew eerily still, an oppressive silence settling between us like a physical weight, pressing down on my shoulders, suffocating in its thickness. It was like a heavy blanket threatening to smother us both.

"Mm... Fate is a cruel mistress," he murmured darkly, his lips twisted into a fierce smirk.

The shade then gestured for me to join him, beckoning me with a single finger. "Come and see," he added, angling towards the mirror. His tone was stern and dreadfully tempting... I couldn't help but step closer.

His long fingers ran across the mirror's surface, and suddenly a flurry of colors flooded its glassy depths. An image slowly materialized inside, so lifelike and vibrant that I had to catch my breath. A mysterious couple stood in an embrace, lost in their own passionate world, oblivious to our presence. Despite the woman's face being obscured by darkness, I recognized him from his silhouette alone.

Their great love was tangible, even through the barriers of time and space. And just as their lips were about to touch, the night seemed to swallow her whole. Existing in a world between dream and reality, he watched helplessly as she evaporated into thin air, leaving him alone in a sea of blackness, too vast to comprehend.

In an instant, the shade's expression shifted from resignation to one of pain and longing. His grip on the mirror tightened before he slowly released it, stepping back with an almost imperceptible shudder.

The dazzling image slowly faded away, leaving behind a hollow, colorless rock. I'd been given a fleeting glimpse of a distant realm, only to have its door cruelly slammed shut in my face.

Aghast, I settled reluctantly beside him. My heart pounded in my chest as I mustered the courage to ask, "Who was the woman in the mirror?"

The air around us became taut with strained silence as his body tensed, his gaze firmly affixed to the floor. His throat rumbled softly with a hoarse and broken voice, "My heart and torment."

I shuddered at the sorrow that tarnished his features—his brokenness as he slumped against the wall, his stare lost and bleak.

"Someone you loved," I mused with a frown. "A torment. How can that be?"

He slowly spun around, and the look in his eyes was that of a man who'd seen too much darkness. His gaze brimmed with grief, and though his voice was low, it carried across the room with a strength that was almost tangible. "Love," he began in a whisper, "love can bring all the joy in the world—but it can also cause unbearable pain." He paused, as if gathering his thoughts before continuing. "It has a way of sinking deep into our souls and anchoring itself there for eternity, yet its presence never seems to linger long enough."

Realization reverberated through me like a clap of thunder. I forced myself to speak plainly, "You come here to remember her... Like the pomegranate seeds in the palace, the mirror grants you a glimpse of home." Even as I spoke, I sensed the faintest hint of nostalgia in the air, heard the echoes of stories long since forgotten ringing within my chest. And it dawned on me then, that perhaps my lack of memory as I wandered in the Netherworld might actually be the greatest blessing.

His eyes met mine with such tenderness that a spark passed between us—a silent understanding beyond words. When he finally spoke again, his voice was but a whisper, asking me in disbelief, "Why do you follow me?"

I shivered, fear creeping up my spine as confusion clouded my mind. I could feel his piercing gaze on me, and I swallowed nervously before I opened my mouth to say anything.

"I'm not following you," I managed to say, voice trembling. "I wanted to..."

But before I could finish, he cut me off with a stern demand. "What *do* you want?" His tone was sharp, his words chips of ice cutting through the cool air.

My heart raced as I tried to think of a response, but the pressure to answer made it difficult for me to form words.

He watched me intently, waiting for an answer that wouldn't come.

Finally, I found my courage and turned to him, speaking slowly so I wouldn't stutter. "To find the way home," I said, my voice choking as anxiety still lingered in my throat. "I was told I could find it through this labyrinth."

His head tilted at an angle that made the light reflect off his chiseled jawline. I couldn't fathom what he was thinking and his enigmatic expression confused me. "And *who* told you that?" His voice dripped with honey as he spoke, a hint of amusement playing on his lips. It was like he was trying to break through my façade, to uncover all my secrets, and his voice held an ocean of emotions behind every single word.

I took my time considering his question, hesitant to answer. "A servant," I finally murmured, trying not to invoke the name of the god who had sent me this advice.

His mouth twitched with mocking amusement, though

it did not reach his eyes. "They lied," he declared simply. All vigor and mirth vanished from his expression.

My heart plummeted at those words, but the certainty of his gaze kept me from surrendering to despair.

The stillness of the cavern weighed heavily between us. The rocks that encircled us reflected back our haggard figures, but his gaze shifted and met mine with a fiery resolve. "But I agree. You must leave this place." He spoke in a hushed tone that reverberated through the chamber, his words laced with determination. "It's too dangerous for mortals like you."

I clenched my jaw. "No," I insisted, refusing to give in. "I won't leave you here like this. You should come with me." My pulse raced as I bravely reached out and offered my hand to him, not daring to brace myself for it. The moment our skin met, a jolt of electricity shot through me, like being struck by lightning—my heart felt as if it stopped beating.

His reaction mirrored mine as we stood there in that moment of stunned silence, his hand still gripping mine tightly.

"We'll find a way out of the Netherworld," I breathed heavily, unable to suppress the wave of anger that surged through me at his snort of dismissal. "You deserve more than this—you deserve happiness."

He pulled away from me then, shaking his head morosely with a hollow chuckle that sent heat boiling up inside me.

"What's so funny?" I said indignantly.

"Happiness is something I lost long ago," he answered with a wry smile.

Undeterred by his words, I squared my shoulders and lifted my gaze to meet his boldly. "I refuse to believe it," I stated fiercely and leaned forward, guiding us back into the conversation at hand. "So, how do these mirrors work exactly?"

He whispered, a low, worshipful note in his voice. "These aren't just mirrors. They're cursed stones, once owned by the mountain nymph Echo and stolen by Hades himself." His words were full of meaning and cut through the air to settle in my bones. "They've been imbued with their own mysterious magic to hold reflections of our pasts." His gaze was piercing as he looked up at me, like he wanted to trap me within its ferocity. His eyes remained riveted on mine, until it was as if we held each other in a trance.

I stepped closer to the towering black pillar, my heart pounding in my chest. "Then perhaps they'll show me the truth about myself..." I lifted my hand, cautiously moving it closer to the shining surface.

He shook his head, his voice full of warning when he spoke. "Don't bother. They won't."

But something compelled me forward. I stretched out my palm onto the smooth stone, hoping it would uncover my secrets. I waited with bated breath, eagerly hoping for a single image to appear; a moment of clarity in this murky void. Yet nothing came. No matter how desperately I wished it, the opaque nothingness lingered on.

A self-satisfied smirk crossed his face as he chided sarcastically, "I told you so."

I spun around to glare at him, anger coursing through me. "Why are you granted the power to explore your past while I am denied?" I questioned, my voice shaking with frustration.

He shrugged, uncaring. "You are mortal." His voice was eerily calm and his stance shifted from lax to rigid in a single breath. "I am not." He slowly straightened, looming over me.

I lifted my chin, steeling myself against his powerful presence. "Who are you?" I asked, my voice firm despite the unease building in my chest.

A single brow rose over his piercing eyes. "Have you not

heard?" His lips curled into a sinister smirk as he spoke. "We have no names in the Netherworld."

"There must be something I can call you," I insisted, unable to tear away from the eerie draw of his gaze.

He tilted his head towards me and tapped a finger on his chin musingly. "Daegal," he said at last with false nonchalance. "Do you like it? It means *Dweller of Darkness*. Fitting, isn't it?"

I nodded readily. In that moment, it seemed like the perfect name for him—impenetrable, mysterious, powerful. Then I realized I'd yet to answer my own question. "And what should I be called?" I murmured, almost afraid of the response.

The corners of Daegal's mouth tugged upwards into a humorless grin. His voice was low and rumbling when he spoke again, dark eyes boring into mine. "Beauty," he said simply.

Fire suddenly flared inside me, burning bright and sure. I kept my face carefully neutral, trying to pretend that the warmth of his words hadn't unraveled something inside me. "What is this place, Daegal?" My voice was softer than I'd intended it to be, almost reverent.

Daegal squared his broad shoulders, a portrait of fearlessness as he declared, "A foregone prison where Hades tortured his fallen foes." His arm extended outward, encompassing the dismal landscape that surrounded us.

"His personal dungeon," I uttered, a chill spreading through my limbs.

"Mm-hmm," he agreed curtly. "Filled with horrors from the Netherworld." He nodded, a hint of delight curling his lips.

I tensed up at the thought. Sheer black dread came bubbling to the surface as I uttered, "The minotaur..." I clutched the necklace tight and turned a wary glance at my surroundings.

He cracked a smile, though it was not unkind. "Don't worry about Asterion," Daegal said in a tone that exuded confidence. "That monster is long gone."

The words brought me faint relief. "Are there any others?" I asked, my gaze searching his face for the truth.

Daegal's eyes smoldered with an insidious delight as he held my gaze. A chill ran down my spine at the sinister energy emanating from him. He paused in silence, relishing in my unease. "None that should concern you," he finally said.

His dark eyes flickered down to the chain around my neck. "That looks familiar," he murmured, his voice rough like stones tumbling together.

"It holds the way out of this labyrinth," I answered hastily.

"We don't need it," he said quietly, a strange fire in his gaze that hadn't been there before.

His features were illuminated for a moment, and I could see the strength and confidence radiating from him as he spoke. "I know the way out."

## 25
## BEAUTY

*M*y heart raced as we plunged into the unknown depths of the cavern. The burnished black marble walls glittered in the darkness, refracting the meek light of the torches and creating a disorienting kaleidoscope that seemed to stretch on forever.

The stale air was heavy with dread and ancient pain, the labyrinth itself alive with unseen presences. I could barely hear myself think over the echoing of our clambering footsteps, our own breathing gasping against the oppressive silence. Every crevice whispered secrets of long-forgotten mysteries; promises of danger lurking in every corner.

"You seem to know your way around here," I finally spoke, looking around at all the twists and turns that seemed so familiar to him.

Daegal only hummed in response, then stopped abruptly, spinning on his heel to face me. His eyes shone with something akin to mischief and his lips quirked in a smug smirk. "Of course I do," he murmured, his voice deep and smoky like a midnight breeze. "I've prowled in the Netherworld for ages."

His eyes were sunken into their sockets, as if he'd been battling with himself in the dark for all that time. His jawline was hard and sharp, chiseled by the hardships weighing on his soul.

"I'm sorry about that," I whispered, imagining the burden of being so trapped and desperate for an escape. Fear crept through my body like cold fingers, wondering what kind of fate might await me here.

"Don't be." Daegal stepped closer, his eyes never leaving mine. "Being stuck here has its perks," he continued, his voice low and with no inclination. "I've had time to think, to really understand what I want."

I couldn't help but feel a pang of sympathy for him, even if he seemed in comfort with his loss and pain. "And what do you want?" I asked, my own voice a mere whisper now. "Freedom... riches…" I paused. "Love?"

Daegal inched even closer, his body's warmth radiating on my own. My heart raced in my chest as he lifted his hand to gently cup my cheek, and with stern determination whispered, "I want it *all*."

The air around us crackled with electricity as he leaned in, his lips seconds away from brushing mine. A tingle of delight shot through my core as his mouth promised a passionate kiss, full of fire and obsession. And just as my lips were about to meet his, Daegal's head snapped back and he stepped away from me.

"It's this way," he quietly said, renewing our stroll.

All breath left me. I wanted to turn back time and freeze that moment forever—the weight of anticipation suspended between us. But it was gone now, leaving a hollow chill in its place.

He gestured us forward into the dark abyss, and all I could do was follow.

A hard lump lodged in my throat, my lips as dry as sand.

Powerless to look away from him, I rasped, "Don't you find it tiring?"

Daegal glanced at me from the corner of his eye. He hummed thoughtfully, his steps slowing just enough for me to reach his side.

"To wander forever in the humdrum of the Netherworld," I choked out, my voice barely making it through the tightness in my throat. His presence was too overwhelming, like a fog that seeped into my veins and caused me to shiver despite the warmth of this realm.

"The *humdrum* of eternity," he purred with dark delight. His smirk held a hint of danger, and his stare burned into me with fierce intensity. "Ah, Beauty..." Daegal's voice shot a thrill down my spine. "Rest assured, I sweep away the drabness of the Netherworld like a gust of wind. For none are quite like me in this domain."

I edged closer, my eyes wide with a maelstrom of emotions. Curiosity sparked and an underlying fear threatened to overtake me, but I pushed through. "I find that hard to believe. I've met *many* lost souls in this realm since my arrival." The words rolled off my tongue and I immediately regretted each one.

He lifted an eyebrow, a hint of amusement in his deep-set gaze. "Perhaps disbelief is more your thing," he said. "But you misjudge me. I am no mere specter." It was then that for the first time, I heard something in Daegal other than disapproval or scorn. It was pride. And it made him even more alluring.

The corners of my mouth twitched. "Oh?" I said, goading him on.

He halted at a fork in the tunnel and straightened, grandly spreading his arms. "I am the embodiment of the night, come to ravish those foolish enough to partake in an immortal dance." He then mockingly bowed.

My lips curled into a sly grin. "You've certainly ensnared me, Daegal. But be warned—I too am no ordinary creature." I pressed my finger against his chest, firm and unyielding.

In a flash, his hand caught mine and tugged it close to him, to the place where his heart thudded wildly. The look on his face was something I couldn't quite process—surprise mixed with wonder and admiration.

"What makes you so extraordinary?" he asked, almost to himself. A shiver ran up my spine at the intensity of his gaze, locked onto me as his eyes burned with an unnatural fire. He spoke in a voice so lyrical, like he was one who could haul the moon out of the darkest clouds.

I swallowed hard and took a deep breath before answering with an air of confidence, "My passion for shedding light on shadows."

His grip loosened slightly as he cocked his head to the side, curiosity engulfing him like a wave crashing on the shore. I could only smile in response.

Daegal's hand slid away from mine, leaving trails of warmth on my skin. My fingertips grazed his sculpted ribs through the black silk of his shirt with a reverence I'd never felt before.

A mischievous smirk spread across his lips. "A challenge?" he purred, admiration and desire blazing in his gaze. His eyes seemed to pierce through me, as if he could see the secrets buried in my soul.

Daegal paused, pondering the depths of my thoughts. His voice was a gentle whisper, sending tingles down my spine when he said, "Do you always guard your deepest truths so carefully? What other mysteries lie beneath your flawless exterior?"

The unspoken connection between us sparked alive, like a radiant surge of electricity. My heart pounded against my ribs, threatening to break free from my chest. I opened my mouth to say something—anything—but all that came out was a hoarse crack. "We should move on," I finally managed, despite the thrum inside me begging for more time with him.

I moved towards the path ahead, but a force greater than myself pulled me back. His hand twined with mine and a bolt of lightning rushed between us. My heart raced, my skin hot and alive. His touch lit up a part of me that had been dark—an unknown world of sensation that filled me with both terror and delight.

Winded, I stared at him, mesmerized by the sheer power and beauty radiating off him, like the wild stag in the woods. His hand, still gripping mine, was like a brand on my skin— and I did not want him to let go

"There," he said in a voice full of confidence, as his long fingers moved over my palm before finally slipping away.

Up ahead, I glimpsed it. A sliver of moonlight, a glimmer of hope. It cut through the shadows, giving us just enough light to see our way out. Daegal gestured for me to follow him, and I hesitantly obeyed. Step by step, we inched closer to escape, the reflection of silver guiding our path.

When we finally escaped the labyrinth, a sliver of moon illuminated our path and revealed the sprawling expanse of the Netherworld stretching out before us. We stood atop a high cliff, ringed by ancient ruins that had been there for centuries, dark in silhouette against the night sky.

A gust of wind raced past me, snaking through my light hair. My lips parted in a smile, and the delicate smell of salt water filled my lungs, setting my spirit alight with joy. "The sea..." I breathed, and without a second thought, I followed the sound of the waves, eager to witness their power firsthand.

My feet flew across the craggy rocks as if guided by an unseen force, closer and closer to the edge of the cliff. A sudden crack echoed through the evening air and my body trembled as I realized I was standing on crumbling ground. But before I could take another step, a pair of strong arms embraced me, steadying my shaking frame and anchoring me to safety.

It was Daegal. His presence was my lifeline, saving me from the perilous fall. His touch brought forth a stream of warmth that ran through every inch of my body, easing my dismay like a soothing balm.

We stood together in silence, overlooking a breathtaking view: the glittering black sand reflecting the silver moonlight while salty foam crashed against its smooth surface below us. The ocean beckoned me to its shore, promising peace and serenity for those who answered its call.

A wistful tear rolled down my cheek as I beheld such beauty. Something within me finally settled into place. The view sang to me—at last, my soul was complete. Here lay an escape from all pain, an eternity for hope.

I whirled around, my breath catching in my throat as our eyes met. His gaze shone like precious garnets in the moonlight, his arms tight around my frame, strong and steady and comforting. Daegal's features were drenched in a soft ethereal glow emanating from him that seemed to twist the air between us into something strange yet familiar.

"You're safe," he whispered, his voice a soothing melody amidst the thunderous waves. "As long as you're with me, nothing will ever harm you."

A swirl of safety and vulnerability surged through me. I could not tear my eyes away from his. "I never imagined such danger... Not in this place," I murmured, relief evident in my voice. Alongside it, an inexplicable connection began to grow.

His mouth curved up slightly in delight. "The Netherworld holds the unexpected, my Beauty," he said softly. "It is a realm where the line between danger and enchantment often becomes blurred."

A sudden warmth surged through me, so powerful that I instantly recognized it for what it was—the pull of a kindred spirit. "Daegal," I whispered, my voice barely audible amidst the crashing waves. "There is something about this place, about you… something drawing me in."

He tightened his embrace, reassuring and electrifying all at once. "There are forces at play here that we cannot fully grasp," he said quietly. "But one thing is certain—together, we can find light amidst the bleakest shadows."

The words hung in the air, a declaration of a blossoming love that transcended the boundaries of time and realms. And as we stood before that black, glittering beach, embraced by the Netherworld's enchantment, Daegal drew me closer. "I've struggled with this endlessly." His voice rumbled low, his dark eyes roving my face before setting on my lips. "I'm done fighting it."

Before I could take another breath, his mouth was on mine, sending tremors through every nerve ending in my being. Every part of me melted into him, our bodies fitting together like pieces of an exquisite puzzle, igniting a fire that could never be quenched. In that moment, we were one and our souls connected across time and space as our kiss deepened.

The sound of our ragged breathing filled the air as Daegal held me tighter still, his hands roaming down to the small of my back while mine tangled themselves in his hair. The force of passion between us was overwhelming, like being swept up in a current with no hope of finding the surface again.

When he finally broke away, gasping and shaking, I saw a look of desire etched into his features—one that mirrored my own hunger for him. I knew nothing would ever be the same again. But then, fear flashed through his eyes, sparking with desperation. "Forgive me," he begged between puffs of air. His head shook as he stepped back, muttering, "I shouldn't have... I shouldn't."

"Daegal..." I breathed, my throat tight with emotion and my chest torn in two. I wanted to plead with him to stay, but the terror that coursed through me locked my tongue into silence.

He murmured something so softly I could hardly make it out.

"You should go back to the palace," he added with haste. "They'll be searching for you soon."

His gaze held mine for a moment longer before he bowed his head in shame and swirls of shadows enveloped him without another word.

## 26
## PHILLIP

The twilight sun was a furnace buried deep in the horizon. Each day, I grew to love the sunrise more fiercely, an ache in my chest until I could witness again the light breaking through the darkness and pushing away the shadows of the night. And when that moment came, I would stand there, watching as the colors shifted and blended until the world was swathed in a soft veil of dawn. And only then, I would feel the power of the sun burning through my skin and radiating into my soul…

"Phillip!" Eloise called out from somewhere outside, the sharpness of her voice bringing me back to reality. "I see land!"

My heart raced as hope surged through my veins. Finally, I was closer to finding Aurora and completing this quest. Once and for all.

I scrambled out of the cabin and up the rigging of the ship, my body appearing weightless in the air. When I reached the helm, Eloise stood there, her frame silhouetted against the bloodred sunset. She pointed eastward, her golden hair streaming behind her.

"Can you make out any details?" she asked, her voice laced with excitement as she peered ahead.

I squinted my eyes, searching for any signs I recognized on the muddled horizon. But all I could see was an undefined mass. "It could be anything," I said, furrowing my brow with confusion.

"Whatever it is, it's closer than we've been in days." Eloise smiled, her gaze still locked on the horizon. "It may not be Aurora, but I see an adventure ahead." She turned to me with a determined look in her eyes. "Let's find out what awaits us."

There was an eagerness to my agreement, and I moved with speed as I adjusted the sails and steered us closer to our destination. The sea raged beneath us, but we made greater progress than before.

As details of the island came into view, a wave of wonderment overtook me—its black sand beaches glinting in the setting sun, its hillsides covered in lush vegetation, air that was sweet with salt from the sea breeze caressing my skin. This was no ordinary isle.

"So this is the Realm of the Dead," I whispered, my eyes devouring the unfamiliar landscape. Not what I had expected, not dismal or disheartening, no. This land was beautiful beyond compare.

"Will you look at that..." Eloise uttered softly, admiration shining in her sapphire gaze.

Our ship sliced through the waters of an abandoned cove, each wave lapping against the hull like an offering from Poseidon himself. We had finally arrived—weeks of dangerous travel culminating in this strange realm. I couldn't deny a certain presence here, as if fate had pulled our strings and brought us to our final destination. Perhaps the gods were in our favor after all.

As our vessel touched ground, I opened my satchel and

clutched a fistful of Princess Iseult's posies. "Eat these, Eloise," I commanded, standing close enough to glimpse defiance in her eyes.

"Don't tell me you believe in the Sea Witch's riddles," she sneered, sliding her sword into its scabbard.

I stepped closer and held her gaze, relentless as I spoke. "The Dark Prince is lying in wait and I won't risk our lives by letting him catch us in his trap. So eat up. Now."

"Fine," Eloise growled and snatched a pinch of petals from my hand, tossing them into her mouth with disdain.

I followed suit, the taste of buttery sweetness on my tongue more intense than expected. I let out a surprised sound, and said, "It tastes like..."

Eloise finished for me, "Cake frosting." A barely-there smirk tugged at her lips.

I couldn't help but smile, remembering all those late nights huddled in the pantry gobbling down Cook's creations and talking until dawn. I glanced at her with a knowing look. "Like the ones we used to steal from the palace kitchens."

Eloise adjusted her bracers, but her gaze was far away. In a soft voice, she whispered, "It's not the cakes I remember— it's the conversations. When my mother had just died and it felt like no one in the world understood what I was going through... but you did."

I nodded, my throat tight with emotion. "I remember," I admitted lowly.

A wistful smile fluttered across her lips. "Those were the sweetest days of my childhood," she whispered, her eyes distant. "I'll never forget them."

The moment was almost too much to bear and I had to break it before we said more than necessary. Clearing my throat, I forced myself to speak. "I think we're ready now," I murmured hesitantly.

She blinked, returning from her dreamy reverie. "Yes," she agreed softly, clicking the latch on her satchel shut. "Let's go."

We dropped anchor and descended onto the pebbled shore, the hush of anticipation tangible in the air. Our gazes sprinted over the strange terrain before us: endless curtains of emerald trees, a turbulent river that cut through a mountain range in the distance, ancient ruins crumbling beneath the oppressive mist. Even as experienced travelers, we couldn't help but pause for breath, in awe of our surreal welcome to this undiscovered land.

The sun slowly sank below the horizon, painting the night sky with a soft golden hue. The hills stretched in majestic beauty for miles, lush with deep green trees standing tall like bygone sentinels. Everywhere was a sense of peace and tranquility... too much tranquility.

A shiver ran down my spine as we moved further onto the shoreline, the fog rising around us like an ominous cloud. Eloise marched forth unafraid, her steps sure and unwavering. "Our destiny is upon us," she said calmly, but with an unnerving cheerfulness. Then meeting my gaze, she added, "Steel and courage."

"Steel and courage," I repeated, fingers closing tightly around the hilt of my sword.

I glanced back, my gaze lingering on the bay we'd left behind. The Dragon's Breath hugged the contours of the cove, tucked away under a canopy of ancient trees. The waters were still and silent like they'd never felt our presence. Here we remained hidden, invisible to prying eyes and far removed from those who would wish to see us fail.

The fae sisters' warnings echoed in my mind as I stared into the depths of the forest ahead. *The palace lies at the heart of the Netherworld*, they'd said.

The sun disappeared behind grey clouds, vanquished by

the Realm of Death. A sharp ache stabbed my heart as we ventured deeper into this unknown realm. Our every movement was weighted, tense—the air growing increasingly colder until I felt like I could barely breathe in the icy mist.

I could feel Eloise's unease as she moved beside me, her steps unsteady on the slick ground. The mist clung to us like a shroud, our labored breaths the only sound that cut through the stillness. Every corner seemed darker than the last, danger lurking within each shadow.

We kept walking, and the horizon lit up with a bewitching sight. On a hilltop miles away, there stood an ancient temple in all its dilapidated glory. I could sense its mystery from a distance, and my finger pointed east without hesitation.

"We should head there," I said into the evening gloom, lightning flashing in the sky.

Eloise's eyebrows were scrunched in concern. "Are you sure? It looks like it's been abandoned for years."

The first raindrops hit the ground as I nodded resolutely. "We need a place to rest for the night," I murmured, tempting her further with, "Who knows, there might be something of value inside."

She graced me with an assessing look before finally nodding her agreement. "Let's go, then."

Our feet flew over the ground, spurred on by a nameless fear and eagerness to reach our destination. We moved quickly through the woods, Eloise leading the way with her sharp eyes ready for danger. I followed close behind, my grip on my sword growing tighter with each passing minute.

The chill air carried an unfamiliar scent—citrusy and sweet—but underneath crept something darker and more sinister; something that made my skin crawl.

"Do you feel it?" I whispered to Eloise, my hand tightening around my sword. She silently said yes, her gaze alert and searching for whatever lurked in the darkness. When her eyes locked with mine, I glimpsed the fear and excitement brewing within her.

"Ready to face whatever comes?" My voice was no more than a murmur, but it held strength.

Her lips thinned into a tight line as she nodded her agreement. "You know it," she breathed, releasing her sword from its scabbard in one smooth motion.

# 27

# BEAUTY

*D*aegal faded abruptly from view, forced by the flash of lightning, and in its wake came the deafening rumble of thunder, shaking me right down to my bones. The rain began as a light patter, but quickly escalated into a fierce onslaught, consuming me with its icy chill.

The last vestiges of light fled from the sky while I stood in the drenching rain. I held myself tightly and glanced around, half expecting to find Daegal reemerging from the shadows. But the night was empty. Even the storm seemed to know that I was now quite alone.

I sought refuge inside the forlorn ruins of the temple, my heart pounding in time with the tempest outside. The warmth of Daegal's kiss still burned on my lips, cruelly, for with it came an intense longing. I shivered, desperate for his touch again.

Once, I'd been afraid of losing my own name and becoming a ghost within the palace walls, but now the dread of a thousand lifetimes descended upon me as I imagined being away from him.

My spirit shattered, the joyous sensation of his nearness

replaced with this prickling angst. A single droplet of salty water quivered on the edge of my lashes, threatening to betray me.

Confusion waged war on my heart. How could he profess his undying love and then vanish into thin air? Was the agony twisting in my chest proof that I loved him too? The thought made me sick with anxiety. My need for answers only grew stronger.

"I must find him," I muttered fiercely into the night air. My pulse raced as I stood on the brink of the unpredictable, one foot suspended above moss-covered stones. A desperate need driving me towards Daegal surged in my veins.

Before taking a step forward, I closed my eyes, gathering every ounce of courage I had left. And as I tore away from the temple and darted into the wilds of the forest, I did it with a newfound resolve—to find him no matter what it took.

I pushed on through the darkness, relentless and determined, even when many times I stumbled over clinging vines or felt sharp branches scrape my face.

The roar of the ocean chased me in the distance, thunderous and rumbling in my core. A mountain of conflicting emotions rose within me—the past urging me to turn back, while the future pulled me ever onward.

I wandered in the woods for hours, until exhaustion crashed over me like an unrelenting tide, and the depths of night gave way to yet another dusk that bled on the Netherworld's horizon. But I trudged on, pain and frustration coiling within me like a tightly wound serpent.

Tears stung my cheeks as I screamed for him—his name choked from my throat amidst sobs. "Daegal! Where are you?" My voice shattered the silence of the storm, but still, no answer came.

Dread enveloped every inch of me, a heavy weight threatening to drag me under. I should have turned back then and there, but something deep within me urged me to press on.

At last, a break appeared in the endless wall of trees, and my heart soared with hope. Could he be waiting for me beyond the thick evergreen trunks? My legs pumped faster, my lungs burning with the effort as I barreled towards the answer to my questions when suddenly, I halted. An unnatural quiet settled around me. The trees abruptly shifted, taller and ominous, their shadows looming like faceless sentinels.

A chill raced down my spine. *I should not be here.* Slowly, I dragged a foot behind me. I tried to run away, but it was too late. Before I could blink, an iron grip wrenched me off my feet and slammed me down onto the forest floor. I whimpered, helpless terror coursing through me as I lay on a bed of shed leaves and daisies, shaking beneath the hulking figure that loomed above me.

My gaze traveled up the warrior's powerful frame, a tremor of fear... and something more... coursing through me. Tall and muscular, his chiseled features were thrown into relief by the moon's glow. His eyes gleamed like silver shards, cold yet entrancing.

I scrambled away from him on shaky limbs, but he stalked closer, aggression radiating from his every move. My heart pounded frantically against my chest as he reached down and grasped my arm, hauling me close. I gasped at the clenched grip, unable to pull away as his free hand unsheathed a dagger.

"What are you doing here?" His voice rumbled low, sending an unwelcome shiver through me.

In this nearness, I took in his frost-pale hair, arched brow, the cruel yet sensuous curve of his smirking lips. He was terrifying but undeniably beautiful. A lethal and alluring predator.

He narrowed his gaze, the dagger still clutched in his

grip. "Are you a prowling *shade*?" he snarled and the ground trembled beneath us as he dropped to his knees. In a flash, his legs straddled my waist, capturing me between his powerful thighs. The air swiftly thickened, the stars my sole witnesses as he held me captive beneath the might of his will.

I gasped for breath, fear lodging in my throat like an impenetrable stone. His face was inches away from mine now and I could feel every raw emotion emanating from him—anger, mistrust, sadness… Even with all this power surging around us, I found myself transfixed by the odd gentleness behind those fiery eyes.

I froze, and my heart plummeted as the slim hope of freedom slipped away. The sharp sliver of steel glinted before my eyes. My breath hitched. And at once, the blade plunged down in silver fury, its icy kiss searing deep into my shoulder. Crimson blood oozed in steaming rivulets from the gash like burning lava, while a cry of agony tore from my lips.

The warrior leaned closer, long snowy tresses spilling over his shoulders, shimmering in the moonlight. His fiery stare betrayed the deepest abyss of shock and disbelief. "You belong with the living," he breathed, and without pause, he scooped me in his strong arms and strode away with me draped over my shoulder.

# PHILLIP

*A*ncient ruins rose from the mists as we trudged
through the sodden woods, a forlorn relic of ages
past. Ivy snaked up cracked columns, which fronted empty
alcoves where statuary had long turned to dust. Behind
loomed the dark mouth of the inner sanctum, promising
secrets or doom.

A ruthless storm unleashed upon us as we mounted the
water-slick steps. Thunder shook the very earth. That's when
the guttural growls arose, seeming to echo from everywhere
and nowhere. The sound raised the hairs on my nape, primal
and hungry. Something inhuman stalked us from the
shadows.

Sinister shapes danced across the moss-eaten walls as our
torchlight guttered. The scent of decay choked the damp air.
This nightmarish place reeked of death and darkness. Most
would flee its creeping ruin. But desperation drives men
beyond fear.

And then, we saw them. Two hulking beasts materialized,
fur midnight black, eyes aflame with rage. The reek of battle
surrounded them, primitive and ferocious. My heart

hammered, but Eloise gripped her sword without hesitation. I followed suit, swallowing back fear.

In an instant, the creatures pounced forward, their maws snapping within inches of our faces. We pushed them back with every ounce of strength we had, and stepped back to back, our chests heaving as our swords remained ready in front of us. The two beasts prowled around us, their menacing growls reverberating off the stone beneath our feet.

Then both flew forward in unison. One targeted Eloise while the other made a beeline for me. I brought my sword down with a mighty force, but I was too slow. The beast knocked me onto the ground, its jagged teeth glinting in the light as it prepared to devour me alive.

But Eloise was faster. With a decisive move, she drove her sword deep into the creature's side, tearing from it a painful bellow. It stumbled away from me, giving me a chance to regain my footing and slice my own sword against its neck. With heartless precision, the monster fell to the ground, lifeless.

The other beast, enraged by the passing of its mate, attacked us with relentless ferocity. We fought as usual, like warriors, our blades gleaming in the torchlight—able to cause injury multiple times although the beast refused to give up.

With a menacing growl, it pounced on Eloise, jaws closing tight around her arm. She cried out in suffering but didn't relinquish her sword. With trembling hands, she plunged it deep into its throat, ending its life.

We stood there for an eternity, breathing heavily and drenched in blood. But we survived. And we won.

"Eloise..." I managed hoarsely.

She let out a shuddering breath, stumbling over an exposed root. Catching herself on a nearby stone, Eloise sat down heavily, pressing her hand against the angry red line of blood on her arm. "I'll be fine," she said, though the tremor in her voice belied her words.

"Wait," I grumbled as I studied the ragged gash marring her pale skin, guilt twisting my gut. If not for me, she would be safe at home instead of shedding blood in this hellish place.

Wordlessly, I grabbed my waterskin, rinsing away the blood to reveal the deep cut beneath. I then tore a strip of linen from my tunic and gently wrapped her wound, staunching the crimson flow. She watched me work, mouth pressed into a pained line. But she did not pull away.

I secured the bandage with a knot, then clasped her shoulder. "Ready to continue, Captain?" I kept my tone light, hoping to raise her spirits.

Moorskill gave me a grim smile that didn't reach her eyes. But she lifted her chin with stubborn pride and nodded. "Onward it is. Can't keep the hordes of darkness waiting."

I smiled back, pride swelling in my chest despite it all. However dire the odds, Eloise never wavered or complained. Her unbreakable spirit put steel in my spine when doubt crept in.

With a grunt, I helped her to her feet. Side by side, we pressed deeper into the forest, moving towards salvation or oblivion. But we would face both together, united until the bitter end.

"We're almost there," I gasped, my breathing ragged.

Eloise gave me a faint smile, and we set our sights on the wilds that lay before us. The mountains seemed to swallow up the sky in the distance, their craggy edges resembling the teeth of some unstoppable beast. Everywhere we looked was full of life—but also danger. What other terrors could lurk within this murky abyss? Still, we pushed through, knowing we had no other choice.

We walked through a land of never-ending wonders.

Majestic trees towered over us, and exotic flowers lit up the foliage in hues I'd never seen before, so vibrant they almost glowed. Their citrus sweetness haunted me, soothing my worries and weaving its way through my veins until it was all I could smell or taste.

As we ventured deeper, the air grew thick with an enchanting presence. The soft rays of moonlight filtered through the dense canopy, casting an ethereal glow upon the moss-covered ground. It was then that I caught sight of movement among the ancient trees.

Eloise and I exchanged wary glances as a hushed whisper drifted through the air, beckoning us closer. Stepping quietly, our senses heightened, we approached a cluster of aged oaks, their massive trunks standing like guardians of a bygone secret.

"Phillip!" Eloise breathed, her widened gaze locked behind me.

Slowly, I turned. And there, amidst the towering sentinels, they revealed themselves—the elusive dryads. These graceful tree spirits emerged from the bark, their shapely forms seamlessly blending with the gnarled branches. Their skin glowed with a radiant emerald shade, reminiscent of the vibrant leaves that adorned their arboreal counterparts.

I stood in awe as the dryads regarded us with eyes that mirrored the wisdom of ages. Exquisite foliage hung from their head, long like luxuriant tresses, and cascaded down their backs, intertwining with the delicate tendrils of the surrounding foliage. With each gentle sway, the leaves whispered secrets known only to these ethereal beings.

The dryads watched us from a distance with curious eyes, captivated by our every movement. Every gesture was met with amazement, as though we were worthy of their admiration—we, the mythical creatures lurking in the woods.

I slowly raised my hands, palms facing outward in a clear

gesture of peace. "We have no intention of causing you harm," I murmured, watching cautiously for any sign of movement.

No answer came. But one dryad, in particular, drew my gaze. She leaned gracefully against the trunk of an ancient oak. The tree bark's delicate veins intertwined with streaks of green in her hair, as if she were an extension of the very woodland she called home.

The dryad approached with liquid steps, studying me with ageless eyes. I stood paralyzed as she trailed one smooth, moss-flecked finger along my jaw, reading my essence through touch alone. Satisfied, she withdrew and glided back to her arboreal guardians.

A gentle breeze then swept through the clearing, carrying the faintest whisper: *"You may pass."*

In that moment, the rest of the dryads followed suit and returned to the trees, blending with them until each solidified as one. Not a trace of the spirits remained. It was a fleeting encounter, a glimpse into a realm where the boundaries between mortal and myth blurred.

Eloise and I stood in silent reverence, the weight of the moment lingering in the air. The dryads had granted us passage. So with newfound awe and respect for the sacred woodland, we continued our journey, knowing that with each step we took, the forest embraced us.

We had been trekking through the dense woods for what felt like an eternity before the full moon finally cast its silver hue across the trees.

As we continued down the path, Eloise's question hung in the air like a dense fog. "Do you think those dryads might alert Hades of our presence?" Her voice was tight and her brows were knit together in worry, making my heart lurch.

"I doubt it," I answered, pointing ahead with my chin. The stars sparkled in the night sky, and the pathways that had been hidden beneath shadows moments ago were illuminated in a gentle light. "If they favored the Dark Prince they would've stopped us by now. I don't think they much like him."

We marched steadily onward, swords at the ready and spirits high despite our weariness. With a newfound surge of strength, we eventually reached the forgotten temple.

As we approached, the battered stone walls of the temple became more visible in detail. Intricate carvings showed scenes of battles and sacrifices, so vivid that we could almost feel them around us. A pair of large statues carved from the same stone as the walls rose up on either side of the crumbling entrance. Firelight from burning torches flickered in their hands, pushing back against the fading storm.

The heavy wooden doors were partially ajar, inviting us to explore what lay within. We crossed the threshold, our footsteps reverberating unpleasantly in the abandoned chamber. A layer of grime blanketed every surface, and cobwebs cloaked the ceiling.

"Finally, a place to rest," Eloise muttered, her words weighted with weariness. "We've been walking for what feels like an eternity."

I dragged my fingers through my hair, trying to clear away the fog from my mind. "Yes, you're right."

She yawned, pausing to rub her eyes. "That sickly fragrance must be getting to me," she mumbled, "or maybe, I'm just exhausted."

"We've put in a hard effort today," I admitted. "Let's set up camp. I'll just look around first, make sure we're safe."

Eloise opened her satchel and pulled out a blanket. "Sounds good to me," she said, settling on the mossy ground and leaning against the single stone pillar.

"I won't be long," I assured her before making my way ahead.

The sweet scent of the world around us slowly faded, either that or my senses grew accustomed to it. I trekked for what felt like miles, meeting a flurry of black and blue in my path, yet stillness filled the air. It was as though nature itself held its breath at our presence.

I raced the nightfall as the moonlight beams lit up a distant river. The silver light glittered across the rippling surface, and I followed it until I stumbled upon a secret spring. It was nestled between two towering trees, hidden away from prying eyes.

Fate had bestowed a blessing on me, and I wholeheartedly accepted it. Neither gods nor monsters deserved my worship on this day; my faith lay only in my sword arm and the courage within me. I'd stumbled into a sacred refuge that would provide respite from the chaos of our journey, and for that, I was grateful.

Dropping to my knees, I stared in awe at this long-forgotten place, and with trembling hands, I cupped them to take a drink from its waters. Its life-giving fluid filled me, and I marveled at its beauty.

"How dare you drink from this sacred spring?" The voice was as soft as a rushing breeze, but its words struck like a war hammer.

I unsheathed my sword faster than lightning as I straightened, my heart pounding hard in my chest. "Who are you?" I demanded, every inch of my body taut in alertness.

I sharpened my gaze, scouring the dark waterside. There she was. A woman of myth and nightmare, lounging on a throne carved from the riverbank's stone.

"There's no need for your sword," she purred, her slim body stretching like a tigress as she spoke. "It can do me no harm."

"It's harmed a god before," I said in a low dispassionate voice, gripping the hilt of my blade until my knuckles turned white. "A feat I wouldn't mind repeating." I paused. "I'll ask again. Who—are—you?"

She rose from the throne with effortless grace, a gossamer gown of emerald and silver cascading down her curves. "I'm *not* a god," she spoke in reassurance, but the power of her words still sent a shiver down my spine.

Her delicate hands knotted at the nape of her neck and pushed a ripple of dark hair that tumbled down her shoulders like a curtain. As if walking on air, she descended from the mound of stone and grass, leaving behind a faint trail of glittering sparks.

My brows drew down in a fierce scowl and I took a step back. The cold metal of my blade felt heavy and reassuring against my palm. I sucked in a deep breath, but my heart continued to race as she moved closer. "What are you then?" I challenged, squaring my shoulders and readying myself for whatever would come next.

She stepped into the river, a deity come to life. Her dress billowed around her, shimmering in the light of the stars as if she wore the night sky itself. The water lapped against her sun-bathed flesh, sparkling like diamonds as she approached. Her movements were effortless yet commanding, a sight both beautiful and fearsome to behold. And then, with fluid grace, she stood before me, a goddess in human form.

Her jade gaze seemed to pierce my very soul as she prowled around me with a predator's grace. Her husky voice tickled my ear as she uttered one word, "So?" For an endless moment, I was suspended in time, and her heart beat in tandem with mine. "What am I?" she whispered, her breath warm against my ear, and it felt like a question of fate.

I remained frozen in place, my throat too tight to utter a single sound.

A delighted smile played upon her lips. "Why, don't you think I'm beautiful?" she asked sweetly.

My gaze lowered to the ground. "Without question, my lady," I answered humbly.

She let out a low chuckle and examined me carefully, from head to toe. "Quite impressive..." Her eyes glimmered with amusement. "Although every now and then someone finds their way here, none have ever been as handsome as you."

As I took in the sight of her, my gaze was pulled towards her remarkable features. Her skin shone like a pearl, as if lit by moonlight and a thousand stars. Dark tresses were woven with strands of emerald green, twinkling with life force like the vines of some divine enchantment. They fell past her shoulders, lending a touch of vibrancy to her breathtaking appearance.

This stunning woman had an aura of mysticism around her, so alluring that it enraptured me. Her eyes were dark pools of wonder and knowledge, as if she had glimpsed eternity and held on to its secrets. They glinted with power and mischief—the same sparkle of authority held by the gods. Her lips carried a rosy hue tinted with green, hinting at forbidden promises and whispering untold mysteries.

"Tell me your name," I managed, subdued by her beauty.

The corner of her lips curled up in mischief. "Can you tell me yours first... *human*?" she goaded lightly with a raised brow.

I sheathed my sword and squared my shoulders before I replied, "I am Prince Phillip, the Ruthless Steel Lion, Ruler of the Iron Provinces, and Heir to the Kingdom of Steelborn."

My words seemed to shock her, and she gasped, eyes wide. "Dear me," she breathed. "You've not lost your name."

I gave her a wry smile. "That's true enough—but now, I'd like to know yours. What should I call you?"

She stifled a laugh, but couldn't contain the amusement

in her voice when she replied, "I'm afraid my given titles are nothing compared to your own. All I can offer is *Minthe*. I am a nymph."

"Are you the keeper of this place, Minthe?" I asked inquisitively, scanning my surroundings. My gaze fixed on the cascading waterfall behind her.

"You could say that," she replied, insouciant. "Hades banished me from his palace to this wretched zone ages ago. It's been so long, I can't even recall why."

"Hades?" Shocked, I blurted out, "Where can I find him? Where is this palace you speak of?"

"Why the urgency, Prince?" she asked innocently.

Rage blazed through my veins like wildfire, burning away all other emotions. "He has taken my fated love and dragged her away to his fortress," I spat. "I'm here to reclaim her and take my vengeance."

A sly grin curved her supple mouth, and watching me in sheer delight, she added, "Your bravery compliments your beauty flawlessly."

Minthe radiated grace and danger in equal measure, a reminder of the duality that lived within the Netherworld. Her aura hinted at both fragility and strength, like a rare flower blooming in shadows.

An icy gust fluttered through the willow trees, suffused with moisture, as the distant growl of thunder echoed in the distance.

"Tell me where he is," I insisted softly, yet no less fiercely.

Her hands rose slowly, her wrists bereft of a single shackle. And there, across her pale skin, were golden vines intricately twisted like bracelets. "Set me free from this imprisonment, Steel Lion," she begged in a whisper, "and I will take you to the palace gates myself."

A sharp breath escaped my lips at the injustice of it all— Hades' cruel punishment. How could he exile a creature as graceful and gentle-hearted as Minthe, only to seclude her in this forlorn sanctuary? I glared into the depths of Hades' realm, my expression hardening with resolve. "What must I do?" My voice echoed throughout the sanctuary with urgency, and my heart longed for vengeance against the Prince of the Netherworld for his wicked deeds.

Minthe's face brightened with hope. "The only way to break my curse is with a key that lies behind the waterfall—guarded by Charon. Wait for the blood moon. He will be away then. Slip into his den and bring back his key. Once I'm free, I will help you in your quest."

I nodded, determined. "I will not disappoint you," I said.

"Oh... We'll see." Her brilliant smile shimmered through the air, enhancing the beauty of this land and reflecting her name. Minthe—a nymph whose very essence embodied the strength and grace of nature itself, her scent of mint and earth lingering long after she was gone.

# 29

# BEAUTY

The sun-kissed sand was a blanket of crushed diamonds beneath my feet, a million glimmering grains that glowed in the midday light. I treaded with a joyous sense of serenity, my toes sinking into the warmth of the beach. The crisp sea breeze blew against my face, and the shimmering ocean stretched out before me like a sapphire dream.

I was not alone. A presence suddenly beside me. He had tigerish eyes—blue like the ocean—and his hair, golden like the sun. His strong jawline made him look almost regal as he reached out to take my hand. Together, we strolled along the shore, our feet crunching against the sand, until we could make out a grand castle in the distance. We walked towards it, our steps growing lighter as we drew closer to our destination.

I blinked, the dreamlike atmosphere evaporating around us. A sudden pang of confusion swept over me, my head aching from the mysterious landscape. But then the man smiled at me tenderly, his sapphire eyes never leaving mine. He squeezed my hand ever so slightly and opened his mouth to speak. His lips curved into a tender smile as he uttered, *"It's time to wake up..."*

"Time to wake up." The voice, like velvet-laced iron, reverberated around me.

My eyes snapped open as sheer dread surged through my veins. Confusion fogged my mind... Where was I? In the arms of the towering stranger with long frost-pale hair who carried me down a chilling passage.

I swept my surroundings with a frantic glance. The dungeon's walls gleamed bloodred from the flickering flames in each recess, and pooled darkness filled the gaps between them.

He cast me into the damp cell with a finality that felt like a death sentence. The warrior stepped back and glanced at me with his stormy gaze, cold and emotionless. His eyes gave nothing away, leaving me to imagine my fate.

An instinctive chill ran down my spine, and without thinking, my hand flew to the spot on my hip where a sword would have been—except there was nothing there. Fear kept me frozen in place, unable to move even an inch.

A cruel laugh escaped his lips as his eyes bore into me. "Your blade is not welcome here," he declared, the smoothness of his words clashing against the might of his presence.

I scrambled to my knees from the cold stone floor, cringing away from him as he stepped closer. The throbbing pain from the wound on my shoulder winded me, and fear threatened to consume my very existence. My heart pounded against my ribs as I implored myself for answers, but none seemed to come.

My captor drew nearer and I stumbled back, panic clouding my vision. He set his jaw menacingly, but then something in his expression softened and he stepped aside. I could feel something stirring deep within him as he motioned towards the prison gate. The exit was so close. All I had to do was make a run for it. And yet, I froze.

Noticing my hesitation, he held up his hand, beckoning me closer with an unspoken command. I warily straightened and stepped towards him, struggling to trust this sudden change in demeanor. He slowly leaned forward and whispered a single word into my ear: "Run."

I wavered for a moment, still unsure whether to trust this stranger or not. But the fear that had been gnawing at my gut told me that staying in this cell was not an option. I took a deep breath and bolted towards the gate.

A chill ran down my spine as a spectral blue light filled the dungeon. Suddenly, cold metal binds appeared on my wrists. Chains formed from the air, pulling me back before I could cross the threshold. I was anchored to the floor, and his harsh laughter echoed off of the damp walls.

I wouldn't cry. I wouldn't show him any more weakness than I already had. My voice trembled with outrage and fright as I forced myself to ask, "Why am I here?"

He arched a single platinum brow, gaze narrowed and calculating. "Isn't it obvious? You're my prisoner." He reached for my wrists, fingers tight around them as he added gruffly, "Don't even think of escaping. No one ever has."

A sudden rush of despair flooded my veins as I looked upon the dismal walls surrounding me. My throat tightened and tears threatened to flood my eyes again, but I forced them back. I couldn't let him see me this way.

My gaze swept the other cells frantically as I searched for something, anything that could help me escape. But all I saw were piles of bones—human bones. Despair filled the air, chilling me to the core and making my heart heavy with fear.

The clattering sound of metal bounced off the walls as the cell door slammed shut behind him.

The stranger's echoing footsteps faded into nothingness as he turned away from me, his last words ringing through my being like a death knell: "You'll stay in my tower until I've decided your fate." His armor shone like stars in the dimly lit dungeon as he stormed away with an air of confidence, his frosty locks whipping around his head.

I bit back my screams, knowing nobody would hear them. Alone now, all hope seemed lost. How would I ever escape this wretched place? I refused to let myself fall into despair. A single ember of hope still shone in my chest. Taking a long steadying breath, I steeled myself against the coming trials. No matter what happened, no matter how hard it was, I would never give up.

I sat there on the cold stone floor for hours, feeling the life slowly drain out of me. The putrid smell of death hung in the air, sickening me to my core. I couldn't help but think of the ones who'd died here before me, trapped in this hellish prison with no hope of escape.

Exhaustion eventually took hold and I drifted into a fitful sleep plagued by nightmares. I slipped in and out of consciousness, unsure if minutes or hours were passing. The cold seeped deep into my bones. My dreams were filled with haunting echoes of screams and weeping, the cries of those lost souls who had perished in this terrible place.

It wasn't until the first flicker of light danced across the cell walls that I realized how long I had been sitting there. A small window high up let in a soft beam of silver moonlight, casting eerie shadows across the chamber. My stomach growled, and I was suddenly hit with the realization that I hadn't eaten in days.

I lurched onto my feet, my body screaming in agony, and scrambled desperately towards the prison bars. Tears streaming down my cheeks, I bellowed a desperate plea for freedom. But no mercy befell me—my words were nothing more than a muted wail, lost amidst the clanging of chains and iron.

"Please!" I sobbed, pain shooting through my back and my arm throbbing with every beat of my heart. But my cries went unheard in this cold, unforgiving prison.

I collapsed into the dirt, a guttural wail of anguish escaping my trembling lips. A stray pale light beam spilled over the dark marks on my shoulder, where I'd suffered the savagery of my captor's blade. The skin around it had healed oddly, weeping black ink that snaked down my arm in a winding thorny vine.

My arm absently lifted towards the moonlight, and I gasped as I took in what I saw. The strange markings etched into my skin throbbed with a life of their own, as if dancing to an unheard tune. I shuddered at the thought of what it might mean, but deep down, I knew the truth. I was cursed, and this prison was my eternal punishment.

# 30

# PHILLIP

As I returned to our campsite, I navigated the rolling hills and dense forests, until I stumbled across a clearing, sprawled out in front of me. It was a savage courtyard of sorts, teeming with fruit trees—oranges, peaches, pears, apples, and plums bursting at the seams.

A rush of warmth filled my veins. I cracked a smile and nearly laughed out loud, barely able to contain my excitement. Quickly, I loaded my pockets with as much as I could carry. Eloise would be so thrilled. I couldn't wait to tell her about this unexpected trove I had stumbled upon.

In the distance, the ancient temple stood against the sky, its aged stones covered in moss and tangled vines. I hurried closer, anticipation thrumming through my veins.

Another dusk set on the horizon as I reached our small haven. Lowering my head, I stepped across the threshold, instantly spotting her as I looked up.

Eloise lay still and peaceful beneath her woolen blanket, her pale skin dusted with freckles in the warm firelight. She was sleeping, and I couldn't help but think of all she had overcome to slumber so deeply.

Soundlessly, I piled up the fruit on the broken altar. I sat down next to her, and the warmth of the fire engulfed me. And for one blissful moment, I simply contemplated her as she slept. The flames danced and flickered across her face, casting shadows that played delicately along her gentle features.

She was a queen in her slumber, her aura of grace and power enveloping the room. Her beauty was both delicate and strong, like porcelain sculpted from iron. Despite this regal visage, I had seen the warrior within her—the one who could wield a blade better than any knight. She was untouchable and wholly admirable, and perhaps it was time for me to tell her how I truly felt.

I reached out to brush a wisp of fair hair from her face, and my fingers lingered, tracing the curve of her cheekbone. Eloise stirred slightly, and rattled to the core, I flinched away.

My heart was ready to burst from my chest, so long had I kept her in the dark about my feelings. As we ventured through a place of eerie shadows and dismal perils, I couldn't bear the thought of one more day without her knowing the truth.

I parted my lips, trying to force the words out that had been lodged in my throat for years. My breath quivered in the air between us as I mouthed, "Eloise…"

She stirred, fair eyelashes fluttering against her porcelain skin. Blue eyes like sapphire pools caught and held me, and suddenly I was unable to move.

How could I speak the truth silenced inside me? How, when she'd opened her heart to me merely days ago, and out of sheer dread, I'd denied my true feelings? Now my heart beat wildly, heavy with the knowledge that if I spoke, our entire world would change and I might lose her.

My soul ached to speak the truth. Those three words sat on the tip of my tongue, begging for release. *I love you,* I wanted to say. *I want nothing more than to protect you from the harshness of this world and keep you safe from the cruelty of a crown.*

"Phillip, what is it?" she asked, her voice as soft as a dove's wings.

I swallowed hard and forced myself to speak, "Look what I found," I said, gesturing to the abundance of fruit stacked before us. "Peaches, apples, pears—a feast fit for a queen."

A whimsical smile graced her lips, her soft laughter tinkling like bells in my ears. "It's perfect," she whispered, before turning away from the food and towards me. Her eyes filled with hope as she reached out and grabbed my hand. "Help me up?"

My flesh burned and tingled with her feather-light touch, as if I'd been struck by lightning. As Eloise stood before me, a tidal wave of longing rushed over my being, pushing me to inch closer. Our time together in this wild ancient realm had silently been building up towards this moment, and all I could think about was kissing her.

And oh, her eyes—they were so bright and sparkling as they bore into mine; yet so tender, so captivating. The intensity of it all was almost too much to bear. One last deep breath filled my lungs, and then I felt myself slowly slipping away from her hand.

*Get out of here now. Leave before it's too late.* I stumbled towards the entrance, my feet clumsy and barely moving me forward when all I wanted was to flee.

"Phillip—wait," Eloise said urgently. "You just got here. Don't leave."

I turned around and found her gazing at me with a million questions mirrored in her pale blue eyes.

My heart pounded so loudly that I could barely hear my own thoughts. "Eloise," I breathed out, feeling exposed in a way I had never before experienced. "I've been meaning to tell you something." The words were out before I could stop them.

Confusion flickered on her face as she replied. "You just did, with the fruit. What more do you want to say?"

My tongue stumbled on the words. "Want to go on an adventure?" I asked, my throat closed up tight as I recoiled from the courage it had taken me so long to find. It was not fickleness or weakness that had stopped me, but the fear that our journey would at some point take me away from her. No matter what, Aurora and I were bound together by the fate that had been set before the moment of our births.

Eloise took her time peering over the delicacies laid on the table. Finally, she chose an apple. Her sleepy voice was so soft when she asked, "Does it involve fighting?" She then bit into her piece of fruit.

My lips curved into a smirk as I replied, "Yes."

Her head tilted forward so that her brilliant blue eyes were locked on mine. In the lowest of voices, she asked, "Is it dangerous?"

"Very," I said with a nod of emphasis.

Eloise held her breath for a beat too long before asking the question on both of our minds. "Will it get us off this island?"

My lips pressed into a thin line. I had to be sure of my answer. "It will help."

Determination and hope flashed behind her gaze. Without a moment's delay, she spoke, "I'm in." A hint of a smile danced across her lips as she bit into the apple, savoring its crispness.

I stumbled back, gaping at her sudden agreement. "Wait," I said, hand raised in protest. "Don't you want to know the details first?"

She gave me a half-hearted shrug, unconcerned, as she stepped into the pale light of the tall window. She tugged tighter the woolen blanket that hugged her slender arms and back, fierce gaze meeting mine as she answered with cold resolve. "It makes no difference. Tell me who to kill, and I'll do it."

Stunned at her sheer loyalty, I cursed under my breath as I stalked towards her, grabbing an apple on my way over to join her. "It's going to be more complicated than that," I said gruffly. "I made a deal with a river nymph. She'll show us the way to Hades' palace. But there's a catch—we need to steal a key from a god who dwells nearby."

My words were met with a scowl. "*Steal* a key? Are we thieves now?" she asked, her voice sharp as frost and laced with accusation. "Is that what it's all come up to?"

I couldn't help but smirk at the sight of her pout—it was hard to stay mad at her. "We can fight him if you want," I teased, hoping to lighten the mood.

Her glare could have cut through steel, but I bravely held my ground. "If there's no other choice," she muttered, relenting only slightly.

Taking my cue, I finished off the story. "The nymph said we should strike on the blood moon. Charon will be gone then."

A heavy silence descended between us before she finally nodded slowly. "All right. We've got enough time. Let's make a plan."

## 31

## BEAUTY

Sunsets came and went, and weaker and weaker I grew, slipping in and out of consciousness, my breaths coming short and shallow. Although no longer bleeding, my shoulder throbbed with a fiery intensity that showed no mercy. But I refused to give up. I could not let the pain overtake me; I had to keep fighting. And so, with every ounce of strength left in me, I pushed through the agony until it became a mere afterthought, fading into the backdrop of my being.

Tucking my legs beneath me, I shrank back against the unyielding stone walls of my cell, trying to make myself as small as possible. Fear and dread coiled in my chest like a cold snake.

The night waned, and I was all alone in the prison of this forsaken tower. The only sound that kept me company was the scratching of rats along the walls. I clung to every glimmer of hope, but I was so weakened, so broken... How long must I remain here before I could flee back to my life in the Midnight Palace? With each passing day, the possibility of freedom faded further away.

A sudden searing jolt of pain shot through me. My scream echoed off the damp stones. I collapsed onto the icy ground, a sharp sob tearing from my throat. I felt it—the abhorrent agony radiating from my shoulder, ten times worse than before. And it was as if his blade had sliced again, each ragged edge ripping its way through my flesh.

The merciless blow finally ceased and my entire body shuddered with ache as I heaved, desperately attempting to draw a single breath.

"You're still alive," he murmured, disbelief in his voice. That gentle timbre was the same as before, wrapping around me like velvet yet holding the sharp edge of a heart made of ice.

He stood at the bars of my cell, his shining, silver eyes locked on me. He seemed utterly transfixed, almost as if he were in awe of what he saw. Yet, despite the strange admiration radiating from him, something sinister was lurking beneath his expression.

Gone was the silver armor that had marked him as a warrior. Instead, regal bloodred robes swathed his form and emphasized the taut muscles beneath.

My chest heaved with each breath I took, my voice scratchy from lack of use. "What do you want?"

His lips twitched ever so slightly as he huffed a quiet laugh, his stormy eyes fixed on me and unreadable. "I've been watching you," he said softly. "You won't give in, even under these conditions... It's remarkable."

My scoff was nothing more than a dry exhale from between pursed lips. "What good does that bring me now?"

He stepped inside, the thunder of his steps echoing off of the cold walls. The metal door slammed shut behind him with a force that made my stomach clench in fear. I met his gaze, and dared to show no sign of weakness; icy gray eyes bared down upon me, daring me to defy him. His presence pressed against me like a physical weight, almost as if he was challenging me to find the strength to confront him.

After what felt like an eternity of painful silence, he finally spoke. "It's time for you to go," he said gruffly.

My stomach dropped. I got to my knees, trying to wrap my mind around what he had just said. Was this some miracle? Could I really be free? But why would he suddenly grant me my freedom? It didn't make sense—unless something darker was going on here.

Rage unleashed through me, and I spat out, "You promised me freedom once before. But you lied. I won't be fooled again—I refuse to play your twisted games."

The corner of his lips twitched into a sneer as he exhaled a daunting breath. "Rise," he roared, punctuating the command with an oppressive wave of his hand. His voice was laced with deadly intent and my body trembled in response. Still, I forced my feet to move and conquered the pain that lingered within me.

"Come," he said wearily. "Follow me."

With a deep breath, I willed my legs to move and stepped out of the cell. We walked in silence down the prison hallway until we arrived at a winding staircase. Finally, we reached the ground floor of the tower. In silence, he led me towards an old wooden door at the back of the room and opened it, motioning for me to enter.

My pulse quickened as I stepped into what appeared to be a small library. My eyes swept over rows upon rows of books, some so ancient they looked as if they were about to crumble into dust at any moment. The walls and shelves were lined with leather-bound volumes that seemed to contain centuries of knowledge and secrets from history's past.

"Sit there." He spoke so quietly, it was barely audible. But the power behind his words left no room for indecision—it was a command. His finger jabbed in the direction of an unassuming desk and chair behind me.

I sighed deeply before doing as he'd asked, but inside, I bristled with defiance.

He paused at a wall near the back corner, sliding his finger along a row of titles until he stopped on one particular book—the oldest-looking one in the room. He pulled it off of its shelf and opened it, revealing page after page filled with hand-written runes and symbols that looked alien even to me. I couldn't help but feel there was something special about this ledger, something powerful within its pages that gave me pause as I looked at it.

With a snap, he closed the book and pushed it away, never explaining why. "I have an offer for you," he said, each step closer bringing him farther into my personal space. He didn't even look me in the eyes as he said it. "Serve me, and I'll give you anything you desire."

I narrowed my gaze skeptically, my mouth forming a suspicious line. Who was he to make such a request? I wanted to ask, but the fear of reigniting his wrath prevented me from doing so. "Serve you?" I asked, though it was more commentary than an inquiry.

"Your freedom can be yours again," he intoned, as he slowly stretched out a single arm to the side. "But perhaps you'd like to have dinner first?"

My heart stopped when I noticed the table beside me, laden with steaming delicacies. At once, the sweet aroma of roasting veggies and freshly baked bread filled the air around me. My mouth watered. I yearned for just one bite of the savory feast before me.

I studied him cautiously, the hollow of my stomach aching with hunger and my heart pounding with the prospect of freedom. His words were an invitation, a demand for something far more than just dinner. I forced away my uncertainties and asked as calmly as possible, "What if I refuse?"

He stood before me, looming so tall that his shadow engulfed me in its darkness. His words were deep and menacing as he declared, "Then you'll remain here until you rot away. Your bones will join the others."

I shuddered as his words hung in the air. It was a cruel fate, and I had no choice but to trust him... But how could I?

"Think about it," he said softly, taking a step towards the door. "But don't take too long. You wouldn't want to make the wrong decision."

The lock clicked behind him, and then the door melted away with a swish of sound. Bookcase after bookcase, the entire library faded, until all that remained was the prison cell, and I realized in a rush that everything had been an illusion.

I'd been inside the prison all along.

I lay there in the darkness, my mind racing with fear and doubt. What would he ask me to do? And even worse, what if I agreed?

The thought of giving in to his offer made my blood run cold. To serve someone as cruel as he was, knowingly and willingly? No. I wouldn't do it. Not just because I feared what might come next, but out of respect for myself and my freedom. I had been held captive long enough, and the time had come for me to take control of my destiny.

I refused to be cowed or manipulated by his offer, no matter how tempting it seemed. There was to be no payment for servitude, no way that I could buy back my freedom through any other means than sheer determination and strength of will. My vow echoed in my mind—freedom would be mine on the terms I chose, and not those imposed on me by an overbearing tyrant like him.

Most of all, one thought lingered in the back of my mind: if he was as powerful as he'd shown me, why ask for servitude? Couldn't someone as mighty as him just *force* me to obey?

# PHILLIP

The endless night was split by the thunderous roar of the River Styx plunging over the cliffs, crashing into the valley below. Before us yawned the cavern mouth, dark and hungry behind the churning veil of water. Frigid mist soaked our hair and clothes as we picked our way down the slick mountain path, drawn inexorably closer to the waterfall's fury.

Tonight was the night of the blood moon. The time had come. Eloise and I stepped into the deep, dark shadows of the ancient Netherworld forest. The air was heavy with secrets and old magic. We both knew what we had to do. Two weeks of restless preparation had led us to this point—a quest for the key that would break Minthe's curse. We could not predict the dangers that awaited us around every turn. But no matter how wary we grew, nothing could distract us from our ultimate goal.

At last, we reached the bottom of the mountain, a realm of shifting shadows and bone-numbing dampness. There lay the gateway to the depths of Charon's domain.

I cast my mind back to Minthe's whispered instructions,

her warning etched upon my memory. *"The key you seek is hidden deep within the mountain. Bring it to me, and I will reveal the way to the Dark Prince's lair."*

Beside me, Eloise silently searched the cascading water for some hidden passage beyond the reach of the ferryman. I envied her composure, a foil to my own spinning doubts. But our purpose remained fixed. Failure was not an option we could countenance.

"There it is." Eloise's arm shot up, a finger pointing at the metal door embedded in the mountainside. Thick ivy crept around it, cloaking it from the world—from all, except those who knew to look for it.

Drawing a bracing breath, I turned to Eloise and forced conviction into my hushed tone. "We'll find the key, somewhere deep in that mountain. And once we take it to Minthe, she will unlock the secret of Hades' lair." I swallowed hard, voicing the thought we both shunned. "It shouldn't be too hard, right?"

Eloise's answering smile was grim. She heard the hollow ring of false confidence in my words. But we had come too far to falter now.

"Right?" I insisted, a bit rattled by her silence.

"Whatever is out there waiting for us," she replied with no inclination, "we'll be ready for it."

I agreed with a swift nod.

Steeling ourselves, we descended into the chasm. The darkness covered us like a blanket as we shuffled down small rocks and loose stones. The walls glistened in hues of blue and purple from the edges of small glowing plants that had taken root on either side of us.

We stopped in front of the ancient metal door, barred by a lever. I frowned at its simplicity. "Is there really no lock?" I murmured.

"No need for one," Eloise said softly, blue eyes scanning

the doorway with tension. "No one in their right mind would dare venture inside."

A chill scurried down my spine, and I shivered. We both knew what was beyond this door—a power that could swallow us whole.

"Well... let's give it a try," she breathed, pulling on the lever. It clicked open with an echoing creak that seemed to echo through all ages past.

We stepped into the darkened doorway, bracing ourselves for what lay ahead. The chamber was unlike anything I had ever seen before. The walls were adorned with a kaleidoscope of precious gems, while the ceiling shone like a starlit sky. Unfamiliar creatures frolicked and cavorted as if they had been here since the dawn of time. In the center of the room stood an imposing altar surrounded by aged stone columns; cloaked in mist and draped in shadows, it concealed its mysteries from prying eyes.

The stillness of the cavern was interrupted by a sudden, hot gust of air that whipped around us. Our gazes fixed on the molten red lava that snaked around the room like an omen, capturing our faces in its eerie shadows.

Atop the altar, a golden relic sparkled with an unearthly light. "There's the key," Eloise said, pointing at the altar. No sooner she started to move towards it, than I grabbed her arm, stopping her midstride.

"Wait," I muttered darkly, my misgivings rising like bile in my throat. Something was wrong—this was far too easy. Shaking my head, I added, "I don't like this."

"Come on, Phillip," she sighed in exasperation. "Pull it together."

But as we trudged down the winding path towards the dais, my apprehension only increased. Whatever lay hidden in this temple could be of immense power and danger, yet there was no one to protect it. I shivered, feeling the weight of countless gazes on our backs, yet when I twisted around there was nothing but empty air and deepening shadows.

We finally reached the altar, glimmering before us with an otherworldly light, emanating from the mysterious object that lay within.

I stumbled forward, mesmerized by the gleam of the archaic artifact. Its aura was filled with a power so ancient it was almost tangible. The moment I touched it, its energy surged through me like streaks of lightning. My feet rediscovered a strength I had forgotten existed. All the trials, all the sacrifices… all of it had led to this. I turned to Eloise and saw the spark of wonder reflected in her eyes.

But our exhilaration vanished in an instant. A powerful tremor shook the cave, like a warning from the gods. I heard it then—the sound of hounds on the hunt. Growling and snarling echoed through the tunnels as if they were closing in.

Fear, stark as death seized me. I grabbed Eloise's arm, terror gripping my throat like a vice and cutting off my voice. "We must flee and quickly," I howled with urgency, yet it was already too late. The thundering paws of the hounds could be heard getting closer by the second.

"Don't worry," Eloise dismissed my concerns with a casual flick of her wrist. "We've vanquished these hounds before."

Their eyes burned a fiery red, embers in the darkness. Eloise and I prepared ourselves for battle as thick fur bristled across their bodies and they lunged forward. What we *hadn't* expected was the three-headed beast that stepped out of the shadows—a mammoth of unearthly proportions.

"Eloise…" I said, bringing my sword up and pressing the tip in between us. "You were saying?"

"Oh, all right!" she spat before thrusting her blade forward.

The tunnel rumbled with an ominous roar, loose pebbles skittering down the walls. Before our eyes, the hulking beast shuddered, then split apart into three snarling hounds, each bristling with fangs and claws.

The first lunged at me, hellfire eyes alight with lethal intent, but I was ready. I swung up my blade, barely parrying vicious teeth aimed at my throat. The force of its attack nearly knocked my feet from under me, but I held my ground.

Planting my stance, I let the creature's momentum carry it forward onto my waiting sword point. Mortally pierced, it collapsed with a pained yelp, ichor pooling on the stone. But two more circled, ready to avenge their fallen packmate.

Eloise engaged the second, her movements swift and deadly. She dodged gnashing jaws and spun away from swiping claws, fighting with breathtaking speed and skill. In a blur of motion, her sword flashed, slicing through thick fur and hide to pierce the hound's heart. It was over in seconds.

But I had no time to admire her flawless technique as the third beast charged towards me with blistering speed, hell-bent on ripping my throat out. My pulse raced as I watched it carefully—the way it moved, the way it attacked—seeking some weakness. But its intelligence seemed far beyond anything we had ever faced before. It was almost like it could predict our next move before we had even made it.

We exchanged a flurry of probing blows, neither able to gain advantage. Its skill matched my own, with savagery compounding its deadliness. I realized with dawning dread— this was no mortal hound, but a demonic familiar bound to a dark master's will.

Sensing futility, I tried to disengage, to draw it after me. But it anticipated the feint, snarling triumphantly as it herded me back against the stony wall. Muscles bunched for the killing pounce.

In that hopeless moment, Eloise's cry rang out. She flung herself between the hound's leap and my exposed flank, taking the full force of its lunge.

"No!" Horror welled in me as she fell heavily, the thing's vicious fangs going for her throat. With a bellow of rage, I ripped my sword across its maw, forcing it back just shy of her life's blood. Before it could recover, I sank my blade through its skull, pinning it lifeless to the cavern's ground.

I whirled to Eloise, pulse thudding. By some miracle, she still clung to consciousness, though bright scarlet spread over her tunic. My hands trembled as I tore my shirt off and pressed the bundled fabric against her wound, desperately trying to stem the steady flow of blood.

Gently, I lifted her head, hands slick with her vital liquid. "Why?" I rasped. "Why take the blow meant for me?"

Through cracked lips, she whispered simply, "Couldn't lose you." Eloise's eyes flickered open for a moment—long enough for me to catch a glimpse of fear in their depths—before she succumbed to unconsciousness.

Tears burned my eyes, but I blinked them back. Gingerly, I bore her weight and stumbled onwards. The hounds were vanquished, but a more ruthless beast awaited: failure and its terrible price.

By my sword and my life, I would see Eloise through this. I would carry her to the ends of the earth if I must. Her sacrifice would not be in vain—I swore it on my soul. Failure was not an option. For her, I would conquer the impossible.

## 3 3

## BEAUTY

*J*woke with a start, my pulse racing as faint red light poured through my cell's tiny window. Dread clutched my heart as I rose to get a better view of what awaited outside, my widened eyes meeting the most terrifying sight—the moon, round and full, glowing an eerie crimson as if its surface had been painted with blood.

The burning sensation of dread and utter despair choked my screams of mercy as I felt myself collapsing to the ground in complete exhaustion. Yet, even then, I would not allow myself to accept my inevitable fate.

A faint melody suddenly broke into the dullness of my prison. Instants later, flashes of blue, green, and yellow light danced across the cell walls as firemagic exploded in the evening sky.

*The gods will always find cause for celebration,* I realized with a sinking stomach.

The dazzling flares of color lightened the oppressive atmosphere, bleeding through the air, sparkling against my skin like a gentle caress. That's when I saw it—the inky vines that once crept up my shoulder and slithered down my arm now appeared to be stagnant, as if they'd finally received their fill of me. A shiver of comfort rushed through my being, though I couldn't decide if it was a warning or a hopeful sign.

I lost count of the days since my captor had last been here. He left me with meager provisions—scraps of food, drops of water—just enough to keep me alive but never enough to satisfy my hunger. His presence seemed to linger in every corner of my cell, his taunting whispers reverberating through the air like a haunting echo. Empty promises of rewards and dire threats, if I refused, resounded in my mind, blurring the line between fear and desire.

I jolted alert as a distant hum reached my ears, steadily growing louder. The sound morphed into an eerie, mesmerizing chant that sent a chill up my spine. Heavy footsteps echoed down the hall, pounding ever nearer like thunder. I sensed a presence before the cell and saw a hooded figure gazing at me. His eyes glinted delightedly from the shadows as he asked in a raspy voice, "Are you ready to leave?"

Instinctively, I backed away from him. I didn't trust his offer—it seemed too good to be true.

"You mustn't be scared," he said in a gentle voice, almost as if he could sniff my fear. He reached out with one hand and opened the door. A sly smile spread across his face. "I will defend you from whatever comes our way."

The unyielding clang of my chains shattering against the jagged stones filled the chamber. I stumbled forward, my bare feet cold and raw on the slimy dungeon floor.

Terror lanced through me when I met his hooded face, veiled in shadows. I could tell he was something otherworldly —something ancient and dark that chilled me to the bone.

But I had no choice. I would never bow to the guardian of the tower, and I could never allow myself to rot away in this prison forever.

Forcing a shuddering breath into my lungs, trying to ignore every ounce of reason that whispered for me to flee, I squared my shoulders in determination and stepped forth into the darkness.

## 34

## PHILLIP

*B*ehind us, the tunnel we had slipped through to enter Charon's lair was now sealed shut, caved in during the titanic battle. Our only choice now was to forge on into the unknown, traversing this lightless labyrinth in search of an alternate exit.

The path ahead seemed endless, a twisting maze with no promise of escape. But I refused to yield to despair. With Eloise cradled limply in my arms, I took a faltering step forward, then another. Giving up was not an option—not when her life and our quest hung in the balance.

My footsteps echoed through the desolate cavern, answered only by the whispers of ancient stone. In the smothering dark, it was easy to surrender to doubt and dread. But I clung to hope, knowing that together Eloise and I could withstand even this.

Shadows grasped at us as we ventured through the Netherworld's depths. This cursed place conspired to crush the spirit, to entomb all hope. But I vowed to defy it, to fight our way clear of this abyss and back into the light.

I would remain relentless until Eloise was safe, until our

destinies were ours to shape once more. Darkness may have surrounded us, but it would not prevail.

Eloise stirred faintly in my arms, brow creased with pain. Her skin was deathly pale, clammy to the touch. With every laborious breath, crimson bloomed anew across the ragged gash in her tunic. Hot blood seeped into my own clothes as I held her fragile frame.

Panic threatened to choke me, but I choked it back down. She needed me steady and sure.

"Don't give up on me, Eloise," I entreated through bloodless lips. "We've sacrificed too much to falter here." My wide eyes desperately scoured the shadows for some route of escape. "Just stay with me..."

But my pleas went unheard, her head lolling limply against my chest. Still, her shallow breaths proved she yet clung to life. And with life, there was hope.

"I'm taking you to the nymph's sanctuary," I promised in the silent caverns. "Minthe will heal you. I know she will."

We had not come so far, braved so much, only to be defeated now. Gathering my fading strength, I forced my aching legs onward, refusing to fail her.

The twisting tunnels seemed to taunt our feeble progress, shadows writhing in monstrous shapes to bar our path. The wan glow of crystals illuminated little, serving only to distort the darkness into strange visions.

Eloise's breaths grew more ragged, each one daggered through my heart. Still, I pushed my exhausted body to its limits, desperate to outpace the icy talons of death that grasped for her.

Just when hope guttered to its last flicker, I glimpsed it— the faintest sliver of moonlight piercing the gloom ahead. New urgency surged through my veins. We were so close.

"See that light, Eloise?" I whispered fiercely to her ashen face. "It's the way out. Stay with me. We're nearly there."

The slash of moonlight swelled ahead until finally, we emerged into the open air, twilight's lingering warmth chasing away the damp chill of the caves. Still, Eloise did not rouse, and fear came crashing down on me like a guillotine.

I pulled her close. "We're getting out of here," I said, my voice brimming with earnest determination. "Trust me, my dearest. We shall overcome. I promise you, when this is over, we'll feast in the Dragon's Breath. Just you and me, drunk on Bloodmoon Red." I sniffed. "We'll play that silly lyre of yours and you'll sing your favorite songs... Fires of the Netherworld —I'll sing to you myself!" I uttered a brief laugh, tears gathering in my eyes.

"Don't... bother," she groaned. "You can't even carry... a tune." When at last her blonde lashes fluttered, joy welled inside me, so sudden and sharp it was painful.

Voice thick with emotion, my trembling fingers brushed the tangled hair away from her bruised face. "I thought I'd lost you."

Chapped lips cracked into a hint of her crooked smile. "Not yet..." she rasped. "...takes more than that..."

I let out a ragged laugh that was half a sob. "Just rest now, my fearsome warrior. You've earned it."

Eloise sighed, eyes slipping closed once more as bone-deep exhaustion finally won out. But her chest rose and fell in a steady rhythm, each breath a small miracle.

As she nestled weakly against me, I cradled her close and stroked her hair with infinite tenderness. "I've got you," I whispered.

Onwards I trekked through the gloom, the bleeding full moon lighting the way, and my precious burden secure in my embrace. The shadows could not touch us now.

# 35

# BEAUTY

*M*y heartbeat thundered in my ears as I crept through the shadowed dungeon hallway, pressed close behind the stranger's cloaked form. Days of near starvation had left me lightheaded and weak, but determination fueled my steps. We were so close now—escape waited just ahead if I could keep pace a little longer.

I kept my body in motion, desperate to maintain the hooded form in sight. Who was this mysterious benefactor who knew the way out, and why risk himself for me? But such questions mattered little if they led to freedom.

*Freedom.* Fear coiled in my gut, paired with exhilaration. If the stranger's plan succeeded, I could soon be free of this dreadful prison and the cruelty of its master. No more enduring the mocking laughter that echoed outside my cell each time his footsteps faded.

I shuddered at the memory of his last visit, when frigid fingers had trailed down my neck, his serpentine voice promising I would learn to appreciate his personal attention. Revulsion and dread churned inside me. I had to get out before my captor made good on his threats.

I shuffled numbly down the withering corridor, my pace sluggish and labored. The stone walls were lined with dark prison cells, shadows that seemed to stretch endlessly in either direction. A chill of dread shuddered through me, for I knew what I had done could never be forgotten or forgiven. Any moment now, my captor could appear from thin air and mete out punishment for my treachery.

Just ahead, the stranger halted, raising a hand for silence. He peered around a corner, then beckoned urgently before pressing on. The outer door was near, past a sleeping guard. Our hopes hung by a thread, perilously close to fruition.

The hooded figure turned to me, his voice low and commanding. "Hurry."

I forced myself to nod silently, too weary to do anything else.

A shiver rushed through me. There it was—the massive steel gate that served as the entrance to this nightmarish fortress. The man stepped forward, unlocking it with ease. At once, a gust of frosty air swirled around me, raising goose-bumps on my skin. As an expanse of glittering stars unveiled beyond, tears of awe and disbelief pricked my eyes. The outside world. Was this real?

With a guiding hand, the stranger led me across the threshold into the crisp night air. Then his voice came, unexpected and familiar. "You're free now."

My fingers brushed the doorframe's cold steel, and a thrill shot through my veins. As I stood on the threshold to freedom, a flurry of firemagic lit up the prison grounds like a thousand bursting stars.

Holding my quickened breath, I warily whispered into the darkness: "I'd like to thank you, but you've not told me your name."

The man ground to a halt. He spun around, a slow, knowing smile stretching across his handsome visage. I stared up at the cowled face, and even under the concealing hood, I could make out his strong jaw, his piercing hazel eyes that glinted in the moonlight like precious amber jewels.

My breath lodged in my throat as recognition struck me. *Impossible. Impossible...* It was him.

Inch by inch he drew closer, until the hood finally fell back, trapping me beneath his mesmerizing gaze. A single word escaped my lips. "Hypnos?" My voice shook as emotion surged within me.

The corners of his mouth curved in a relieved smile. "I've come to take you home, my lady," he said warmly, but the joy and delight saturating his voice was like a shout.

In a single heartbeat, he scooped me up into his arms and took off running from the prison walls. All fear fell away into the night as we flew over the lush grass, my breath gasping with every step he took. His embrace was a shield from the darkness around us, carrying me closer and closer to freedom.

The moon shimmered across his face, silver light cascading in his eyes. It was like looking at the stars— nothing but love and compassion that promised a new beginning.

For an instant, I dared to look back and locked eyes on the tower that had imprisoned me. Its high walls seemed to stretch endlessly above, as if reaching for the night sky. An oppressive atmosphere hung heavy in the air, and I shuddered, unable to believe that I had finally escaped.

The thought of what could have been set my heart thundering in my chest, but Hypnos had taken me away from that place and now we flew across fields and forests, the wind whipping around us with the crisp scent of the river and fresh leaves. My skin tingled as I gasped in sheer bliss. I was truly free.

"We can rest here for a while," he said, tilting his wings to guide us into a gentle landing.

Our feet touched down softly on the banks of a secluded river, surrounded by swaying palms and lush foliage. Moonlight filtered through the fronds, dappling the white sand shore. The murmur of water over smooth stones was soothing after the grating clangs of the dungeon.

I drew in a deep breath, filling my lungs with the clean scents of water and night-blooming flowers. "It's so peaceful," I whispered in wonder, trailing my fingers through the clear stream. After the oppression of my cell, this place felt like a dream.

His arm draped across my shoulders, the divine tattoos inked on his skin glimmering with magic as his wings folded back and buried themselves within the artwork. We stood in a silence heavy with unspoken emotion. His voice was gentle but thick with relief as he said, "I've been searching for days. I thought you were gone forever..."

The words rang out into the emptiness. As our eyes locked, an overwhelming sensation of gratitude washed over me. I gave him a faint smile and whispered, "Thank you for finding me."

His gaze softened and he pulled me closer, surrounding me with warmth. His silent sigh vibrated against my ear, and I breathed in his presence. And there we stayed, embracing under the stars for a little while.

Around us, the palm trees towered, their branches whispering in the warm breeze. I closed my eyes and inhaled deeply, drawing in the smells of fertile earth and wildflowers, feeling as if I'd been reborn.

With a graceful hand wave, Hypnos showed me a blanket of crimson petals on the grass behind us. A basket brimming with succulent berries, luscious grapes, and exotic fruits lay beside it.

We sank into the lush grass beneath the hulking palm tree. Its mighty trunk rose like a wall, its emerald leaves spreading out to form a protective canopy around us, enfolding us in its quiet serenity.

His gaze glinted with concern as if he knew how much I'd struggled. "Eat this," Hypnos said, offering me a handful of berries. Their tart taste burst over my tongue, and warmth spread through my body, slowly easing my weariness.

I grabbed a handful of berries from the basket beside me, letting my gaze drift up to the night sky. The stars twinkled and shone fiercely and the distant flares of firemagic flickered, painting a colorful star-speckled canvas across an ebony backdrop.

"What are they celebrating now?" I murmured, a stark tone hanging in my voice.

Hypnos' brow shot up in surprise. "It's a blood moon," he said with a shrug. "The night when the gods are free from all worldly concerns. Our own holiday, if you will."

"That explains why he wasn't there," I whispered. "My captor found me in the Veiled Forest. I never should have left the palace..."

He stared at me intently. "Why do you leave? Do you find no solace in the temple?"

I scrunched my brows, taken aback. "A temple... is that what it is?" I heaved a sigh. "I was looking for—"

"What *are* you searching for?" he asked. His voice was soft, captivated, and concerned. But he asked the wrong question. It wasn't what, it was *who*—and I stayed quiet as a wave of sadness crashed over me. Daegal was the first thing on my mind, followed by the memory of our kiss that had kept me going in the days of captivity.

Hypnos cleared his throat and plucked a grape from the basket before him. "I feel for you, my lady," he said quietly. "I truly do. But let me assure you, outside the Midnight

Palace, all you'll find are evergreen woods, dull cliffs, and cascading waterfalls."

As a slightly sad smile tugged at my lips, despite myself, I quipped back, "Well, that doesn't sound too frightening now, does it? You'll have to come up with something better if you want to scare me."

His expression hardened. "If gods and monsters will not frighten you, my lady," he murmured gravely, "what will?" He paused. "Think carefully. Beauty unaccompanied often fades away. Who knows how long Prince Hades will hold an interest in you? Although you are his guest, his favor could shift at any moment—would you wish to be abandoned then?"

I rolled my eyes, tossing aside a handful of berries. "Hades hasn't even shown himself yet. I doubt he'd even notice me."

Hypnos yelped in alarm, swiftly assessing our surroundings with a frantic glance. "Don't court fate like that! You never know who might be listening."

His words sent an icy shiver down my spine, triggering memories of my harrowing imprisonment. "He called me a *'prowling shade'*..." I murmured, my voice hollow. Dread and relief collided in my heart, as I recalled the fear instilled by my captor.

"A shade?" Hypnos said thoughtfully, something unreadable in his tone. "I can understand why he'd believe that. It's this recent imbalance in the Netherworld... We've been dealing with so many wandering shades."

My heart raced as I gathered my courage and asked, "Is *he* the Dark Prince?"

"No, my lady," Hypnos said softly. "The one who captured you is Thanatos. He's the Guardian of the Dead... and my brother."

Shock ripped through me like lightning. "Your...?" I

breathed out, barely able to comprehend it. "Your *brother*?" Then came the fear, making my body tremble uncontrollably.

"Shh..." Hypnos pulled me into a tight embrace, an iron-clad barrier to the turbulence that haunted me. His strength flowed through my body, his heart beating a comforting rhythm as he rocked me protectively. "We're nothing alike. I assure you," he murmured against my hair.

"The Guardian of the Dead," I whispered. The words drifted in the air, an understanding filling my chest. Suddenly, it all made sense—the reason why Thanatos was so irritated with me, why he couldn't control me, and why he'd asked me to agree to serve him. I posed a frustrating hindrance to him, given the fact that I *'belonged with the living'* as he'd so bitterly mentioned before.

Hypnos drew me into his warmth, one hand cradling my chin so he could whisper softly into my ear, "Sleep now." His lips touched my forehead in a gentle kiss, and my eyelids grew heavy at his voice's lulling melody.

Strong arms encircled me as my legs gave way. I sank gratefully against Hypnos' chest, soothed by the steady rhythm of his heart beneath my cheek.

"You're safe with me," he said, his quiet tone spinning me deeper into slumber's web. "No harm will find you now."

His promise echoed as exhaustion claimed me. Hypnos had come for me through the deepest darkness. In his healing embrace, I had nothing left to fear.

# 36

# BEAUTY

*I* awoke to an unfamiliar room, its ancient ochre walls accented with midnight-blue tiles and a sturdy wooden door with an iron handle in the center. A strange yet comforting light spilled through tall windows, and I heard the distant trickling of a fountain.

Footsteps rounded the corner, accompanied by hushed tones that brimmed with uncertainty. The snippets of conversation that reached me were full of dread and worry, their urgency unmistakable.

I stirred, groggy and disoriented. As I slid from the lavish burgundy kline, the rough spun prisoner's garb I wore no longer rasped over my skin. I glanced down—and froze in astonishment.

Somehow in my sleep, the crude rags had been replaced by an elegant ivory gown. The silken fabric draped gracefully off my shoulders, hugging my arms in long split gossamer sleeves. Exquisite embroidery swirled across the bodice and hem.

A gentle knock sounded at the door, and then all fell silent.

The door creaked open, and I stared at the threshold fixedly, my heart hammering hard against my chest. But my worries waned the minute I glimpsed Hypnos, gallant in azure robes embroidered in gold. "I'm glad you're awake," he said quietly. "I trust you slept well?"

He gently took my hands into his own, sending tingles up my arms. "Actually... Yes," I said on a breathy exhale. "Yes, I did." And for that, I had Hypnos to thank—or blame.

He gave me a brief smile. "I'm glad to hear it."

Chronos loomed behind him then, towering yet somehow not intimidating or unkind. "I was wondering when I'd see you again," he said with a hint of teasing in his voice. His golden locks glistened in the candlelight, and his robe shimmered green and gold in its own muted glory. "You've been quite the elusive sleeping beauty."

My cheeks flushed and my mind scrambled for answers, as I tried to remember what had happened and how I'd arrived here. All I could manage was a feeble "Where am I?" before my gaze settled on the floor.

"This is the home of a trusted friend," Chronos whispered, gentle and reassuring. "Do not worry."

Hypnos stepped forward. "I believe this belongs to you."

My eyes flew open in delight at the sight of Voidbringer, resting peacefully in his hands. I gasped in relief and accepted it eagerly. I quickly sheathed her against my hip, feeling almost like a homecoming after being so long apart.

Chronos's piercing gaze raked over me as he delicately brushed my hair aside. He stared at the thorny vine entwining my arm, and I couldn't help but shudder at the memory of how it got there.

"How did you land yourself in trouble?" Chronos asked, his voice smooth as honey.

"I followed your advice and went into the labyrinth," I replied, bracing myself for their reaction.

"Labyrinth?" Hypnos piped up, astonished.

My lips parted to say more, but before I could continue, Chronos cut me off with a dismissive wave of his hand. "Clearly, the girl is delirious," he pronounced.

My jaw dropped as I stared at him in disbelief. The door opened again, though neither of us paid it any mind.

"Ah. Here you are, Hecate," Hypnos said with a sly smile. "I take it my message intrigued you?"

Hecate strode into the room, her wild auburn hair swaying around her face. Her purple robe was laced with intricate gold trimmings that matched the chains on her wrists and neck. She was panting from her frantic run, but her eyes were lit with curiosity and anticipation. "Very much," she said breathlessly. "Where is it? Show me."

Hypnos stepped aside, and there she was—Hecate standing in front of me with a determined gaze and flushed cheeks. I couldn't help feeling an odd sense of admiration as I gazed upon her.

"We meet again, my friend," Hecate said, her slender fingers wrapping around mine. "I wish that it wasn't under such dire circumstances," she added sadly.

Hypnos and Chronos both tensed when Hecate touched the vine inked onto my arm. I felt a sudden blast of pain as she ran her finger up to the stem at the top of my shoulder before I yanked my hand away.

Hecate's expression softened in sympathy as I rubbed at my shoulder.

"I can do little for you here," she murmured regretfully. "The brand marks you as one of Thanatos' own now. The immortal has claimed you, and nothing can undo that fate."

"*Claimed* me?" I echoed with a frown. "What do you mean?"

Sighing heavily, Hecate led me to the kline. She settled beside me and captured my hand in hers. Warmth and kindness instantly poured over me as her soft gaze met mine. "Once death has touched you, it never truly goes away," she explained, fingertips brushing my cheek. "My dearest, from this moment onward, you will never be the same." She paused. "But *this* can make things easier…"

As she spoke, warmth spread out from her palm and through the tendrils of the thorned vine on my arm. They writhed and slowly dissolved into nothing until only an intricately designed rose was left in their place. Its stem seemed fused to my skin, burying the scar left by Thanatos' dagger deep within my veins.

"Thank you, Hecate," I managed, not fully understanding what her gift had done.

Delicately, her hand came to rest on my cheek. "I only wish I could do more… *Beauty*." The word was barely a whisper as her lips curved in a mischievous smirk.

My heart clenched as Hecate spoke Daegal's name for me. How was it possible? I opened my mouth to speak, but before I could utter a single syllable, the goddess gracefully rose and said, "Now, I must go attend to other matters."

The goddess paused at the doorway and slowly spun to face me, amethyst eyes fixed on mine. "Remember, my dear," she said. "Death may have claimed you, but that does not *define* you. Your destiny is yours alone to determine."

With a final nod, Hecate turned and disappeared from the room.

Hypnos and Chronos shared a concerned glance, and I knew they were both considering the implications of Hecate's words.

Chronos finally spoke, hesitantly breaking the silence. "What now?"

In that moment, a newfound energy surged through me —a conviction stronger than I had ever felt before. With unhesitating confidence, I rose to my feet and stood in the center of the room. I stared them both straight in the eyes and declared adamantly, "We return to the palace. Hecate is right. I won't let Thanatos control my destiny."

Fear clouded Hypnos' face as he asked quietly yet desperately, "Does this mean you won't leave us again?"

I squeezed his hand reassuringly. A faint smile broke out across my lips and I murmured, "No more running. I'm ready to face Hades—even if *he* isn't."

Despite my attempt at reassurance, dread still flashed in Hypnos' eyes.

"Back to the palace, it is." Chronos nodded in agreement and started walking towards the door with renewed purpose. Hypnos and I trailed after him closely, an oppressive silence blanketing us like a smothering mist.

# 37

# PHILLIP

*M*y heart thumped in my chest with sharp apprehension as I half ran, half stumbled up the overgrown path to the nymph's creek. The closer I got to the mountain, the more familiar my surroundings became. There it was. The same stone dais, nestled in a sea of wild-flowers, encased in a faint luminescence and draped in delicate ivy strands.

Eloise hadn't stirred or spoken again since we'd escaped from Charon's cave, yet her bleeding had ceased long ago, and in that fact, I took hope.

I stopped at the foot of the dais. Hesitantly, I tucked a few stray strands of her fair hair behind her ear and whispered, "We've made it. You're going to be all right, my dearest. I'll be right back." I spoke softly, though I knew she didn't hear a word. But I wanted her to know—to feel—that we were there, and she was safe from the nightmare at last.

As I eased her down upon a bed of daisies, I noticed a small symbol etched into the stone. It was one I recognized from tales of old, but never had I seen it before. I tentatively reached out to touch the symbol and was rewarded with a loud rumble from deep beneath the earth. Fast as lightning, the stones shifted and revealed a secret underground chamber.

Taking a breath to steady my racing heart, I descended into the darkness below. "Minthe!" I shouted as I entered the sanctuary, my voice bouncing off the barren walls.

Time itself seemed to stand still as I waited, until at last, her answer came.

"Ah, my handsome warrior," she purred in delight as I watched her materialize from thin air. Her sensual figure was draped in the finest gossamer and embedded with diamonds that sparkled like morning dew on leaves. Streaks of jade shimmered through her ebony hair, which she delicately swept back with an offhanded pass of her hand. When she stood before me, the sweet smell of woods after a summer rain filled the air, washing away all my worries and woes.

"So tell me," she asked slyly, "was your quest successful?"

I nodded, pulling the key from my pocket and placing it in her waiting hands. She gasped in delight, twirling around before enveloping me with a long hug. Tears streamed down her cheeks in joy at the sight of this trinket, the relic that would grant her freedom from her paradisical prison.

She almost danced back to the throne, pressing the key carefully into its slot at its base. A familiar metallic jangle filled the sanctuary, followed by the grinding of machinery that startled against age and disuse. Then there was a screech, loud enough to make us both jump, as metal clanked and the bracelet vines snapped free from around Minthe's wrists with a loud hiss.

Minthe shouted in pure joy, spinning around before barreling into me for another exuberant hug. "Valiant Steel Lion, I am so grateful for your service!" she said, parting from me briefly. "I could kiss you!" Her hands moved to my neck, her full lips mere inches away from mine as her icy breath brushed against my face.

"That would be an honor, my lady. But if I may humbly suggest, would you consider exchanging that kiss for something else as a token of gratitude?" I asked, careful not to offend her.

"Go on," Minthe replied, her voice filled with curiosity.

A single step forward and I descended the dais, my every sense aware of the nymph that followed. A quiet plea left my lips, "I need you to save my friend, Eloise—she's been wounded."

Minthe stood a mere breath away from me, and I could feel my heart rate quickening as doubt ran through my being. Could she really help her? Was there any other way? There was no time to think. I had to move forward in faith alone.

The nymph paled, and the green of her gaze turned dark with hurt. Jealousy and suspicion were written in the single line between her brows. "You should have told me about *Eloise* before you left for this journey," she choked out through clenched teeth as she spun away.

I stepped back, startled by her sudden shift in mood. But I refused to give up hope. Desperately, I seized her arm and uttered a broken plea, "Please... save her." There was no doubt in my mind that Eloise's existence stirred Minthe's all-consuming suspicions and clouded her with bitterness. I bowed my head imploringly, attempting to reach any ounce of kindness that still resided in her heart. "Without Eloise, I would have never succeeded in freeing you at all. Please, my lady, we need your assistance."

Minthe's expression was a turmoil of doubt, jealousy, and something far more menacing. Her lips settled into a disgruntled line, her gaze lingering on my hand as it slowly slipped away. Eyes narrowing, she spat bitterly, "No. I don't think so."

I swallowed the lump in my throat and mustered courage. "I would be forever grateful if you could help us," I declared boldly, "Please—if it is within your power to heal her."

Minthe seethed with anger at my words, her slitted green irises burning with hate. "If?" she spat. Wearing a grimace of disdain, she slowly stooped until our gazes met. "Do you doubt my power, human?"

I shook my head. "N-no. Of course not, my lady." I needed no other reminder that Eloise's life hung in the balance. "But we need help quickly."

Minthe hesitated, her gaze like a blade piercing my soul. Finally, she straightened, a small smirk tugging at the corner of her lips. "Very well. I will help your friend. But only under one condition."

"Anything," I breathed out in despair.

She grinned wickedly. "You must swear your loyalty to me," the nymph said, her voice smooth and sultry.

My heart sank at her demand, but I knew I had no other choice. "I swear my loyalty to you, my lady."

Minthe accepted it with a satisfied smirk, and bade me to follow her back into the underground sanctuary while Eloise lay in my arms, pale and motionless. When we reached a small chamber, Minthe gestured for me to lay Eloise on the stone bed covered in moss.

My heart pounded hard against my ribcage as the nymph stepped closer, hands glowing with an eerie green light. As her hands moved over Eloise's body, mending and restoring warmth where there was once coldness, time seemed to stand painfully still.

Finally, Minthe stepped back, her hands resting on her hips as she surveyed her work. Eloise's color had returned, and she was breathing peacefully.

"She will live," Minthe announced triumphantly, and locking her jade eyes with mine, she added fiercely, "But remember your oath, my prince. Your loyalty is now mine."

I silently vowed to accept whatever consequences would come with this bargain. Eloise's life was worth any price I could pay. And as we made our way back to the surface, one thought rang through my head: what would she ask of me next? Would I have to betray my own kingdom for her sake?

But even as I watched Eloise, cocooned in the nymph's grotto, my heart glowed with an all-consuming love. A love that would propel me to whatever lengths were necessary to keep her safe.

"You can remain here for the night," Minthe murmured, her voice a soothing balm. "Your safety is guaranteed while you're within these walls."

I thanked Minthe and settled down on a pile of soft furs, my eyes never leaving Eloise's sleeping form.

The night drew on, and my thoughts kept returning to the oath I'd sworn to Minthe. What would she expect in return for saving Eloise? Would she ask me to lead my troops into battle against her enemies? Was it possible that she wanted information about my kingdom's defenses?

A chill ran through me as I considered another possibility. What if she demanded something more personal instead? Something that might break the faith Eloise already had in me?

The thought made my blood turn cold. I couldn't bear the idea of hurting Eloise, not after all we'd been through. Yet I was bound to obey Minthe's every command, no matter the cost.

Dusk crept in, and my resolve grew stronger. As my head hit the pillow, I knew I'd sworn fealty to the sorceress—but I *also* knew where my heart belonged.

## 38
## BEAUTY

*H*ypnos lingered in the doorway as we entered my familiar chambers, glancing around as if to assure himself all was still well. Satisfied, he turned to me with a tired smile.

"Get some rest. Hecate's potions take a toll even on immortal flesh." His eyes were shadowed by the memory of my ordeal. "I'll come to check on you soon."

After a final squeeze of my hand, his footsteps faded down the hall, leaving me alone with my thoughts. I began to pace, emotions colliding within me. Relief at my deliverance from Thanatos. Lingering weakness from Hecate's purging spell. But most of all, frustration.

My steps echoed against cold obsidian walls as I stalked back and forth like a caged beast. Hades still hid from me, indifferent to my suffering. Yet the answers I needed were locked away inside him.

Even were I to draw him out, did I have any hope of escaping this place? All roads here led only further into darkness. None offered a way back up into the light. Or perhaps I only lacked the vision to find it.

SILVANA G. SÁNCHEZ

A fierce determination kindled within me, fueled by my brush with oblivion. I would find a way to survive this ordeal. I would open Hades' eyes to the truth. And I would reclaim my freedom, no matter the cost. They had not broken my spirit yet.

My stride settled into purposeful steps towards the balcony. If I could not sway Hades, I would appeal to his true love. Gazing out over the vast midnight domain, I whispered my plea into the shadows: "Lady Persephone, hear me. Lend me your wisdom, I beg you. Help me endure this trial."

Somewhere beyond the gloom, I had to believe she listened. And maybe, just maybe, she would take pity on another caged soul. I clung to that fragile hope with everything I had left.

As I paced the room, my thoughts consumed by the heavy weight of uncertainty, a cold breeze stirred the balcony's gossamer curtains. It was then that I noticed an eerie silence had settled over the courtyard. The usual sounds of birds and the trickle of water were nowhere to be heard. It was as if the world outside had ceased to exist altogether.

Suddenly, a shiver ran down my spine, as though a thousand icy fingers had traced their way along my skin. I turned to the door, half expecting it to burst open and reveal some unspeakable horror lurking in the shadows. But nothing came.

I tried to shake off the oppressive feeling that had abruptly descended upon me, but the more I fought against it, the stronger it seemed to become. Only then did I notice a faint red glow emanating from the brand on my arm. My shoulder wound blazed like unquenchable fire.

I held my breath as I stared at the glimmering inked rose, my pulse racing and the hairs on the back of my neck standing on end. I could feel a presence behind me, seeping through the walls like fog.

240

As I reached out to touch the blooming crimson rose, a voice spoke from behind me. *"Why would you refuse me?"* it whispered, its breath cool in my ear.

My body shook with fear as I recognized the voice of Death. I clenched my jaw, feeling courage swell inside me, and spun around, my hand gripping the hilt of my sword. But the room remained empty. I was completely alone.

*"You should have taken my offer,"* Death hissed, passionless and menacing.

I swallowed hard. "I'm not afraid of you," I spoke into the dark. Heart pounding hard in my chest, I added, "I know who you are... Thanatos."

A sudden knock on the door sent a jolt of terror through me. I stared fixedly as the heavy slab of wood slowly creaked open. Had Thanatos come to drag me back to his lightless dungeon, where cruel amusement awaited? I steeled myself for his icy voice, the bite of his bruising grip...

But instead, a masked servant waited on the threshold, a golden tray laden with fragrant delicacies balanced carefully in her hands. "Lord Hypnos sent me, my lady," she said, but I could detect a hint of fear in her voice when she met my gaze. "May I come in?"

I let out a long breath. "You're not the usual servant," I said, my voice a broken whisper. "Where is she?"

The woman simply shook her head with uncertainty and strolled into the room, delicately placing the tray on the bedside table.

Without missing a beat, she began to draw a hot bath and laid out my nightgown on the bed. "Lord Hypnos has asked me to convey his wishes for you to have a peaceful evening tonight," she said in a soft voice that belied her steely demeanor, "but he eagerly anticipates your presence at tomorrow's dinner."

My pulse raced as Thanatos' warning echoed in my mind. "Very well," I replied tightly.

As the servant left the room, I could feel a weight lifting off my shoulders. I grabbed one of the treats from the tray and took a bite, savoring the sweetness on my tongue. I walked over to the terrace, light rain falling softly outside, painting the world on a moody canvas.

My heart warmed as I thought of Hypnos, but it was soon iced over with the realization that Thanatos was his brother. Doubt crowded my chest and filled me with a hollow dread. However, I chose to trust him and push away my wariness, and so I forced those thoughts away from my mind. After all, I had no reason to doubt him; he'd been nothing but kind to me.

But the memory of Thanatos' warning refused to leave me as I undressed and sank into the warm bath. *You should have taken my offer.* The words resounded in my soul.

As I settled against the ample pond's rim, a chill snaked up my spine. And even as I closed my eyes and let out a sigh, I couldn't shake the feeling that something was coming for me. Something terrible.

## 39
## PHILLIP

That night, sleep eluded me. The shadows seemed to move around me, alive with Minthe's spirit watching my every move.

I tossed and turned, until finally, I opened my eyes and was met with a breathtaking view. Eloise stood before me, her beauty almost too perfect to be real. Her blonde tresses cascaded down her back, and her eyes were aflame with an aura of mystery and temptation that left me unable to look away.

A sheer gossamer gown clung to her curves, shimmering in the twilight air. Her voice was a whisper in my ear, her words a sweet caress as she said, "My fearless Steel Lion, you have been so generous to me... Let me show you something only the gods know." She climbed atop me, her thighs pressing firmly against my waist.

Anticipation and passion tangled in my veins. My breath shuddered as I stared into her eyes and sensed myself yielding to my darkest desires. Her lips were tantalizingly close, and promises of pleasure seared down my spine.

Every part of me wanted to indulge in the temptation, to

take what Eloise offered and freefall into a night of bliss, but I knew she deserved more than that. No matter how desperately she called to me, or how much I ached to touch her, my love deserved better.

Trembling under her gaze, I managed to whisper, "Eloise... I can't."

"Oh, I think you can," she hummed, her breath tickling my ear.

Eloise began to move above me, her body writhing with a dangerous grace. Her skin was soft and cool to the touch, like silk under my fingertips. I closed my eyes and allowed myself to be lost in the sensations—her scent, the sound of her breath, the warmth of her body... all of it was consuming.

But even in my abandonment, guilt still coursed through me. I wanted Eloise too much. Her innocence, kindness, beauty... all of it made me feel undeserving and debased. My mind screamed at me to flee while my body begged for more. But she held me tight, her motions relentless and demanding until I was wild with desire.

"My dearest love," I growled against her lips, my hands clawing into her hair as I kissed her. A wildfire blazed inside me, brighter and hotter with each beat of my heart. I could no longer restrain the ferocity of my emotions for her.

She clung to me and pulled me tighter into her embrace. Her touch seared into my soul like a white-hot branding iron and sent a molten wave through my veins.

I forgot everything in that moment. The reason for our presence in the Netherworld was eclipsed by Eloise's warmth and the scorching intensity of her kiss.

A shuddering groan escaped me when she shed her robes, exposing curves that drove me wild. I couldn't resist tracing them with my fingertips, savoring every inch of her bare skin. My lips followed the curve of her neck, my teeth grazing it as her breathing grew labored with pleasure.

Eloise's fingers tangled in my hair, tugging me closer to her as if we were one, bound by an invisible force. She was giving herself to me completely, and although part of me feared I might be unworthy of such a gift, all my doubts and worries disappeared the second I took her into my arms. All that mattered was the rapture we found in our union.

Her lithe body moved with mine, our ardor accelerating until the world around us seemed to ignite in flames. We fell into the rhythm of one another, our bodies fusing together in a primal dance of desire. Every moan that escaped her only fueled my own cravings further—the feel of her, the taste of her, every scent and sound that belonged to only her was maddeningly intoxicating.

As her embrace deepened, a sudden spark ignited within me that sent pain like jagged shards of glass ripping through my veins. I stumbled back instinctively, only to discover the ground around me was littered with thorny vines snaking around my feet. My gaze snapped up to find not Eloise, but *Minthe,* staring back at me with malicious satisfaction and an eerie gleam in her eye.

"What enchantment is this?" I demanded, trying to keep my rage in check.

Minthe's lips curved into a smirk as she spoke in a deep and husky voice. "My darling, you should know the Realm of the Dead is full of surprises. I am no ordinary nymph, but the daughter of a god of the Netherworld himself."

I stared at her in disbelief, the thorns still piercing my flesh. My mind raced as I tried to come up with a plan to escape, to get back to Eloise, who was probably still sleeping, oblivious to the danger I was in. But Minthe seemed to read my thoughts, and before I could make a move, she raised her hand and whispered a spell.

My vision faded to black, and when I blinked open my eyes, I had been transported to some far corner of the

Netherworld. The thick air was laden with the stench of decay and despair, turning my stomach as I stumbled to a halt. My feet sank into something sticky and warm, and as I looked down, terror shot through me like lightning—I was standing in a pool of blood.

At once, Hades appeared from the shadows. His footsteps were slow and deliberate, but they seemed to make the very ground shake beneath them. He stood tall before me, his burnished black armor gleaming with an otherworldly sheen that spoke of power beyond measure.

Everything around him hushed in acknowledgment of his presence, as if nature itself couldn't bear witness to his devastating presence.

His wings exploded behind him with a boom of thunder —black feathers spread wide like outstretched limbs, rustling slightly in the fiery breeze that seemed to follow his every move. His raven hair, tousled by unseen forces, cascaded around his face, lending an air of fierceness to his already formidable presence.

But it was his eyes that held me captive. Obsidian orbs, deep and unyielding, glinted with fiery embers, reflecting a flickering inferno that burned within. They seemed to penetrate my very soul, their gaze unrelenting and merciless. As he regarded me with a ruthless smirk playing upon his lips, it sent shivers down my spine, a chilling reminder of the power he possessed.

"Well, well, well..." he drawled, his lips curving into a cruel smile. "What have we here? A mortal, wandering in *my* realm without permission?"

I tried to speak, but my throat felt dry and parched. Hades advanced on me, his eyes glinting with a hunger that made my skin crawl. He circled me, his fingers trailing along my arm, sending shivers down my spine.

"You should know better than to cross Minthe," he whispered in my ear, his breath hot against my skin. "She belongs to me, you see."

I tried to pull away, but his grip on my arm was too strong. Panic engulfed me as I realized the gravity of my situation. I was trapped in the Netherworld, at the mercy of its ruler and his twisted desires.

A growl escaped through the tightness of my throat, and Hades leaned in closer, his lips brushing against my neck. I struggled to break free, but it was no use. He was too powerful, and I was nothing but a mere mortal.

"Relax," he murmured, his hand sliding down my chest. "I promise to make it worth your while." A slight pat on my shoulder. Slowly, he inched close to my ear, and added, "You're not going anywhere, mortal. You should know better than to meddle in the affairs of gods."

My mind raced as I desperately tried to think of a way out of this situation. But before I could even begin to form a plan, Hades raised his hand and muttered an enchantment. A searing pain shot through me, and my vision blurred as darkness consumed me once more.

When I came to, I was back in the real world, lying in a pool of sweat. Eloise stood over me, concern etched on her face. "Phillip, are you all right?" she said softly. "You were having a nightmare."

"Eloise! You're all right!" I struggled to sit up, my heart racing. It had all been a dream... hadn't it? But the thorns etched into my chest told me otherwise. "I need to tell you something," I said, my voice hoarse. "About Minthe..."

"Who is Minthe?" Her voice was plaintive, echoing in the clearing.

I couldn't answer. I just clamped my jaw shut and looked around us. Gone was the lush creek of a minute ago; gone was the stone dais and the nymph's sanctuary. We were back in our old campsite, as if nothing had happened.

My chest tightened, and my fists began to tremble with anger. "Where is she?" I gritted out through clenched teeth.

Eloise stepped closer to me, sky-blue eyes watching me carefully. "Phillip, you're worrying me," she said softly. "It's just you and me here. Nobody else."

Refusing to look at her, I gathered up my satchel and rolled my fur blanket tightly under one arm. I nodded sharply, my voice like ice. "Pack your things. We're leaving —now."

Eloise blinked up at me, her hands stilling on the blanket she'd been gathering. "Now? Shouldn't we rest first? We have a long journey ahead of us."

A spark of something wild flashed in my eyes, daring her to argue. "I bet we're closer than you imagine," I bit out through clenched teeth as a thrill raced through me at what might be—surely close enough to draw Hades' attention. "Come on. Let's go."

# 40

# BEAUTY

The song of blackbirds lured me out of my bedroom just as the sun began to kiss the horizon. I'd been unable to find sleep all night, convinced Thanatos was waiting for me in the corner, ready to drag me back to his watchtower prison. But even when I did manage a few moments of oblivion, my nightmares were still filled with scenes of the Lord of Death's wrath should I ever be bold enough to escape him again.

I stood on the terrace, mesmerized by the sky above, with stars shifting and twinkling in complex patterns I had never seen before. I marveled at the beauty of it all and felt myself relax for a moment in its calming embrace. And then, as if responding to an unspoken whisper, a shooting star cut through the sky like a blade through silk, leaving a stream of glittering stardust in its wake.

I couldn't help but feel that this celestial display was meant just for me. It seemed to be a beacon of hope, an unspoken promise that if I kept on trying, I would find freedom and solace at last.

My heart quickened as I descended the obsidian steps

into the courtyard, drawn by some irresistible compulsion. The shadows seemed to whisper and stir as I passed, tugging me towards the still Midnight Lake at the garden's heart.

I halted at the mossy shore, pulse racing though, I knew not why. Ripples lapped gently against stone in a hypnotic rhythm. What had drawn me here this moonlit night?

A flash of otherworldly light beneath the surface made me catch my breath. There, just under the veil of water—the gleam of iridescent scales. I started, disbelieving but unable to look away as those shimmering colors rose closer. My breath caught in my throat at the sight of the mermaid's gracefulness as she glided effortlessly through the dark blue depths, moving with such speed that seemed to defy nature.

I moved closer, captivated by this incredible creature, and dipped my fingers into the cool water. This palace also served as home to these wondrous nereids, beings that any other god would have seen fit to enslave, yet Hades showed them mercy. The thought struck me—how could a cruel god offer such kindness? Maybe Hades wasn't so cruel after all. Maybe there was more to him than myth ever implied.

A flood of sensation overcame me as her cold fingertips brushed against mine. Her hair was like liquid fire as it swayed in the current, ebbing with the underwater rhythm. I watched her nimbly glide away, feeling the strength of her powerful tail rippling beneath my skin with each stroke.

Her preternatural voice surged from the waters, a sound so soothing yet otherworldly that shot gooseflesh up my arms.

*"Oh, Beauty, Beauty, feel the whispers' grace,*
*In hushed tones, secrets I do embrace.*
*Draw near, my dear, let curiosity unfurl,*
*A secret held close, that will make your heart whirl."*

A moment later, she reemerged from the depths like a stunning sea goddess, instantly trapping me in a daze. Her skin was pure alabaster, ivory dusted with moonlight. Small gills thrummed gently at her throat, and her eyes were jewels of aquamarine that stared into mine intently. She was something ethereal and captivating, I knew I'd never be able to look away. I opened my mouth to compliment her beauty, but no words escaped me.

"Do you want to hear a secret?" The mermaid's voice drifted in the evening air, smooth and preternatural, her slender frame suddenly bobbing into view.

I tensed, waiting for the question I knew was coming. "Can you keep one?" she finally added.

The blood froze in my veins. Mermaids were mischievous creatures—never to be trusted until they could trust you first. I'd heard the stories from Hypnos and those had come as the harshest warning.

"I don't know." I spoke honestly, and narrowing my eyes, I cocked my head to the side, and asked, "What do you have to tell me?"

The corners of her lips tugged into an enigmatic smile as she languidly shook her head. "Ah-ah. Mermaids never share," she chanted in a low hum that sent warmth radiating through my being.

"I'm sure you must know many secrets," I said.

From beneath the surface of the water, she nodded slowly. With exquisite grace, she raised an arm out, a delicate finger pointing past me. Confusion creased my brow. I turned and surveyed the forest behind me. I glimpsed nothing out of the ordinary. The same precious footpath led into the Veiled Forest, swallowed by an untamed jungle... What was I supposed to see?

A snicker echoed through the air, and when I whirled around, she was gone.

"Wait!" I shouted, my hands slapping against the ledge as my head hung low over the rippling water.

But it was too late. She'd vanished like a ghost in the night. A pitiful moan escaped my throat as I slammed my fist into the lake's murky surface. "Fantastic," I grumbled in frustration.

Suddenly, my screams pierced the air, even before I realized what was happening. Out of nowhere, a swift hand reached up from below and grabbed my wrist in an icy grasp that threatened to drag me into the depths with it. My heart jolted into a gallop and I clung to the edge with my free hand, too frightened to utter a sound until it finally let go and I tumbled back onto the walkway.

My shuddering eyes fixed on the rippling water as dread coursed in my blood. And then, eerily, I watched as the mermaid ploddingly resurfaced—her face lit with a devious grin. "Find my secret," she egged me on, her voice a rush of foamy waters crashing on the shoreline.

The bleakest silence fell upon us then. And I started when she added, "GO TO THE WOODS!" her voice thundering and resounding in my chest.

Wicked laughter scattered in the night.

Taking a graceful leap out of the water, she twirled in midair, defying gravity as her glittering tail transitioned seamlessly into a mass of tangling red hair that sparkled, weaved with thousands of precious gems.

With one last splash, the mermaid disappeared beneath the surface again, leaving me short-winded, stunned, and afraid—but also *keenly* aware of a curious thrum stirring inside me.

I scrambled onto my feet, gasping in shock. "A secret in the woods..." I mumbled, looking back.

A flicker of light barely visible through the dark trees made my heart pound with anticipation. Could I trust this mermaid? Why did she seem so intent on persuading me? I had to find out.

Breathless, I pushed forward, taking the first steps that would lead me to the Veiled Forest. Voidbringer was by my side, ready to help if disaster should strike. I was determined. Whatever surprises lay ahead, I was ready.

As I stood at the threshold between Hades' courtyard and the wilderness of the Netherworld, the wind whispered around me, gentle and reassuring like the embrace of an old friend. *"Do not be afraid,"* it said, *"for you are meant for greatness."*

My gaze followed the path of the breeze, searching for unseen speakers—but there were none. Only a feeling of warmth and something larger than myself, something… magical.

I saw it then, a flicker of light scarce feet ahead. A spark of unknown power beckoned me into the wood. The iridescent blue light seemed to draw me forward, a strange and captivating pull that I couldn't resist. Fear welled up within me as I stepped closer, and excitement too. What kind of enchantment was this? Perhaps Hades had finally decided to grace me with his presence, and he would finally release me to the Realm of Man.

I trudged through the sea of wildflowers, their colors dim and swathed in gloom. Lavender and roses filled my senses with their sweet perfume as I glanced around the clearing where tall, ancient stones stood guard like sentinels, forming a circle of power beneath the dusky sky. The light guided me to the center, where a beam burned bright from above.

I gaped in wonder, enchanted by the light as it danced with the clearing's dust motes, glittering with golden flecks of sunlight suspended in the fading dusk.

As soon as I stepped foot into the ring, the mermaid's melody filled my ears, rooting me in place with its beauty and charm. I couldn't help myself from singing to its tune.

The first notes sailed through my lips, and at once, the

previously dull and colorless woods bloomed around me. A rain of rose petals sprinkled over me in shades of red, orange, and purple. Vines twisted with newfound intensity, buds blooming at a dizzying pace, petals scattering like confetti beneath my feet. Every hue I'd ever dreamed of was present, as if it had been held back until this very moment.

It was then I realized this magnificent transformation was coming from me—my voice had brought these woods back to life. But just as I started to revel in my newfound power, the snap of branches pulled me out of my reverie.

I froze, and the wonderful enchantment steadily faded.

My eyes locked on the shaking shrubbery ahead and my heart raced with fear.

I was not alone. Someone else marauded in these woods.

41

# PHILLIP

Fury burned like wildfire in my gut as I ventured into the dense forest, hunting while Eloise set camp at our new location. Minthe's betrayal had rocked me to my core. How could I have been so foolish to trust a nymph?

My bow tightly gripped in one hand, I scanned the shadows for signs of small game. Moss-covered trunks rose up around me, their ancient arms reaching for the sky like sentinels. Dusky sunlight filtered through the canopy in glimpses of emerald green, and the woods sang with life all around me. Movements from creatures unseen made rustling noises behind thick carpets of ferns while tiny birds chirped happily above.

The air was thick with the scent of soil and damp moss. Everywhere I looked, beauty bloomed in vibrant colors across the forest floor, and majestic trees stood tall against the sky. Yet my chest burned with a deep-seated rage as Minthe's betrayal bore into me like an arrow.

The frustration had reached a fever pitch when I realized

that finding food for Eloise and me would make it easier to get to the Dark Prince's palace sooner.

Years of war had made me a survivor, able to face down any challenge life threw my way. In long strides, I set off towards my goal, confident that I could navigate whatever lay ahead.

I stopped midstride, keenly aware of the sound that echoed from the clearing. Rabbits had been scurrying around all afternoon, but this was different. It was… music?

My skin prickled with curiosity and I moved through the brambles with caution, my hunting knife tight in my grip. But then it changed—it sounded gentle. Someone humming a quiet tune.

I had to find out who it was.

## 42

# BEAUTY

*D*ried leaves crunched beneath my feet as I peered into the dark woods, eyes narrowed, searching for something hidden in the shadows. The foliage stirred and shuddered in an unfelt breeze, and I inched closer, driven by an unknown force.

I turned into stone, transfixed, when I saw the figure emerge from the woodland—a mane of golden hair that shone like wheat fields in the midday sun, piercing eyes the color of a summer sky that deepened from sapphire to violet, sculpted lips that slowly parted in wordless wonder.

Every line of his visage slammed into me like lightning—from the powerful jut of his jaw to the magical blue of his eyes that were like oceans crafted from glass. He was a flame dancing amidst shadows, a burst of sunlight in this realm of darkness.

A thundering silence descended over us as his gentle gaze locked with mine, his breath coming in slow heaves as if he could never inhale enough air. Everything inside me trembled in shock, mirroring the staggering emotion glaring back at me. The world around us faded to nothing—just me and him, standing beneath the trees' leafy canopy. Nothing else mattered but this divine instant. And I was lost in it, willingly drowning in its grandeur.

I spoke first, my voice barely audible. "I know you..." I breathed as recognition settled. "I walked with you on sun-kissed shores by an azure sea. Once, in a dream."

His handsome face drained of color, throat bobbing as he tried to force words past tightness. "Can this be real?" he whispered, bewildered awe spilling from him like rain.

My heart jolted into a gallop as I smiled shyly and replied, "It's the strangest thing." I bit my lip, not daring to say more lest I break the fragile spell that held us both captivated.

He stepped closer, until I felt the warmth radiating off his skin. And then my senses flooded with his fragrance, and he smelled like the forest after the first summer storm—enticing, refreshing.

"Is this a dream?" he asked, and his voice was smooth like velvet.

"Maybe it is," I said. My cheeks burned immediately, embarrassed by how forward and vulnerable I felt, yet utterly unable to look away from him. "My dreams are often so real."

A warm smile tugged at the corner of his lips as he responded thoughtfully, "Then let us not wake..." His hand grazed mine, rough yet achingly tender.

My breath hitched as his touch slid up my arm and eased along my jawline—so familiar, a balm chasing away the night's chill. In this nearness, I became lost in his gaze, unable to tear myself away from the violence of our connection.

I wanted nothing more than to linger in this moment, but a flicker of apprehension shot through my being, and I forced myself to step back. "Are you a shade?" I blurted almost soundlessly into the night, fear knotting inside me, knowing what would happen if Thanatos came across him.

His lips moved, though no words emerged.

"You can't stay here," I warned him lowly as memories of Thanatos's brutality stole my breath. "Guardians are close by, keeping steady watch. They show trespassers no mercy." My eyes remained trained on his face as I paused before whispering desperately, "You must go."

"My lady?" someone called, an all-too-familiar voice ringing through the forest. *Hypnos.*

I whirled, gaze searching frantically for the Lord of Slumber. Then, I turned back and saw him—the beautiful stranger, his hard jawline set in a resolute frown that kept his sapphire eyes locked on me.

"Wait," he commanded gravely, a cautious hand held in the air.

Dread snaked up my spine at the sound of twigs snapping beneath firm footsteps. Hypnos trudged through the woods, heading directly towards me. "My lady!" he called once more, his voice ringing out somewhere to my right.

My mouth dried as I faced the stranger again. Fearing for his safety, I all but hissed at him, "Go away or he'll destroy you!" His eyes widened in shock as I shoved him back into the thicket, where he toppled down and thankfully disappeared from sight.

I whirled seconds before Hypnos stepped into the clearing, a disapproving look etched on his face. "Wandering off again?" he said, puzzled.

I met his gaze, mastering a calm expression while anxiety ate me from within. "No. Of course not," I said firmly. "Just taking a stroll." My boots scuffed against the ground as I moved away from the undergrowth, where the stranger was hiding.

Cunning Hypnos swept the grounds with an appraising

stare before finally nodding. "The Dark Prince won't be pleased if he finds out about this," he gently warned me, offering an arm.

My heart lurched at his words. But I took a deep breath and forced a steadiness into my voice as I accepted his offer, tangling my fingers in the crook of his arm.

The wind picked up, twirling around us and causing my golden locks to swish around my shoulders before they settled back into place. "Then we mustn't tell him, must we?" I whispered in mischievous confidence. Though a small smile graced my lips, the sharpest apprehension flooded my veins.

Hypnos' gaze softened and he offered a small, careful smile. "I don't mean to pry, my lady," he amended in a warmer tone, tinged with caution. "But it could have been my brother who found you."

My heart froze at the thought, and I forced a laugh that sounded foreign even to me as I bounced lightly on my toes. "Lucky for me he did not," I replied lightly. My fingers twitched, anxious around his arm as I stepped back. I tugged him with me towards the palace—as far away from this clearing as possible.

As I stepped away, I chanced one last look back. The man was still there, his gaze fixed on me with shock. I only felt a tinge of relief, but my heart ached for him—Hypnos would not have given him such mercy as he'd offered me.

But something else blossomed in my heart, a gentle warmth that seemed both foreign and familiar—like a forgotten memory being rekindled. I had no name yet for this feeling. All I knew was that in that sunlit instant beneath the trees, I had glimpsed a vision of something more. It lingered with me, even as I let the darkness close in once again. A single moment of light to sustain me as I returned to the shadows.

*I* trudged through the mud and foliage, desperate for some semblance of peace after my devastating discovery. My axe bit into the ashen wood as I chopped kindling for the chill night ahead. Each stroke punctured my memories of Aurora's desperate wish to explore new lands, a longing that I'd worked so hard to suppress out of concern for her safety, back when we were among mankind. Now, in this desolate Netherworld—the place where all hopes and dreams are laid to rest—I feared there was so little I could do for her.

Fury simmered within me as I pictured her walking away from the clearing on the arm of that odious god Hypnos— the one who'd damned her to an ageless sleep, shattering our lives and plans of marriage. That she could not recognize me or recall our story only deepened the twisted dagger in my chest.

Tears of stern determination blurred my vision. After years of surrendering to her curse—a prisoner of an endless slumber—she deserved freedom and adventure, impossible as it seemed. My heart burned with resolve; I owed Aurora this much, and no amount of fear was enough to stop me from making good on my promise.

My legs trembled as I approached the campsite. The darkness around me seemed to move with a life of its own, a thousand eyes watching my every move. The trees loomed ominously with trunks of ivy-covered bark, twisted branches reaching up to a sky aglow with stars like I'd never seen before. Each step I took was met with a hollow thud, the ground uneven beneath my feet.

The campfire in the distance beckoned me, its flames burning brightly against the night sky. But as I drew nearer, the fire seemed to be consuming itself, trying to suck away all its warmth and light into nothingness... A chill raced up my spine.

This realm leeched away all vibrancy, smothering it under ceaseless gloom. Even Aurora's radiance had been dimmed, though her poise and confidence remained untainted. She had shown no hint of fear or surrender earlier, facing the shadows with astonishing grace. Still, the pall over this place had muted her light.

My boots stumbled over the stones, my heart cracking with every step. A dull ache settled in my bones ever since our meeting—an ancient pain, a soundless grief.

More than anything, I wanted to rush back to Aurora's side and take her hands in my own. To tell her who I really was, why I'd come—to let her know how much I cared for her, and that I would do anything for her. The thought almost made me stagger before I could contain myself again, straightening my shoulders as I nearly reached our campsite.

Everything seemed different now—darker and oppressive, the shadows thicker than before. Something had changed. Something new settled inside me that chilled me to the core. My heart was heavy with memories of what had been, but could never be again.

Lost in thought and too exhausted to move on yet, I silently set up camp for the night, the feeling of nostalgia and loss lingering around me like an ever-present veil.

"You come empty-handed," Eloise began, her voice gentle yet tinged with wariness.

She rested beside me, but I could not find solace in her presence. Instead, I threw my hands out to the fire, searching for comfort that would not come.

Our eyes met and her lips curved into an almost mischievous smirk. "You've brought wood but no game to cook over the fire..." she added, a teasing lilt softening her words.

My throat seized up, cutting off any chance of speech. Grief had sunk its claws on me and refused to let go.

Eloise released a breathy sigh. She shifted forward, hugging her knees, and her smile became more pronounced. "It seems a troll has caught your tongue?" she asked sweetly, though her eyes held a glimmer of concern.

Once my gaze met hers, I couldn't look away. Firelight danced on her sun-kissed skin and sparkled in her ice-blue eyes—fathomless wells of everlasting peace. She was my refuge from the darkness, my safe haven in the chaos. Effortlessly, the words that had been stuck inside me suddenly erupted, unbidden.

"I saw her," I said simply, feeling as if my broken soul was shattering even more.

Eloise's soft brows tangled in a frown. "Saw who?" she hurried to say. "Not your mermaid friend?" She forced a laugh, but it was heavy. "Don't tell me she's found a way to walk now."

But the sternness of my expression remained unchanged. "Aurora," I breathed out. "I saw her in these woods."

Eloise's eyes widened in disbelief.

"She... She did not recognize me," I mumbled with an empty stare. "The dark god Hypnos was guarding her. He addressed her as a commoner and she allowed it." I shook my head in confusion.

"The mermaid said that all who enter this realm lose their name," Eloise said thoughtfully, and then turned to me with resolve in her expression. "In the Netherworld, she *is* no one, Phillip. There are no titles in this realm—save that of the Dark Prince. You mustn't blame Aurora for not remembering you."

My heart quivered, determinedly thawing at Eloise's words as I realized a faint glimmer of hope had not yet been extinguished. "But how am I supposed to save her if she doesn't even remember who she is?" I rasped, my throat constricted with desperation and hopelessness.

Eloise stared into me, her eyes holding nothing but conviction as she spoke the truth. "You must make her remember," she said quietly but firmly. "Our lives depend on it."

The weight of her words sank through my skin, an icy chill creeping up my spine as I accepted the gravity of them. Gritting my teeth, I steadied myself; if there was one thing I had learned from my travels in the Netherworld, it was that anything was possible if you put your mind to it.

"I'll do whatever it takes," I said resolutely.

Eloise smiled, a glimmer of longing shining in her eyes. "Then let's start by finding her," she said. "If you ran into her in these woods, then the palace must be nearby. We're almost at the end of our journey..."

I squared my shoulders, emboldened by her words. "Tomorrow, I will march back to the clearing and unearth Hades' palace," I declared.

Minthe's spellwork flashed through my mind, as did the first time I laid eyes on the Dark Lord himself. Revulsion churned within me as I pictured that cruel, heartless god who had stolen Aurora away. Hades ruined everything he touched, destroying lives and kingdoms on a mere whim. He had ripped my world apart when he took her, dooming both our realms to decay in his wake.

"I will not rest until I find his lair," I declared through gritted teeth, hands curling into fists. Aurora would be freed from his clutches if I had to tear down his palace stone by stone. Nothing would stop me from rescuing her, not even the ruler of death himself. I was prepared to battle Hades with my final breath if that was what it took.

Eloise's sharp gaze met mine, glowing with fearless strength. "We both will, Phillip," she said, her gentle hand softening mine. "You're not alone."

A knowing nod was all that I could offer her. I leaned back, my muscles weak and weary from the tension, but didn't allow myself to succumb to sweet oblivion. The unknown future ahead of us was darker than anything I'd imagined. And yet, despite my worries and fears, slumber found me—dreams of me rescuing Aurora from this terrible place pervading my mind.

## 4 4

## BEAUTY

*I* said my goodbyes to Hypnos, the pleasant taste of ambrosia still lingering on my tongue. Weariness caught up with me as I strode down the open halls and up the Midnight Palace's grand staircase, familiar steps feeling like home beneath my feet.

Dim sconces lit the hallway, casting haunting shadows and flickering light against the lavish tapestries that lined the walls. In the distance, I heard the faintest melody, though it wasn't the usual strains of the bard that often lingered in these grounds. The tune was strange, and strange was all I thought about as I sauntered down the final corridor. My days had been so long with worry and the most trying challenges, and all I wanted now was to rest in the safe haven of my bedroom. But as I reached the entrance, something in the air shifted. An unsettling knowledge crept into my being.

I was not alone.

I moved across the threshold, my steps measured and deliberate, my heart pounding hard against my chest. Every inch of me went taut and even the air froze in my throat as I lay eyes on the figure standing near the terrace, his tall and strong frame silhouetted against the fading moonlight.

He didn't move as I entered, and I had to fight the urge to run to his arms the second his gaze found me. I couldn't break free from his spellbinding presence—and the truth was, I didn't want to. Desperately, I longed to know why he'd stayed away for such a long and agonizing length of time.

At last, he spoke, his voice deep and determined. "I've been waiting for you," he said. His words were a discreet declaration of an unknown fate, the mysteriousness of his delivery both exciting and fearsome.

He paused expectantly, inviting me to ask my questions. But I was too mesmerized to speak.

"Daegal," I finally breathed, my voice wavering between the bliss of our reunion and the sorrow of his unforeseen departure.

His lips twitched in the hint of a smile, and my heart fluttered with joy. His gaze was soft, his expression confident and knowing.

Daegal stepped forward, an impossible hesitation visible in his movements. Reaching out, his fingertips slowly swept across my cheek, like a single snowflake drifting through the evening sky. "I've missed you," he whispered, and with those three words, the agony and misery tucked away deep in my chest gently dissipated.

He took my hand, and I followed him into the night without hesitation. Gleaming butterflies fluttered in the warm breeze, carrying with them a heady fragrance of dahlias and jasmine. The courtyard was a place of hushed and bewitching beauty, where colors bled into shadow, edges blurred like half-remembered reveries.

His gaze locked on me, watching as I took in the evening's splendor. He then inched closer, the heat of his breath fanning my cheek. And cradling my face with both hands, he looked deeply into my eyes with a tenderness that warmed my soul before leaning forward to press his lips against mine.

It was a kiss, unlike anything I'd ever known—gentle, yet an inferno of reckless passion, blissful yet demanding and all-consuming. We stayed there for what felt like an eternity. Until finally, we pulled apart, both of us lost for words as we let out matching sighs of contentment. And then our brows gently kissed, and we smiled at each other, our hearts over-flowing with love and soundless understanding.

"I told myself to stay away," he murmured, his voice barely loud enough to be heard. "Again and again, I fought it —but my feet still led me here. To you." His fingers curled around the side of my face in a reverent caress. His maroon eyes held mine, dark with desperation and longing. "You are my beacon of hope, my Beauty—my one true love, my dearest desire. You are my sun in this darkened world. I can no longer draw breath without knowing you are mine."

The graze of his fingertips on my skin ignited the flames of passion within me, and I clung to him, wanting to remain in his embrace forever. "I'm yours," I whispered, tears of joy welling in my eyes. "From this moment until eternity." My lips curved into a slight smile. "I believe I was yours long before I realized how much I loved you."

"Oh, Beauty," he murmured, his mouth grazing mine and rekindling the blaze between us. "My darling Beauty." He drew me fiercely against him once more, claiming my lips with unrestrained longing. I surrendered completely to his fervent kiss, lost in blissful sensation as his hand trailed down my arm, coming to rest gently on my shoulder. But even that delicate touch sent agony lancing through me. I cried out, the sound muffled against Daegal's mouth.

He pulled back sharply, eyes wide with concern. "You're

hurt," he gasped, gaze raking over me for some visible sign of injury. "What happened?"

I sagged against him, the thrill of our reunion fading to reveal the true extent of my wound. "It's nothing," I lied weakly. "A mild bruise..."

But I could not conceal the truth from Daegal. Grim understanding settled on his features as he carefully pushed back the heavy locks of my fair hair. His jaw tightened at the sight of the mottled skin and ragged gash beneath the black thorned rose. Raw fury blazed in his eyes.

"Who did this to you?" he demanded. "I swear on my life, I will make them pay for every tear you've shed." His voice thundered with fury, yet his eyes glistened with unspilt tears.

Despite the pain, I raised a hand to soothe his wrath. "The past is done. What matters is that you're here now, with me." I touched his face, gentling the fearsome intensity of his emotions.

"Give me a name," he said in a softer tone, though his expression remained masked in icy rage. "I will bring them to their knees and make them suffer tenfold for the harm they've caused you." His voice lowered, promising retribution.

Ferocious rage and vengeance flashed in his eyes, but the gentle curve of his lips softened as he gazed upon me.

Tears trickled down my cheeks in a steady stream as I whimpered, "No, Daegal." I wished I could give a better answer, but words eluded me. The pain was too fresh, still raw in my heart.

His firm hand glided along my jawline. "My love, the kindness of your heart will not deter me. Know that it will take however long it takes—*I will find them*," he whispered, his voice like a lullaby, while its intention clear and cutting.

Tenderly, his thumb brushed away one of my tears. "Tell me who it is."

Finally, I gave in. "The Lord of Death," I replied helplessly.

"Thanatos?" Daegal gasped, aghast. He staggered back, a tremble running through his frame. But the shock of discovery was short-lived, as his sword whispered free from its scabbard in a silvery blur.

My heart raced with fear. "Please don't," I begged, reaching for him.

Daegal stood resolute at the garden's threshold, and casting one last glance over his shoulder, he said, "Do not fear for me, my love." His handsome face twisted into a savage sneer. "Pity *him*, if you will, for my wrath is unfathomed and knows no forgiveness." Although smooth as silk, his words harbored the promise of destruction. And with that, he descended the stairs and strode purposefully into the grand courtyard.

The world slowed down until I jolted upright, my heart pounding against my ribs and dread flooding my veins. "No, no, no..." I breathed, my soul splintering at the thought of Daegal facing off against this fearsome fiend.

I pushed forward with haste, screaming for him to stop. "Daegal, NO! He's a GOD! He will DESTROY you!"

I burst down the stairs, my feet pounding out a frenzied rhythm. I had to reach him before he disappeared into the night, my beloved whose silhouette was already blurring in the darkness ahead. Yet something halted me as I reached the courtyard—an invisible force that held me back. I stumbled to a stop, chest heaving and heart pounding. The garden spread before me, moonlight gleaming off so many secrets that threatened to consume us both.

A bone-chilling scream ripped through the evening air, magnified by thousands of stars. "THANATOS!" Daegal roared into the darkness, and a shockwave reverberated to my very core.

Sheer dread coiled around me like a viper as the Lord of Death stepped forth from the shadows. His presence alone riveted me in place, my heart thundering against my chest as I watched him stride forward. Thanatos stood tall and proud, his intimidating aura carrying undeniable authority. "You summoned me," he said softly, although with stern conviction.

Daegal's face contorted with rage as he raised his sword, his first swing ringing in the air. "How dare you?" he seethed, stalking forward with no regard for the powerful deity. "How *dare* you touch her?!" The second strike punctuated the air with a sharp clang as the god sidestepped nimbly, narrowly avoiding the attack.

"Fight me!" Daegal bellowed, tossing his weapon away. Muscles tense and fists curled tightly, he challenged the dark god into submission. "Fight me, now!"

But Thanatos remained silent. His searing silvery eyes slid past Daegal to meet my own, and I quaked beneath their fire.

Fury spasmed beneath his skin as his gaze broke away from me, focusing back on Daegal. "You've chosen her," he said, his voice deceptively steady despite the storm raging inside him. "I did not know." Subdued, he stepped back, bowing his head until massive obsidian wings unfurled behind him with a deafening crack of thunder. Shadows curled around the god, swallowing him whole before he vanished, leaving only silence behind.

Daegal and I stood in the stillness of the garden, broken only by the soft patter of rain.

"Daegal," I managed, my voice hoarse with distress. My feet stumbled over the cobblestone ground as I raced to him, and relief nearly overtook me when his strong arms encircled my frame. We fit together like two pieces of the same puzzle, and for an instant, it felt like coming home.

"Dear gods," I gasped, anguish in every syllable as I pulled away to look him in the eyes. "I thought... I thought I'd lost you."

But Daegal looked away from me, with eyes downcast and a detached expression. Moments before, he had challenged Thanatos for my sake, staring defiantly into the face of Death itself. Such flaming courage, such passionate devotion... and yet now, he seemed lost in solemn thought, distant and cold.

A dreadful possibility slithered into my mind like a dark snake... poisonous and *maleficent*.

"Daegal?" I whispered, my limbs quivering. "Why would he not fight you? Why did Thanatos recoil from you?" Fear rushed through my veins like ice water, freezing me in place.

"He knows you..." I took a quivering step backward, understanding dawning on me. "He *bowed* to you."

An oppressive silence spread between us, broken only by the distant rumble of thunder in a now starless sky.

"Daegal," I whimpered, my voice fractured with raw pain. "Tell me the truth!"

He slowly raised his head, and met my stare with harsh obsidian eyes. With an impassive expression and an unwavering voice, he spoke. "Thanatos would not take my challenge because..." He paused, letting his words hang in the air for a moment. "*I* am the ruler of this realm."

A wave of disbelief crashed over me. "You're the Dark Prince?" I stammered, my insides shredding at his words. "*You*—are Hades?"

His expression softened, edged with sorrow. Withheld tears shimmered in the faint light that surrounded him. "Beauty..." He tilted his head, painfully subdued.

Wrath swirled inside me like a tempest, swelling with

each breath. "You lied to me!" I spat the words, unable to contain the clash of my emotions. I stumbled backward and away from him, all hope inside me shattering like glass. "All this time..." Despair ripped through me as I closed my eyes, the countless moments we had shared flashing in my mind. "I thought... I trusted you!"

He stepped closer, his voice shaking with sheer agony. "My love, let me explain."

"No!" I lashed at him, once again putting distance between us. Each word that left his mouth felt like a dagger stabbing through my core. I hugged myself tightly, my gaze still locked with his as I spoke in a low voice. "One thing, and one thing only, is what I want from you now."

"Name it and it shall be yours," he pleaded urgently.

My throat was too tight to speak, but finally, the words spilled out of me. "Give me back my name."

Hades stared at me with confusion that soon melted into worry and fear.

"I want... my name," I said again, hot tears prickling in the corners of my eyes. "I should never have been here!" My voice grew sharper now, more desperate.

He spread his hands in surrender. "Beauty, I would never force you against your will," he argued frantically. "You summoned me. You *asked* to come to the Netherworld!"

The truth struck me like a slap across the face—it made my knees weak and my lungs feel hollow. It stole every ounce of strength from me until all that remained was undiluted fear. "Who am I?" I asked, shivering in terror.

"My darling, I cannot tell you," he replied, his voice soft with sorrow. "Some boundaries even *I* cannot cross. There are rules..."

Anger blazed through me like wildfire. "Break them!" I screamed at him, rage coursing through my being.

Hades stepped closer and locked eyes with me, his

expression shifting between anger and desolation. "What you ask of me is impossible," he said slowly, each word packed with barely restrained wrath.

"You're a *god*," I exclaimed, the words resounding in the courtyard. "Find a way!"

His chest heaved with silent fury. "Do you *presume* to command me?" he seethed through gritted teeth, and before I could even process what was happening, fiery embers ignited his eyes and powerful black wings burst from his back, slowly spreading wide until their shadow fell upon me. "I will remind you, I am the Netherworld's one true ruler. I *bow* to no one." Ire contorted his face, a thick vein pulsing in his neck.

My gaze angled upwards, for the first time daring to look upon his divine fury—an overpowering dark force that made my stomach twist in knots. Even then, I found the courage to whisper, "Prove me your love's worth or I shall never see you again."

"Beauty..." Hades reached out for me, but then stopped as tears trailed down my cheeks. Anguish softened his glare but for a moment before I took two steps back. "Beauty, don't leave like this!"

But it was too late now. His desperate cries followed me down the stone steps as I hurried away, until all that remained was the echo of a heart-wrenching farewell forever branded in my soul.

# 45

# BEAUTY

*A* staccato thundering of footsteps echoed through the hallway, Hypnos gracefully strolling down. The beat stopped when he stood at the doorway, intense hazel eyes gazing down as he found me sitting on the cold marble floor, barefoot with my drenched lavish gown billowing around me.

"Mm…" The sound rumbled deep and mysterious like a whisper from the dark corners of the five realms. His vibrant eyes gleamed with secrets as he prowled closer, his presence as heavy and grand as a storm cloud. "So you *found out*, didn't you?"

My bloodshot eyes flickered upwards to meet his. "Hypnos, you mischievous creature…" I breathed out shakily, my heart breaking as the salty taste of tears trickled down the corner of my lips. "You knew." I paused. "You knew he was Hades all along and said nothing."

He leaned against the bedpost, a smoldering smile gracing his lips and creasing his cheeks. "Mischief does seem to be my second calling," he mused, dark amusement lingering in his voice.

My brows tangled in confusion. "And what would you call your first?" I asked, curiosity lacing my words.

His lips twitched into a cunning grin as he gave me a careless shrug. "Divinity, my lady," he replied with an air of confidence.

I heaved a heavy sigh. "You should have told me," I murmured, barely audible beneath the crackling firelight.

"No. I should *not* have," he asserted with a stern shake of his head. "Angering the gods is never wise—*especially* Hades. He brooks no foolishness." His words hummed with quiet caution.

"Your warnings have come far too late," I lamented. "But even if they had come sooner, I doubt they would have discouraged me." The words tumbled out faster than I could keep up with—like pebbles cascading down a steep mountainside—and there was no stopping them.

He threw me a secretive look from beneath his deep-brown lashes. "Nothing ever could, I think," he replied fondly before producing a golden vessel from within his coat pocket. Candlelight glinted off its contents enticingly as he waved it in the air. "I brought some wine, if that helps any."

Hot tears pooled in my eyes, my broken heart aching with Hades' betrayal. "Ambrosia?" I begged, hopeful.

"Is there anything else worth drinking?" he returned with a smoldering glance.

I echoed his words just as sharply. "Is there?"

"Maybe the elusive Bloodmoon Red…" He sighed wistfully, pausing for a moment to appreciate the mere mention of the rare liquid. "It's nearly impossible to find in these parts since it is man-made. A true weakness of mine, I can't deny it."

I inhaled deeply, letting out a drawn-out breath before continuing. "So for tonight, let's make do with ambrosia," I said. "Come, sit with me."

A contented smile spread across his face as he settled into my side. "Gladly."

"I've asked Hades for my name," I muttered despairingly, watching him fill my cup with the golden elixir.

"Oh?" He raised one sculpted eyebrow quizzically and passed me my drink. "And how did that go?"

I groaned in frustration, my frown deepening even further when I answered him. "It's too soon to tell. I don't think I properly asked—I *demanded* it... He'll never help me now." Taking one long sip of the nectar, I closed my eyes and savored its smoothness as it coated my throat.

Hypnos licked his lips, and leaning closer, he murmured softly, "As you said... It's too soon to know the answer." He held up his glass and met my gaze. "Let us drink then. Until we have the courage to find out."

I forced a smile at the corners of my mouth. "That's..."

"What?" he prodded, inching closer with his usual intensity.

"Uncommonly sober," I replied, quirking a brow. "Not your usual exquisite poetry, I'm afraid."

Hypnos let loose a bark of laughter. "Don't tell me you enjoyed hearing all that lyrical nonsense."

"No, I surely did not enjoy it." I shook my head, feeling the heat creep up my neck. "But it's kind of grown on me."

"Mm. I do have a poetic vein inside me, don't I?" he replied with a hint of pride in his voice.

"Hypnos..." I stared pleadingly into his eyes to just finish the toast and let this moment pass between us in peace.

His expression softened, eyes darkening as his voice gained strength, sailing into the night: "Let us not forget the shadows that lurk within, for it is when all light seems lost that we must be guided by their glimmer. And so, we fill our cups to overflowing with this blissful ambrosia. May its fire remain forever burning in our hearts."

I sat there awestruck, barely able to speak. "Hypnos, that was beautiful," I finally said.

A smirk tugged at his lips as he glanced at me over his shoulder. "Bottoms up," he said nonchalantly.

Our glasses clinked in a symphony of sorrow. The luxurious golden liquid flooded my mouth, but it was not enough to wash away my despair. I sighed wearily and said, "I don't think one glass will be enough to ease the ache in my heart."

His grin widened in mischief, his words lingering in the air like a promise. "Oh, there's plenty more where that came from."

"Hypnos..." I uttered, my voice a gentle request in the hushed room.

He turned to me, his gaze delving into mine.

"I don't think I've ever asked you... how did you get the scar on your cheek?" I said cautiously, my finger lightly tracing the thin silver line that cut across his cheekbone. "You're an immortal; why do you bear it?"

A moment passed with no sound but our breathing in the stillness of the room. "I bear it because I *chose* to keep it," he said gravely, his conviction tangible in the darkness around us. "It's a reminder of the one who gave it to me," he continued, his gaze never straying from mine. "When next we meet, I will know it was him." He paused. "Now, sweet girl... Drink your wine and forget your troubles."

My throat clogged as emotions threatened to rise up, and I took a shaky sip of the wine. Hypnos watched me intently, no doubt reading my inner turmoil.

"I need your help," I said quietly, setting down the glass.

The god's expression changed, morphing from thoughtful contemplation to concern.

"Hypnos... Would you kiss me to sleep like you did in

the forest?" My voice was almost pleading, desperate for a reprieve from the pain Hades had caused.

He frowned at me, his gaze concerned. "Do you earnestly wish this?" he asked in a whisper, searching my face for an answer.

A single tear escaped when I nodded.

Hypnos sighed heavily. "Oh, my darling…" His delicate fingers inched close to my face as they pushed back a stray lock of hair behind my ear. "You truly love him, don't you?" he murmured gently, his eyes full of sorrow.

I leaned into his palm, taking what little comfort I could from his touch. "I do," I confessed brokenly. "But he has shattered my heart beyond repair."

His thumb delicately brushed away the trail of my tears. For a moment, I saw turmoil warring behind his stoic mask. At last, he straightened with resolve.

"I believe this conversation has come to an end," he said, rising and offering me his hand. "Come. Let us find you some rest."

## 46
## PHILLIP

We ventured into the woods of the Netherworld, a sense of foreboding enveloping us like a suffocating cloak. The atmosphere grew thicker with an eerie stillness, broken only by the occasional hushed rustle from lurking beasts. Every footfall sank deeply into the sodden earth, as if the very ground resisted our intrusion.

The air carried a chilling breeze that wailed and whispered through the gnarled branches of skeletal trees, sending a shiver down my spine. Heavy mist clung to our surroundings, distorting any landmarks and concealing the path ahead behind a swirling wall of obscurity. It was as if the very fabric of this realm conspired to keep us lost within its treacherous embrace.

Deeper and deeper, we descended into the abyss of darkness, until the air was thick with its oppressive weight. The Dark Prince's presence loomed larger as we traveled further, his words from our last meeting ringing in my ears—promises of destruction and pain. He had made himself master of this immortal wasteland, and I could feel his menacing hand steering every inch.

"Eloise…" I breathed, ridding myself of the unearthly mist that clung to my clothes. "There's something you need to know."

She stiffened, her deep gaze locking with mine. "What is it?"

I hesitated, feeling my insides churning. "Hades knows we're coming for him. I'm sure of it."

A swirling gust of air escaped Eloise as she sighed. Her lips curved in a smirk, her eyes sparkling with amusement. "What made you think that, Phillip? We've not caused nearly enough trouble for him to take notice," she said with a dismissive hand wave. "Besides, the gods don't pay attention to anyone but themselves." Her shoulders slumped and she started forward.

My heart pounded with uncertainty as I caught up with her. But perhaps she was right. Perhaps my confrontation with the Dark Prince had been nothing more than a nightmare, an enchantment contrived by Minthe solely to torment me… The raw sting of shame coursed through me as I remembered how willingly I'd fallen for the nymph's deception.

But even in the midst of my doubts, the memory of almost losing Eloise remained deeply engraved in me, a reminder of the only truth that mattered to my heart. Part of me wanted to speak out, but I could not bring myself to spill my foolishness. So, I held it all in, locked away in the depths of my soul.

"You're right," I conceded, raking the land with a careful glance. "Let's keep our wits sharp and hope that whatever lurks in this fog remains undetected."

We pressed on, walking for what felt like an eternity with no end in sight. Everywhere we looked was shrouded in fog, making it impossible to judge the distance we had traveled. The only other presence we encountered were occasional hares scurrying through the undergrowth, their fur blending eerily into the shadowy terrain.

Eloise slashed the dead branches between us, her expression tense. "I can't wait to get out of this forest," she mumbled under her breath.

"It *is* kind of boring and uninspiring," I replied, looking around at the fog-shrouded trees that seemed to stretch into eternity.

A wry smile tugged at Eloise's lips. "I don't mind that in the least—though I am getting a bit hungry, and hunting with all this fog would be pointless."

"*Pointless*," I mouthed the word silently, barely allowing myself to grin at the irony of it all.

I halted midstride. Eloise froze beside me. A cruel stillness pressed down on us like a blanket—yet beneath it, faint and haunting, a melody began to drift through the air. "Eloise, do you hear that?" I whispered, barely daring to breathe.

"I've heard it before," she replied to my astonishment. "But never this close."

The music seeped around us, as dense as the fog, winding its way between the trees like an ethereal specter with no earthly home. Goosebumps broke out across my skin as I listened to the howling wind and mournful notes, coming together in an unearthly harmony that set my teeth on edge. Beside me, Eloise shivered, her eyes wide with unease as she strained to listen.

Eloise and I exchanged tense glances, our determination unwavering but our hearts heavy with the weight of the somber tune. The music swirled around us, each note, a sigh of lost dreams and forgotten secrets.

Growing louder still, it wrapped us in its tangible grief,

the ethereal notes seeping into our souls, captivating and enthralling us with their melancholic allure. It was as if the deepest sorrows of the Netherworld resonated in a wistful whisper.

"Keep moving," I said, my breaths shallow as sheer trepidation quickened the blood in my veins.

With each step, the music grew sonorous, a clamor entangling around us like a spectral snake. It echoed through the desiccated woods, howling hints of forgotten tragedies and abandoned dreams.

"It's hopeless," Eloise murmured, her voice barely audible above the melody. She stumbled back and slumped against a tree trunk. "To challenge the gods was a dream too grand for me to ever realize." Her gaze cut to the leafy ground. "I wanted to become a legend, but this quest was always beyond my skill."

"Eloise?" I knitted my brows as I approached her side. "What are you talking about?"

She pressed her back into the bark of the tree and sank to her knees, light sobs escaping her lips when she buried her face in her hands. "I've been a fool," she choked out. "How could I pretend to outwit Hades? He's the Dark Prince of the Netherworld. We have trespassed his realm of death and now we are doomed." A stifled cry escaped her lips.

Fear lodged in my throat at her words and I crouched beside her, my heart twinging with sympathy. "Eloise, don't say that." Such despair was alien to me—completely unlike the Eloise I knew.

The Netherworld's melody lingered in the air like ice, seeping into our bones and casting a pall of gloom upon our spirits. Suddenly, the path that had seemed so promising only moments before had been swallowed by the encroaching shadows, and the trees stretched high around us, their gnarled branches resembling bony fingers reaching out to ensnare unsuspecting prey.

I stumbled to the ground, my sword discarded at my side, as unforeseen weariness swept over me. A mysterious voice spoke in my head, reminding me how brashly I'd ventured into this journey, leaving behind my kingdom and forsaking my people. With bitter irony, it reminded me that I'd risked it all in search of glory...

Wait. Suddenly I was aware of something. "It's that rotten music," I said aloud, realization dawning on me. Fiercely, I grabbed Eloise's shoulder and shook her lightly. "Eloise, it's that melody! Don't listen to it!"

"Melody? What melody?" She stared at me, bloodshot eyes shuddering with confusion.

I pressed my hand against my chest, trying to steady my frantic breathing and clear my mind. "The Netherworld's melody," I explained, desperation creeping into my voice. "It's meant to lure us in, make us lose our will. We must fight it."

Eloise's eyes widened as the bewitching tune finally reached her ears. She inhaled sharply, a sigh escaping her lips. "Gods," she murmured softly. "It's so... beautiful."

My jaw clenched tightly and I grit my teeth, willing myself to ignore the captivating tune. Desperation was rising in me. My voice cracked as I said urgently, "Don't listen! We have to keep moving!"

With a great heave, I managed to stumble back to standing and reached out an arm for Eloise. She took it with a reassuring squeeze, and we proceeded forward, the music growing in volume as we trudged on.

The night seemed to press in around us with a crushing force, its weight smothering me. The thunder of my heart pounding against my chest practically reverberated through the forest trees. Clinging tightly to each other, our fingers entwined, we fought back the power of the Netherworld that threatened to consume us with each step we took.

"We can do this," I said resolutely, wanting desperately to believe that these words would be enough to sustain us until the end of this arduous journey. But the Netherworld's whispers remained constant, a melancholy song carried by the wind and sent to haunt our every thought. It surrounded us with its siren's call, beckoning us even as it sapped away our courage and strength. An overwhelming sensation of despair clung to us, but still, we moved ever forward.

"Keep going," I murmured weakly, my eyes growing heavy with weariness from this unwinnable battle. "We're almost there—we're almost out of these wicked veiled woods!"

Eloise nodded, her gaze zeroing in on every detail of the dense woods around us. There was something almost feral about her vigilance that made a chill run up my spine. Our journey through this cursed land felt never-ending, and though neither of us spoke of our exhaustion, it was there between us. Eloise had to feel as tired as I did.

As if summoned by a prayer, the fog gradually began to lighten and we spied a clearing ahead. The sorrowful music that had haunted us during our journey softened and we staggered into the open air. Uncontrollable relief flooded through me and tears stung at my eyes. Eloise sighed heavily, standing tall as she embraced the blooming twilight.

I hit the ground hard, as if it had been waiting for me. Pain flared in my lungs, still struggling to comprehend what had just happened. I whispered the words I never wanted to say, "Hades blocked our way..." We had worked so hard and for so long, and yet here we were, beaten once again by the nightmare god.

Eloise sat stoically by my side, her gaze unassuming yet knowing. I couldn't tell if she was understanding my plight or sympathized with it, but either way, I felt secure in the moment.

"I believe you," she exhaled a breathy whisper after a few moments of silence had passed—her voice so steady and unwavering despite the storm brewing in her eyes. The unease swelling within her was all but tangible. "But I also believe there's more to this story than what you're saying."

I bowed my head in response, feeling the tightness cinch around my throat as I slowly began to speak. Eloise deserved to know everything if we were going to have any chance of making it out alive from our descent into the Dark Prince's palace.

"There is..." I started carefully, remembering all too well the sting of Minthe's deceit when I had come face to face with its reality only days before. But now, having Eloise beside me, it almost seemed worse—as though it was twice as painful to be speaking these words out loud.

She needed to know everything.

*Everything.*

# 47

# BEAUTY

The room was cloaked in shadow, the dying embers in the fireplace offering little comfort to the otherwise silent air. Unease slithered down my spine.

Slowly, I sat up, peering into the gloom. There—a shifting silhouette at the foot of my bed. I stifled a cry, my fingers clenching the sheets.

The figure moved closer with predatory grace, menacing and alluring. Moonlight glinted off sharp eyes, full of cunning and malice. Recognition dawned within me, colder than the starlight.

Thanatos. The god of death had come for me.

He looked down at me with an unreadable expression, curiosity and contempt entangled in his cruel gaze.

My chest tightened as I tried to keep from freezing, fumbling for the sword by my bedside. Voidbringer gleamed red in the shadows as I seized it tightly in my trembling hands.

I shuddered as he approached, unable to tear my gaze away. Thanatos grinned menacingly, drawing his own sword with a metallic ring. "Such a pretty toy," he said mockingly, gesturing towards the obsidian sword. "But tell me, mortal, what will you do with it? Strike me down?" His brow rose in challenge as he taunted me.

Terror pulsed throughout my veins. My heart raced and I stumbled back, the bedframe creaking beneath me. Gripping Voidbringer, I used its weight to anchor myself as a sudden quake shook the room.

I shrank back against the headboard, willing my voice not to shake. "What do you want from me?"

Thanatos tilted his head, assessing. "Such spirit," he mused. "I begin to understand why he chose you." His words were inscrutable, yet threaded with mockery.

My breath caught as I met his icy silver gaze.

"It's just you and me this time," Thanatos murmured, his deep voice smooth and resolute. "No one is coming to save you."

The Lord of Death stepped forward, his sword at the ready. I stumbled off the bed and raised mine in defense. For a heartbeat, we stood there, blades crossed between us, and all the while, I knew this was a fight I could not have prevented.

"Let's find out what you're made of," he tersely challenged, and without notice, he lunged forward with lightning speed, his sword whistling through the air. I barely managed to block it with my own blade, feeling the shock of impact course through my arms. Fighting Thanatos was like battling against a hurricane—his strength, inexhaustible; his movements, effortless.

I struck back with what little skill I owned, but my attacks were clumsy and uncoordinated. Thanatos merely laughed and deflected them easily, moving ever closer with each passing moment.

At last, my sword flashed in a practiced arc, but Thanatos blocked the assault with ease. I held my ground as our swords collided in sparks. He pushed forward, close enough that his minty breath fanned my face. His free hand boldly scurried along my jawline, pulling me to him. "That's a good girl," he purred in a low growl, his eyes smoldering with silver flames. "But not nearly good enough."

I started, an unwelcome shiver blasting through my being.

Lazily, his sword grated away and he stepped back, watching me with an air of authority. "You see, mortal," he murmured, voice like liquid silk, "you can't win. You are playing with forces beyond your comprehension. Give up now, and I promise to make it quick." The corner of his lips curled up in dark delight, waiting for an answer.

But I wouldn't surrender. I set my jaw and fought on, bravado belying the fear coursing through my veins— parrying and striking with all my might, until the sweat was pouring down my face and my arms trembled with exhaustion. But it was all for naught. Thanatos was simply too powerful, and I was no match for him.

A dark smile crossed his handsome face. "Have you had enough?" he taunted, unfaded by the fight.

I stared at him, hopeless and drained, yet unrelenting.

"Because *I* have," he added, and in one cold move, his blade sliced through my chest like hot butter. Pain as I'd never experienced surged through me in one searing wave and my knees buckled beneath me. My vision blurred, and I fell to the ground, gasping for breath.

Thanatos stood over me, watching as my lifeblood spilled onto the floor. "You should have listened," he said softly, as everything went black. "Now, you belong to me."

A scream sliced through my being.

I jolted awake, my heart hammering in my chest. An icy breath of fear escaped through my lips. The scream that had awoken me still echoed through the air. Tears streamed down my face, and I heaved a shuddering sob as fury replaced the terror inside of me.

A chill ran down my spine as I realized that Thanatos had somehow found a way to haunt my dreams. Hypnos' magic must have mistakenly opened the gates to his brother's malice and deceit. I'd already been through so much pain at Thanatos' hands, and I refused to suffer any longer.

Gripping my sword so tightly that my knuckles turned white, I tossed away the heavy comforter and crept out of bed, then threw on only my boots and a cloak for protection. With no sense of hesitation or fear, I marched outside the room, through the darkened courtyard, and into the fathomless shadows of the forest surrounding it.

A low whinny startled me into alertness. There, in the woods, a pristine white mare awaited, saddled, as if expecting me. With no time to lose, I mounted swiftly and spurred the horse into the shadowed depths of the forest.

The mare flew through the trees, her hooves striking sparks against the stones. I leaned low over her neck, urgency lending speed to our flight as the cool night air lashed my face and tangled my unbound hair.

A light thunderstorm fell as we followed the course of the river, tracking back the journey of my escape, until I found myself standing in front of his dreaded watchtower.

The tower stood tall, its ebony walls rising defiantly into the night. Its architecture echoed the somber grandeur of the Netherworld itself, with sharp angles and intricate carvings that seemed to come alive under the moon's haunting glow. As I gazed up, the structure disappeared into the heavens, as if reaching out to touch the gods themselves.

At its peak, a solitary beacon burned with an eerie blue

flame. The flame danced with an otherworldly grace, casting a soft, ethereal light that illuminated the surroundings, shedding long shadows upon the land.

As I stood there, a soft breeze swept through the darkness, carrying with it the haunting whispers of forgotten souls. I couldn't help but feel a sense of trepidation and amazement, mingling together in a delicate dance.

Memories of when I'd been held captive here filled me with anxiety, but not enough to sway me from my purpose.

The entrance door opened with a rusty creak and I stepped forward, scurrying down the long obsidian hall until I reached the threshold to Thanatos' chambers. He was unaware of my presence at first, his back still turned to me as he stood there. In an instant, all apprehension left me as I charged forward towards him, sword raised high above my head. A battle was about to begin.

He whirled to confront me, his eyes alight with a fiery rage. "You foolish mortal," he bellowed. "What makes you think you can stand against my might?"

"I'm not here to play your games," I asserted, finding strength in the words as my voice held steady. "I'm here to challenge you, once and for all. I will *not* cower before you."

The silence between us seemed to stretch on forever before Thanatos gave a slow nod. "Very well," he said in a low rumble. "The quicker we get this over with, the faster you'll be in my thrall."

With an explosive cry, we both lunged forward. Our blades clashed with an intensity that shook the very walls of the chamber. We fought with wild abandon, neither one backing down nor relenting in our attack. Sparks flew from our weapons as they met again and again; the clanging of metal, like thunder in the air. My arms ached from the effort, and fine beads of perspiration ran down my face, but I didn't stop; I *couldn't* stop until one of us lay defeated.

My strength was waning more and more with every passing breath, and I knew that it would only be a matter of time before Thanatos claimed victory. My mind raced as I desperately searched for a way to turn the tides, some way to end this battle before it was too late.

Just when it seemed all hope had vanished, my eye fell upon a chance. A tiny chink in his armor, exposed in the heat of battle—a possible escape from this nightmare. My lungs burning, my muscles screaming, I launched forward one last time, and with a final burst of energy, I thrust my sword into his side.

Thanatos staggered backwards, a look of disbelief and agony clouding his features as he realized what had happened. His weapon clattered to the ground as he collapsed to his knees, unable to bear the pain any longer.

I stepped forward, barely able to stand after the strain our fight had put on me, but still feeling victorious nonetheless. Keeping my blade raised proudly above him, I declared my victory over him in a soft voice.

"You… have been bested," I said through grinding teeth, the pained exhaustion still present in my voice, "by a mere mortal." My flushed cheeks still burned from the night's exertion, and with a defeated huff, I spun on my heel and hastened away from that cursed place—never wanting to set eyes upon Thanatos again.

"You have proven yourself worthy tonight," he said, a tinge of respect in his tone. "It seems I underestimated you, after all."

I proudly sheathed my sword and stood tall. "It's over," I declared, my voice bouncing off the chamber's walls like a peal of thunder, and all my fears seemed to dissipate with those words. "No more death. No more terror. I have a new life now, and it begins today."

A wicked smirk curled the corner of his lips as he

regarded me with amusement. "A new... *life*?" he echoed cruelly. "Do you truly believe that crossing over into the Netherworld will be enough to free you from my grasp? Don't let yourself be fooled, my lady—when it comes to me, there is no escape." His words hung in the air like a warning before dissipating into nothingness.

But I shrugged them off. His body lay vanquished beneath me—a symbol of my determination and strength. I had won this battle and I was going to take ownership of my new beginning. An unfamiliar strength flooded my veins as I turned away from him and took my first steps towards freedom. No god or wraith could influence my destiny but me.

# 48

# PHILLIP

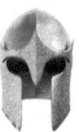

*I* left nothing out, boasting of the mighty fight we'd won against the devilish hounds in Charon's cave, and how I had almost lost her. Then, came the part that made all my muscles tense as I spoke—the way Minthe had seduced me after freeing her from her chains, only to prove she was still loyal to Hades.

Eloise's eyes glittered in the night as she finally finished listening to my story. "I nearly died?" Carefully, she tugged up her shirt, exposing what were once jagged gashes across her ribcage—now thinned pale lines. "I figured it was a scratch, and thought no more of it," she mumbled, puzzled, tracing them with her fingers. "I can't remember a thing."

"Your memories were sealed by Minthe's spell." I sighed heavily, throwing another birch log into the flames.

"And you've been with her?" Eloise asked incredulously, confusion written all over her face.

"I thought..." The words drifted into silence. With all my being, I wanted to tell her the full truth; that when I'd seen Minthe at first glance, I'd mistaken her for Eloise. That I'd trusted all too easily without looking deeper. But I knew such a confession could cost us our friendship, so instead I clumsily lied. "She tricked me too."

Eloise regarded me gravely before speaking again. "You were right Phillip," she said softly. "Hades *is* onto us. We must be careful from now on and trust each other completely."

We locked eyes then and despite the fatigue taking hold of me I felt a spark of determination in my chest. We would see this through—together. A silent agreement passed between us as Eloise folded her delicate hand over mine, infusing warmth into my being.

"We'll make it out of this," she murmured reassuringly, when a howling gust of wind tore through the haunting forest, its plaintive cries ripping at my heart. As it wailed, a chill spread in its wake, extinguishing the fire, sweeping away any remaining warmth. Darkness crept steadily inwards, until only the faint light of dusk remained, struggling to penetrate the dense canopy above.

The trees around us twisted and bent under the force of the winds, their skeletal branches reaching out like clawed hands ready to ensnare unsuspecting prey.

My gaze sharpened as an unfamiliar snap struck from an unknown source. Eloise and I both shot to our feet, my fingertips brushing my sword's hilt.

I stepped forward, "Who goes there?" My voice echoed off the ancient trunks, yet no reply came back to us.

I whirled around to search for Eloise only to find her gone without a trace. Taking a deep breath, bracing myself with every ounce of strength I had left, I prowled closer towards the sound. But nothing could have prepared me for what I saw next. Nothing could have steeled me for the wave of emotions that surged through me when our eyes met.

A vision stood before me, her beauty an incandescent blaze that stirred memories of lullabies sung just for me in the days of my childhood. Tears stung my eyes, unraveling a warmth I hadn't even remembered until this moment.

"Phillip, my sweet boy," she breathed, her voice a frail blessing that filled the air with a silvery glimmer of forgotten wonder. "Oh! How I have yearned for you, my beloved son."

My heart swelled with bittersweet nostalgia. I'd been yearning for her comforting embrace ever since our last farewell. "Mother—" Tears welled in my eyes, a blend of deep joy and overwhelming sorrow. I ached to take her in my arms and feel her warmth once more. In an instant, memories of her tender kindness flooded back, replenishing the hollow crevices of my broken soul that craved nothing but her love.

As I stepped closer, enticed by her familiar perfume in the air, my mother extended her ethereal hand towards me. Her touch was as gentle as a butterfly's wings brushing against my skin, and yet, an icy shiver raced down my spine.

"Mother, it's been so long," I uttered softly, torn between conflicting emotions. "I have missed you, more than mere words can express."

She bowed her head, overcome with emotion. Her tender blue eyes found mine, and her voice trembled with longing. "Oh, dearest Phillip... The pain of our separation has weighed heavily upon my soul. But fear no longer. I am here now, guiding you through this maze of shadows."

Her words enfolded me in a blanket of fortitude, granting solace amidst our bleak surroundings. I followed her lead, mesmerized by her aura, oblivious to whatever danger might be lurking beneath my feet.

We delved deeper into the forest, cloaked in a hazy mist. My mother's voice filled the air like a luscious symphony, recounting past moments of our lives, of laughter and love we had shared together before time stole them away from us. As she spoke, her stories painted vibrant pictures of bliss and adoration, filling me with warmth and nostalgia.

The ground grew more treacherous as we wilted further into the woods, yet I was held captive by its deceptive beauty. Shimmering evergreens blazed through the fog, while soft mosses and colorful wildflowers donned the terrain. The chill of the mist clung to my skin, but I was too enraptured to care—if only I could reclaim my bond with her.

"Phillip, my darling," she whispered, her voice tinged with a touch of urgency. "Come closer. Let me hold you as I used to." Her familiar scent of lavender and orange blossoms permeated the air and filled my senses, and I stumbled towards her without hesitation, the allure of her embrace overpowering all reason.

As I wrapped my arms around her, something shifted beneath my feet. My mother's form instantly flickered, and her eyes glinted with an unworldly light that sent shivers down my spine.

The words tore out of me like a plea. "Mother, you were always an honorable and wise queen." I wanted to linger in this moment, knowing it could well be my last. "You *shouldn't* be here," I continued through gritted teeth, my expression hardening as I braced myself to face reality. "You should be at rest at the Elysian Fields." Tears brimmed my eyes, and finally one fell down my cheek, the truth unraveling before me like a tautly wound thread.

The woman standing in front of me was not my mother. This twisted scene was nothing but a cruel ploy conjured by Hades to keep me from his palace. Anger seethed through my veins as I watched the figure dissolve in my arms and the earth shifted beneath me, my feet giving way to a dark abyss and I felt myself fall—a sharp gasp leaving my lips as I plunged into the depths of stygian quicksand.

Panic thrummed through my veins as I kicked against

the relentless pull, trying to grasp something—anything at all —to help me escape.

But before I could succumb to the black void, a voice pierced the inky night like a beacon. Eloise's urgent warning, cutting through the cacophony of my fear. She'd fallen prey to Hades' trickery as well, and we were both doomed if we couldn't find a way out.

Gathering every ounce of strength that remained within me, I began struggling upwards—towards the surface where Eloise lay, prey to the same evil as me.

"Eloise!" I called desperately. "Are you all right?"

"I'm not dead yet," she shouted back. "I saw my father! He tricked me!"

"That was not your father!" I grunted, pushing against the suffocating grip of the sand as it crept up my body. "It was a trap from Hades!" Untamed fury blazed through my veins like wildfire.

"Do not fight it or it will drag you further down!" Eloise warned urgently, her words slicing like blades into my desperation.

I stilled my frantic movements, saving my energy as best I could while I sunk further into the quicksand's grasp. Terror threatened to overcome me but I held on tightly to Eloise's words and the sliver of hope that together we would make it out alive.

A sudden hush descended upon the woods, and a golden radiance pierced my vision. A figure emerged from the light —beautiful and regal, shining with an untouchable air of power and knowledge. Her youthful face gleamed with a splendor that time could never age.

The goddess approached me, her mere presence commanding enough to cause the stygian quicksand to shudder in her wake. Her eyes were a captivating shade of green flecked with gold, and when they locked with mine,

I felt as if she could uncover all my secrets with a single gaze.

Long locks of golden blonde hair cascaded in luxurious waves down to her waist, shimmering like strands of sunlight.

With a wave of her hand, the ground rumbled beneath us and the cursed quicksand began to recede. The goddess then spoke, her voice like a gentle breeze carrying a promise of freedom. "Fear not, mortal souls," she declared in a tone that commanded authority. "I shall not let Hades capture you."

The sand shifted at the goddess' command, but I was still sinking deep. Sand swirled around my ankles, climbing higher with every second as I sank further under. The relentless suck of the quicksand threatened to swallow me whole when out of nowhere, a hand clasped mine.

Eloise's grip was firm and unwavering. I reached out my other hand, our fingers intertwining, and as I emerged from the treacherous quicksand, gasping for breath, our eyes met in silent understanding, acknowledging the bond that had formed between us in the darkness.

The goddess turned her gaze upon us, her face illuminated by an otherworldly glow. Her voice was a soothing melody that filled our souls. "Beware," she warned, "for Hades' realm is fraught with treachery. But do not falter, for you shall not tread alone in your quest. I shall watch over you."

Eloise and I remained still, her gaze keeping us spellbound and silent, reverently offering our admiration.

"Go to the mountain," she commanded with a voice that echoed through the forest. "I shall protect you there from the Dark Prince's prying eyes."

Before I could thank the goddess or even ask her name, her form started to dissipate into the mist like a fleeting dream. As she vanished into the night, her parting words whispered through the woods: "Remember, hope will be your guide through the shadows of despair. Now... RUN!"

At that, a deafening roar scattered in the woodlands, as if enraged by her divine presence. The ground shook beneath our feet and the distant growls of predatory creatures rumbled through the trees, making us shudder in dismay.

And so, we ran.

I reached out and grabbed Eloise's hand, never looking back. The Netherworld's worst was hot on our heels, its growling beasts snapping at us through the trees. I dared not look over my shoulder, I just pushed forward; my body driven by fear and wild determination.

As we scampered into an evergreen forest, the air around us grew lighter, the oppressive weight of the Netherworld's gloom giving way to a gentle breeze that carried with it a scent of fresh earth and blooming flowers. Gradually, the dense forest thinned, revealing a majestic mountain range in the distance, its snow-capped peaks towering high into the heavens.

The menacing roars that had chased us soon faded away, a reminder of the goddess' protection as we made our way along winding paths towards the safety of the mountain.

We scaled the mountainous layers, a chain of vibrant green foliage crashing into stony cliffs and jagged rocks. But with each step, I could feel her presence around me, bringing ease to my racing heart.

At last, we stumbled upon a secret sanctuary hidden within the mountain's embrace. I gasped at the sight of its beauty. Illuminated by the soft moonlight, an ivory fortress lay before me, a haven of tranquil refuge amidst the treacherous wasteland. The sparkling waters of a nearby stream danced around us, offering solace to our weary souls.

Our haven rose like a titan at the edge of the mountain,

its gaze surveying the Netherworld far below. An imposing portico of fluted columns greeted me at its grand entrance—their capitals adorned with intricate acanthus leaf motifs, beckoning me closer.

I stepped through the threshold and into an atrium that seemed to stretch endlessly before me, its mosaic floor displaying scenes of mythological victories and celestial beauty. In the center, a courtyard framed with elegant colonnades offered a brief respite as beams of muted moonlight streamed down from above, filling the space with a majestic ethereal glow.

The structure was carefully designed to blend with its natural surroundings, with open balconies and terraces allowing one to become immersed in the beauty of the landscape.

I passed archway upon archway—each one expertly carved with intricate detail. Frescos lined the stone walls, depicting scenes of mythical battles and grand heroes, while ornate furnishings draped in rich fabrics provided luxurious comfort.

From my elevated vantage point on the terrace, I surveyed the land and glimpsed as the river wound its way through the valley in a brilliant azure ribbon. The mountain's edge towered above me in breathtaking beauty, light and shadow cascading over its rocky face—a testament to something greater than us here on this immortal plane.

"Oh, dear goddess!" Eloise all but shrieked behind me.

I spun around, a wondrous sight greeting my weary eyes —a large, sturdy wooden table stood in the center of this glorious place, piled high with fragrant and luscious treats. Glimmering fruits from all corners of the world spilled forth from shimmering bowls, tantalizing us with their vibrant colors and sweet aromas. Piles of velvety peaches and succulent plums beckoned us, their ripe scent filling the air with an enticing promise of delectable indulgence. Intricate pastries and creamy confections sat upon golden platters, each crafted by skilled hands, promising heavenly flavors with each bite. Our feast was fit for royalty, a majestic exhibition of sights, scents, and flavors.

"Look!" Eloise exclaimed, lifting a goblet from the oaken table. Candlelight glimmered and danced off its golden surface, as I marveled in amazement at the dozen more that were filled to the brim with vibrant, sparkling nectar.

"At last," I sighed, grabbing one of my own and raising it in a silent toast.

Laughter of relief echoed between us as we clinked our goblets together in victorious celebration. Despite the suffering of weeks passed, here was something to savor.

The drink's velvety texture slid down my throat like a river of joy, and its sweetness burst across my tongue like an eruption of firemagic.

"It's no Bloodmoon Red," Eloise jested with a smirk and gulped down another swallow. "But it'll do for now."

"It'll do..." I echoed, delighted as I settled into the plush chair. Scattered clusters of grapes littered the tabletop before me and I grabbed a handful of them before leaning back with contentment.

Eloise drifted past me with light steps, the goblet heavy in her grip. She came to a sudden stop and, with a swift kick, opened an old forgotten trunk. "Blessed be the goddess," she murmured softly, looking up at me with shimmering eyes. Reverently, Eloise plucked from the depths of its contents: trousers, leather armor, boots—all of it once cast aside and now in her possession.

"What is it?" I asked from behind a pile of provender.

A joyous spark lit up her face as she held out the boots for me to see. "I can finally wear something that befits my station," she breathed in rapture.

I let my sweet drink with a bittersweet smile. Ceridwen had outdone herself in providing the most exquisite gowns for Eloise, but even without them, I could see the beauty radiating from her delicate frame.

Wasting no time, she darted into the next room and gasped at what lay inside.

"Oh. Now, this is too much," she mumbled in awe. "There's a small pond too!"

Before I could say a thing, a loud splash resounded and a contented sigh floated through the air. A thought crossed my mind, mischievous and tempting—what I wouldn't give to join her in those waters. But instead of indulging myself, I downed my drink and grabbed another off the table.

# 49

# BEAUTY

*I* trudged up the stone steps to the palace, my clothes clinging to me and mud caking the hems of my garments. My long hair hung like a waterfall of wet rain down my back, weighing me down with weariness and hunger.

The gentle hum of conversation emanated from the dining hall. My stomach grumbled in response to the delicious aromas that wafted through the air, promising sustenance and companionship from my beloved friend Hypnos.

My shoulders slumped with exhaustion as I took a deep breath and leaned my full weight against the heavy doors. With the last dregs of my strength, I pushed with all my might. The doors slowly swung wide open with an awful groan.

I froze at the doorway, stunned, as it was not Hypnos who sat at the head of the table, but Hades himself. The Lord of the Netherworld reclined upon his throne-like chair, a regal presence amidst the lavish feast spread before him. Pomegranate seeds glistened like rubies in a golden bowl, their crimson allure captivating my gaze.

I couldn't stop myself from despising him for his trickery. He had deceived me in the cruelest way. Yet, beneath that layer of disdain, lay the deepest truth of my feelings—a magnetic pull, an undeniable attraction that had woven its way into the fabric of my being. Despite all the pain and heartache he'd caused, I loved him still.

Our eyes met across the table, and for a fleeting moment, the air crackled with a tension that neither of us could deny. Hades arched an eyebrow, his chestnut eyes glinting with something darker than delight, something that mirrored the conflicted emotions swirling within me. An unspoken understanding passed between us—a deeper recognition of the turmoil that entangled both of our hearts.

"Oh..." I uttered, as I watched him lounging on the armchair, so careless and informal, popping pomegranate seeds into his mouth. "It's you." My tone came off indolent but my stomach churned and my knees trembled at the sudden sight of him.

"You were expecting someone else," he mumbled, eyeing me sidelong as he continued to pick the ripest seeds. "Someone more *likely* to drown himself in ambrosia, I believe." He spoke these things with such disdain that it set my blood aflame with fury.

My skin prickled with indignation. My heart raced in my chest, pounding frantically against the delicate walls of my ribcage. I clamped my jaw shut and swiveled around, taking swift strides towards the door.

"Where were you?" The question sailed through him drenched in conceit and reverberated in the vaulted room.

My hands curled into tight fists. "You're the god who rules over this realm," I seethed through gritted teeth. "Shouldn't you know the whereabouts of those in your kingdom?"

"Careful there," he purred, his voice as smooth as silk.

"That tongue of yours stings like a blade tonight." Hades heaved a heavy sigh. "Yet here I am, offering you this sumptuous feast." His arm swept around him, showcasing the room.

I faced him once more, determined not to let his words rattle me. "You can spare me the pleasantries, Hades," I said. "I know your game. This feast is just another one of your elaborate schemes."

A wry smile played at the corners of his lips as he plucked a pomegranate seed from the bowl, his gaze never leaving mine. "You wound me with your suspicions. Can't a Lord of the Netherworld simply enjoy a meal without ulterior motives?"

I scoffed, unable to resist stabbing him with a dry answer. "Ulterior motives seem to be your specialty. But let's not pretend this is anything other than a calculated move to manipulate me."

He leaned back in his chair, regarding me with an intensity that sent shivers down my spine. "Manipulation?" His dark brows tangled in confusion. "No, my dearest. I simply wish for us to share a meal together. Is that not what civilized beings do?"

I fought against the treacherous tug of his spell, reminding myself of the pain he'd caused, of the walls I'd built around my heart. "Civilized beings don't deceive the ones they claim to care for," I said, stepping closer. "They don't toy with their emotions like a puppet master pulling strings."

Hades exhaled heavily, the sound carrying a hint of regret. "You have a lethal way with words, Beauty. But trust me when I say that my intentions are not as black and white as you make them out to be. There is something far more daunting at play here than what your eyes can see. A deeper purpose to all of this." This time, his voice was earnest and true, free from pretense.

I hesitated, my resolve waning as his words seeped into the cracks of my defenses. The conflict within me intensified, torn between the love I still harbored and the pain he had inflicted. "What purpose could possibly justify your lies, Hades?"

His eyes softened, a rare vulnerability flickering within their depths. "A purpose that seeks to protect you. To keep you safe from forces far more dangerous than me."

My heart thrummed with a fragile flicker of hope in the wake of my chaotic emotions. "And what if I don't believe you?"

Hades rose slowly, his steps measured and purposeful. He extended an outstretched hand that was both commanding and gentle. The air seemed to part around him as he spoke, his voice deep and full of conviction. "Then stay, Beauty," he breathed. "Stay and witness the truth for yourself. Judge me not by my past actions, but by the future that I offer."

I looked into those abyssal eyes, searching for sincerity, for a glimpse of the man I had once loved. And in that moment, I made a choice. I reached out, my hand trembling as it nearly met his, almost bridging the chasm between us. And as his hand drew closer, mere seconds away from brushing mine, I pulled it away. Just remembering the sheer intensity of it, the streaks of lightning coursing through my being each time we touched, I knew that with a single graze, I'd be lost to him forever.

"I'll stay," I whispered, the weight of my decision mingling with the unspoken promise hanging in the air. "But Hades... you're playing with fire."

A smoldering smile curved his lips as he drew closer, our destinies entwined once more. "Oh, my dear Beauty," he purred in a low voice, his darkened stare drinking in the sight of me, "fire has always been my domain."

He dragged the chair next to him, an unspoken invitation. I sat, uncertainty tangling with anticipation inside of me. I waited for him to join me, wondering what fate would befall us after crossing this threshold together.

A sinister stillness settled between us, threatening to smother our very souls. The candlelight flickered wildly, illuminating the room with its fiery brilliance and weaving a web of shadows that shifted and shimmered with each passing breath.

The feast before us on the heavy oak table was fit for kings and queens, yet our eyes never left each other's. Hades' obsidian gaze held me in its grip, black pools of swirling emotion that dared me to look away. His power and presence seemed to consume me, drawing me deeper into his captivating abyss.

His jaw hardened as he muttered, "You think you've seen the depths to which I can sink. But don't be so quick to judge me by my darkness."

My grip tightened on the silver fork as I stabbed him with a glare and all but hissed, "I know all too well what hurt your words can cause."

He leaned forward, his voice filled with striking sincerity. "I am aware that nothing I can do will make up for the pain you've endured. But if you give me a chance, I promise you will see a different side to me—a side devoted to protecting those it cares for."

The tenderness in his voice pulled at my soul, the moments of our purest love flooding back into my mind. "How can I ever open myself up to you again? How can I believe this is not another web of deception?"

He reached across the table, his hand hovering over mine before retreating, as if uncertain of his own touch.

"Trust takes time, Beauty. But perhaps we can find a way to mend what has been broken," Hades murmured, his voice low and inviting. His smoldering eyes locked on mine, unleashing a shockwave through my veins. "Would you want that?"

His words stirred a longing within me, a flicker of hope that danced amidst the remnants of my shattered trust. I took a deep breath, meeting his gaze as apprehension and yearning tangled inside me. "Perhaps, Hades. But trust must be earned, not freely given."

A fleeting smile touched his lips. "Then allow me the opportunity to earn it," he purred, lifting a glass high. "Ambrosia?"

My hand shook slightly as I accepted the offer, but my instincts screamed at me that a single drink was not enough to walk out of this dinner unscathed.

The night unfolded serenely, our stories peeling back the layers of our souls. The more we spoke, the more I glimpsed the vulnerability behind his stoic façade. Our banter soon shifted from barbed exchanges to shared laughter, the lines blurring between enemies and potential allies—Hades was my only way out of this realm, after all.

As the night drew to a close, Hades stood from his throne with an outstretched hand. "Shall we stroll through my garden?" he asked in honeyed tones, his grin sending shivers down my spine. "The Netherworld is most enchanting just before twilight."

I hesitated for a moment before accepting, my heart racing as he led me through the labyrinthine paths of his domain.

We walked by each other's side, my sopping garments clinging to me like a second skin. I couldn't help but grimace, the fabric sticking to me in all the wrong places.

As if aware of my train of thought, Hades halted on the

terrace. "You are such a magnificent creature," he murmured, his stare never leaving mine.

I gazed up at Hades, admiring his silken voice until my gaze narrowed. "Your words are sweet as honey," I murmured with a small smile, "but actions speak louder."

A glint of mischief flickered in his features as he leaned in close. "Oh, I intend to prove myself to you, my Beauty," he rumbled darkly, maroon eyes boring into mine. "One—action—at a time." The intensity of his words gave rise to a different meaning that shot a thrill through my core and left my knees trembling.

"Let me show you your own power," he breathed, his fingers burning a trail along my shoulder. "See yourself through my eyes."

Before I could take a breath, the rain-drenched courtyard shifted—sodden earth giving way to verdant gardens, rain replaced by the heady perfume of blossoms. I glanced down and saw not my muddy boots and damp clothing, but an exquisite black gown, embellished with shimmering golden brocade. My hair no longer hung in wet tangles around my face, but had been twisted and curled into an intricate braid that draped gracefully over my shoulder... But all of this magic paled as I tilted my face to the gray sky, and the clouds suddenly parted. And the golden light of sunrise spilled over me for the first time in what felt like an eternity, banishing the gloom.

# 50

# BEAUTY

*M*y breath stuttered as tears welled in my eyes, the vision both familiar and strange after so long a time spent in shadow. I refused to let them fall, not wanting to spoil a single moment of this dreamlike vision Hades had created for me.

"This might be your greatest gift yet," I said, struggling to contain my emotions.

"I'm trying my best," he whispered, a glint of amusement in his gaze. "It seems like it's working."

My heart soared at the allure of his darkness. Every fiber of my being ached to run into his arms then and there. "Maybe," I replied with no inclination, giving him a feeble smile before venturing towards the garden. "I've never been to this courtyard before."

A devilish smirk spread across his lips, and he guided me towards a side garden. A wispy glow of sunlight beamed through the lace-like branches of pomegranate trees, their brilliant blossoms glimmering against an azure sky.

"This is my own little corner of bliss," he murmured softly.

I gasped in awe—the beauty of this place was beyond words. It was like discovering an oasis that I never knew existed. "I thought I'd seen every inch of this palace," I said, unable to contain my shock as I followed him down the winding footpath.

He snickered, a low sound that filled my heart with warmth. "Yes, you do like to explore, don't you?" He paused, dark eyes smoldering with barely concealed rage as they regarded me. "Now, tell me where you were earlier tonight." His voice was as smooth as velvet, yet a chill filled the air—a warning of what could come to pass should I choose the wrong answer.

I held my tongue and refused to utter even a word. I dared not speak of Thanatos with this man. I'd seen how quickly his temper could flare and I had no wish to tangle with it again.

"So, you've chosen silence then?" His expression darkened at my refusal to appease him. "Each time you step out of these palace walls," he said in a low, dangerously level tone, "you are practically begging for trouble. I brought you here to protect you from the dangers that lurk outside, and I cannot do so if you keep making your way further and further away from me."

"Can't you?" My gaze met his head-on, and I arched an eyebrow in challenge.

His anger slowly melted away into a twisted sort of amusement—darkly delighted by my defiance. That seemed to please him more than any answer I could have offered.

I sauntered away, my shuddering heart hammering hard against my chest. Hades followed behind me as I stepped into the orchard. "You're a god, Hades. No matter where I go, you could always find me," I said, masking my anxiety with a veneer of nonchalance.

The air halted violently around us and Hades stopped

dead in his tracks. He glowered at me from behind, a savage curl forming on his lips as he leaned closer with a menacing growl. "Oh… yes," he crooned wickedly into my ear. "I could always hunt you down."

My heart threatened to burst out of my chest as I remained resolutely still. "Like you hunt the shadowhorns?" I asked in a spiteful challenge, my voice carrying a façade of boldness despite the trembles that wrecked my very being.

Hades moved closer until his face was mere inches from mine. His fingers lightly traced the curve of my neck while his hot breath ghosted across my cheekbone. "With the same fierceness," he murmured silkily. "Yes."

My knees felt weak as his penetrating stare locked with mine—a mixture of both anxiety and longing building within my chest as an unnamed emotion took root inside me. "And what would you do if you could catch me?"

Without warning he wrapped his strong arms around me, crushing our bodies together until nothing but heated desire separated us. His lips curved into a wicked grin as he whispered darkly in my ear, "I would take pleasure from you until you screamed in sacred agony."

A chill spread up my spine as his presence threatened to consume me. I should have wanted nothing more than to take a step back—to run away. However, I stayed. "I would only run away from you again," I replied softly.

"You would defy a god?" he asked darkly, shooting endless ripples of desire through my being.

I gripped the edges of my dress, steeling myself against his nearness. And refusing to cower in the face of his presence, I managed a swift nod.

He was inches from me now, his lips so close that I could feel them like a whisper on my skin. His captivating scent enveloped me, and my breath caught when he spoke again, the deep rumble of his words washing over me like an invisible caress. "Then I will find you and ruin you—again... and again."

The longing that thrummed through my veins was almost unbearable with him so close. His cold breath felt like a whisper against my neck, tempting me to take one step closer to the fire of his kiss. I shivered in anticipation, trembling for something more than this tantalizing torment.

His strong arms reluctantly dropped away, icy emptiness instantly taking their place. Hades stepped back then, but not far enough that I couldn't still feel his warmth.

An invisible force between us yanked me towards him, beckoning me with an unbreakable draw. It was as if our souls had been entwined since the dawn of time. A voice whispered in my heart that he was my moon and stars, my solace and strength—but he was also the source of all my pain. The startling understanding overwhelmed me and hot tears welled in my eyes.

"Have you found a way to break the rules?" I said, my voice quavering as I tried to forget what I wanted most—*him*.

"Yes," he murmured tenderly, his voice soft yet with a fierce intensity that made me shiver with pleasure.

Possibility and hope surged through me. "You've found a way..." I whispered in sheer awe. "You'll give me back my name?"

He slowly walked away, shoulders slumped in defeat, and sat on the stone bench behind us. "Something like that. Yes."

I settled next to him, my legs crossed and fingers entwined. "What do you mean?" I asked, my voice barely above a whisper. My heart pounded against my chest like a caged beast, but I forced myself to remain seated. My hands shook slightly as I clenched my gown over my knees.

Hades stared ahead, his gaze distant. "As I explained to you before, I do not make these rules. I have no control over such... undesirable designs." His eyes flickered upwards and his lips parted with a sigh.

"Zeus?" I asked, tremulous at the thought of the mighty god's possible involvement. "Is he the one behind this?"

He shook his head slowly, his sadness all but tangible. "My mother Nyx," he said wearily. "She has demanded that you face a challenge."

"But what does she want from me?" I breathed, transfixed.

He released a heavy sigh and finally looked at me. "You must prove yourself worthy of your name through your own strength and will," he said solemnly. "She allows no other way."

"What is this challenge?" I asked, my voice tingling with unease.

"A riddle that will set you off to the beginning of your quest," Hades replied, wounded and subdued. His words sent an icy shiver down my spine. "If victorious, your name shall be yours, and with it, your freedom." His sorrow-filled gaze met mine briefly before he reached into his pocket and drew out a small scrap of parchment bound with a thin red ribbon. He held it out for me without a word.

Trembling, I carefully unwrapped it to find a cryptic message written within:

*An abyss-bound treasure holds secrets and might,*
*In darkness deep, its keeper's out of sight.*
*Steal from shadows to find what's concealed,*
*In a wheel of power, the truth is revealed.*

My brow furrowed, confusion and hope tangling in my core like slender vines. The answer to this riddle was the key that could open the gilded cage of this realm, granting me the freedom I so desperately craved. Yet solving it would also unlock the shackle between myself and Hades, severing us irrevocably.

I hesitated, gripped by indecision. Could I bring myself to turn the key in that lock, sundering us for eternity? My mind recoiled from the thought even as my heart yearned for release.

I closed my eyes, cheeks damp with silent tears. This was a choice no heart should have to make. Yet make it I must, if I wished to see the sun again.

"Hades..." His name slipped past my lips in a whispered plea, lingering in the scented air. But when I lifted my gaze, he had vanished like mist under sunlight.

The lush orchards disappeared with him, the vision crumbling away until only the rain-drenched courtyard remained. Morning's radiant glow faded back to dreary twilight. My resplendent gown transformed into sodden, mud-spattered clothes once more.

I hugged my arms around myself, suddenly cold to my core. The tender interlude in the gardens had been but a beautiful illusion. Now stark reality closed in again, the burdens of the past settling heavily upon my shoulders.

Shivering, I tilted my face up to the weeping sky. The rain mingled with my own tears, which fell steadily, soundlessly. I mourned the lost dawn, my stolen name, my shattered hopes—and the love I had so foolishly believed in.

That love had bloomed like a rose in my heart, full of promise. But it had been nurtured in poisoned soil, and could not survive such darkness. And so it had withered, its last lovely petals scattered by betrayal's bitter wind.

I sank down upon the wet stone, heedless of the chill seeping into my bones. There was no solace to be found, neither in this realm nor in my own heart. Both had been transformed by sorrow into strangers to me.

The dream was over. The light extinguished.

I was alone.

## 51
## PHILLIP

*H*earty laughter filled the air as we sipped on sweet wine and soaked in the divine bliss of the meal before us. I dearly treasured this moment of respite, this fleeting interlude of calmness before we plunged back into our treacherous journey. And yet, I couldn't shake being mindful and cautious, questioning the mysterious goddess' aid. Quickly, I'd learned to trust nothing and no one in this realm of darkness.

But for now, I pushed back those thoughts and relished enjoying Eloise's company. The perils we'd faced head-on during this journey had breached the deliberate distance I'd once forged between us, each new day in this remote waste-land shattering the walls I'd raised around my heart.

We sat across from each other at the rustic wooden table adorned with an array of succulent fruits and a bottle of exquisite wine. The dim glow of the candlelight played upon Eloise's features, accentuating the delicate lines of her face and the glimmer in her eyes. The tension between us hung thick in the air, as tangible as the lightning that crackled in the stormy sky outside.

I cleared my throat, trying to break the silence. "Quite the spread we've got here," I remarked, gesturing towards the colorful banquet.

Eloise smiled, her eyes twinkling mischievously. "We deserve a little indulgence after all we've been through, I think."

I couldn't help but snicker, the sound mingling with the sputter of the hearth. "I suppose we do," I said. "The goddess has been generous to us. And on that note, I must say, you look absolutely divine in your new attire."

A blush colored Eloise's cheeks, and she averted her gaze for a moment, resting on her crisp white shirt and trousers before meeting my eyes again. "Flattery will get you nowhere, Phillip. But I must admit, the Netherworld's eerie charm brings out the best in you."

I raised an eyebrow playfully. "Oh, so you're saying I have a certain *allure* in this gloomy realm?"

She nodded, a taunting smile dancing on her lips. "I guess it's the way you tackle adversity with such courage and determination." Her eyes sparkled with merriment, but all signs of joy faded away as her expression became more serious. "It's quite hard to ignore."

I leaned in closer, my voice lowering to a husky whisper. "And what about you, Eloise?"

Her cheeks flushed pink and she nervously averted her gaze, fair lashes fluttering in the low light. "What *about* me?" she nervously said.

"You hold an allure of your own," I continued unfalteringly. "The way you fearlessly face the unknown, the way your eyes shine with an unbreakable spiritedness in the face of danger... All of it enthralls me." I spoke in all truthfulness.

Eloise's lips parted at my words, her breaths coming faster. Longing flickered in her countenance as she tilted even closer, mirroring my forwardness. Heart pounding, I reached out to brush a windblown curl from her cheek. Her skin was like satin beneath my fingertips.

The air crackled with anticipation, the weight of our unspoken desires hanging between us like a delicate thread. It was a dance of temptation and restraint, a battle against the undeniable attraction that pulsed in our veins.

The fear of loss and the urgency of our mission faded into the background, leaving only the two of us in the present moment.

"Eloise," I voiced with newfound courage, my gaze helplessly roving her face, "may I have this dance?"

She started, surprised, though she quickly recovered with an impish grin. "You know Phillip, I don't think anyone has ever danced to the sound of howling winds and thunderous rain before."

Clasping her hand in mine, I lifted her up and weaved her towards me. Her body moved into mine as if drawn by an invisible string, our hands intertwined delicately like silk ribbons. Holding her close, I pushed back her long mane of light blonde hair and said with determination, "Then let's be the first. Let's create our own melody out of this storm."

The wind wailed its rhapsody around us while our movements harmonized in perfect bliss. Our souls synced in a rhythm only they could comprehend, and for a precious few seconds, we were lost in each other—dancing to the song of our hearts.

At one point, we stopped moving. I did not know when, or for how long we stood standing still, locked in each other's arms. I folded my hands over hers, and brought them to rest against my chest. Our brows slowly touched, and I murmured her name with undying reverence.

"Eloise," I whispered. "Sometimes, in this absurd world of ours, something beautiful blooms from chaos. And you are that beauty. You encourage and challenge me more than anyone ever has. When I am with you, I truly feel alive."

She smiled timidly at my confession, those gentle pink lips reflecting an uncertain happiness I'd scarcely ever witnessed. "And to think, you almost stopped me from joining you on this journey," she uttered softly with a nervous yet playful grin. "We make excellent partners on this quest, and any other." Her hand shook slightly beneath mine.

My tone grew serious as I pulled back briefly. "That's just it. I want us to be *more* than partners on this quest... I want our lives to be entwined, for us to live each moment together."

Her eyes widened in surprise before they glossed with bittersweet tears. The delicate blush that covered her cheeks reached deep into my heart; a heart that had been closed off but was now overflowing with emotion that threatened to burst out of me at any given second.

She grasped my hand tighter as she stared up at me. "You have no idea how long I've waited to hear these words," Eloise managed through trembling lips and breathless sobs. But then her demeanor shifted and she abruptly pulled away, her voice laced with disbelief. "But can you mean them? After all this time... Phillip, I won't be your second choice."

My heartache mirrored hers, and guilt filled me for not having realized or acted sooner on what thrummed between us.

"I've felt this way about you for so long," I began, my hand reaching out to touch hers. "I was only scared of the consequences should I act on my feelings. Everything stood against us from the start—your rank in the Royal Guard, my duty to the Crown... But above all, I could never risk losing you forever." My voice lowered as I trailed off, trying to find the right words. "It has taken me walking in the land of death to finally understand all of it doesn't matter."

Lifting my hand, I cupped the side of her face. "Life is too fleeting, my love. I cannot waste another second of it without you."

"But Aurora is your destined one. Not me," she said in the lowest of voices, sheer pain lacing the words.

My gaze held hers as I spoke earnestly. "It may be fate that chose her—but *I choose you*. In silence, day and night, I have chosen you all along."

Her eyebrows furrowed in confusion. "Then what of this quest?"

"I owe it to Aurora to free her from the Netherworld," I began slowly, taking her hands tightly in mine. "However, it is with you that my heart lies."

"But, all those dances... All those journeys to feasts in distant kingdoms... You hardly ever saw me," she uttered.

I had hurt her deeply, and I was determined to make it right. "Eloise," I breathed, my eyes burning into hers. "I have never been blind to your beauty or your grace. I have seen you all these years, and right now before me, I see everything that I could have had if I had taken a chance on us sooner and I don't—" The words caught in my throat, but I pushed through in a heartfelt whisper, "I don't want to live without you in my life a moment longer."

She looked up at me then, tears spilling down her blushing cheeks. "Do you mean that?" she asked softly.

"My precious love, I swear it," I replied, tears prickling in my eyes as I leaned down to capture her lips with all the pent-up passion that had been building inside me for years. Nothing in the world could ever come between us again.

Our kiss was sweet yet passionate, conveying all of our repressed feelings as we fought to be free from our tumultuous past. Tenderly, I pulled back briefly and brushed away a stray lock of hair from Eloise's face before claiming her mouth again. And this time, my hands explored every inch of her body, tracing and memorizing the warmth she offered as my soul enveloped hers in its depths.

With each passing moment, I sensed her doubts fading until none remained, and I drank in her scent of honey mixed with cinnamon as her hands found their way to my neck and she clung to me tightly.

"Do you want me?" I murmured against her sultry mouth.

"Yes," she replied breathlessly.

Surging forward, I seized her in my arms and raised her high—every touch a shock—then cradled her in my embrace as I stumbled towards our alcove of furs and bliss.

I eased her on the bed, the firelight etching an ethereal halo around her sensual body, granting her skin a warm, glowing sheen. I took a moment to admire her beauty—the way her blonde tresses fanned out over the pillow, the rapid rise and fall of her chest.

"I've always wanted you," I vowed, and I kissed Eloise hungrily, my hands gently peeling off her clothes, exploring her curves as she moaned into my mouth. I teased and tantalized until she was writhing beneath me, her fingers clawing at my back, urging me on.

My own desire raged, an inferno inside me. I tore at my garments impatiently, desperate to feel her skin on mine. As I bared myself, vulnerability and longing swept over me. This was more than just blazing passion—I was unveiling my soul before her.

Her widened eyes gazed upon me, hesitantly flickering her awareness between my face and the length of me. A gentle blush bloomed across her cheeks and she shyly glanced away.

Gently, I turned her chin back. I could feel her tremble, sense her nervousness reflecting my own.

"There's nothing to fear, my love," I whispered, gliding my hand along her jawline. "I would never hurt you."

She nuzzled against my palm, her body relaxing into my touch. "I know," she murmured, desire smoldering in her gaze.

"Do you trust me?" I breathed.

"I trust you…" she said, the tension easing from her frame. Her lips parted slightly as she drew in a shaky breath.

My heart swelled, overflowing with emotion. Ever since we'd arrived in this bleak realm, she'd been my sole comfort amidst the shadows. I would give her the same solace in return, show her that with me she was safe.

"We can stop anytime," I whispered, my racing heart hoping she wouldn't.

Her eyes locked with mine, dark pools of desire banishing any doubts. She reached up, trailing her fingers along my jaw. "I don't want to stop," she said, conviction erasing the tremor in her voice.

At her breathless consent, relief and elation washed over me. My mouth claimed hers, reveling in her softness. I wanted to treasure this moment, draw out each touch and sensation.

Desire gripping my veins, I explored her body with blazing deliberation. Starting at the graceful arch of her neck, I pressed hot kisses to her delicate collarbone and heard the small sigh that escaped her lips. My fingers brushed lightly along her sides before skimming over the curves of her breasts. Her back arched in response, silently begging for more.

A smirk tugged at my mouth as I lingered everywhere but where she wanted me most. I nipped and tantalized until she was mindless with want. My lips and hands teased her body as I descended lower, softly pressing kisses into the curve of her waist. Her gentle insistence sent thrills down my spine, but I refrained from rushing things. A low chuckle escaped me as I felt her anticipation rising beneath my touch.

I finally gave in, my kiss exploring the sweet place of her pleasure, my tongue hungrily giving it the adoration it deserved. Her soul-shattering cries echoed around us as I worshipped her body. Drawing her closer to me, I showered every inch of that sacred place with gentle attention until she was trembling with delight.

My own pleasure intensified, and I took her mouth in a passionate kiss, our tongues tangling together. Her quiet moans of rapture were music to my ears and my lips trailed down her neck and chest as I brought her to the brink of completion again. I wanted her to know how deeply I felt for her, that I would always care for and protect her.

Only when she was ready did I finally settle between her thighs. Our stares locked as I slowly entered her, groaning in sweet agony as her warm tightness enveloped me. Her body trembled against mine as I moved in and out of her unhurriedly, discovering her as I worked my way deeper inside. I took my time, exploring the boundaries of her pleasure and giving her a chance to adjust to me. With each thrust, I brought us closer together, lost in her warmth and sweet caresses.

She moaned my name, her hands tightly gripping my back and her legs wrapping around my waist as we explored each other without fear or hesitation. Her body quivered beneath me as I quickened my pace—we both gasped and moaned in pleasure as our passion erupted in a wave of blissful ecstasy.

We moved together in perfect harmony, her sensuous curves molding to the hard planes of my body. My own passion rose inside me, the tension building until I was barely able to hold onto control.

Trembling in godless delight, our breaths came in

quick, shallow bursts. Steadily, I moved inside her, increasing my pace as her breathing grew faster, her pleasure rising with each thrust. And as I sensed her climbing towards the peak of delight, I allowed her to reach it instants before mine followed—a rush of ecstasy blazing through my being in waves, pulsing through my veins as I shuddered against her.

When the flood of sensation began to fade, I collapsed beside her, my chest heaving in pleasant exhaustion. Her eyes were half-lidded with bliss as she looked up at me, a small smile playing across her lips.

"That was…" I whispered, between panting breaths.

"Everything I've dreamed and longed for," she finished for me, and cupping the side of my face, she pulled me near, and pressed her lips against mine. And I seized the chance to steal from her a dozen slow kisses. Each one, a symbol of my endless devotion.

We lay there in silence, our bare bodies entwined together in perfect bliss. The room echoed with fading sighs of passion, the air still heady with the scent of our lovemaking.

I lazily trailed my fingers through Eloise's golden tresses as she rested her head on my chest. Her skin was flushed, glowing with spent desire.

Overcome with emotion, I pressed a kiss to her damp temple.

*"I don't think there's ever been a time when I haven't loved you,"* I whispered against her brow, echoing the words she'd spoken as we first stepped into this journey.

Eloise tilted her face up to meet my gaze, eyes shimmering. "Oh, Phillip…" Her lips brushed against mine in a feather-light caress.

I shivered at the soft touch, rekindled desire coursing through me. I drew her closer, one hand tangling in her silken tresses while the other spanned the delicate curve of her waist.

"Even before I knew what this feeling was," I continued, eyes boring into hers, "my heart recognized you as its missing piece, its one true home."

She gazed up at me through lowered lashes. "Shut up and make me yours completely," she whispered in a sultry tone.

Unable to resist, I captured her lips in a searing kiss. She melted against me with a throaty moan, returning my passion twofold. Our kisses deepened, speaking wordless vows of longing and devotion.

My hands roamed her supple curves as our bodies molded together, and when we finally parted for breath, our chests were heaving. Eloise trailed her fingers down the line of my jaw, eyes hooded with desire.

"I need you, Phillip," she murmured, voice laden with lust.

My blood heated at the sultry plea.

The night awaited, full of tantalizing promise. Our lips met again and again between murmured endearments as we gave ourselves to each other, erasing all distance between us, until we were one flesh. One soul.

We loved with aching thoroughness, expressing with hands and lips what words could not convey. I worshipped Eloise with touch and taste, learning the beauty of her form until it was etched into my soul.

Each kiss was a line of poetry, a verse in a love letter I wrote on her skin. And I sought to compose a masterpiece, one that would sing of my devotion through all the ages. One that would remain engraved on her heart if ever we were forced apart.

# BEAUTY

The first crimson streaks of twilight seeped through the thick canopy of oaks in the Netherworld as I stepped into the courtyard. A hazy light settled in the air as the chirps of crickets waned and birdsongs stirred inside the treetops.

Hades had offered me a way out, and I could barely wrap my head around the kindness of his heart. He'd been cruel to me, no doubt in that. Time and time again, he'd vanished into the night, fleeing from his feelings. Each time, wounding mine. His lies and deceptions were too many to count, yet inexplicably, something inside me wanted to believe in him again.

My heels clattered against the cobblestones as I paced through the courtyard. I moved forward blindly, desperately hoping that my restless pacing could somehow help me solve the riddle quickly. But part of me still secretly wished for Hades to appear in the garden maze.

I shook my head in an effort to clear my mind and focus on the task. *"An abyss-bound treasure holds secrets and might. In darkness deep, its keeper's out of sight..."* I mumbled as I hurried along the treacherous path. "In darkness deep." As I scoured my surroundings for hints, a chill scurried down my spine—darkness lurked in *every* corner of this realm.

The memory of his obsidian eyes burning into mine filled me with longing and fear simultaneously. Hades had asked me to trust him, but how could I? If only I could find a way out of this realm and restore my name and freedom without leaving him behind...

I froze. My skin prickled with alarm, each nerve ending screaming a warning. The air sizzled with tension, like the silence of a storm before the strike of lightning. Dread twisted around me, icy fingers encircling my spine as it crept through my body and settled in the pit of my stomach.

I crept slowly towards the end of the hedge maze, my heart hammering in my chest. When I stumbled into a clearing, I stopped short. There was a figure standing there. Her silhouette was a stark contrast against the pale marble, draped in wisps of ivy and moss. At first glance, she seemed like a sculpture delicately carved from the finest stone. But as I approached her, I finally recognized her for what she truly was.

The woman's jade eyes glittered with triumph as she held my stare. Her lips curved up into a sly smirk, and an uneasy chill snaked through me.

"So here you are," she said, her voice smooth as silk. "What an honor to finally meet a legend." The woman pushed herself away from the fountain's pillar, her predatory gaze taking me all in.

I furrowed my brow, my words edged with suspicion. "I've not seen you here before. What brings you to Hades' palace?"

She stalked around me in a slow circle, eyes blazing with a strange power. "Oh, my dear, I could ask the same of you." Her voice was smooth and heavily accented, which only heightened the thrill of danger that crept up my spine. "Are you so brave as to march into a monster's den?"

I eyed her cautiously. The woman was divinely composed, like an ancient goddess born of earthen mint and verdant moss. Each jade-streaked dark lock of hair was perfectly placed, framing a face of sharp angles and curves that were softened by a captivating hint of green in her skin. Not quite human.

Despite her unique beauty and the subtle allure of her enticing perfume, the ancient and mystifying aura of darkness about her unsettled me to the bone. Something sinister lurked within.

"Who are you?" I finally forced out.

Her lips turned up in a smirk as she glided closer still. "What does it matter?" she said with a voice like honey and lightning. With a light shrug, she added with indolence, "I am here."

A shudder rippled down my being as she let out an insidious laugh. "So, you're the one who has caught Hades' eye and stolen my beloved's heart? I'm almost envious of you, dreaming of taking my place."

My façade of indifference faltered, but I still managed to keep up the pretense. "I assure you, I have no intention of taking your place—whoever you are. All I seek is to reclaim my name."

The woman's gaze sharpened as her eyes scanned me. "A name is such a fickle thing—so easily twisted and manipulated by those in power." Her chiseled nose wrinkled in clear disdain. "But tell me, what does *he* call you?"

My mouth was dry as I forced myself to answer. "Beauty."

The fury that crossed her features was unmistakable, unfathomable; although she did her best to conceal it. "Do you truly believe you can unravel the secrets of the Netherworld and reclaim your identity?" she asked coolly. "Such a feat has never been attempted before. Yet here you stand."

I lifted my chin, courage swelling in my chest. "I may not have all the answers yet, but I am determined to find them."

Her lips curved in a furtive smile as she stepped closer, invading my personal space. "Ah, you truly are a naive one, *Beauty*. Hades may have fallen for your grace, but that does not grant you any power here." Her voice dropped to a whisper, her wicked gaze roving my features. "Do not forget —you're a mere mortal in a realm of gods... *and monsters*." Her eyes flickered, sharp pupils stretching high like a serpent's.

Although taken aback, I held my ground, refusing to let her recognize any fear in my stance. "I understand the obstacles I'm up against. But your attempts to threaten me won't work."

Her crisp laughter pierced the courtyard, a haunting sound that echoed off the stony walls. "Threats?" she said with feigned surprise. "Oh no, that should be the least of your concerns. The secrets of this realm could make even the bravest quiver. Are you sure you can withstand the darkness awaiting you?"

I took a step back, putting some distance between us. "Maybe I'm not fully prepared, but I'm willing to face whatever comes my way."

Minthe's eyes bore into me, her expression a mix of disbelief and disdain. "We shall see, Beauty. We shall see if you can resist the trials that await you. Just remember, in the realm of shadows, not everything is as it seems."

"Even so..." I breathed, "I must prevail." There was no other choice.

Her laughter echoed through the courtyard, cold and bitter. "Oh, Beauty," she gasped, her amusement swiftly fading away. "Hades is not one to release his grip so easily.

He keeps secrets within secrets." This last part, she drawled, hissing like a viper.

Her words deeply unsettled me. But I refused to waver. "I will find my answers," I said, determined.

The woman started, confused. "And how will you do that?" she asked, but before I could utter a sound, she continued. "Oh, don't tell me. He's offered you a challenge?" Slightly, she leaned towards me, her brows lifting softly.

I started. How could she know? Swallowing the knot in my throat, I nodded. My walls suddenly crumbled. "He gave me a riddle," I admitted quietly. "He said it's the only way for me to reclaim my name and find my way home."

She smiled—a guileful, dark grin—as her words filled the air. "I know this story so well..." Then suddenly, vines of dark green ivy appeared from nowhere and wrapped around her wrists until they interweaved, tightly enough to make her skin pale white beneath them. "I know how it ends," she said quietly. With purposeful movements, she lifted her arms so that her tied wrists caught the light. "You see here? I've played Hades' game too many times."

Shock raced through me, paralyzing me in place as her warning settled around us. This woman had been deceived by Hades more than once. Who was to say he wouldn't do the same to me?

As she held back her amusement, the vines binding her wrists disappeared, leaving a golden pattern traced on her skin. "But perhaps... you might be able to win this one," she said thoughtfully, taking a step closer. Ice skittered down my nape when her lithe hand settled on my shoulder, and a tingle raced up my neck as her cold fingers trailed along its slope. "With my help, of course."

She pulled away, a piece of parchment pressed tightly in her hand. "Oh, I do love riddles..." she purred before unrolling it and beginning to read.

My stomach twisted as I realized my own parchment with the riddle was gone from my pocket. "Why would you help me?" I asked hesitantly, but she gave no answer.

"Well, *that* was easy," she said with a hint of disappointment, discarding the parchment fast.

Suspiciousness churned in my gut, but my need for answers burned brighter than my caution. "Tell me, what is the answer to the riddle?" I pressed.

A small smirk curved her lips. "Your task awaits in the maze of shadows," she said, resolved. "Beneath it lies a hidden path. It is through the Veiled Forest that you shall find the key to your identity." Batting a pair of long and delicate fingers in the air, she added, "Follow the winding passage in the woods until you reach the ancient oak tree atop the hill. There, beneath its roots, lies the name that you seek."

I could barely believe what I was hearing—yet somehow, I knew it must be true.

The woman stepped aside, pointing the way to the Veiled Forest. "Quickly, now," she urged. "There's no time to waste."

I swallowed hard, then sucked in a deep breath, garnering my resolve. But before I could take a step forward, a voice thundered through the courtyard, freezing me in my tracks.

"STOP!"

The voice belonged to Chronos, the god of time, who appeared before me in a blaze of golden light. Even the woman shied away from his commanding presence and piercing gaze.

Chronos fixed her with an uncompromising look. "Minthe, your deceit ends here. You will not mislead Beauty."

"Minthe?" I echoed with a frown.

"You should not be here!" Chronos continued, pointing

at her with a denouncing finger. "Hades banished you from these grounds for a reason."

With those words, Minthe's mask of composure finally cracked and her jade eyes flashed with fury and dread. "Chronos, you have no right to interfere!" she snarled, revealing sharp-edged ivory fangs. "I'm simply offering help."

"By deliberately sending Beauty to the minotaur's den?" Chronos spat, infuriated. "Your help is tainted by jealousy, Minthe. Beauty's path is her own, and you will hinder it no further." His tone was firm and final. "Leave now or I shall cast you to the barren lands, where you will wilt away into oblivion." At this, Chronos took one step ahead of me and brandished a resplendent golden sword and shield, promising the fiercest battle if Minthe dared oppose him.

I shuddered in dread, realization washing over me. Minthe had almost succeeded in leading me to the vilest fate in the minotaur's lair. When I shot her a glare, the nymph quietly slunk away, anger emanating off her like smoke from a fire.

My focus then shifted to Chronos. Appreciation flooded me. "Thank you," I said sincerely.

He rewarded me with a warm smile and an even warmer gaze from those wise green eyes. "You are destined for greatness, Beauty." He nodded sagely. "But beware... Many will seek to stand in your path. Do not let them discourage you. Your journey has only just begun." His iron grip closed over my arm in reassurance. "You won't be alone. I will be watching over you."

I sighed in relief and refocused my determination on the path ahead of me—a treacherous road, but one that I was now ready to take on with newfound strength. The riddle awaited, and so did the key to unlocking my fate.

## 53

## PHILLIP

*A*s the sun dipped below the horizon, spilling dazzling oranges and gold throughout the sky, I knew our time was coming to an end. The stone walls were illuminated by soft flickering candlelight while inviting aromas of sweet fruits and delectable treats filled the warm air. Our eyes connected in one last shared glance full of sorrow for that which was ending and joy for that which had been found.

"Are you ready?" she asked, her voice barely audible, like a whisper in the wind. Eloise's ice-blue eyes held mine captive as she searched for my answer.

My hands entwined with hers, and I pulled them close to my chest, gently bringing her towards me. We locked brows as I breathed out softly, "With you by my side, I'm ready for anything."

A hair's breadth away from each other now, I sealed her mouth with mine in one long and slow kiss. Unfathomable, was the newfound freedom of having spoken our truth aloud. Knowing we both reciprocated these feelings gave us strength to face even a dozen Netherworlds with no fear of consequence. But such awareness drove me to fight for our future together more than ever before; a future that awaited us in the Realm of Man.

Eloise stepped back, her fingers grazing the grip of her sword before securing it in its sheath. "It's practically downhill from here," she murmured, an edge to her voice. A mischievous glint sparkled in her gaze as she glanced at me over her shoulder. "*Literally*," she added with a smirk. "I've seen the palace turrets."

Delight danced across my expression. "Are you being serious?" I asked, barely containing my enthusiasm. "But, when was this? Last night... We were—"

"I'm an early riser," Eloise confessed with a shrug, a hint of amusement touching the edges of her lips.

Before I could refrain, I strode forward and seized her waist, drawing her body against mine. "You'd walk away from our bed and leave me?" I growled softly, my lips hovering above hers in anticipation of a sinfully sweet kiss.

"Don't worry, my love..." she whispered breathlessly into our shared air. "I'll always be there to protect you."

A quiet laugh escaped us before our lips met in a passionate kiss. My hand glided along her soft jawline to cup her cheek as we savored the moment, knowing that once we ventured outside, it would become life or death as we battled through the hostile terrain.

As we parted briefly, my brows rose at the challenge. "Downhill, you say?"

"Mm-hmm." Eloise nodded, her eyes brightening with eagerness. "We're nearly there."

I clenched my fists and gave her a bold smile. "Then let's see this adventure through."

Her countenance brightened in sheer delight as she stepped back, heading towards the entrance. "I studied the terrain last night, and I've figured out the way in," she said, her confidence clear.

I stood there in silence, marveling at her, in awe of the tenacity that coursed through her veins. Her skill and resolve on the battleground were undeniable; it was her truest passion and obsession, and I loved her for it more than anything.

The corners of my mouth twitched as I shook my head slightly. "Of course, you did," I murmured, then stepped forward to meet her at the threshold, and together we set off.

We plunged into the dense woods once more, our senses heightened in sheer alertness. We'd left the safety of our haven behind and were now facing the unknown. Our steps faltered, though we moved forward unsurely. The forest air seemed to press against my skin, and even I could feel the unnatural stillness of the woods. My heart raced, and my throat went dry with trepidation.

"Eloise," I said softly, unable to keep my unease contained any longer. "I think we should—"

But before I could complete my sentence, a low rumble filled the air around us. It was distant at first, but quickly grew louder until it shook the very ground beneath our feet. We froze in place, exchanging wary glances.

We were so close now—close enough to know that whatever was out there, it was watching us intently. Still, we journeyed deeper into the darkness, fear no longer an obstacle, only pushed aside by courage and determination.

The rumbling grew louder and more intense as we ventured further down a sinuous path shrouded in trees that seemed to come alive with each passing second. Shadows from hidden creatures slithered between the foliage as Eloise pulled me closer against her body for support.

And then, a sudden stillness settled in the forest, and our steps came to a stop.

There, amidst the verdant leaves, stood a creature that embodied both grace and power—a magnificent stag, twice the size of any beast we'd ever seen. Its coat shimmered with an otherworldly sheen, while mighty antlers branched from its regal head. And its eyes, like liquid gold, held an ancient wisdom filled with untamed spirit.

"Look at that," I whispered in awe and excitement. "Have you ever seen anything so extraordinary?"

Beside me, her eyes gleaming with wonder, she nodded.

But our shared admiration was short-lived, as bleak terror swept through our beings when the stag began stomping its hooves menacingly against the ground. Without conscious thought, I stepped forward, drawing my sword as I prepared for a fierce confrontation.

But Eloise sprang forward, her grip like iron on my arm, halting me before I could raise my blade against the beast. She slowly pivoted around to face the majesty of the creature before us, and shook her head in warning. "I don't think a sword can get in the way of a beast like that," she breathed, her voice laced with fear.

The moment the stag's eyes met ours, a deathly silence descended upon the woods. I could feel the air thicken between us, as if nature itself was holding its breath. But then, with a heart-stopping roar came a sea of stags from all sides—a frenzied horde with wild and relentless eyes.

The beasts snorted violently, their sharp hooves pounding hard against the earth. Sheer dread coursed through me as my mind raced for a plan—any plan—but nothing came. We were hopelessly outnumbered and outmatched, yet these magnificent creatures barred our way to safety.

"Eloise," I shouted, my veins running hot with shock. "It's either fight our way out or find it!"

A roar of battle cries filled the air, and Eloise yanked me away from the looming danger. As soon as we were far enough, she commanded with a calm, yet firm tone, "We must leave now!"

Gathering whatever courage I had left, I followed her lead into the woods. Quickly, the forest had become a living nightmare, every rustle of branches and crack of twigs driving terror deeper into our hearts. We ran as fast as we could, fear coursing through us in waves as the wild baying of our pursuers echoed closer.

When the rocky face of a mountain towered before us, Eloise and I were forced to stop. "It's a dead end," I said, my eyes searching the surrounding trees for any sign of escape, but there was none.

My head snapped up to the chilling chorus of snarls. Wrathful stags emerged, advancing slowly in formation.

"Remind me to add *'surviving a forest horde'* to our ever-growing list of adventures," Eloise said wryly, her voice laced with steel as she gripped her sword.

That made me laugh, even as the antlers around us glinted dangerously in the weak light. "Duly noted, Eloise," I said, readying my bow and arrow. "Just make sure we live to tell the tale first!"

Without hesitation, she stepped forward, her every movement saturated with courage. I could feel it radiating from her body like heat. We would survive—or die trying.

The horde advanced closer and closer, their guttural roars rumbling like thunder through the air. My heart was racing as I glanced around—we were *vastly* outnumbered. Then my gaze settled on a single stag standing nobly amidst the rest. His antlers gleamed with a fierce light beneath the moon, and his eyes were sharp and wise. I knew he was their leader.

The monsters encircled us with a relentless intensity that made my skin prickle.

I steeled myself, and taking aim with my bow and arrow, I muttered under my breath, "That's the one we want." My fingers trembled as the horde closed in on us. It felt like the end. Even with my bow drawn taught, I could feel my own fear start to rise. But then something miraculous happened— a light started to seep from the forest depths, sending a spark of hope through my veins.

Scintillating light beams speared through the trees, dispersing the monsters like dust in the wind. Suddenly, three figures emerged from the enchanted woods. I knew them well. I'd met them when we'd first arrived on this island of death.

"The dryads!" Eloise whispered in utter relief.

The one I recognized as their leader lifted her hand into the air, and a path of moss and stones materialized in the forest, leading away from danger.

"Thank you," I said, bowing my head in respect as I stood before the deity, towering over me several feet high. "We owe you our lives."

The dryad nodded regally. "The woods always protect their own," she said softly, her preternatural voice sounding like a gentle breeze. "Remember—tread here with respect, and the forest shall be your ally."

And just like that, they vanished back into the trees. Eloise and I were left standing, awe-struck over how beauty and peril could coexist in death's realm.

My heart was still pounding, but I managed a smile as I turned to Eloise. "Another grand adventure for us to add to our list," I said. "I wonder if the goddess had anything to do with this."

A soft smile tugged at her lips as her eyes twinkled with hope and worry. "I don't know. But I'm sure we'll find out," she murmured.

"Come on. Let's go!" She charged ahead and I followed close behind, ready for whatever awaited us.

# BEAUTY

*I* should have known it was too much to expect—to hope—that Hades would be there. But it wasn't Hades waiting in the dining hall for me that evening, stunning in regal blue and gold. It was Hypnos.

He flashed me a smile as I descended the last flight of stairs. His body leaned against the doorjamb as his eyes tracked my every movement. "How fitting, the name he gave you," he murmured pensively. "Your beauty rivals the splendor of the gods."

My cheeks burned, even though he'd meant it only as an observation—a detached appraisal typical of all deities. They appreciated the world without passion, without fervor, without *human* emotion.

"Impressive, how news spreads like wildfire in the Netherworld," I murmured, flustered as I glided a hand down the silky golden sheen of my train. I couldn't resist the temptation. The way it glimmered in the candlelight was simply enchanting.

A scowl creased his brow. "My dearest, such bitterness in you is most unbecoming." Without hesitation, Hypnos reached forward and took my hand in his. Inching closer, his hazel eyes locked on mine as he sternly said, "I won't allow it."

I blinked, confused as he stepped away from the doorway. As we moved down the corridor, I caught the alluring fragrance of his skin, a burst of invigorating citrus mingled with a hint of spicy warmth, lively and energetic. It was like a breath of crisp, sun-kissed air on a spring morning, awakening my senses and igniting a spark of anticipation.

"Where are we going?" I asked, unable to contain my curiosity.

"I've arranged a special dinner for us," he answered, pausing at the terrace that opened into the garden. "Here. In the courtyard."

Our eyes met for a moment in understanding. He smiled at me with tenderness. "Perhaps it will help lighten your mood?" He spoke warmly, teasingly, as he squeezed my hand before guiding us down the steps of the stone staircase.

When we reached the bottom, the breathtaking view of the lake spread out before us, and on its island at the end of the bridge, stood the pavilion where we'd once danced together.

As I set foot onto the ancient structure, my gaze was captured by a wondrous sight. Twinkling fairy lights lined the bridge, guiding us through the velvet night like stars come to earth. Vibrant blossoms adorned the parapets, a riot of color amid cold stone. The perfume of roses enveloped me, mixing with the scent of moonflowers and lilies that shone like pearls beneath the endless sky.

The pavilion came alive as we arrived, the silken curtains swaying in the cool breeze, and a thousand candles blazing like stars. The shadows they cast moved across the columns in a captivating luminescence.

A feast of delights awaited me inside. Sparkling crystal

glasses, gleaming silver cutlery, and pristine porcelain plates were laid out before me in glorious array. Jewel-bright fruits glistened beside chocolates and pastries draped with swirling spun-sugar lace, their sweet scents wrapping around me like a fragrant embrace, daring me to sate my desires.

I drew a trembling breath, spellbound by the splendor. "It's... just like a dream," I whispered in awe.

"It very well may be, for dreams are my specialty," Hypnos purred in my ear, sending tremors across my skin.

I whirled around to face him, dread coiling in my stomach despite the admiration that flickered in my chest. "Won't it bother *him*?" I whispered, my voice shattering our blissfulness like glass against stone.

Hypnos narrowed his eyes as he comprehended what I was asking. His gaze gradually became soft and gentle, almost innocent, as he asked quietly, "Hades?"

My palms started to sweat as a wave of dread consumed me, yet I forced back the emotion that attempted to break free from its tethers.

He let out an audible sigh, guiding me towards the table with firm hands. "It's not likely," he mumbled. "He knows me better than my own shadow does. He understands I would do anything to make you happy."

A whirlwind of emotion blew through me at his words, fierce and powerful like a hurricane. I stopped walking near the pavilion's columns, causing Hypnos to cease as well. Our eyes locked for an eternity before I spoke again. "Would you...?" I whispered, "Do anything to make me happy?"

The corner of his lips curved upwards in a gentle smile and he nodded without hesitation. "Anything," he assured me.

An unexpected idea suddenly came into my head—a plan that might just work if Hypnos agreed to it. Taking a deep breath, I stepped closer to him and finally uttered, "Hypnos... I need your mind."

His eyes widened in shock and bemusement, his usually serene face filled with alarm. "What did you say?" he croaked out softly. "You need my... *mind*?"

"I have a riddle," I declared, and finally the trepidation left his body as understanding dawned on him. "Perhaps you can assist me in solving it."

He scoffed in disbelief. "*Perhaps*?" Hypnos shook his head. "My dearest Beauty, your lack of faith in me is cruelly disheartening."

I mustered a small smile. "I'll rephrase," I said, my fingers skimming lightly over his arm. "I'm *sure* you can solve it. Please, help me?"

"We can discuss it over dinner," he suggested, pulling out a chair for me. His fingers brushed my wrist as I sat down, and I felt a strange jolt of electricity shoot up my spine. "But why ask me? Why not Hades?" he continued as he took the place in front of me, swiftly sweeping off the table a glass brimming with ambrosia. The liquid shimmered like diamonds in the light. "I'm sure if you ask, Hades will be more than willing to offer his help."

It was a reasonable suggestion, but how could I possibly explain myself without sounding foolish? My cheeks burned at the mere thought of it. In the end, all I could do was shrug my shoulders and say, "I highly doubt it." My gaze drifted down as I studied the desserts laid before me. Choosing amidst them seemed almost impossible. "He's too... too intimidating."

Hypnos laughed softly, his hazel eyes twinkling as he lifted the glass to me. "But surely you must know there is nothing to fear from Hades," he murmured after taking a sip himself. "Not for you, at least."

I glanced down shyly, my cheeks flushing. "Well..." I replied quietly, tipping some of the drink into my mouth, "he's earned his reputation for a reason."

We shared a knowing look before bursting into laughter.

Hypnos gave me a knowing look before we both burst into laughter. When we finally settled down again, he reached for the glimmering tray nearby. Resting on top was the most perfect dessert I had ever seen—an intricate combination of exquisite textures and layers. The cake's golden crust was crisp and inviting, beckoning us closer with its subtle chocolate topping shimmering like liquid silk.

An enigmatic smile tugged at his lips as he placed the tray between us. "Why do I feel there's more to this than what you're sharing?" he asked, narrowing his hawkish eyes. As he sliced into the masterpiece, a tantalizing fragrance wafted through the air, filling my senses with anticipation. Silky smooth vanilla cream mingled with whispers of fragrant spices, enveloping my senses in a dance of sweet ecstasy.

"The truth is, Hades is either unable or unwilling to help," I said, my hands curling into fists with frustration. I glanced up at Hypnos, who pushed his dish forward served with the glistening slice of chocolate cake, in a silent gesture of solidarity. Without a word, I accepted the offer, though I was unsure how I would get the food down.

"It doesn't matter anyway," I spat out bitterly. "He's a lying, cruel god who takes wicked pleasure in playing with my heart—and hunts shadowhorns, on top of it. He deserves nothing but my contempt."

His eyes flew open in shock. "Whoa!" Hypnos started, an appeasing hand held in the air. "That's a lot to unpack in a single breath!"

I let out a humorless laugh and I blushed, wishing I was invisible instead.

"What do you mean, he won't help?" he pressed.

I drew in a quivering breath. "I suppose he's yet to tell you this," I began. "His mother sent me the riddle. It's my only hope of reclaiming my name and my freedom." I paused, my throat tight with emotion as I recalled that excruciating moment, having Hades so near, and yet holding back from embracing him and reliving our last kiss. "He just gave me the riddle and vanished without saying a single word. I haven't seen him since."

"I can imagine why," he mumbled, raising a finely groomed eyebrow.

I flinched. "What?"

"Beauty," he said in a low voice, and I felt a stab of guilt at his use of my assigned name. "Surely you can see how much this hurts him? He cares deeply for you, and yet, he's offered you an escape from this realm—an act completely unheard of! My dearest, Nyx is darkness personified. If Hades got that riddle out of her... believe me, it was not easily done. I'm sure it cost him dearly."

The blood froze in my veins. "I didn't realize..." I breathed, but Hypnos carried on.

"And Hades—hunting shadowhorns?" Hypnos winced skeptically. "My dear, I'm sure you're quite wrong about that too. Shadowhorns are sacred guardians of the Netherworld. They keep the souls of the living at bay, consuming them to protect our hallowed lands. Hades would never sacrifice one of his loyal guardians; they're far too dear to him."

I swallowed past the tight knot in my throat. "They *feed* from the souls of the living?" I said incredulously. My heart twisted at his revelation, as I understood then that Hades had sacrificed the stag, not out of sport, but to spare *me* from its maw.

As everything fell into place, I was reminded of how

much suffering had been etched on Hades' expression upon that day. The kill had weighed heavily on his soul, and he'd never spoken about it. Not once. No matter how cruelly I'd tormented him with my harshness after that day.

Tears pricked my eyes as I recoiled in disbelief. Oh, I had misjudged him in almost every conceivable way, and understanding he'd sacrificed so much for me shattered me to the core. Hades had loved me from the start, and had proven his love more than once—only I'd been too blind to realize it.

"My lady?" Hypnos asked cautiously. "Are you all right?"

I swallowed hard, willing myself back into the present. "I'm not sure I am…" I mumbled, pressing my fingers against my lips.

Hypnos cleared his throat. "But since we're here," he carried on, unfolding the napkin and laying it on his lap. "Tell me about this riddle." He then dragged a fruit plate closer to him, picking at the berries with lazy fingers.

I sucked in a deep breath. "The riddle," I said. Mindlessly, the words spilled from my lips, my heart too rattled to focus on little else. I had no choice but to force myself to focus and steel my heart against its anxieties.

With a shaking hand, I retrieved the tiny scroll Hades had given me and held it out to Hypnos. He took it gently, brows furrowing as he unrolled the parchment and scanned the cryptic verse written within.

*"An abyss-bound treasure holds secrets and might…"* Hypnos echoed with a frown, adorable as his mind whirred, spurred by the challenge to his divine ego. *"In darkness deep, its keeper's out of sight."* He remained silent for what felt like an eternity, until finally, a small smirk curled the corner of his lips.

"A treasure in the dark abyss," he said thoughtfully as if speaking to himself. "Of course." Hypnos nodded to himself, a knowing amber glint burning in his eyes.

I leaned forward in my chair, unable to remain still any longer. "Do you have the answer?" I blurted out eagerly.

But Hypnos merely shook his head, that knowing glint still in his gaze as he rose from his chair. He gestured for me to follow him, and with a mysterious air, he said, "I've got something infinitely better."

# PHILLIP

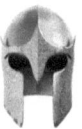

"*I*f there's one more monster for us to slay, I'm afraid I'll scream," Eloise growled from behind me as we trudged downhill. "It feels like it's been centuries since our last skirmish! My sword thirsts for divine blood…"

"Your lust for battle will do nothing but bring danger your way," I murmured, my blade hacking through brambles and thickets blocking our path. "The gods have all the time in the world. Whatever they're doing, wherever they are, they could be planning something even now…" My steps came to a sudden stop.

Eloise and I stood at the edge of the veiled woods, greeted by a sight that held us captive. Hades' domain spread out before us like a tapestry, a magnificent courtyard leading up to an obsidian lake that reflected the stars above. The air around us was saturated with dark energy, sending shivers down my spine.

"Is this it?" I whispered, awestruck by the dark grandeur before us. "Have we finally reached the palace?"

"I believe we have," she answered solemnly.

"Let's go closer and see if we can find a way inside," I

suggested, my voice barely above a whisper. "We must seek out the weakest point."

She nodded her agreement and we began to move forward when suddenly, an almighty voice boomed through the night air.

"HALT! INTRUDERS!"

The ground rumbled beneath us as Hades himself appeared in all his fearsome glory—darkness and power incarnate. His eyes blazed with the fires of the Netherworld, with such intensity that almost seared my very soul.

"How dare you enter my domain?" he snarled. An invisible force swayed his locks of raven hair as he straightened, tall and proud in faultless black burnished armor. Imposing wings stretched out behind him, vast and dark, a tangible presence that weighed heavy on the air around us.

But I would not cower before him—this fiend who'd come into our realm and stolen my dearest Aurora away under the veil of darkness. I braced myself, summoning the courage that could only be reaped by the wildest fury, and brandishing my sword, I spoke. "I've come to claim Princess Aurora Stonewall!" The words left my throat in a roar of grief.

Hades' lips curled into a cruel smirk as he scoffed. "I will never allow it," he spat, venom dripping from his words. His cold eyes gleamed with hatred as he continued, "I have done everything in my power to see you fall. *Why won't you die,* human?" He sneered in contempt, reveling in his own wickedness.

"I have overcome your traps, finished your beasts, and I will not rest until Aurora has been returned to her rightful place on the Stone Throne with her people!" I righteously declared, my voice steady and unwavering despite the oppressive atmosphere that enveloped us.

His dark gaze narrowed at me, his fury burning hotter

than the depths of Tartarus. "Your arrogance will be your downfall, mortal," Hades snarled. "I will crush you for daring to tarnish my realm with your presence. I will doom your soul and your swordswoman's to a life of eternal banishment in the barren lands. Your eyes shall never glimpse the foothills of Elysium." A maleficent laugh sailed through his lips, shooting a shiver down my spine as he continued, "But before I've doomed you, I will give you the slow and painful death that you deserve…"

My heart pounded as his sinister words filled me with courage—and dread. Taking a breath, I met his gaze with determination. "You speak too much, Hades," I challenged him, brandishing my sword in silent defiance. "Face me now. Just you and me—I'm as ready as I'll ever be."

Hades snickered again, the sound sending spikes of terror through my body. "Arrogant human," he jeered. "You presume to be worthy to stand in my presence. My guardians shall take care of you."

But before Hades could unleash his guardians upon us, a voice reverberated through the woods. "He's not alone, Prince Hades," came the mighty clamor of the goddess herself, stepping forward from the shadows like a wraith.

Hades' eyes widened in surprise. A hush descended on the spot as all eyes turned to the goddess, her figure illuminating with an inner light that was more than divine—unfathomably beautiful.

"Demeter? What business have you here?" he demanded.

"Demeter?" Eloise mumbled in shock beside me, eyes wide.

At last, the goddess' identity clicked into place. She who loved nature and the harvest—no wonder the forest had aided us. Eloise and I owed her a greater debt than we knew.

The corners of Demeter's lips curled into a mysterious smile. "My business is my own," she said coolly, her frighteningly powerful gaze never straying from Hades. "The human has stated his demand. The princess is his betrothed, his fated love. You cannot stand in the way of fate."

An angry red stained Hades' face as fire ignited behind his brown irises. The earth trembled beneath our feet in response to his wrath as he clenched his fists and growled with an intensity that was both feral and divine. "I can and I will," he spat out between gritted teeth. "Your meddling has cost me great losses before, Demeter. You know very well there's a sole reason I've not once raised a finger against you —but if you insist on interfering in my affairs any further, you too shall suffer my ire. Now *go away!*"

The tension between them crackled in the air like lightning while Eloise and I stood ready, our resolve unwavering even when faced with two deities at war. It seemed inevitable that their clash would tear apart heavens and earth alike.

The air was electrified with anticipation, the atmosphere thick and pulsing. Hades and Demeter stood facing each other, their combined power clashing like two opposing armies ready for war. Tension hung heavily in the air, like a brewing storm on the horizon.

Demeter stepped forward, her voice unwavering and full of courage. "Hades, you cannot deny the bond between Phillip and Aurora. It is written in the stars, destined to be," she stated, unrelenting. "Release her from your clutches and let them fulfill their fated bond!"

"You've made your choice," he answered darkly. "Combat it shall be."

I watched as the gods engaged in their epic battle, the very ground beneath us quaking in response to their divine powers.

Demeter summoned a shield of foliage to protect herself, vines stretching through the air like hungry tentacles, while leaves spun around her in a swirling cyclone.

Hades, clad in his burnished black armor, exuded an air of ruthless confidence. With a flick of his wrist, dark shadows coalesced around him, forming a shield that absorbed the blows of Demeter's elemental attacks. He retaliated with bolts of malevolent darkness that shot towards Demeter's shield with deadly accuracy.

With every clash of forces, shockwaves reverberated throughout the forest, trees shuddering and birds taking flight in an explosion of terrified feathers. The very wood seemed alight with ethereal energy, magical sparks cascading through the tangled foliage.

"Your attempts to defy me are futile, Demeter," Hades sneered, his voice dripping with venom. "The Netherworld is mine, and nothing you conjure from your precious forest can stand against the might of my power."

Demeter's eyes narrowed, her voice resonating with authority. "The forces of nature are eternal, Hades. They will never bow to your darkness!"

With a wave of her hand, Demeter summoned a whirlwind of emerald and ivory, enveloping Hades in a swirling vortex of vibrant greens and browns. But Hades had other plans. With a sinister smile, he unleashed a torrent of dark flames that consumed the swirling tempest, incinerating the chaos until all that was left was ash.

The ground beneath them quaked as Demeter unleashed her true power. Roots erupted from the earth, intertwining to form massive tendrils that surged towards Hades. But he countered with a blast of chilling cold, encasing the roots in ice and shattering them with a single strike.

Their battle escalated, the very fabric of the forest bearing witness to their clash. Lightning arced through the night sky, illuminating the scene with its electric glow. The air sizzled with tension as the gods traded blows, their powers colliding in a dazzling display of magic and might.

Despite Demeter's valiant efforts, Hades proved to be an adversary of formidable strength. With a final burst of dark energy, he unleashed a shockwave that sent the goddess crashing into the earth, her form momentarily obscured in clouds of dust and the debris of their battle.

My lungs burned as I held my breath, the sound of my heart thundering in my ears. Demeter stood tall amid the wreckage, rendered speechless by Hades' might. She staggered forward, a deep gash on her forehead the only visible reminder of her struggle. Yet, despite the intense pain she must have been enduring, an unyielding determination remained in her emerald gaze.

"You may have won this day, Hades," she finally spoke, her voice laced with defiance and exhaustion. "But know this: nature's power is indomitable, and one day, you will face the consequences of your actions."

Hades smirked, his obsidian eyes glinting with triumph. "We shall see, Demeter. But for now, I'll have my way."

I cautiously approached Demeter, concern marring my expression. "Are you all right?" I questioned, my voice filled with worry.

She offered me a weary smile, a faint trace of her divine power still radiating from within. "I will heal, Prince Phillip," she replied gently. "But the journey is not yet over. You must press on and reclaim what has been stolen."

Her words ignited a renewed sense of determination within me. I nodded grimly, steeling myself against the insurmountable challenges that lay ahead. I would face whatever obstacles came our way, and reclaim Aurora from Hades' grasp. Nothing would stop me, no matter the cost.

Wings flaring in a daunting display of darkness, Hades glared darkly at us with a mix of fury and reluctant acceptance. His voice resounded like thunder as he spoke his warning. "Your alliance with Demeter does not guarantee your triumph, savage mortal. The threads of fate are fickle, and I will not rest until I have taken my revenge."

With a flicker of darkness, Hades vanished, leaving Demeter standing amidst the remnants of their battle. The forest fell silent, the echo of their clash fading into the depths of the woods.

The ground quaked violently as if in response to Hades' departure, and then suddenly, out of nowhere, a thick wall of obsidian thorns burst out of the earth with deadly precision. The thorns spread wide, thick, and sharp, lacing in an impenetrable barrier.

We stared in shock at the formidable obstacle that stood between us and our goal. The wall of thorns served as a stark reminder of Hades' power and his burning desire to keep us at bay.

My heart quivered as I glanced at Eloise, my eternal vow of courage and devotion clear in my eyes. "We'll make it through this," I declared firmly, the blistering heat of determination coursing through my veins. "We're so close. Hades will not stand in our way."

Demeter stepped forward then, her face aglow with an unidentifiable emotion. "Do not underestimate Hades' power," she murmured quietly, as if the very wind carried her warning. "Stay true to your fated love, for it's your greatest weapon against the darkness that lies ahead." And with that, she faded away like a summer breeze.

Eloise's gaze became glassy and distant. She choked on a gasp, her lips trembling at Demeter's message. "*Your fated love...*" she breathed, wounded as she wandered off into the woods.

"Eloise..." My voice was barely above a whisper as I stumbled after her retreating figure. But it was too late— she'd already disappeared between the trees.

# BEAUTY

"The Midnight Lake…" Hypnos, standing beside me, pointed towards the mysterious expanse of the fathomless waters, anticipation and caution flickering in his eyes. "*There's* your treasure," he said, his voice laced with a hint of mystery.

I stood at the precipice, my gaze locked on the abyssal depths that lay below. The freezing wind whipped around me, picking up locks of my fair hair, whispering a promise— what lay beneath the murky waters could set me free, if I was brave enough to follow where it led.

My pulse quickened, excitement and terror rushing through my veins. Diving into the abyss could bring either freedom or destruction; it was all a matter of how far I was willing to go. I knew the risks involved, the dangers that lurked beneath the surface, but my desperation to break free from this realm outweighed my fear.

Without a second thought, I kicked off my heels and prepared to leap into the unknown. A thrill coursed through my being, pushing me towards the edge. But before I could take that fateful step, Hypnos moved with a swiftness that belied his laid-back nature. At once, his strong arm encircled my waist, pulling me back from an imminent fall.

"Are you out of your mind?" he roared, the force of his words shaking me to my core.

"Hypnos, let me go!" I pleaded in dismay, struggling against his iron grip as I fought for freedom, desperation warring with fright. But no matter how hard I thrashed or kicked, nothing seemed to break him away from me. *"Please!"* My voice grew ever louder, and still it begged for answers.

The air around us stirred up like a whirlpool of chaos, my leg suspended over a precipice so deep that all sound within it had been silenced.

"Have I taught you nothing?" Hypnos growled, his chest heaving with quickened breaths. "Mermaids are not to be trifled with! They are fierce protectors of their treasures, and they will defend them with voracious might. And let's not forget, such a fall would be fatal! You would seal your stay in the Netherworld permanently, a fate I'm sure you do not desire!"

I stopped struggling that instant. His words cut through the haze of determination that had clouded my judgment. Reality crashed down hard upon me, and I shuddered at the memory of my previous encounter with a mermaid. Their beauty masked a ferocious nature, and I knew firsthand the danger they posed.

Taking a step back from the edge, I allowed Hypnos to guide me away from the precipice. The excitement that had coursed through my veins moments ago began to subside, replaced by a startling sense of caution. At the same time, an ache settled in my chest, the knowledge that I was so close to what I wanted, yet so far away.

Hypnos led me back to the grand pavilion. We strolled in silence for a long while until he finally spoke, his voice laden with concern and wisdom. "Beauty, you must understand," he began, his tone softer now, "the Netherworld is a realm of tests and challenges. Nothing comes without a price or an obstacle to overcome. It is not a place for reckless actions or impulsive decisions. To face the mermaids and claim your answer, you must be prepared."

His voice lingered in the air like fog, a reminder of my need for careful strategy. I had been so desperate to find the truth that I had almost let myself be drawn into danger without thought. But Hypnos had saved me from myself yet again.

I bowed my head in agreement.

We returned to the elegant pavilion, its beautiful façade a contradiction to the perils and evils waiting beyond its walls. Hypnos motioned towards an ornate velvet cushion, and I sank into it as he gracefully dragged a tray with two shimmering golden teacups full of fragrant, steaming tea.

"I've seen so many souls come and go," Hypnos said, his voice filled with a mix of melancholy and wisdom. "And those who succeed in their quests are not the ones who rush headlong into danger, but the ones who approach with caution and careful thought. You must be ready, both physically and mentally, before you face the mermaids."

A thick curtain of steam rose from the cup cradled in my hands, its pungent aroma blurring the space between us. As I breathed it in, his words swam through my mind until they finally made sense. "You're right," I uttered, tears welling up in my eyes. "I know... It's just too much to bear."

He wrapped an arm around my shoulders and pulled me into his embrace, but no matter how firm and warm it was, it failed to quell the ache rising inside me. My throat tightened with the force of emotions that clogged it, and then they did unleash. I was sobbing uncontrollably against him as he murmured soothingly into my hair, "These trying times won't last forever. I promise you, my dearest. You'll get rid of us, soon enough."

I clung to Hypnos, my body trembling as I wept into his chest. "That's just it," I finally managed to choke out between sobs. "I know what I must do. More than anything, all I want is to find my name and reclaim my freedom, but I..." My voice died away as jagged fears roared through me.

Hypnos pulled me closer. He released a long exhalation, his breath ruffling the hair at the nape of my neck. "Shh... it's all right," he whispered, running his fingers gently through my fair tresses. "Tell me what troubles you so."

I took a shuddering breath, trying to calm my sobs enough to speak. "I... I want to know who I am," I managed. "I want to solve the riddle and reclaim my identity. But..."

My lips trembled. How could I tell him that during my time here, I had come to care for him, and Hades, and all the others? That the thought of regaining my freedom now carried a bittersweet edge?

Sensing my turmoil, he slowly pulled back and tilted my chin up with a soothing hand until our eyes met. His hazel gaze was filled with understanding and compassion. "You don't wish to leave us," he said softly, not asking but knowing.

I nodded, fresh tears spilling down my cheeks. "I don't know what to do," I whispered brokenly, feeling completely lost.

Hypnos pulled me close, resting his chin atop my head. We sat there in silence for a long moment before he spoke again. "The heart often wars with the mind," he mused softly. "But sometimes, we must let one win out over the other."

The gravity of his cryptic words hung heavy on me and I tried desperately to make sense of them—was he trying to tell me that I should listen to my heart's desire to stay, or my mind's call for freedom? Tears continued streaming down my face as I felt torn in two directions.

But before I could ask, a wild gust of wind swept through the pavilion, tearing countless cherry blossoms from their branches above us. Bright pink petals danced and twirled in the moonlight as I looked up, my gaze drawn to the source of the disturbance.

Hypnos and I leapt up in surprise. Through the whirlwind of petals, a dark figure appeared against the star-strewn sky—a winged steed with a coat blacker than midnight. The creature's sleek muscles glimmered in the moonlight, but it was its rider that transfixed me.

Hades.

Entranced by his presence, my heart skipped a beat.

The stallion's hooves pounded against the earth with thundering force and grace. Hades' face was etched with urgency. His presence commanded the space around him, his imposing stature and aura of darkness sending shivers down my spine. He sat atop the horse with an air of authority, his eyes blazing with an intensity that matched the fierce gleam of his armor. Locks of raven hair fell in disarray around his chiseled features, and even with his wings concealed, he exuded the promise of swift retribution to any who defied his will.

"Hypnos," Hades called gravely, his voice cutting through the air. His words carried a sense of urgency, a hint of concern.

I turned to Hypnos, who stood beside me, his expression shifting between surprise and uncertainty. "Hades?" he mumbled, clearly taken aback by the unexpected appearance of the Dark Prince. "What is it?"

"Outsiders have breached the palace grounds," Hades growled. "They've brought an ally with them... *Demeter.*" His voice dripped the venom of hostility. "They won't be easily found. Bring them to me—take your brother with you."

"It will be done," Hypnos said, bowing his head in prompt resolve. The god of sleep took one step back, ready to fulfill his task when Hades called him.

"I want them alive," Hades said, and the words sailed through gritted teeth.

Demeter. The name echoed in my mind, and a surge of restlessness assaulted me at the thought of suffering the goddess' fury. But as quickly as that fear had bloomed, a seed of doubt began to take root. What danger had we stumbled upon? And why did Hades seem so concerned?

No sooner had my lips parted to voice my questions, than Hades turned his attention to me. His piercing gaze bore into mine, and his voice held a sense of haste. "You need to leave the palace," he told me, his words resonating with an undercurrent of authority. "Now!"

His strong grip closed on my waist, and before I could protest, he effortlessly lifted me and tossed me over the back of the winged stallion. The beast beneath me whinnied, its powerful hooves gently pounding the ground, ready to take flight.

As I found myself perched atop the creature, fear and anticipation coursed through my veins. I turned my gaze back to Hades. Subdued and somber, he stroked the stallion's neck with a firm hand, his touch both gentle and commanding. His fingers lingered near the creature's ear, a silent communication between them.

"Take her to safety, dear friend," Hades said, his voice filled with a rare tenderness.

"Aren't you coming?" I breathed, pulse quickened and voice strained with concern.

His firm thumb glided along my jawline. "I'll join you as soon as I can," Hades replied, his voice carrying over the rushing wind. A hint of determination lingered in his words, a promise that he would not be far behind.

He gave the pegasus a light pat on its hind, urging it forward. "Go now!"

I couldn't tear my eyes away from Hades, his figure growing smaller as the winged stallion lifted off the ground. The wind whipped through my hair as we soared higher into the sky, but my heart remained heavy with worry for the one I was leaving behind.

We soared away, and my longing for answers warred with my fear for Hades' safety. But I could only cling to his promise to follow as the winged steed carried me into unknown skies. My heart was torn—would I find freedom? Or had a new danger found us first?

# PHILLIP

*E*loise's name echoed through the eerie silence of the
Netherworld, but still, no reply came. I trudged
through the dense undergrowth, my steps heavy with anxiety
and resolve. The twisted trees groaned with a foreboding
chill, their gnarled branches reaching out like bony fingers.
This maze of gloom and secrets had been treacherous since its
inception, but now it held an added layer of danger, as Hades
himself sought to thwart our mission.

"Eloise!" I called out again, desperation licking at the
edges of my voice. "Eloise, please come back." She was head-
strong, impulsive, but she was also my beloved partner, my
ally in this treacherous realm. The thought of her venturing
off alone sent sheer dread washing over me. The Netherworld
was a cursed land, filled with lurking horrors and malevolent
creatures. Even more so now that our presence had sparked
Hades' wrath.

And then, as if summoned by my distress, two figures
emerged from the shadows. A shiver of unease ran through
my veins as I recognized one instantly—Hypnos, the fiend
who had cursed Aurora with unending sleep. His presence

was both haunting and unsettling. But it was the other figure who drew my attention, a stern and imposing warrior with long frost-pale hair, clad in shimmering steel armor.

The guardian stepped forward, sword drawn in the fiercest challenge. "Who seeks entry into Hades' domain?" he barked out in a shrill voice that rumbled through the stillness of the woods.

My heart throbbed in my chest as I stared at the formidable warrior towering before me. It must have been Thanatos, the fearsome brother of Hypnos, whose reputation as the embodiment of death itself sent chills down the spines of mortals and gods alike. His steely gaze bore into me, his sword poised for battle, and I knew that I stood on the precipice of a fight that could have dire consequences.

"Prince Phillip Steelborn," I replied as I stealthily eased my hand to the hilt of my sword. "I've come from the Realm of Man."

The warrior stared me down, his blazing stormy eyes narrow and sharp. His brows drew together as they roved over my figure and he growled low in his throat, "Are you traveling alone?" The question came like a challenge. He then turned his feral glare away, raking through our surroundings.

"Yes," I hurried to say. But my words were met with silence, the woods seemingly holding its breath as the tension between us slowly mounted.

Malicious satisfaction twisted the god's expression as he drawled, "Liar." My heart shriveled at the thought of Eloise as she roamed the woods alone, unsuspecting of the gravest danger yet to come.

Hypnos stepped forward, gold filigree shimmering on the blue steel of his chestplate and bracers. His amber eyes burned with amusement and malice. "Ah, Phillip," he said, his voice dripping with condescension. "We meet again. How delightful."

My grip tightened around Dawnbreaker's hilt as the memories of our past encounter resurfaced in my mind—the clash of steel, the acrobatic dance of blades, and the mark I had left upon his cheek, a scar etched as a reminder of our unfinished business.

Lowering my chin, I stabbed him with a glare. "I've longed to see the day when the god of slumber falls," I spat, my expression hardening with rage. "It's a privilege to bring an end to your story."

Hypnos' lips curled into a wicked smile, his tone laced with twisted amusement. "I see you don't travel lightly... still carrying your pathetic arrogance, mortal," he taunted, his words like venomous whispers in the wind. "Do you truly think you can best a god?"

My blood ran hot, defiance and fear tangling in its stream, my hand instinctively tightening its grip on my sword. I had come to the Netherworld to rescue Aurora, protect Eloise, and find answers, and now I stood face to face with the very embodiment of my past mistakes. But this time, I was not the same inexperienced man I had been before.

"Your power may be great, Hypnos," I said with stern conviction, "but I've learned much since our last encounter. I will not be so easily defeated."

The tension between us crackled in the air, a tangible force that threatened to ignite into violence. Each moment dragged on, the weight of our past rivalry mingling with the present danger.

Thanatos, ever the silent sentinel, stood beside his brother, his gaze never wavering. "That is enough," he said under his breath, the earth shuddering as he stomped forward.

Hypnos stopped him, a hand pressed to his brother's chest. "He's mine," he spilled the words with a snarl.

The frost-pale-haired warrior's eyes narrowed as he glanced my way, his expression stony and unyielding. "Yours —why?" he said in a breathy voice laced with exasperation.

Hypnos glided a finger along the scar on his cheek, a scar I remembered only too well. "We have a history, you see," he replied, a flicker of dark delight dancing in his eyes.

Thanatos' words were like a whip, sharp and precise. "Fine. I'll go after the woman," he declared, his voice echoing with a steely confidence that filled the woods with leaden anticipation. In a blur of motion, he whirled away, as if the force of his will had taken tangible form.

Icy dread crawled over me as I watched him leave, and I could do nothing but trust that Eloise's years of fighting had prepared her for the threat coming her way.

I forced myself to focus on the task at hand. Hypnos had chosen to face me. Years of animosity and rivalry came down to this one moment. The air around us felt like a deepening silence, simmering with electric tension and hostility.

Our gazes locked in a deadly clash, until time itself seemed to stand still. His laughter echoed through my ears, sending a chill down my spine as his eyes met mine—dark with amusement.

"I've dreamed of this day," he purred, savoring his impending victory.

A blaze of fury surged through my veins, banishing away all fear. Images of Aurora's still body filled my mind, so many years lost where her beauty had lay frozen in time by Hypnos' cursed slumber. My blade thrummed in my palms as I readied for battle. The icy metal felt familiar in my palm—a glimmer of promise amidst the darkness that had befallen Aurora's kingdom.

My fury burned brighter than the stars as I locked eyes with Hypnos and declared firmly, "I'll happily make that dream into a nightmare." A smirk crossed my lips as I remembered the first time we'd met. "My blade has thirsted for your divine blood ever since the day it kissed your cheek."

And then, with a startlingly graceful motion, Hypnos drew forth his sword. Starlight glinted off of its smooth surface, vibrating in the air as if inviting me to reach out and touch it.

The clash of steel resounded through my bones, shooting sparks in all directions and sending shockwaves of dread and memory coursing through me. His attacks were like liquid fire; each thrust more lethal than the last. He was a storm of death that sent chills up my spine. Every move he made was full of purpose, every parry carefully planned. This fight wasn't one born of recklessness but rather of ages-old revenge.

But I held my ground, channeling every ounce of determination and skill within me. I parried his blows with valiant precision, my own strikes propelled by a relentless drive to protect those I loved. Each strike of our swords thundered through the woods, the metallic clang filling the air in an ominous symphony.

Time lost all meaning as we fought, our bodies locked in a dance of danger and defiance. Only the forest bore witness to our struggle, its ancient trees whispering secrets as their leaves rustled in the wind. My muscles burned with exertion, my mind focused intently on each swing of our swords.

The sweet savor of victory hung in the air, taunting me with its presence. With each strike my sword made against Hypnos, I was ever closer to claiming his defeat. My veins hummed with a thrill and my muscles burned with raw, fiery power as I leapt and parried, diving through the air and rolling out of harm's way.

But despite my best efforts, Hypnos refused to surrender. His powers surpassed that of any mortal, and with every second the battle raged on, a weight pressed down on me like a heavy blanket. He moved like lightning, dodging my blows and striking back in one momentous motion. No matter how hard I pushed myself, I could feel the god's strength overpowering me, threatening to overcome my will entirely. He was a god—his strength so much greater than anything I'd ever encountered—and in that moment, I knew he would remain undefeated.

With every ounce of strength left in my being, I lunged at Hypnos. My blade swished through the air with a ferocity that even I didn't know was within me. But Hypnos was no ordinary foe; his divine blood coursed through him like liquid gold, and he evaded each of my strikes with ease. With a final, decisive blow, he disarmed me, sending my sword spiraling through the air and embedding itself deep into the forest floor.

My body, battered and bruised, ached as if pummeled by a thousand fists, but my mind was clear. As Hypnos approached me with a smug grin etched on his face, I dug deep and summoned all my willpower to stand tall.

"Do you see, Phillip?" he sneered, his voice dripping with disdain. "You *cannot* defeat a god."

But as I looked into his eyes, I glimpsed a flicker of uncertainty, a glimmer of doubt that belied his bravado. And refusing to let his taunts break me, I rose from my defeated stance and met his gaze with unwavering boldness.

"I may not be a god," I said, my voice steady as steel, "but I'm driven by love and a purpose greater than myself. And that is a power you will *never* understand."

The god's expression slackened at the courage of my conviction, his eyes narrowing as he regarded me in stern appraisal. Suddenly, the forest erupted into a frenzied whirlwind. Leaves whirled around us in a maelstrom of chaos. The wind howled past my ears, the deafening roar of nature's fury obliterating my senses.

As the breeze dissipated, it gave way to a murky fog that

rolled in like an army of ghosts. The mist clung to my skin, its chill tingling through me, heavy with secrets and whispered woes.

I struggled against the god's enchantments, to no avail, as the weight of drowsiness washed over me. I fought the irresistible pull with all my might to push through it. But it wasn't enough.

My limbs faltered, betraying me at last. "What is this... magic?" I murmured as I crumpled to my knees.

And then, in an instant, darkness descended upon me like a shroud. It was as if the very essence of night had been unleashed, swallowing the world whole. My senses were overwhelmed by an abyss of nothingness. I fought to maintain some semblance of reality but found myself slipping further and further away.

In that moment, defeat weighed heavily upon me like a leaden cloak. Hypnos had proven himself to be a fearsome adversary indeed, his powers of slumber subjugating even my mortal strength.

As darkness closed in around me, despair threatened to conquer me completely. But even in the face of certain defeat, a glimmer of hope flickered within me. For though I fought alone, love was my shield and heart's desire. And I knew that while that flame burned inside me, I would rise again.

# BEAUTY

The night stretched endlessly as Hades' mighty steed raced across the starry sky, hurtling past the vast Veiled Woods until we were soaring higher than ever. I clung tightly to the horse's powerful neck. My skin prickled with delight at its sheer speed and strength that defied even the fiercest winds, staying firmly set on its course.

Soon, a blanket of light clouds surrounded us, caressing me with their icy chill. We drifted closer to a luminous silver moon when I peered down to catch a glimpse of a breathtaking display of shimmering lights scattered on the lands below like glittering diamonds. Little by little, I shed my apprehension, replaced by wonder as my body relaxed and I savored this extraordinary ride.

We dipped further, and amidst the darkness, I spotted a pristine white temple shining brightly from beneath a silken carpet of thick cumulus clouds. Torchlight flickered in a grand courtyard, dazzling marble effigies surrounding it.

Gradually, our vigorous flight softened into an effortless drift as we began our descent. The steed released a low shriek as it stretched out its wings, steadily slowing us down until finally, its forelegs gently touched the ground and we landed safely.

The black pegasus pounded on the stone floor a few times, then stood completely still, its majestic form glistening in the night. It whinnied and bowed its head almost reverently as I stroked its neck, and when I reached for its mane it bent its forelegs enough to allow me to dismount gracefully.

As my feet touched the ground, my sapphire gown gently fluttered with a peaceful breeze that carried a delightful scent —clashing yet complementary notes of lilac and citrus that tickled my nose.

I adjusted the silk of my gown and stared around with wide eyes. An otherworldly gleam bathed this garden. Silver moonlight veiled its every corner and lavish lanterns hung from ornate iron hooks, their shuddering flames projecting dancing shadows upon the cobblestone pathways.

A breathtaking beauty engulfed us, but more astonishing was the exquisite mosaic beneath my feet, forming a perfect circle that seemed to stretch endlessly across the courtyard. In the center, a radiant figure stood tall, surrounded by a halo of golden light. Her flowing robes cascaded around her, while her face, framed by dark auburn curls, exuded serene wisdom —she seemed oddly familiar.

Why would Hades send me here of all places?

"Welcome, my dear," a voice said, fast approaching.

My head whipped towards the sound. It was then that I noticed a figure emerging from the shadows, moving towards me with an air of both grace and power. Her amethyst eyes sparkled with ancient wisdom. Long strands of flowing auburn hair rippled down her back, shimmering copper in the torchlight.

Her gown, a rich shade of purple and midnight blue, clung to her slender form in elegant folds, emphasizing her statuesque silhouette. The fabric shimmered with an inner light of its own, as if touched by magic.

My heart skipped a beat as recognition dawned upon me. "Hecate..." I whispered, surprise and delight coloring my voice. Then, remembering her divine condition, I added, "It's an honor to be in your presence once more." I began to curtsy when her delicate hands curled around my arms and stopped me.

A gentle smile thinned her lips, warmth and familiarity instantly washing over me in pleasant waves. "I'm so delighted you've come," she added in a mellow tone, opening her arms in a welcoming embrace. "What brings you here?" The silver pendant hanging from her neck was shaped like a crescent moon, and twinkled as she briefly parted from me.

I glanced at the pegasus, a shared understanding passing between us. Then, meeting Hecate's eyes with unwavering determination, I replied, "Hades."

"Is anything wrong?" she asked. Her creased brow and concerned gaze told me she already suspected the answer to her question.

"There's trouble in the Veiled Woods," I said with a sigh, the weight of the Netherworld's disturbance resting heavily on my shoulders.

A knowing smirk curved Hecate's lips before she answered. "There's always trouble in those woods. You will be safe in my temple." With a gentle hand wave, she beckoned for me to follow.

The pegasus reared its head, gaze steady and vigilant, as if it was offering me protection with no words spoken. I stepped forward, unable to resist the urge to stroke its muscled neck. Gratitude welled up inside me, but I turned my attention quickly back to Hecate.

"Come," she said, her hand holding mine, "let us not

waste another moment standing out here. I have much to share with you."

We set off together, sauntering along the cobblestone pathway. The courtyard seemed to come to life as we moved —the scent of blooming flowers filling the air, intermingling with the sound of distant laughter and the gentle rustling of leaves.

We walked through the colossal entrance, my eyes widening in awe at the grandeur that met me. Gold enameled ornate carvings and ancient symbols adorned the doors, their intricate designs only hinting at the mysteries beyond.

At length, we arrived at the entrance of a grand library that defied anything I could have imagined. Shelves stretched up into the heavens, filled with countless books in gold and silver lettering. Moonlight filtered in from tall windows, as if this library had been created for illumination alone. Warm candlelight flickered along each shelf, inviting us to explore, and the air held a faint scent of old parchment. This place was like no other, a sanctuary dedicated to knowledge and power.

Hecate sauntered gracefully between the towering shelves, her movements almost reverent. She paused every so often to run her fingers lovingly along a dog-eared spine or a gilded title. Her eyes sparkled with delight as she finally glanced back at me.

"Everything you need to know about sorcery lies within these books," she said softly.

I looked around in wonder. "You've read... *all* of this?" I managed.

Hecate's crisp laughter echoed around the hallowed walls. She held it back and faced me with a mischievous glimmer in her eyes. "What did you think, my dear? Magic certainly is not born out of thin air," she said, her voice full of mirth as she turned away from me again. "You just need to know where to look."

My gaze swept across the expanse of the library, each book an invitation to unravel the secrets of the Netherworld. "Perhaps here I may find the full answer to my riddle," I mumbled to myself, my heart inflamed with the thrill of possibility.

Hecate tilted her head at my words, her features illuminated by the faint glow of the candelabras. "A riddle?" she asked, her voice a mix of enchantment and solemnity. "What riddle?"

I carefully plucked the crumpled piece of parchment from my pocket, the lines etched upon it a puzzle waiting to be solved. "The one that will grant me my name," I explained, placing the paper in her outstretched hand. "Hypnos traced it to the Midnight Lake, where the mermaids hide their treasures."

"Mm... Mermaids are great secret holders," Hecate whispered, studying the lines closely. "If you are to dive into their depths, you will need a spell to resist the lake's cruel waters and armor strong enough to survive their fangs."

Icy dread skittered down my spine. "Is there such a spell?" I asked cautiously.

"My child," she began, her voice full of gentle assurance. "There are *many* spells that will help you on this quest. Come with me."

My feet echoed on the marble floor, a hollow sound that seemed fitting in such a sacred place. Flames licked at the walls, casting orange shadows across the curved hallway. I could feel my excitement growing with every step, knowing that within these hallowed halls, I would find the answers to my questions.

"This is it, Beauty," Hecate said, her godly grace radiating from within. She pointed with a graceful finger to the library alcove, and I gasped in utter awe. It was as if an entire universe had been captured into one tiny room of wonders; old tomes lined the shelves from floor to ceiling, alongside ancient scrolls and mysterious texts.

"Here you will find everything you need for your quest," Hecate continued solemnly, her eyes twinkling with pride. "I've gathered countless volumes that delve into the intricacies of mermaids and their ways."

She stepped aside and beckoned me into the room, allowing me to wander amongst the bookshelves as she explained each text in detail. With every sentence uttered in her melodious voice, I felt something inside of me awaken— a sense of purpose and courage.

When we finished gathering every book on mermaids, Hecate stepped back and regarded me with admiration. "You're all set now, I think," she said, satisfied. "I'll leave you to it." There was something in the way she looked at me— like she could see what was coming next for me. In her presence, I was both small and infinite at once; fearlessly preparing to set off into the unknown while being surrounded by her unconditional love.

As I poured through generations of old tales and myths, the weight of their wisdom pressed down on me. Time seemed to bend, moving ever slower as I studied late into the evening.

My eyes drooped with weariness. With a sigh, I set down the heavy tome in my lap and yielded to exhaustion's gentle lullaby. In the library's quiet embrace, sleep claimed me, and my dreams became a tapestry of warm whispers and swirling fantasies.

# PHILLIP

*I* awoke in darkness, the damp and cold air clinging to my skin. The jarring pain in my head served as a cruel reminder of the chaos that had unfolded before I lost consciousness. As my vision cleared, I realized I was confined within the walls of a dungeon, the iron bars of my small and windowless cell separating me from the rest of the world.

Groaning, I sat up, my head pounding. Hypnos' sneering face flashed through my mind. He and Thanatos had attacked Eloise and me in the woods. I recalled the fight, the magical mist enveloping me... then nothing.

They must have overpowered us after I blacked out. But where had they taken us?

The air was heavy with cloying dampness, and it seemed as though the walls inched closer with every breath I took; oppressive and suffocating. My vision blurred and adjusted to the murky light. There were figures everywhere, shrouded in silence, each an enigma in this shadowy prison.

Something drew my attention then. At the end of the dungeon sat a cell, unlike the others. Thick iron bars ran from floor to ceiling, capped with wicked spikes that gleamed in the dim torchlight with strange glyphs. The stone around it seemed blackened, as if scorched by some fierce heat. This cell was meant to contain a truly formidable prisoner.

Inside, a powerful frame was visible even through the gloom—muscular and broad-shouldered, he stood tall and imposing. What truly caught my eye were the prominent horns of ivory that stemmed from his forehead, branding him as a minotaur. Legends of such creatures passed through generations, whispered tales of mythical beasts of terrible strength. Seeing one so close before me sent shivers racing down my spine. An ethereal aura surrounded him as his foggy breath curled slowly around us. He commanded respect. Not even the dimness of the room could hide his raw power.

Our gazes locked, and I felt a heavy sense of sorrow emanating from his deep steely eyes. His horns curved fiercely above his massive frame, but there was an unmistakable gentleness to the minotaur that shook me to my core. He'd been held in captivity, just like me. I wondered what trials he'd faced that brought him here.

As he stepped closer to the iron bars I glimpsed the intricate tattoos crawling over his muscular arms—stories of courage, battles won and lost inked into his skin. Despite his chains and this endless despair into which we were both thrust, I could see that his spirit remained unbroken, unwavering in its strength.

The minotaur's dark eyes silently searched mine, as if trying to imprint my very being before slipping back into the darkness without saying a word. I remained still, in silent awe. But as my gaze fell upon the figure in the cell opposite mine, my heart lurched. Eloise lay motionless on the cold stone floor, her chest rising and falling in a steady rhythm.

Relief flooded over me at the sight of her, but it was quickly replaced by a surge of anger and helplessness. We were prisoners, at the mercy of our captors, and the weight of our predicament bore down upon me with a suffocating force.

Ignoring the pain in my skull, I staggered to my feet and gripped the bars, peering out. Torches flickered in sconces along the walls, casting wavering golden light. A long hallway stretched in both directions, lined with more cells where other prisoners shuffled listlessly or lay still.

"Eloise?" I rasped, my dry throat protesting. Only echoing silence answered.

Fear lanced through me. I called her name again, louder. "Wake up, my love. We're trapped. We must find a way out of here."

Her eyelids fluttered, and she groaned softly, her voice filled with weariness. "Phillip? Is that you?" Her eyes slowly opened, meeting mine with confusion and concern. She sat up sluggishly, a hand pressed to her temple. "What happened? Where are we?"

"Captured," I replied grimly. "It seems we're in Hades' dungeon."

Her eyes widened in alarm. She crawled to the bars separating us, grasping them with white knuckles. "Aurora. We must find her. She's still in danger, Phillip!"

"I know." Desperation clawed at me, but I strove to remain calm for Eloise's sake. "First," I said, pushing back my matted hair, "we must recover our strength and assess the situation. We must examine if there's any way out."

Eloise nodded, her eyes growing sharper as the fog of unconsciousness lifted. "You're right. We can't let them win. We'll find a way out of here."

As we huddled by the bars, plotting our escape, footsteps drew nearer, and with them, a metallic jingle. Eloise and I exchanged a wary glance, our hearts quickening with hope and trepidation. The sound was unmistakable—the clinking of keys.

A figure emerged from the shadows. My pulse quickened with fury as I recognized him instantly—Hypnos, the god of sleep. He stood tall, hazel eyes gleaming with wicked amusement.

"What do we have here?" Hypnos sneered, his voice dripping with condescension. "The high and mighty prince, in chains at last."

My grip on the bars tightened, anger burning within me. "What do you want, Hypnos?" I spat, my voice laced with defiance. "Why have you brought us here?"

Hypnos snickered darkly, his gaze shifting between Eloise and me. "You think you're so special, don't you? But the truth is, you're nothing." He leaned against the wall, his voice oozing with sadistic pleasure. "You see, the Dark Prince has plans for you, Prince Phillip. He wants you to suffer, to endure a fate worse than death."

My blood ran cold at his words. The Dark Prince, Hades, had spared my life, but only to subject me to unspeakable torment. The realization struck me like a physical blow, and a fire of determination ignited within me. I would not let them break me. I would not succumb to their twisted games.

"You underestimate me, Hypnos," I retorted. "I may be trapped now, but I will not be defeated. I will find a way to escape, and I will rescue Aurora, bringing an end to Hades' tyranny."

Hypnos laughed, a bone-chilling sound that froze the blood in my veins. "Oh, how very amusing," he taunted callously, his eyes glinting with sadistic pleasure. "The prince thinks himself a savior." He paused, drawing closer. "You're nothing but a puppet, and Hades merely pulls your strings for his own gain." His hand hovered in the air, fingers fluttering in a mocking illustration of his words.

Rage built up inside me, fueling my resolve. "You may think that," I spat. "But I refuse to be his plaything. There is good in this world, and I will fight Hades and his darkness until my very last breath."

Hypnos snorted. He raised an eyebrow, mirth dancing in his eyes. "Oh, how *heroic...*" he sneered. And inching closer to the bars, he added, "Let me make one thing clear to you, Phillip. You are doomed. You will suffer, and you will break. Hades will see to that."

I clenched my fists, a surge of contempt flooding my being. "We shall see," I declared, my voice firm and resolute. "I may be a prisoner now, but I will never surrender."

The god's cruel laughter echoed through the dungeon, bouncing off the cold stone walls. "We shall see, indeed," he replied with icy finality. "But mark my words. Your days are numbered, and your fate is sealed."

I could sense the portent of those words, even as the god of death limped into view, one hand clutching his side. Crimson rivulets seeped between his fingers where his silver armor was torn open. His face was drawn, jaw clenched against the pain.

I couldn't contain my shock. "You're injured?" Immortals did not wound easily. What could have possibly brought down a god of Thanatos' might?

Thanatos grimaced, blood dripping from his hand. "Your *captain* fights like a gorgon," he bit out, stabbing Eloise with a harsh glare.

The realization stunned me—Eloise had managed to land a blow against Death itself. I whipped my head around, casting an astonished glance back at her.

Eloise lifted her chin, defiant even as Thanatos glowered at her. "I warned you not to touch me," she said coldly.

Thanatos let out a sharp, pained laugh. "You have a fire, woman," he said, a hint of admiration in his voice. "There's more fight in you than most men I've met. I'll give you that."

He staggered to the iron bars, resentment and grudging respect tangling in his features as he glowered at Eloise. "That blade of yours is cursed. It will be the death of you one day," he added, silver eyes burning with wickedness.

Eloise met his gaze unflinchingly. "Not if I see you dead first."

A tense silence fell. Then, incredibly, Thanatos grinned, baring blood-flecked teeth. "Perhaps you will at that," he said as he leaned heavily against the bars, leaving a streak of divine blood on them. "You did manage to catch me off guard."

Hypnos snickered behind him. "If only your lover had half your fighting spirit," he sneered. "He drops as easily as a fledgling bird."

My blood boiled, my knuckles turning white as I shook the bars of my prison cell with all my strength. "Say that to my face, coward!" I roared. "Unlock this cell and we'll see who drops first!"

Thanatos' smug gaze slid to me. "Such arrogance. You truly have no grasp of your situation." He tisked, shaking his head. "No, little prince. We will *not* be opening these bars any time soon. Not until Prince Hades commands it." He backed away as if he could not bear to look at me. He then lurched back down the hall, calling over his shoulder, "Rest while you can. When Hades is through with you, you'll be begging for Captain Eloise's sweet blade."

Rage flooded through me. I surged against the bars, heedless of how the metal bit into my palms. "Hades will pay for what he's done!" I snarled. "I swear it!"

In a flash, Hypnos was there, so close to me that I could feel his breath on my skin. His hand shot through the bars and clamped around my throat in an iron grip. I clawed at him, choking for breath that would not come.

"You're in no position to make threats, human," Hypnos hissed, face contorted in seething anger. "You live now only through the Dark Prince's mercy. Do not forget that."

He released me abruptly, and I crumpled back onto the ground, gasping for air. Eloise cried out my name but stayed back warily as Hypnos glared at us.

"You are doomed, Your Highness," he said with a deadly sneer, lazily stepping back. "The Netherworld will bleed you dry. Pray that your end comes swiftly."

With those chilling words, the Lord of Slumber turned on his heel, black cloak swirling around him as he departed. Thanatos lingered only a moment, his pitiless eyes promising future pain before he followed his brother.

Silence descended once more. I leaned against the cold stones, shaken but defiant in my heart. We would find a way to escape. For Aurora's sake, and the sake of all the souls trapped here, we had to succeed.

I met Eloise's frightened but determined eyes. Hades had not broken us yet.

I swore it right then. I would not rest until this dungeon ran red with the blood of the gods.

# 60

# BEAUTY

*M*y breath came in ragged gasps as I sprinted through the tangled undergrowth, the sound of my pounding footsteps drowning out the din of the forest. I glanced over my shoulder, my heart skipping a beat as I caught a glimpse of movement—a fleeting shadow that danced between the trees. It was a relentless pursuit, an unyielding chase that seemed to mock my desperate attempts to escape.

The forest closed in around me, the air becoming thick with its oppressive weight. Hidden between the trees and vines, I could feel hungry eyes tracking my every move.

The ground blurred beneath my feet as I fought to maintain my balance, dodging roots and fallen branches in a desperate bid to stay one step ahead. My legs burned with exertion, threatening to give way beneath me, but I pushed on, my determination overriding the ache that gnawed at my muscles.

And then, as my lungs screamed for respite, I stumbled into a small clearing, my body skidding to a halt on the damp earth. The stillness that settled over the space was suffocating, a stark contrast to the chaos of the forest that surrounded it. The scent of blooming flowers filled the air, their sweetness mingling with the dense musk that clung to the soil.

But my relief was short-lived as I sensed a presence, an imposing figure standing at the center of the clearing. I froze, my breath catching in my throat as I turned my gaze towards him. Hades—the Dark Prince himself—had emerged from the depths of the Netherworld to confront me.

His presence was electrifying, his aura crackling with power and peril. Twilight filtered through the canopy of leaves, casting a haunting glow upon his bronzed skin. His eyes, dark and predatory, seemed to penetrate my very soul, leaving me feeling exposed and vulnerable.

To be face to face with him now sent a thrill down my spine, a realization that I was at the mercy of a deity who held the power of life and death in his hands. Even then, my heart raced with longing.

But I would not yield to my emotions. I stood tall, my gaze locked with his, refusing to let my desire consume me. I had come too far, faced too many challenges, to back down now.

He stepped closer, as if drawn by an invisible tether. Without a word, he snatched my wrist, pulling me towards him. His agonizing nearness at once shattered my resolve, and our lips met in a hungry, desperate kiss, his hands roaming over my body with fierce possessiveness. Sparks of gold ignited between us when we touched, a foreboding of grazing something forbidden.

I moaned into his mouth as he pushed me against a tree, his hardness pressing on my thigh. My mind warred between two choices—part of me wanted to pull away, to run back to the safety of Hecate's temple, but the other part longed to

SILVANA G. SÁNCHEZ

surrender completely to him, to let him take me right there amongst the trees and the dirt.

"On your knees," he demanded, his breath hot in my ear.

I bristled at the presumptuousness of his command, my frown deepening in exasperation. "You should know by now... I kneel for no one."

A roguish smirk curled over his lips as he grasped me firmly by the nape, tugging me closer to him. "Not even for me?" His dark eyes scanned over my body seductively. "On your knees or on your back. However I please," he drawled, pausing to gauge my reaction.

"Hades," I whispered, feeling a thrill surge through me at the closeness of his body.

His gaze locked with mine and all I could do was stay entranced in the moment. "It's Your Highness now," he purred smoothly. His strong hands guided me down onto my knees and without hesitation, my tongue flicked out across his flesh. He groaned deep from within his throat and a heat spread rapidly throughout my body as he forced himself further into my mouth.

The woods around us echoed with our passionate love-making—his fingers gripping my hair ever tighter as he reached the peak of pleasure. "Yes... That's it," he growled before spilling himself into me fully and I savored every drop like an elixir, relishing the taste of him still on my tongue.

He grabbed my hips and I clung to him, wrapping my legs around his waist. His fingers danced up the sides of my thighs and scorching heat spread throughout my body.

"Do you want me?" he whispered against my lips, his breath coming in short ragged pants.

I nodded, unable to find the words, and he thrust into me in one powerful move. A soft cry escaped my lips as Hades moved inside me, the sweetest ecstasy crashing through my core in powerful waves, each sensation bolder than the next. I collapsed into him, our breaths becoming one, our bodies knitting in perfect harmony. He moved faster and faster, inside and out, pushing me to new heights of pleasure... I had never felt so alive.

In that moment, I knew I had found something unique —an untamable love, wild and passionate. With him, I had found my ultimate freedom, unlocking at last an all-consuming bliss.

"Beauty," he purred into my hair, instigating my hunger for him. *"Oh, my Beauty..."*

"Beauty," a smooth voice sang through the pitch darkness. "Open your eyes for me."

My soul stirred in my sleep and my eyelashes flickered open. Before me stood a darkened figure and I gasped, jolting awake.

"Hades," I managed, my pulse throbbing hard in my chest and throat. "I was having a dream..." The words stumbled out of my mouth as though they had their own life, flustering me even more as I tried to take in his intimidating presence.

His hand glided higher along the mattress where I lay, his chest tilting closer to me. The narrow distance between us became painfully unbearable.

"Was it a good dream?" he asked, and his voice cut through the air like a blade, his gaze burning into mine as he perched on the bed, nearly on top of me.

The beat of my heart reverberated through my ribcage, sending fire throughout my body. "You were in it," I said in a blurt, then swallowed hard before I could say anything else, regretting each word as soon as it dripped from my lips.

A smirk tugged at the corner of his mouth, setting magic

onto the air with every syllable he spoke. "Then I'm sure it was good."

My cheeks burned warmer than before as I forced a smile, but without any regret this time.

"You're blushing," he observed with surprise lifting his brows. A mischievous grin followed and he purred suggestively, "It must have been a *very* good dream."

I was left speechless, lips parted in shock.

"You're back," I managed, my voice barely audible against the stillness of the night as longing and deep-rooted concern battled for control within me. The words hung in the air before me like a heavy fog, strangling all but the most essential thoughts from my mind. "I was so worried."

He moved closer, filling the space between us with an electrifying energy. Moonlight danced along his strong features, and his eyes sparked with a dark delight that sent a ripple of heat through my veins like molten lava. "You worry about the mightiest god that rules the Netherworld?" His smooth voice wrapped around me like liquid silk, washing away any doubts I might have harbored.

I met his gaze head-on, my courage bolstered by his mere presence. "Have you caught our enemies?" I asked, fearful of what their intentions may have been yet unable to stem the flow of questions.

His expression shifted subtly, though just enough for me to sense something dangerous lurking beneath its surface. "*Our* enemies have been imprisoned and shall be dealt with," he declared assuredly. "You mustn't worry, my Beauty. I won't let anyone harm you." The words carried a weighty promise, a declaration of his fierce determination to protect me—even if it cost him dearly. Yet, there was an edge of danger in his tone, a reminder that the Netherworld was a realm of shadows and secrets, where power and darkness held sway.

"I have a gift for you," he crooned teasingly, slipping an object into my hand.

I cautiously lifted myself up on the bed and opened my hand to find a golden pendant; an oval-shaped charm encrusted with an opal gemstone that gleamed with a preternatural enchantment.

"Look closer," he murmured, firelight dancing across his face. His fingers tilted the locket so that the warm glow spilled across it, revealing the faint etching of a skull—the emblem of his realm.

The gravity of his words descended on me like a blanket, heavy in the silence that perched between us. I took a deep breath, feeling the chill of the locket against my chest as he fastened it around my neck. His touch skittered down my nape, riveting yet tender, and shot a jolt of anticipation down my spine. It was a gesture, a connection that bound us together in ways I couldn't fully comprehend.

"Come what may, promise me you'll keep this with you always," he added. "It holds that which I love most."

"What is that?" I asked breathlessly.

His lips curled into a knowing smirk as he leaned towards me, his intoxicating musk surrounding us. "You," he replied simply, his words carrying the weight of a promise and a dangerous truth.

My mouth moved towards his, lured by the heat radiating off his skin. "Hades," I murmured, our lips barely a whisper apart.

"Mm?" he responded, keeping perfectly still, the air between us charged with longing.

He made no move to close the narrow space between us, allowing me to choose what happened next. I wanted to kiss him so badly, but instead, I held back and forced myself to focus. "I need to know more about the riddle," I said firmly, pushing away thoughts of passionate kisses and caresses from my mind.

"Have you figured it out?" His words were a whisper, and yet they carried like thunder through the air, lingering on my skin.

I dared not look away from him, his very presence drawing me closer. My heart pounded in anticipation. I managed to force out a response, my voice barely above a murmur. "Not completely. I know it leads to the mermaids in the Midnight Lake. But if I take the plunge now..."

He broke away, exhaling as a chill between us thickened. "In my realm, time has no bearing—not unless Chronos intervenes, anyway," he muttered darkly. "What's the point of haste?" He set his jaw in quiet annoyance.

I sat upright on the bed, leveling our stares. "Hades, I need to know who I am." Emotion choked my throat as I begged.

He met my eyes, and a smirk danced on his lips. His gaze was nothing but wildfire as he spoke. "You... you are *everything* to me—my salvation and my downfall. The light that ignites my darkness." With agonizing gentleness, his fingers curled around my wrist, scorching me with his touch. His heated lips then grazed my knuckles in a feather-light caress before pressing a smoldering kiss to my hand, searing into me like a brand.

"You are my most beloved, my most cherished... my most desired one." Gently, his finger skittered along my jawline and pushed a stray lock of hair behind my ear. "My Beauty, you're the beating heart of my kingdom. I would have you sit on my throne with me by your side where I will love you to no end. What else is there to know?"

The air around us hummed with anticipation as he leaned down and claimed my mouth with a kiss. I gasped at the sudden heat, my cheeks turning pink in embarrassment.

But for once, I was glad for his advances. His lips hungrily explored mine until we were both breathless and clinging to each other.

The sweet taste of wine lingered on his tongue as his hands explored my curves with wild abandon.

When I pulled away, my heart hammering in my chest, his face was a picture of pure bliss. His eyes sparkled with love and desire, and his smile was brighter than the stars.

Tears pooled in my eyes. "Hades, you are cruel!" I protested. "You twist my heart with honeyed words, yet refuse to give me the answers I seek!"

His lips parted and his eyes glowed with an inner fire. A thousand unspoken words lingered between us. He wanted me by his side, desired that I rule alongside him—but he knew I couldn't do that unless I knew who I really was.

Still trembling slightly, I squared my shoulders and looked up into Hades' dark eyes. "If you truly wish for me to stay at your side and accept this love of yours…" I sucked in a stuttered breath, "then help me find out who I am."

A gentle warmth enveloped my body as Hades' gaze softened like a winter fog. With utmost tenderness, he cupped my face in his hands and kissed my forehead gently. "My Beauty," he whispered against my skin, "you are much more than what you think you are… much more than just a mere mortal woman."

As I gazed deeply into his entrancing eyes, all fear left me. I waited expectantly for him to continue.

He watched me silently, his expression unreadable. "If it were within my power, I would lay the answers you seek at your feet," he murmured huskily.

*"But this is something I cannot help you with,"* I finished in a whisper, my voice barely audible above the sound of our shallow breaths.

He sighed deeply and leaned back to look up at the starlit

sky, his silhouette cast in the moonlight, making him seem like an angel fallen from grace.

"Let me guess," I said derisively, trying to stifle the fluttering of my heart as I savored this moment with him. "It's your mother, Nyx. She has forbidden you from assisting me." My words hung heavy in the air as he remained silent, unable to refute my claim.

I watched as shame and guilt darkened his expression, but then a soft smile curled the corner of his lips and his gaze softened as he looked down at me. "Tell me more about that dream," he purred, tenderly stroking my cheek with his thumb.

I blushed hopelessly, feeling every part of me affected by his velvety touch, and pursed my lips to keep myself from stammering.

He threw me a knowing look, grinning mischievously as if daring me to challenge his words. "I swear to you, my love," he whispered in a low voice that sent shivers down my spine, inching closer to me until our faces were mere seconds apart. His breath was hot against my skin; sweet and alluring like honey. "The moment I bring you to ruin will be sweeter than any dream you've ever had."

My heart swelled as I teasingly uttered, "Ruin me? Surely you meant *love* me?"

A dark wolfish smirk eased on his lips and his bright maroon eyes sparkled with delight as he responded without hesitation. "I meant every word I said."

The air around us crackled and hummed with energy as an invisible force drew us together and gave flight to our longing hearts. At long last, he bent down and sealed his words with a scorching kiss that left me reeling in pleasure.

# 61

# PHILLIP

*I* ran my fingers along the dewy walls of my cell, in search of an escape from this nightmare. The air was thick with the scent of mildew and despair. My hands came up empty as I found no hidden passage to freedom, no chink in the meticulously crafted stone fortress that trapped us within its walls. Exhausted from my futile efforts, I slumped down, pressing my brow against the unforgiving bars.

Eloise's trembling hand clenched her cell's bar tight, ice-blue eyes locked on mine. "Phillip," she said, her voice low and calm. "We're getting out of here. I promise you. We *will* find a way." Her sole assurance grounded me amidst the consuming darkness that threatened to swallow us whole. Her eyes glinted with a combination of fear and unbreakable will that served as a beacon of hope for my battered soul. For now, all we could do was wait and pray for a future beyond these cold, damp walls.

Time twisted and distorted within the dungeon halls, erasing all distinction between the hours as we languished.

The complete lack of windows or light prevented us from knowing if it was twilight or night. Our conversations were weak and vapid, our minds just barely keeping up with the anguish that filled our being.

And then, as if summoned by our suffering, the sound of heavy feet trudging along a set of jangling keys rung through the hall. A sickening chuckle echoed off the walls and sent an ice-cold shiver straight down my spine. Hypnos, Lord of Dreams and Slumber had arrived.

"I hope they're feeding you gruel," he taunted, his voice dripping with sadistic amusement as he grabbed a bar and leaned against the gate of my cell. "We wouldn't want you to *die* now and be stuck with you forever."

"The gruel here is fantastic," Eloise snapped. She did not miss a beat before she countered him. Her fiery nature made her brave even in the greatest desperation. "A jug of ale would be lovely to wash it down, while you're at it." She threw him a sly smile. "The water isn't bad at all, but I do miss my wine."

"Human wine can never compare to the ambrosia of Olympian feasts," Hypnos sneered with a scowl. And then he paused in thought for a moment. His expression brightened, and wistfully, he smiled. "But I cannot deny that Bloodmoon Red has a remarkable flavor, and I'd even go as far as saying it rivals the sweet nectar of the gods."

Eloise barely lifted one corner of her mouth in a small smirk as she spoke, her voice faltering with the slightest hint of feigned shock. "Bloodmoon Red, you say? How curious... We've got over a dozen cases of it safely tucked away on our ship."

Hypnos' smug expression cooled for an instant. "You lie!" he protested. But even as he spat out the words, doubt lingered heavily in his voice.

A mischievous grin stretched across Eloise's heart-shaped face. Her eyes sparkled as she replied, "Uh... It's true, sleepy-head. And it's such a pity, too. It would be nice if we had a bottle right about now. Phillip, don't you agree? "

I glowered, baffled and beyond bemusement. But she seemed to relish in my reaction, her mouth curling into an even wider grin.

"Bloodmoon Red..." Hypnos said, and his voice took on a dangerous edge. Around us, the shadows seemed to lengthen, as if they, too, had become aware of his burgeoning excitement. He licked his lips hungrily as if he could already taste it. "It has been far too long since I indulged in the pleasures of that exquisite elixir."

Eloise beamed confidently. "The taste of Bloodmoon Red *is* incomparable," she drawled, tempting him further. "Its depth and richness are nothing short of legendary."

Hypnos leaned in closer to her, his curiosity fully piqued. "And where can one find this delightful pleasure?" he asked, his eyes mesmerized by her every word.

"Don't you tell him, Eloise!" I growled, unable to contain my outrage any longer. My being was drenched with frustration.

But my warning only made Hypnos even more intrigued about the renowned drink. His lips curved into a smirk as he waited for Eloise's answer.

She turned to me, her gaze a tantalizing concoction of danger and regret. Although I failed to understand her reasons, I could see just how badly she wanted to do this—desperately enough to take such a risk. Her voice was barely audible when she spoke. "Oh, Phillip... Why not? I'd hate for any of it to go to waste."

Hypnos trailed a single fingertip along the bar until it lightly grazed Eloise's skin. "I might consider bringing you a bottle if you tell me where it is," he said in a low murmur, laced with enticement. "But just for you." An accusing glare speared my way. "None for *him*."

A delighted hum escaped her lips. "I like the sound of that," she mumbled.

The god's face drew nearer. His eyes were bright as amber, narrowed with a wicked glint. "So tell me," Hypnos purred. "Where's the wine?"

With eyes aglow with mischief, Eloise pointed at the ceiling, diverting his attention away from the cells. "Why, in our boat, of course. Tucked away in—"

"Don't!" I roared before she could finish her sentence, my fingernails digging painfully deep into the iron bars as I tried desperately to get their attention.

Hypnos spun around, his voice a low thunder as he prowled towards me. "Look here, mortal," he said in a low growl. His eyes, like fiery gems, pierced through me and I almost cringed against the hard dungeon wall. He stopped just in front of me, so close that I could feel heat radiating from him. "I have an offer for you." The god extended his arm, parchment and ink clutched between his long fingers. "Draw me a map of where you docked the ship, and I shall make sure that your remaining days in this dungeon are more *bearable*." He paused. "But be warned," he added coldly. "Be precise, or I may lose interest in this little game and find another that might cost you dearly."

My pride warred against my longing for vengeance.

Eloise scoffed in the corner, her voice filled with apathy. "Give the god what he wants. It's not like we're getting out of here anytime soon."

My mind reeled with disbelief as Eloise gave me a sturdy nod. I glared at her with confusion, but she remained unphased. Against my better judgment, I sighed in defeat and plucked up the parchment and quill from the dusty ground.

My hands trembled as I began to draft the road that had led us here—this chaotic realm of monsters and gods. In fits and starts, I sketched out our journey among the craggy rocks and ancient trees, until finally, my weary arm was still. Although far from perfect, I thought it would do if Hypnos saw fit to accept it.

Yet as I continued to stare down at my work, something strange came over me—a surge of defiance rising in my chest. No god should interfere with my destiny. With one swift motion, I balled up the parchment and threw it carelessly towards Eloise's cell. It glided through the air in a graceful arc before settling silently at her feet.

Hypnos watched on with bemused disdain, his barely concealed laughter echoing off the walls. "Silly human…" he muttered. But as the god bent down to gather the discarded map, Eloise caught my eye. She flashed me an audacious wink before snatching the keys from Hypnos' belt without being seen, deftly concealing them within her clothing.

My expression slackened, her daunting deed filling me with shock and admiration.

Unaware of Eloise's theft, Hypnos slowly straightened. He stepped back into the hallway, his attention consumed by the haunting promise of Bloodmoon Red. "Well, mortals," he said in a voice dripping with satisfaction. "It seems that having you around is really worth *something* after all."

"What will you do with it?" Eloise whispered her question as though she feared the answer. "Will you drink it all?"

Hypnos let out a booming laugh, his bright eyes twinkling with wickedness. "Drink it? No, no, my dear. I plan to ensure we have something truly spectacular to celebrate when I return!" He held out the precious parchment like a trophy and waved it proudly in the air. "I shall arrange an extravagant feast!" His gaze lingered on the map until it finally landed upon us with an icy glint of triumph. "Sadly for you, you won't be invited."

With a last jeering snicker, Hypnos' form gradually faded away into nothingness as his footsteps echoed down the hallway. Eloise and I locked eyes, a silent understanding passing between us; we both realized this was our chance. At long last, we had found a way out of this prison.

# BEAUTY

*A*s dying embers of sunlight draped the Netherworld in a sheet of molten gold, I found myself leisurely strolling along Hecate's captivating courtyard, escorted by Hades. I'd spent many moons under the sorceress' guidance, and he often kept me company in the evening's dark hours.

Rays of twilight lent hints of orange and purple to the sky, while moonflowers and night-blooming jasmine unfurled their petals, permeating the atmosphere with their sweet scent. Fireflies danced around the flickering lanterns lighting the path before us, weaving a mesmerizing chiaroscuro.

We arrived at a secluded garden, where vines of ivy embraced the walls and pillars, twining their way intricately and shifting with each passing breeze. A small fountain at the center gurgled with crystalline water, its tranquil stream adding a soothing melody to our serene surroundings.

Hades' hand brushed against mine and I shivered, my body craving his touch even as my heart soared at the sight of him. His maroon eyes held something new in their depths that remained a mystery to me. His dark hair tumbled around his face in glossy waves, and his black cloak billowed gently in the breeze, granting him an air of gloom that left me breathless. He was commanding yet tender, dangerous yet loving.

"You could have chosen any of your watchmen's towers to keep me safe, and yet, you chose Hecate's temple," I began, my gaze drawn to the play of emotions in his eyes. His lips curled into a small, secretive grin, and despite the stillness of the cool air, a warm sensation spread within my chest. "You have a fondness for this place, don't you?" My words echoed in the temple's courtyard, its walls of pure white marble aglow with countless flickering lanterns.

He smiled at me knowingly, like he understood something that I hadn't even realized myself. "It holds memories," he replied sweetly, though cryptically. "Memories of ancient times and friendships that have endured through the ages."

I nodded. Some things were better left unspoken, their significance known only to those who held them close to their hearts.

As we strolled through the lush, sun-dappled courtyard, I stopped to admire the dark belladonna blooms, their velvet petals unfurling like shadows coming to life.

Hades stood beside me. A tingle raced up my spine when his fingers interlaced with mine. "And what about you?" he said. His question lingered in the air as his gaze roved me intently, taking in every detail of my expression. "Do *you* have a *fondness* for this temple?"

My throat was too tight to answer. I simply nodded and looked into his eyes with admiration. Hecate's temple was a place of unearthly beauty, where the boundaries between gods and mortals blurred, and all secrets were laid bare like an opened book. The library was spellbinding, and the goddess' kindness had been nothing short of extraordinary. And still...

His firm hand glided along my jawline, persuading me to meet his darkened gaze. Unwavering, he spoke. "Come back to the palace with me." The words delivered a promise of enticing delights to come. "The outsiders have been dealt with. There's no reason for you to stay here a minute longer."

"I can't," I sighed regretfully, torn between my longing to be near him and my determination to face the mermaids. My body craved to accept his invitation and return with him to the Midnight Palace, where I could be by his side once more.

His brow subtly creased, and I could tell he struggled to understand my reasoning.

"I must stay here and learn everything Hecate has to offer on the mermaids," I explained, trying to convey the importance of my quest. "She can give me spells and knowledge that will be essential for their confrontation."

"Oh, I *know* she's eager to help," Hades uttered, his voice tinged with a hint of jealousy. "But you know I would do anything for you. If you wish to learn about the mermaids, I could provide you with information as well."

My heart ached as I slowly replied, "I appreciate it, Hades. But Hecate has knowledge of their realm better than anyone else, and you're forbidden from helping me." I exhaled, grasping for the right words to express my thoughts. "I'm not a goddess whose wishes can be granted at her whim. I'm just a woman, trying to find the truth in a realm of gods… I need all the help I can get."

Hades nodded, though his jaw was taut. "I regret I cannot aid you directly. But know I wish you success in your quest."

His words rang hollow. Did he really want me to untangle my past, risking the possibility that it would sever any ties between us?

I searched his face but found only carefully composed neutrality. He was adept at veiling his true thoughts.

"I wish you could join me on this journey," I said. My admission hung in the silent air between us. I longed for his companionship, but fate divided us once more.

We stood amidst the stone benches that lined the garden, the space between us now feeling insurmountable. Hades stepped closer, tipping my chin up. His thumb grazed my lower lip in a feather-light caress. "I am always with you, Beauty," he whispered, and the silken touch of his fingers trailed down the slope of my neck and rested on my glimmering stone pendant. "Always."

Hades inched closer. His presence was like a raging tempest, the thunder of his heart echoing against mine. I fought the urge to melt into him as his breath tickled my cheek. Dusk was drawing nearer and with it came the duty that waited at the temple, but my soul longed to linger here just a little longer.

Reluctantly I stepped back, breaking the spell of his touch. "Nightfall is coming. I must go."

He glanced up at the bruised sky. "Must you leave so soon?" he asked, pain straining his voice. But something else lingered in his words, and I shuddered as I recognized the slightest glimpse of untamed fury.

I blinked back useless tears. "If I could choose, I would stay with you." I drank in his beloved features, committing them to memory. "But Hecate is waiting. Please understand." I took one more step back, my heart splitting in two.

Hades tensed, his grip on my hands tightening. "You value her company over mine?" His face was a mask of controlled rage, every muscle tensed and drawn tight.

"It's not that way at all," I blurted, wrenching free from him.

"It is *exactly* that way!" he roared, the anguished howl finally breaking through his carefully composed façade. Hades stepped closer, looming over me like an obsidian storm cloud. "Hecate covets you like a crown of laurels—can you not see it? It has *always* been so!"

My brow furrowed in confusion. "But you sent me here..." I said slowly, trying to make sense of his words. "Why would you do so if you despise Hecate?"

"It wasn't my choice!" he exclaimed desperately, his chest heaving as though he'd been running for miles. He inhaled a shaky breath, his fury teetering on the brink. "The pegasus chose your destination—not me!" His knuckles turned white as he gripped the back of the bench.

I studied his profile, unease coiling in my core even as my heart ached to bridge the distance between us. He was holding something back—I was certain of it. "Am I in any danger?" I asked warily.

"I'd never allow you to remain here if you were," he replied in a calmer tone. "Hecate is a formidable ally..." The words sailed into silence. "Please, just trust that I want what's best." His hand reached as if to cup my cheek, then fell away.

I steeled myself against the pull of his pain. "Best for whom? For me?" I challenged. "Or for you?"

At that, Hades drew himself up to his full imposing height. Danger gleamed along the hard lines of his body. "You—belong—with me," he decreed, his words finality itself.

I stepped back slowly, swept by sheer indignation. "I am not a prize to be seized and kept, Hades." Tears brimmed my eyes as a tempest of emotions exploded through me—anger, frustration, and even love. "Not even you can command me so, *Your Highness!*" I spat his title like a curse, the words edged with bitterness.

We stood frozen, chests heaving, the space between us now a yawning chasm.

"In time, my path will lead me back to you. But for now,

I must walk it alone. Try to understand," I pleaded, softening my voice with effort.

Hades turned his face away, bitterness etched on his noble features. "You may think you'll find answers," he bit out, and for once, I caught a glimpse of pain behind his tearful eyes. "But all you'll find is more distance between us."

Sorrow pierced through my anger like a lance. "Why must it be like this?" I beseeched raggedly. "If you care for me, would you not see me free?"

Hades turned his back on me. "I think you should go," he said. "Hecate is waiting." His voice was lifeless, all passion drained away.

Tears blurred my vision, but I would not falter now. My heart was heavy as I stepped away from Hades, his cryptic warning echoing in my mind.

The solace of Hecate's temple called to me across the gloom. What lay ahead was uncertain, but I had to try nonetheless. Too much depended on it—not just my freedom, but perhaps even my soul.

# 63

# PHILLIP

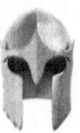

*I* sank to the cold, unforgiving ground of my cell, my back pressed against its damp and ancient stone. The musty scent of dust and mold clung to me like a second skin. I pulled out my makeshift chisel, crafted from a discarded metal piece, and ran my fingers over the rough surface of the wall like I did every day during our seemingly everlasting imprisonment.

Eloise's voice floated in from across the room, her melodic laugh teasing me as she said, "Are you trying to *tunnel* your way out of here, love?"

A soft snicker escaped my throat at the thought. "I wish it were that simple," I said, setting aside the chisel. My hand reached for the small piece of charcoal I had found during one of my explorations early on in our confinement. "But no, I'm just keeping track of the days."

"The days?" Eloise prompted curiously.

I nodded solemnly and began tracing faint lines into the stone as I explained, "Yes, the days until the Bloodmoon Red Feast."

Eloise's hazel eyes widened with astonishment. "You can keep track of time in this windowless cell?"

I showed her the newly etched markings on the monolith walls, a testament to my attentiveness during our imprisonment. "I've been studying the guards vigilantly," I explained in the lowest of voices, "listening intently to their minutiae conversations to glean any information that could benefit us when creating an escape plan."

I narrated my plan for Eloise: the impending Bloodmoon Red Feast was approaching and everyone, even the sentries, was invited. This was our opportunity to flee without raising any suspicion from the guard's heightened state of alertness.

Eloise's gaze flickered from me to the wall, reading it like a quatrain of prophecy. Her face changed from surprise to apprehension. "Do you think we can escape without getting caught? They'll be expecting something during the feast, won't they?"

My lips curled ever so slightly into a smile as I looked back at her with confidence. "That's the beauty of it," I replied. "They'll be distracted by all the revelry, too intoxicated to notice two missing prisoners."

Eloise's eyes glimmered with awe. "My goodness, you're brighter than I imagined," she exclaimed, a lightheartedness lingering in her voice.

"Uh… Thank you?" My lips pulled into a tight smirk, disturbed by her odd compliment. "Anyway," I warned, my words harsh yet laced with caution. "We must take extra care. Those guards may be sloppy in their drinking, but they are still primed with sharp blades and considerable expertise. And Hades, well, he's no common deity."

Eloise nodded in agreement before spinning to take in her exquisite surroundings with an expression of amazement. "This cannot be an ordinary prison," she murmured thoughtfully. "We must be within the confines of Hades' palace itself."

I quirked a questioning brow, my interest piqued by Eloise's deduction. "What makes you so certain?"

Her gaze roamed around the lavish hall, taking in the intricate marble pillars, sweeping across the tapestries hung on the stone walls, admiring the gilded ceiling that seemed miles above us—each detail more extravagant than the last. "Just look at this place," She breathed in admiration. "It is far too grand for it to be any ordinary prison. This is a fortress worthy of royalty."

As her words tumbled from her lips, I nodded in uneasy agreement. We were held captive in the deepest depths of Hades' palace; a world away from the dreariness and isolation one would expect from a dungeon cell.

The truth behind our imprisonment settled heavily upon me—being trapped in Hades' own domain meant untold dangers. But amidst those shadows of danger, there was also hope. "We must be close to where the feast is taking place," I said, feeling my heart swell with anticipation.

A fierce glint lit Eloise's gaze, determination creasing her features. "I believe you're right," she replied, her voice ringing out confidently as she clutched something in her hand. "And luckily, I have the keys."

"If we can find the banqueting hall," I said, my voice wavering with hope, "there's a chance we could rescue Aurora and make it out alive." I shook my head, gloom quickly descending on me. "Why would Hades keep us here? He could easily dispose of us in some far corner of the Nether-world where no one would ever hear from us again."

Eloise's expression turned serious, her brows furrowing in thought. "Perhaps he's got some twisted plan for us," she suggested, her tone laced with trepidation. "Or maybe he plans to use us as leverage against Demeter."

Her words sounded like a dagger piercing through my worst fears, and I nodded slowly as the pieces of the puzzle fell into place. Hades was well-known for his cunning and manipulative nature; it wouldn't be surprising if he had an ulterior motive for keeping us captive in his palace.

The oppressive air of the god's dungeon lingered, like an invisible cloak wrapped tightly around us. My heart raced as I glanced around to make sure no guards were nearby. "We have to be careful," I whispered, my throat dry. "If Hades even suspects that we're plotting something—"

"Don't worry." Eloise cut me off with a shake of her head. "We will be smart about this, Phillip," she said fiercely, her voice strained with emotion. Her eyes glittered in the dim light of the atrium, bright blue pinpoints of courage and resolve. "And we have the advantage of surprise on our side."

I smiled at her, grateful for her resourcefulness. "Then all we need is the right moment," I said. "When the gods are deep in their cups and their guard is down, we'll make our move."

Eloise smiled, the glint in her eyes conveying reassurance. "We'll get out of here, my love," she said with a fierce determination in her voice. Her expression darkened as she added, "All of us."

Gusts of hope stirred my heavy heart, giving me the strength to face the looming shadows in this dank dungeon.

64

# BEAUTY

The days dragged on in Hecate's temple, each one consumed by my burning desire to solve Nyx's riddle. Hades remained aloof and distant, but I was driven by profound determination.

I pored over Hecate's heavy scrolls and texts seeking the answers I needed, until I finally stumbled upon a chart that pointed me towards the mermaids' den. Its contents warned of their traps and battle strategies—information vital for me to succeed.

"Mermaids venture into the ocean just before dusk and return to their lair at nightfall," I murmured, tracing my fingertips over the ancient map etched with elaborate designs. "But time flows differently in the Netherworld, and there may not be enough of it for me to make it back." I whipped my head up and met Hecate's amethyst eyes. "Can you extend the twilight? It's the only way I can reach the mermaids' lair and come back in time."

Hecate's lips curled into a knowing smile. Her eyes gleamed with molten power as she spoke. "My dearest Beauty, I can bestow you with two gifts: The ability to breathe underwater, and the capacity to summon a guiding light that will illuminate your path. But Time... that is something even I cannot control."

The ground suddenly rumbled, the room thrumming with an unforeseen mighty presence. With a quick glance, I discovered Chronos—the Lord of Time—his tall figure illuminated by golden hair and his emerald eyes laced with the weight of ages.

A thunderous voice reverberated through the archives. "I can take care of that."

My heart soared with relief as I greeted him. "Chronos…"

Hecate's gaze lit up with surprise as the Lord of Time strode into the library. She rose to her feet, a spark of anticipation radiating from her body. "Chronos! What a pleasant surprise. What news do you bring?"

A handsome grin spread across his features. "Have you not heard?" he said. His gaze scoured the scrolls on the table before him. "There's to be a feast."

Hecate's eyebrows tangled as confusion crossed her face. "Another feast?" she asked. "So soon? The blood moon only appears once every twelve full moons."

"This isn't a blood moon feast, dearest Hecate," Chronos murmured with a sly smile, perusing the many scrolls. The movements of his fingers were graceful, as if he were weaving together a mythical tale.

Hecate eyed the god and raised an accusing eyebrow. "Well then, what is it?" she asked sharply.

Before Hecate had time to wonder further, the imposing library doors swung open. "A *Bloodmoon Red* feast!" Hypnos cheered as he stood at the doorway, his broad shoulders framed by the setting sun behind him.

I raced towards him in an embrace. "Hypnos! Where have you been? I've missed you dearly."

The god of sleep snickered and swung away, holding me at arm's length. With a twinkle in his eye, he proudly said, "I have traveled far and wide to bring you a wondrous treasure, my dear friends."

My chest tightened at his words and my disbelief was replaced with deep curiosity. Hypnos stepped back and presented his discovery to us with a flourish. "One hundred cases of Bloodmoon Red, ready to be served in our forthcoming celebration," he declared.

The very thought shot a thrill through my being. All around me were looks of great excitement. A deep red glow shimmered in the corner of my vision and when I turned, there it was—a bottle of burgundy resting on the table.

"Bloodmoon Red…" Chronos whispered reverently, while Hecate murmured a warning.

I cleared my throat. "What exactly are we celebrating?"

Hypnos moved closer, eagerness in his gaze. His breath tickled my ear as he purred, "Your victory, love. I *know* you will reclaim your name."

My breathing hitched, the emotion threatening to overwhelm me. I had to swallow hard against it before I could turn to Chronos, and even then hope sparkled within me.

"Chronos," my voice was soft yet determined. "Can you help me buy more time?" The air shimmered with anticipation as I waited for his answer.

He nodded gravely, understanding what was at stake. "I will do all that I can to extend the twilight," he assured me. "But be warned. Time is a willful mistress and its limits cannot be pushed much farther."

"I understand," I said, my resolve strengthening at his words. "With your help, I know I can recover the treasure from the mermaids' den!" My voice reverberated off the library walls.

Hecate's eyes widened with admiration as she realized

what I intended to do. "I guess it's time then," she said, gazing at me with pride. Her lips eased into a smile. "You've learned all I can teach you, my child. You're ready to do what must be done."

She stepped forward, and as her hands rested on my shoulders, a sudden glow cascaded over me. Magic surged through me like lightning, igniting the darkness within and fortifying my courage.

I glanced down in awe—shimmering gold scales had enveloped my body in gorgeous armor. Light as a feather, it clung to me closely like a second skin, with no restrictions on movement. The golden hues sparkled and shimmied before shifting into glimmering aquamarine shades that mirrored the ever-changing hues of the Midnight Lake. The intricate detail and dynamic texture that ran along each scale made it ripple as if I were underwater every time I took a step.

The power of this magical armor was beyond belief. Its mystical energy vibrated beneath my touch, as if the very essence of the ocean itself was woven into its fabric. I would be safe from the mermaids' menacing claws and sharp fangs —they would simply bounce off the barriers of its magical defense.

"This armor is remarkable," I said, my voice filled with gratitude.

Hecate smiled, her eyes shining with pride. "It is a gift from my power and the vastness of the ocean," she said. "Now, take this spell to breathe underwater. It will allow you to traverse the Midnight Lake as if you were one of its own inhabitants."

She handed me a small vial. Its liquid content sparkled like starlight, and as I uncorked it, a gentle sea breeze swept through the room, carrying with it the unmistakable scent of saltwater. "My magic will last until the first ray of moonlight," she warned me. "Use your time wisely."

"And here," Hecate continued, offering me a small scroll bound with a red ribbon, "is the incantation to summon the guiding light. Speak these words, and a luminous orb will lead your way through the depths, and show you the way home."

I took the vial and the parchment, holding them close to my heart. With these gifts, I felt as if I were a part of the lake itself, embraced by its ancient wisdom and fathomless mysteries.

"I will not forget your kindness," I said, my voice firm with determination. "I will bravely face the mermaids, uncover their secrets, and vanquish whatever darkness threatens me."

Hecate's eyes sparkled with pride and trepidation. "Take heed, Beauty," she murmured, her voice quavering with motherly tenderness, "the mermaids are not to be underestimated—they are sly and lethal as the depths of the lake they reside in. Do not be fooled by their beauty, for that is only but a façade to hide the danger within."

I bowed my head solemnly.

She nodded her approval before stepping back to allow me to ready myself for the task at hand. As I examined the spellbinding armor and grasped onto the vial and parchment tightly, an overwhelming feeling of purpose surged through me. Hecate had given me a tremendous gift; one of bravery and courage.

"Thank you so much for your help," I said weakly, tears pricking at my eyes.

She smiled warmly. Her comforting gaze fortified me from within. "You are like a daughter to me, Beauty," she uttered softly, her face aglow with fondness. "May you succeed on this quest."

"Stealth and speed are key," Hypnos advised, his stern voice echoing in the room. "Once inside, move fast but be thorough. Search diligently without hesitation. Get in—find your treasure—get out."

Fumbling for words, I silently agreed.

"Reclaim your name, my friend," he added in a low, determined voice. "We'll be waiting for you." He lifted the bottle of Bloodmoon Red off the table and held it high, promising our imminent celebration. Hypnos stepped back, illuminating us all with his boldness. It was enough to give me courage and fill every inch of my being with strength.

I strapped Voidbringer to my back and stepped out of the room. My boots clattered as they struck the hallway's travertine floor, the sound bouncing off the pristine walls.

No sooner had I left the temple's safety, than a gust of wind buffeted me. A flurry of rose petals drizzled over me in a shower of pinks and crimsons, a wondrous beauty that swiftly faded as the breeze died back, and the courtyard remained in mystifying stillness.

I whirled around, my heart thudding in my chest. Hades stood before me, larger than life—a god of darkness and shadows, his aura both menacingly seductive and inviting.

"Beauty," he breathed softly, his voice haunted by sorrow and longing. "I beg you to turn back and reconsider."

I exhaled slowly, feeling the pull of his gaze like a wave washing over me. Dark and captivating, his eyes were brimming with an intensity I'd never known before. "I know it may seem impossible," I murmured, my voice trembling from the sheer emotion coursing through me. "I know you think I'm being naive."

He stepped forward, and we were so close I could feel the heat radiating off his body. His fingertips brushed against my cheek and I shuddered in response, as if an invisible force was tugging us together.

"I admire your courage," he said huskily, searching my eyes for understanding. "But the Midnight Lake is a hazardous place. There are dangers beyond what you can imagine."

My eyes widened, and I paused for a moment before responding. "And I am ready to face them," I vowed fiercely, warmth blossoming on my cheeks as his thumb caressed my skin.

The air charged around us with an unspoken longing and despair. I could sense Hades battling himself, but he knew I could not be deterred.

"Very well, my love," Hades sighed in resignation. "If you're set on this path, I will not stop you. But promise me this—you will be cautious and take care of yourself."

My heart raced in my chest, torn between his quiet plea and my desperate need to move forward. Gathering every ounce of courage that I had to stay focused on my task ahead, I replied resolutely, "I promise."

He drew me closer to his chiseled frame, and our bodies entwined in sacred stillness. Hades gently leaned in, and closing my eyes, I welcomed a gentle yet lingering kiss that silenced each of my uncertainties.

We parted briefly and looked into each other's eyes.

"I cannot intervene directly," he said regretfully, his gaze never faltering from mine as his thumb grazed circles along my palm. "But I can guide you on your journey."

An influx of power surged around us, a whirlwind of bright sparks skimming our skin as the wind rustled my hair and danced around Hades' frame. Everything became a dizzying blur as I felt myself being lifted off the ground by some unseen force.

Time seemed to stand still until we were abruptly dropped onto the edge of the Midnight Lake. Its tranquil waters stirred in perfect harmony beneath the shimmering canvas of the twilight sky. The stars above glittered in the lake's depths, reflecting infinitely in the tiny silver ripples that lapped against the shore.

"We're here," he breathed, his voice heavy with reverence. His eyes lit up with something—admiration? awe?—as they searched mine.

A plethora of emotions bubbled inside me. Love and gratitude chiefly among them. "Thank you, Hades. It means more than you know," I whispered.

The corner of his lips curved into a comforting smile, and he held my hand gently but firmly in his. "I cannot go with you any further," he said earnestly, "but I will be here to support you. You can do this, Beauty. I know you will."

His words ignited a fire of bravery within me. With his faith and encouragement, I could overcome the most daunting tasks to come.

"I will come back to you," I vowed earnestly, my gaze boring into his. "Once this nightmare is over and my fate is redeemed, I shall return to your side."

Hades nodded slowly, his gaze heartbreakingly tender, yet resolute. He opened his mouth like he had more to say before pausing and whispering, "The gods be with you."

His words clung to me as I whirled away, my gaze fixed on the lake in the distance.

My destiny awaited.

# BEAUTY

The icy water lapped at my ankles as I stood at the lake's shore, peering into its impenetrable depths. Somewhere in its abyssal darkness lay the answer to the riddle—and the key to unlocking my true identity.

I triple-checked the lightweight armor gifted to me by Hecate, enchanted to aid my movements underwater while protecting me from the mermaids' vicious fangs.

My stomach cramped with dread, yet an inner strength kept me going. I had to remember who I was and fight for what I'd lost. In the depths of the dark and mysterious lake, guarded by a creature of enchantment and danger, my fate beckoned.

My lungs seared as I inhaled one deep breath, and without another thought, I plunged into the water. The magical armor Hecate had gifted me shimmered in response to the gentle waves, and it was like falling into a deep pool of stars. I intoned the parchment's incantation, and an ethereal orb manifested just ahead of me, paving the way through the dark depths.

I sliced through the chilly waters, the weight of my quest

pressing on me. But I pushed past my fear and dove deeper, into the abyss. It swallowed me into its depths, cold and shocking at first, then oddly tranquil. I drifted downwards, allowing my body to acclimate.

Save for the soft guiding light, the darkness was lifeless and all-consuming, swallowing me until nothing else existed but its void expanse. Terror threatened to claw its way through my veins. How could I ever hope to find the mermaids' lair?

For a long moment, I stayed frozen. Then, like a dam splitting apart in a sudden flood, a surge of calmness washed over me. I remembered a tracking spell prepared with Hecate's guidance, and my fingers flew to my belt where the vial hung heavy from its cord.

Swiftly, I unstoppered the vial, releasing swirling sparks that hung suspended, shimmering faintly. They twitched once, then shot off deeper into the lake's shadowy womb. I hurried after them, powerful kicks propelling me forward.

As I delved deeper, I knew that my journey was fraught with peril and uncertainty. But I also knew that I carried with me the love and belief of those who cared for me. And that, in itself, was a powerful force that would guide me through the darkest of waters.

Down, down I dove, guided by the wisps of magic. The icy pressure squeezed my lungs, the depths threatening to swallow me. Still, I pushed on.

After what felt like an eternity, the sparks paused, dancing in place above a rocky outcropping looming from the darkness. A cavern yawned in the stone, likely the tunnel to the mermaids' treasure hoard. I shuddered, picturing whatever guardians might lurk within. But it was too late for second guesses. I had to see this through.

As I approached the den, wonder and caution tangled in

my quickened blood. The treasure I sought was here, and with it, the answer to the riddle that held me captive.

I speared into the tunnel, jagged rocks brushing my arms and sides. The way ahead was pitch black but I kept one hand on the stone wall to guide myself forward by touch alone.

At last, a dim glow appeared, casting dancing shadows against the stone. I moved cautiously towards it until the tunnel opened up into a vast underwater cavern, the ceiling lost in gloom far above. The weak light came from glowing crystals studding the walls and pillars of stone.

But more captivating were the heaps of treasure piled high throughout the cavern—chests spilling forth gold coins, jewelry dangling from stalactites, suits of armor, weapons, gemstones, and more. This was the hoard of centuries, salvaged from countless shipwrecks.

I couldn't stay for long. The darkness of the lake was unyielding, and I had to make my way back before twilight faded, or else lose my ability to breathe underwater and suffer a hazardous encounter with the fearsome mermaids.

My eyes desperately raked over the mounds. Somewhere here was the object that would end my turmoil, if only I could find it in time.

I dove towards the nearest pile, sifting through gold and jewels, necklaces and daggers. The minutes slipped away as I plunged through heap after heap, never the right item. Doubt crept into my heart. What if I'd come to the wrong place?

No—I could not afford to think like that. I forced myself onward to the next mound, my movements growing frantic.

I watched with bated breath as the tracking spell's golden dust drifted past me and glided through the cavern, glinting faintly in the gloom. It wafted on an unfelt current, meandering past piles of sparkling treasure before finally settling on one unassuming chest tucked against a carved pillar.

The dust gleamed and flickered brightly for a moment. This was the object of my quest. I let out a shaky exhale, scarcely believing fortune had led me true after so many trials and false turns.

I rushed over, heart pounding.

The chest's lid snapped open, stale air rushing out in a plume. Inside was not a jumble of jewels and coins like the other chests, but a single item resting on black velvet—a polished wooden box with an ornate silver clasp.

Hardly daring to breathe, I reached in and lifted it with trembling fingers. This had to be it. I cracked open the clasp to reveal a ring within, a flawless diamond circled by smaller gems that sparkled even in the cave's weak light.

Was this it? Could this be my answer?

And then, the riddle's stanza came to mind, resounding like a vigorous anthem: *"Steal from shadows to find what's concealed. In a wheel of power, the truth is revealed."*

A wheel of power... My fingers trembled as I held the ring up to the dim light. There on the inside, an engraving: *To my fated love.* The words resonated through my soul.

I started. A shifting shadow rushed along the cavern walls. I had to act quickly.

With no time to lose, I slipped the ring on my finger. When metal touched skin, lightning erupted through my entire being. My mind flooded with a cascade of long-lost memories. I saw my old life play out in vivid detail—the castle, the prince, the fateful night I'd summoned the gods and was swept away by darkness… It all came rushing back in overwhelming waves.

Gasping, I steadied myself against the cavern wall. The truth blazed within me at last. This ring had revealed my identity. Here was the key to unlocking my past, present, and future.

Joyful laughter escaped me, the muffled sound carrying through the cavern. But my cry of victory shattered into cold horror as a bone-chilling shriek answered me. The mermaids knew I was here.

Fear jolted through me as shadows rippled at the mouth of the tunnel. I turned to flee, but too late. Three mermaids blocked the exit, eyes burning with rage, writhing tails primed to strike.

"Thief!" the lead one snarled, baring hooked fangs. "You dare steal from our trove?"

Gripping Voidbringer, I raised my chin. "I've reclaimed what is rightfully mine." My bold words echoed through the cave. "Let me pass!"

The mermaid hissed, sharp and cold. "Nothing leaves here but bare bones!"

With terrifying speed, all three shot through the water towards me. I barely had time to raise my sword before they attacked in a blur of lashing tails and slashing claws. I twisted desperately, Voidbringer biting into scaly flesh to release plumes of inky blood.

The lead mermaid's talons raked my shoulder, slashing through a gap in my armor. I cried out, kicking her back to break free. My heart hammered wildly as I faced the raging creatures. Through the pain and fear, one thought burned bright—I could not fail now, when I was so close.

But her sisters only increased their assault. Together they rushed me from both sides, intending to pin me between them and finish me off. At the last second, I dropped into a spin, feeling the brush of their scales glance off me. As I came back up, I slashed in a deadly arc, opening up gashes along their torsos. Their blood billowed out in crimson clouds.

The injured mermaids fell back with furious shrieks. But

their leader quickly took their place, eyes burning with vengeance. We clashed again and again, her fangs snapping at me between savage blows.

My chest heaved with effort. I knew my time was quickly running out. Even now, my lungs strained painfully, each watery breath requiring more focus. Hecate's spell was nearly spent.

The mermaid seemed to sense it too, and moved faster in response. Soon, I was battered with gashes that sent curls of my own blood swirling into the icy water. I parried and stabbed furiously, but my movements slowed despite my desperate resolve.

Sensing victory, the mermaid let out a triumphant wail and shot forward, fangs bared for the killing blow. With my last ounce of fading strength, I surged up beneath her guard and drove my blade straight through her chest in a burst of black ichor.

Her scream turned wet and gurgling before she went limp, sliding off my sword to sink slowly into the abyssal depths. Her sisters watched in horror, then turned tail and fled deeper into the cavern tunnels.

I hovered in the dark water, nearly spent. But freedom was so close now. Clutching my side, I began pulling myself up the tunnel, away from the remaining mermaids' domain. Each stroke was agony, my breath little more than ragged gasps. Yet I pushed on relentlessly, trailing a winding path of my blood.

My heartbeat roared in my ears, drowning out all else. Just a little farther... but black spots stained my vision. My legs slowed. Against my will, I opened my mouth, instinctively gasping for air. Only icy water flooded my lungs, shocking me.

This was it. I had failed. As darkness took me, I thought only of Hades' face, wishing I could see it one last time...

Then strong hands seized me. Through the haze, I glimpsed Hecate's amethyst eyes as she and Chronos pulled me out of the water and onto the rocky shore. I retched helplessly, vomiting foul liquid as air mercifully returned to my burning lungs.

When at last my vision cleared, I found myself cradled in Hecate's lap. Chronos and Hypnos hovered nearby, faces creased with worry.

"We almost lost you," Hecate chided, though her voice held deep relief.

"The mermaids..." I rasped weakly.

"Gone, for now," Chronos reassured. "Rest, my dear. It's over."

But I forced myself upright, still coughing out acrid water. "No—it worked. I know who I am."

Shaking, I reached out. Could it be true? Bliss erupted within me at the sight of the diamond ring glittering on my finger, perfect as though made for me alone. The missing piece of my soul, restored.

My friends stared in awe as I beheld the relic from my stolen past. No magic could hide me any longer. I lifted my gaze, speaking my name aloud for the first time in this realm like a war cry:

"I am... Aurora."

# 66

## AURORA

*J*stood on my room's terrace, gazing out at the Midnight Lake's shimmering waters as they sparkled under the moon's silvery glow. In the distance, laughter and music drifted on the night air, flowing from the courtyard where the gods and goddesses gathered.

A heavy sigh escaped me as I clutched the diamond ring, its cool metal pressed against my skin—tangible proof of the freedom I had won, yet also a burden. My harrowing journey through the mermaids' depths had restored my identity, transforming me from a nameless captive to Aurora Stonewall once more. But with those decades of lost memories restored came inescapable duties and heartbreaking truths...

What would this mean for Hades and me? I'd spotted him watching from the shadows as I emerged from the lake, triumphant ring in hand. Our eyes had met in perfect understanding before he turned and glided away, cloaked in solitude.

And then there was Phillip, the prince I had abandoned in a desperate attempt to save my kingdom. His face lingered in my thoughts, a constant reminder of my shattered vows.

"My lady?" a voice spoke behind me.

"You may go," I dismissed the hovering servant, desiring to be alone.

I stood clothed in a gilded dress evoking my royal station, though I felt hollow inside its finery. As worries besieged my whirring mind, deft hands had woven my hair into an intricate braid laced with diamonds.

But now the servants were gone, and I could stand the masquerade no longer. I had to find Hades.

In a whirl of silken skirts, I slipped from my chambers, my racing heart leading the way. Each twisting corridor blurred past until I arrived, breathless, at his closed door. Fear and anticipation warred within me. Drawing a deep breath, I steadied myself and knocked.

"Hades?" My voice trembled like a fallen leaf clinging to its branch.

The door creaked open. Hades stood before me, his dark eyes meeting mine in shock as he took in the glittering dress, the ring... Recognition dawned on his handsome features.

"My love," he rasped, hope and sorrow mingling in those two words.

"It's me," I confirmed, drawing strength from his gaze. "I found my name, Hades. I know who I am."

We stood in heavy silence as emotions flickered across his face—awe, longing, pride... and something deeper I could not name.

My heart galloped wildly as I awaited his response. Finally, he spoke, voice hushed. "You have your name. I'm glad." His hand tenderly cupped my cheek. "My feelings remain unchanged. But what about yours..." His thumb traced my skin reverently, a wordless plea, "Aurora?"

Relief unfurled within me. I leaned into his touch. "I

don't want them to change," I confessed sincerely, eyes burning.

His response was to draw me inside, into the shelter of his embrace. "Then they shall not," he vowed.

As soon as the door closed behind me, Hades' arms enveloped me with desperate longing. I clung to him, my tears rolling down my cheeks.

"You don't understand," I choked out between sobs. "I'm promised to another. Prince Phillip is my destiny."

My chest tightened at this realization and I pulled away from Hades, too afraid of his answer. But his arms encircled my waist fast, and his lips grazed mine as he purred, "Your mouth whispers that you're promised to him, but your body screams you're bound to me for all eternity."

My heart raced as his words sunk in. "Please, don't..." I begged, yet an unexplainable pull kept me rooted in his arms.

"Do you want me?" he murmured against my ear, and I shivered under his touch. He smiled knowingly and continued, "Do you want me now? Inside of you?"

I gasped at his smoldering intensity and my face flushed with embarrassment. For a moment, there was nothing left but the two of us—no promises or fates standing in our way.

A soft sound escaped my lips as I surrendered to his touch, the heat radiating from him like fire and desire coursing through me until all I wanted was for him to consume me completely.

"Say it," he commanded, his lips almost brushing mine.

"Love me or ruin me..." I murmured fiercely against his mouth. "Make me yours."

Hades stared down at me, his dark eyes searching mine for something hidden in the depths of my soul. "You're already mine," he declared in a low, husky voice that sent shivers running down my spine. "But I will have you again and again, until there is no doubt left in your mind."

My body ached for him with every breath, and I moaned in response as he pressed me against the wall. His strong hands held me firmly in place as he claimed my mouth in a heated kiss. His tongue explored every inch of me, and I felt myself melting into him as he kissed me deeper and deeper until I was left gasping for air.

Hades pulled away, his lips curved up in a knowing smile. He brushed the hair out of my face and tucked it behind my ears, and for a moment, I sensed myself floating in complete bliss.

"I've waited for this for too long," he whispered and he kissed me again, this time softer and more tender than before. His hands roamed over my body, caressing my skin as he explored every inch of me until we both were lost in a passionate haze.

He swept me in his arms and cradled me against his chest as he carried me to the bed. His heart thrummed like a drum in my ear, sending ripples of warmth through my veins. He laid me down gently and then, without warning, he was on top of me, and I shivered at the sensation of his hard muscles crushing into mine. His lips burned on mine, and I surrendered to his kiss with a low moan.

I shuddered as his touch glided up the smoothness of my thighs. His fingers rode up the silken fabric of my gown when a thunderous knock echoed through the room, reverberating off the walls and rattling through my bones. My breath hitched as I heard a deep voice warning that the feast could not begin without us.

We froze—our breaths panting, chests heaving. His gaze burned like fiery garnets as he whispered fervently, "They won't go away." With one soft motion, he tucked a lock of hair behind my ear. "Not until the feast is done with."

Another forceful slam echoed through the hall. "Your Divine Highness, they're awaiting you," the guard declared.

Hades shut his eyes. When he opened them again, a rumble reverberated from his chest and he reluctantly parted from me. My body thirsted for more of his intoxicating nearness, but I knew we must carry on. Then offering me his hand, he gestured for me to follow.

We traversed the winding stone corridors, the only sound being the clicks of my heels against the faded marble floors. As we emerged from the palace, the darkness seemed infinite, like it would never end until we reached our destination. Even then, I felt nothing but anxiety as I was ushered down a cobblestone pathway, and turned into an open courtyard surrounded by pristine white marble columns, bathed in the firelight's mesmerizing amber glow.

As we approached hand in hand, a sense of anticipation filled the air. The gods and goddesses had gathered, their eyes fixed on us as we made our way through the crowd. Starlight glittered like a million diamonds, sparkling above us, and the terrace was ablaze with torchlight and the shimmer of elaborate gowns and gleaming armor. It was a sight that took my breath away, and I couldn't help a thrill of excitement at the thought of being part of this world.

When we reached the threshold, the crowd erupted in ovation, a symphony of cheers and applause that echoed in the night. I glanced at Hades, who wore a proud and regal expression, his dark eyes shining with satisfaction. A rush of pleasure streamed through my veins, knowing that I stood by his side, his equal in the eyes of these powerful beings.

But as the cheers died down, a figure emerged from the crowd. It was Hypnos, holding a wineglass in his hand.

The Lord of Slumber raised his glass, catching everyone's attention. "As the moonlight's tender glow graces this majestic courtyard, we gather to honor a tale of triumph and courage," he began. "Tonight, let our glasses rise in celebration of Princess Aurora, whose heart blazes with the bravery that conquers darkness and emerges victorious."

A wave of warmth washed over me as Hypnos praised me, his words a testament to my journey. I smiled, feeling a sense of acceptance and validation from the gods and goddesses around us as they murmured with delight, punctuated by sporadic cheers and claps of approval. Hypnos nodded, and the mumbling grew lighter as he continued. "Beside her stands the formidable Prince Hades, the embodiment of strength and steadfastness. A ruler of unwavering heart, a pillar of support. Together, they form a harmony of power and grace, unquestionable proof of the greatness within every soul."

Lifting the glass higher he added, "To Aurora, warrior of heart, whose flame of courage lights our way, and to Hades, eternal ruler, whose strength and constant heart inspire us all. May their love echo through the ages, reminding us that in darkness, bravery and love always shall prevail." He paused. "May their legacy shine brighter than the stars above."

Hades and I raised our glasses, acknowledging the toast. "To new beginnings," he said, his voice low and intimate.

"To new beginnings," I echoed, meeting his glittering stare, and we clinked our glasses before taking a sip of the rich, red wine.

Music began drifting through the hall, and Hades extended his hand towards me. "May I have this dance, Princess Aurora?"

I placed my hand in his, excitement coursing through me. "Of course, Prince Hades."

We moved to the center of the room, the crowd parting to make way for us. The music swelled, and we began to dance. Hades swayed with grace and elegance, and I followed his lead, feeling as though we were floating on air.

As we danced, I could feel the eyes of the gods and goddesses on us, their gazes curious and intrigued. But I paid them no mind. In that moment, there was only Hades and me, the world around us fading into the background. It was a dance of two souls entwined, of past and present colliding, of destiny fulfilled.

"I'm honored to have you by my side tonight," he said, his fingers gently brushing against mine as we twirled.

"I'm honored to be here," I admitted, awe and adoration in my voice. "I never imagined I would find myself in the company of gods and goddesses, let alone dancing with the Lord of the Netherworld."

Hades smiled, a warm and genuine expression that softened his usually stern features. "And I never imagined I would find someone like you," he said, his voice laced with emotion. "Brave, fierce, and unyielding in the pursuit of what she believes in."

My heart skipped a beat at his words. "I couldn't have done it without your encouragement," I confessed.

Hades nodded, his gaze never leaving mine. "You are strong, Aurora. Stronger than you know," he said, his tone earnest and sincere. "And I have no doubt that you will be a formidable ruler in your own right."

"I hope to be a worthy partner to you," I said, my voice barely above a whisper.

Hades drew me closer, his hand resting against the small of my back. "You already are," he purred, with a tenderness that took my breath away.

A sense of belonging and completeness that I'd never known before washed over me. With Hades, I had finally found my place, my home.

He leaned down, his lips meeting mine in a tender, passionate kiss. Suddenly, the world stood still, and it was just the two of us, bound together by fate and love.

As the dance came to an end, the crowd erupted into applause once more. Hades and I stepped back, smiling at each other, our hearts filled with a newfound sense of joy and belonging.

The celebration began in earnest, a grand celebration that would last through the night. The gods and goddesses feasted and reveled, their laughter and merriment filling the hall. I found myself surrounded by well-wishers and admirers, each eager to congratulate me on my victory.

But my attention kept drifting back to Hades, who stood at the center of it all, a powerful and enigmatic figure. He glanced in my direction, his eyes locking with mine, and a soft smile tugged at the corners of his lips.

He raised his glass towards me, a silent toast to the future we would build together. I smiled in response, knowing that I'd found my place in the Netherworld and that I was exactly where I was meant to be. With Hades by my side, I was ready to embrace my new life as Princess Aurora, and together, we would rule the realms with love, strength, and unity.

# 67

# PHILLIP

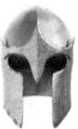

The distant pounding of revelry filtered through the stale air—the gods were busy feasting above. Our chance had come. I crept to the bars, muttering hoarsely, "Eloise. It's time."

Her eyes widened, kindling with fragile longing. "Now?" she breathed.

"Now or never," I affirmed grimly. "We may not get another chance."

Resolve eclipsed fear on Eloise's face. Wordlessly, she drew out the stolen keys, her hands faintly trembling. This was our sole chance to escape these fetid dungeons. Key glinting, she approached the lock.

I watched, barely breathing, as she slid the key home. Freedom beckoned past that corroded gate... if we dared seize it.

As I met Eloise's anxious yet staunch gaze, I knew we would brave any peril to reclaim our lives. Tonight, we had taken the first step towards defying the gods themselves. Whatever came next, we would face it arm in arm.

Our fate was no longer theirs to command.

# AURORA

*L*aughter and music filled the royal courtyard, the sweet scent of Bloodmoon Red perfuming the balmy air as the gods celebrated my triumph. Hades stood tall beside me, exuding confidence—together, we were an image of unity and strength.

But then the firelight began to dim, casting menacing shadows. A bone-chilling wind swept the grounds, extinguishing the torches one by one. The cheerful music faltered as darkness encroached.

Apprehension clawed up my spine when the distinct aura of ancient malice preceded Nyx's entrance. The primordial goddess glided into view, her fathomless black gown drinking in all light. Her presence smothered the finally dying embers of gaiety—in mere moments, she leeched all traces of warmth and mirth from the courtyard.

Where there had been joyful revelry, now despair and bleakness reigned. The very air felt heavier, bearing down with unspoken threat. None could stand against Nyx's power; she consumed hope as effortlessly as light.

Her very presence shook the foundations of the realm. A

hush fell over the crowd as she glided forward, her voluminous cloak swirling about her like the vast night sky given form. Her fathomless eyes pierced all they beheld, pools of fathomless darkness.

Each deliberate step of hers sent a spike of dread through me. But worse still were the figures that followed in her wake. The Keres, dark-haired bringers of violent death. Their sullen, beautiful faces promised merciless fates to any who incurred their mistress' wrath.

My throat went dry at the sight of these harbingers of doom. Their presence could not bode well. I sensed Hades tensing beside me, on edge as the ageless creatures approached. This night's joyful revelry teetered on a precipice, threatening to plunge into darkness.

A heavy pall settled over the gathering as Nyx took her place, the atmosphere now laced with both reverence and dread. As goddess of night, she held dominion over existence itself. Her ancient gaze swept the assembled deities, and for a moment, unease flickered in my core. But then her darkened eyes locked with Hades', and something passed between them—something that spoke of ancient grudges and silenced disapproval.

"Mother," Hades greeted her warily with a nod, guarded in her imposing presence.

"Hades," Nyx returned, her voice cold as the endless dark she ruled. "I've come to offer congratulations, though I regret not being invited."

"An oversight," Hades dismissed tersely, unwilling to reveal more.

The tension between them was a tangible force—ancient secrets and bitter history veiling their relationship from view. Nyx's stare turned to me, assessing and inscrutable. "And who is this mortal who has ensnared your heart? Has she finally found her name?"

Hades' jaw clenched in a way that betrayed far more than his discomfort.

I stood taller under that crushing scrutiny. "I have," I confirmed, steel in my tone. "I am Aurora, rightful heir to the kingdom of Stonewall above. I claimed my past by deed and valor."

Amusement flickered in Nyx's impenetrable eyes. "Aurora," she repeated, her voice softer than before. "Such a fitting name for one who brings light to the darkness." Her gaze slid to Hades knowingly. "But fate often lives to surprise us. Enjoy this victory—it may prove fleeting."

As the crowd stirred uneasily at Nyx's veiled warning, another figure emerged from the shadows—Thanatos, radiating both elegance and menace. His frost-pale hair flowed in the chill breeze, and his stormy eyes seared into mine, sending a shiver down my spine.

"Too many stake their claim on you, mortal," Thanatos uttered, his voice like a whisper in the wind. "But you belong to me, and no other."

His ominous words clutched my racing heart in icy fingers. His demand spoke of power beyond my comprehension.

Rage spasmed across Hades' face, only to be stifled as the Keres sprang upon him in a blur. With fearsome claws, they slammed him back against a column, holding him fast, their depthless eyes warning against resistance.

Hades strained furiously against their merciless grip. "Release me!" he commanded through gritted teeth.

Nyx smiled cryptically, untroubled by his fury. "I've come to offer congratulations, my son. But I've also come to remind you where your loyalties lie." Her midnight eyes fixed on me once more, freezing me in place. "This is a dangerous game you play, mortal. The realm of gods is not to be trifled with."

Her soft-spoken admonition was more chilling than any scream. As Hades struggled helplessly, stark truth dawned—we were but motes of dust caught in the hands of capricious and pitiless cosmic forces. Fear threatened to crush me in its fist... but I forced my spine rigid. I would not show weakness before these ancient creatures.

Tension coiled through the silent courtyard as we awaited the next move in this lethal dance between mortal and gods.

In a flash, Thanatos drew his blade, its razor edge gleaming cold and bright as moonlight.

"Don't you dare!" Hades snarled against the Keres' unyielding grasp, fury and despair tainting his voice. But his warning went unheeded.

I knew then what had to be done. With trembling fingers, I freed Voidbringer, its familiar steel cold in my grip. Fear gibbered within, but I forced it down, steadying my sword arm through sheer force of will. Yet again, I must face the god of death himself.

Thanatos circled like a starving wolf, his predatory gaze intent on me. "I admire your defiance, mortal," he purred, voice smooth as velvet. "But fortune is not with you tonight. You won't leave here alive."

I ground my teeth in false bravado. "I don't need to defeat you. Just resist long enough to make a difference."

His smile came razor-sharp. "Such boldness. You believe you can alter destiny?" One pale brow lifted as his stare cut to the merciless Keres.

Our swords crashed in a deadly refrain—his movements fluid and precise, targeting weaknesses, while I parried desperately. The gulf between god and mortal was clear with each ringing blow.

I knew I was outmatched, yet still, I resisted. If these were to be my final moments, I would face them with

434

courage. Let Thanatos cut me down—I would show no fear. Some acts of defiance matter more than victory.

"I don't believe in fate," I shot back through gritted teeth, muscles straining at the clang of our swords. "I believe in fighting for what's right."

Steel rang against steel, sparks erupting. Though my body ached with exhaustion, I refused to yield. There was too much at stake to surrender to darkness.

Thanatos laughed, the sound colder than winter's breath. "You're only mortal, Aurora. You cannot challenge the will of gods."

"You hold no power over me or my fate," I retorted defiantly.

For an instant, respect flickered in his icy eyes. "You have courage. I grant you that," he conceded. "But courage alone won't save you."

Mustering my remaining strength, I launched into a frenzied offensive, striking with all my skill. Each ringing blow echoed through the silent courtyard. The gods watched, frozen in awe and dread, as we danced across the stones locked in fatal combat.

But mortal flesh could only endure so much. In an elegant flurry too fast to counter, Thanatos feinted left then right in a blur. Too late, I realized his maneuver. With casual grace, he flicked his wrist and disarmed me, his sword sliding effortlessly through my heart.

Agony exploded through me. I staggered back, useless tears blurring my vision, Hades' anguished roar ringing in my ears. My knees met unforgiving stone, then the courtyard tiles rushed up to meet me.

Shadows closed in as Thanatos loomed above me, triumph etched across his beautiful, merciless face. He had won. I was at the mercy of the god of death. Strange, how the end comes not in a blaze of glory, but on bended knee, alone and in pain... I tilted my head up one last time to gaze at the indifferent stars. If this was where my thread was cut, I would face that final night with courage unbroken...

The gods recoiled, their expressions torn between disapproval and sorrow. They yearned to intervene, to spare me from Nyx's cruel decree. But duty's fetters bound them fast—they could only watch, helpless, as events raced towards tragedy.

A tear scurried down my cheek when Hades' devastated gaze found mine. His eyes swam with anguish, torn between protecting me and obeying his mother's will.

"Nyx..." he forced out, voice ragged with pain. "This was not meant to be. I won't let you take her from me."

Nyx merely smiled, cryptic as ever. "She chose her path," she stated in an icy tone. "Now she must face the consequences."

As my vision darkened, I clung to memories of triumph and joy on my journey—each treasured moment a flickering candle against encroaching night. I thought of the friends I'd made, the love nurtured even in darkness...

My story ended here, life bleeding out onto cold stone. Though my dreams would die with me, perhaps my name would live on, kindled in the hearts of those who knew me. One last defiant spark against the endless night.

I focused on Hades' beloved face, determined to hold onto his visage as long as I could...

With that image in my heart, I closed my eyes, ready to embrace whatever fate awaited me beyond the mortal realm. And as the gods and goddesses looked down in silent reverence, the night stretched on, unyielding and eternal.

# PHILLIP

*E*loise reached through the bars, her delicate fingers faintly brushing mine. She summoned a brave smile, though it flickered like a guttering candle. "Whatever horrors await, we'll face them together," she vowed, voice eerie in the gloom.

I squeezed her hand, nodding. Despite the uncertainty ahead, I had faith in us.

My cell door screeched open, the harsh sound ricocheting down the dim passage. But no guards came—our escape was unhindered.

I stepped out, only to be engulfed by the prisoners' anguished cries for aid, a wretched chorus besieging me.

"This way!" I urged Eloise gently but firmly, gesturing towards freedom.

But she lingered, her eyes clouding with uncertainty as she stared at the haggard prisoners.

"Eloise?" I prodded, unease churning within me.

She hesitated, then stepped back, shattering my hopes like glass. Helplessly, I watched her move with grim purpose from cell to cell, unlocking each gate, and freeing each mythological being trapped in this dreadful dungeon.

My heart hammered as sheer pandemonium ignited around me. The inmates—docile before—now shrieked with savage liberty, the stench of fear and rebellion choking the air.

"Eloise, what are you doing?" I whispered desperately, barely audible over the din.

She turned to me, eyes blazing with insurmountable conviction. "They don't deserve to be caged like animals," she declared vehemently. "No one does."

"But they're dangerous!" I grumbled, eyeing the wary minotaur, who'd kept its steady gaze fixed on us.

Eloise touched my arm soothingly. "Only because captivity tainted them," she reasoned gently. "They've endured enough torment. It's time to show them mercy."

I hesitated, torn between craving freedom and dreading the chaos these creatures would unleash. "This wasn't the plan!" I growled wretchedly.

Eloise glanced at the minotaur, muscles rippling under bronze flesh. "It was *always* the plan," she refuted passionately. "I told you, Phillip—we're *all* getting out. Chaos is our only route now."

I wanted to argue, to protest that our chances of escape were now even slimmer, but her resolve was iron—no convincing her otherwise. With a shuddering breath of resignation, I nodded acceptance.

The prisoners watched us in awe as Eloise moved among them, unlocking creatures long resigned to their shackles—satyrs, harpies, centaurs, and more. Tentative fingers reached to graze her skin, as if needing to confirm this dream made real.

Keys clashed, gates groaned open. With each unlocked cell, Eloise granted not just freedom, but flickering hope long-denied. Apprehension churned within me at the swelling chaos. But greater still was my admiration for this remarkable woman who found light in such darkness.

Where I wavered, she charged ahead, heedless of risk, compelled by compassion. She had awakened something in these wretched beings—and in me. Perhaps she was right... Perhaps real change came not through timid steps, but daring leaps of faith.

Ahead shone a gilded cell unlike the others, golden ivy winding its bars. I shuddered, recognizing the vines that had once bound the nymph Minthe. A figure stirred weakly inside.

"Eloise," I warned softly.

She turned, shocked. "Phillip..." she breathed, hand stretching uselessly towards the prisoner. Moonlight revealed a weeping woman huddled inside. Pity lanced through me—to suffer such isolation was a fate crueler than death.

Eloise unlocked the gate with a groan of metal. Slowly, the woman raised her head, disbelief etched across her drawn features.

"Prince Phillip?" she rasped, recognition filling my name.

Tears stung my eyes. "Demeter," I managed, voice breaking. Here was the fallen goddess I had once adored, now chained by pitiless fate.

Eloise approached and Demeter's eyes glistened with tears. "Hades cursed you, stripped your powers," she whispered in startling realization.

Unable to articulate her relief, she simply nodded. Demeter's fingers fluttered to her throat, pondering whether she could speak again. "I've been silenced," she managed, "powerless to warn you all this time."

I met her haunted eyes with gentle assurance. "None of this is your fault. We're here now—we'll free you from this place."

We locked our fingers with hers and heaved her to her feet. Demeter leaned between us, her body trembling with heavy humility that seemed to soak through our palms. Her gaze was dull and distant—she wasn't the same deity who'd carved history into stone. This was an ancient goddess, weary from the years of battle.

"Thank you," Demeter said through spilling tears.

Eloise's sad smile acknowledged we could only do so much. "No need for thanks," she assured Demeter gently. "Now go." Our resolve renewed as we watched the goddess disappear down the dark passage.

At last, we faced the minotaur. Rage simmered in its feral eyes, flaring nostrils sampling our scents. The air thickened as it regarded us warily.

Key poised, Eloise hesitated, conflicted.

The beast's breath came out in a foggy exhale as it peered down at us with unsettling intelligence.

"I am Asterion," he finally rumbled after an agonizing pause. His voice was a deep, guttural scrape that sent tremors through me.

I remained frozen, pulse racing as the massive creature regarded me with its baleful gaze. It took a lumbering step forward, the ground trembling beneath its hooves. I flinched back instinctively.

The beast's lips peeled back, revealing rows of jagged teeth in a mockery of a smile. "You and I are not so different," he continued, each word deliberate. "Hades wronged me too."

His words struck an unexpected chord, hinting at a shared pain I did not fully comprehend yet. I hesitated, torn between fear and curiosity. What twisted history lurked behind this monster's existence?

Asterion watched me closely, as if gauging my reaction. I

shuddered, icy dread coiling within me while Eloise's knuckles whitened around the key.

"Are you sure?" I asked nervously. She met my gaze, ice-blue eyes blazing with determination. Nothing could stop her now.

The lock squealed open. "Go," Eloise whispered. "You're free."

Asterion paused, as if considering her words. Then with a deafening roar, he charged forth, the ground quaking violently beneath his massive hooves. Each thunderous footfall sent tremors through the stone halls as he stormed into the shadows and out of sight.

I shuddered, awed by the risk Eloise had taken—a bold, courageous risk that would forever alter the course of our escape.

"I don't know what comes next," she confessed, voice firm yet kind. "But I won't stand idle. We must seize our chance, whatever it may bring."

I nodded, a bittersweet mix of hope and sorrow welling within me. We had opened the gates. Now we must see our defiance through.

Taking Eloise's hand in mine, I led us up the winding stairs, away from the fetid dungeons. The distant revelry swelled louder with each step as we ascended towards the world above.

I glanced back one last time at the chaos we'd sown—dangerous creatures unleashed, ravenous for long-overdue freedom... and revenge. Whatever fate awaited us above, we had cast our lot.

*D*arkness shrouded me as I lay on cold stone, the distant clashing of steel ringing in my ears. Through my body's crushing agony, I felt Hades' hand entwined in mine, his warmth a lifeline. His ragged cries resonated in my heart—grief-stricken words of devotion as death's shadow crept over me.

"My radiant Beauty," he choked out, voice thick with torment. "My queen..."

I struggled to open my eyes, to glimpse him one last time. But pain's weight pressed down inexorably, dragging me under. Still, I clung on, unwilling to lose a single precious moment with him... more so if it was our last.

"I cannot bear to lose you," Hades whispered, his lips grazing my ear. "I've waited lifetimes for you... I can't let you go. I can't—" His voice broke into a sob.

Tears slipped free as I listened, his anguished heart laid bare. I longed to tell him my soul would love him to no end. But my voice failed, my body weakened beyond remedy.

"You are the light in my darkness. The hope that sustains me," he rasped, each word tremulous with devotion. "I have loved you for eternity, and I will love you for eternity to come. You will always be my beating heart, my every breath... my all."

His words were a balm to my wounded soul. For a fleeting moment, I forgot the pain, the fear, the uncertainty. All that mattered was the love that flowed between us, a love transcendent and immutable.

Hades' grip on my hand tightened fervently, then he leaned down to press a gentle kiss on my lips. "I am yours," he vowed, voice thick with conviction. "No one can take you from me. Not even Death."

I knew then that he would fight for me, that he would never give up on me.

Another voice pierced the haze. Hypnos, his beloved timbre kindling hope's fragile flame within me. "The brand on her shoulder... it's fading away."

A single whispered word came in response—"No..."— etched in ice. With each second that followed, Thanatos' presence diminished, as if dissolving into the ether. And as the Lord of Death's presence faded, strength gradually returned to my limbs.

My eyes fluttered open, vision blurry. I could make out figures hovering over me, their faces slowly coming into focus.

Hypnos was nearest, his handsome features creased with concern. But as awareness returned, his expression shifted to surprised elation.

"Aurora, you're alive!" he exclaimed, shock and joy mingling in his tone.

I blinked, trying to clear the fog from my mind. I opened my mouth to speak, but only a ragged rasp emerged.

Hypnos grasped my hand, features lit with a relieved smile. "Just rest, my lady. You're safe now."

Before I could respond, Chronos appeared beside him,

emerald eyes heavy with care. "Lady Aurora," he said gently. "You were struck down by Thanatos... killed by his hand."

*Killed? Thanatos?* I winced as dim recollection kindled. But somehow that couldn't be right. Bewildered, I whispered hoarsely, "You call me Aurora... who is this girl you speak of?"

Understanding dawned on Hecate's face as she swept forward. The sorceress dipped into a graceful curtsy before me. "My lady," she breathed. "You've returned to us... at last."

At her words, realization transformed Chronos and Hypnos. Their faces turned to stone as her meaning hit them. Together, they sank down in reverence, echoing in hushed voices, "My lady..."

I looked down at myself, taking in the ruined state of my gown for the first time. Dark stains blossomed across the once pristine fabric. With growing horror, I realized it was blood.

My hands shook as I examined the damage. Great rends had been torn in the delicate material, caked in dried crimson. It flaked off beneath my fingertips, turning them rust-colored. Bile rose in my throat.

So much blood, and none of it appeared to be mine. The implications of that sank like a stone in my gut. Cold, visceral fear slithered through me. What catastrophe had I awoken to? What fate had befallen my love while I slept?

I had to find Hades. Wild panic pounded through my veins now. I tried to stand, limbs leaden and sore, desperate to begin my search. Nothing else mattered but ensuring his safety first and foremost.

"Where is Hades?" I asked urgently, forcing myself upright despite the lingering pain—a fading memory of fathomless agony. My throat tightened with anguish, desperate to know that he was safe.

Hypnos steadied me, concern creasing his brow. "Where is my husband?" I repeated. This time, louder, as stark dread coiled inside me.

"It *is* you," came a beloved voice that turned my legs to water. I whirled to find Hades, all grief gone from his face.

"Beauty... Aurora..." His tearful eyes searched mine despairingly. "It has *always* been you. My love. *Persephone*."

Warmth cascaded through me at the sound of my name sailing through his lips—a homecoming I'd only dreamed of. I rushed into his arms, soft sobs of relief escaping me. "Oh, Hades," I whispered fervently against his chest. "I remember everything now."

He held me close, our racing hearts beating as one.

The gods surrounding us erupted into jubilant cheers, the courtyard swelling with joy. But then an icy glare stabbed between my shoulders, marring our perfect bliss.

I spun to find Nyx and her Keres lingering at the courtyard's edge, little more than shadows themselves. With an arcane gesture from Hades' mother, the ageless creatures began dissipating into the night that birthed them. No words, no farewells—simply an air of ominous finality.

It was as if the darkness had reclaimed its own. They vanished utterly, leaving only a lingering chill in their wake.

Hades squeezed my shoulder, relief and regret mingling in his voice. "They're gone."

"For now," I murmured uneasily. "But I suspect we'll meet again."

Hades nodded, his burning gaze never leaving mine. "Perhaps. But let us revel in this love we've reawakened, and the truth that has set us free."

I smiled softly, twining my fingers through his. No matter what the future held, we would face it together.

Hades caressed my cheek, a faraway look in his eyes. "Dance with me," he murmured. "As we used to, long ago."

I nodded, heart swelling. He drew me close as haunting music began to drift through the moonlit garden, seemingly from nowhere and everywhere at once.

The night breeze swirled around us, perfumed with the heady scent of night-blooming flowers. We moved as one, attuned to the rhythm of each other's hearts, steps gliding across the travertine stone.

Centuries fell away as we danced. Time itself blurred until it was just us again—goddess and god, souls entwined. The music wrapped us in its spell, beautiful and aching, underpinning each graceful turn.

With his hand warm at the small of my back, his eyes only for me, it was as if we'd never been apart. Our past, present, and future converged here.

A roguish smile played at his mouth. "At last, my soul is complete," he murmured, and leaning in, his lips brushed against mine in a searing kiss. The touch sent shivers down my spine, igniting a fire within me that only he could quench.

As Hades led me through an elegant turn, a tingling warmth suddenly spread across my skin. I glanced down to see my tattered gown dissolving, fading into glimmers of light that danced over my body.

Delicate new fabric spun into being, draping gracefully over my form. Shining like liquid night, my dress transformed into a regal ballgown embellished with intricate swirls of gold thread. The smears of blood and grime disappeared, leaving behind pristine splendor.

I gasped, marveling at the magic that had reshaped my ruined garments into a majestic dress fitting for a queen reunited with her king. The midnight hues reflected the colors of our realm, marking me unmistakably as Hades' bride.

He tilted my chin up, pride and admiration glinting in his eyes. "Perfect," he pronounced with quiet satisfaction.

Joyful tears pricked my eyes. After endless hardship, once more we danced beneath a canopy of stars. I had come home, at long last wearing the mantle fate had woven for me. Never would we be sundered again.

The garden resounded with merry cries, divine voices raised in chorus. Gods and goddesses danced in our honor, rejoicing in this union of two souls. They sang with joyous fervor, despite any misgivings in our differences. And I basked in their approval, knowing I was home.

The cacophony dimmed as Chronos lifted his glass, commanding attention. "Esteemed friends. We gather on this night to bear witness."

All eyes turned to Hades and me as we stood hand in hand amidst the revelers. Nervous excitement fluttered inside me.

"After arduous journeys, our kingdom's rightful rulers are reunited." Chronos' voice rang loud and clear. "We celebrate their ascension to the thrones of the Netherworld!"

Rapturous cheers erupted, shaking the courtyard's very foundations. As they faded, Hecate glided forth, an ornate crown resting on a velvet pillow. Countless rubies glittered in the firelight, polished to a brilliant gleam.

Solemnly, Hades knelt before her. With elegant grace, Hecate raised the crown and placed it upon his bowed head. "Hail King Hades, Ruler of the Dead, Keeper of Souls," she proclaimed.

Thunderous applause followed as the newly crowned King of the Netherworld rose. The goddess then turned to me, lifting the smaller diadem intended for his queen.

I trembled, poised on the cusp of destiny. As the circlet touched my brow, Hecate's voice rang out in declaration: "All hail Persephone, Goddess of Spring, and our Ruling Queen!"

The words resonated through my very bones.

Hades turned to me as cheers filled the courtyard, his eyes brimming with emotion. "No words can express what it means to finally stand beside you as King and Queen," he said, his deep voice laden with fervor.

I squeezed his hand, my heart nearly overflowing. "We've endured every trial imaginable to reach this moment together," I replied. "Now a new age dawns for us all."

Drawn as if by a magnet, we leaned closer, the din of the feast fading until only we two existed. When our lips met, the gathering collectively gasped at our profound intimacy.

The kiss was a seal, a promise, a reunion. In it, we poured every ounce of our love and dedication. The long years apart fell away, replaced by a boundless, bright future. When we gently pulled back, eyes still closed, I knew I'd never tire of the exquisite joy of his kiss.

As our eyes opened, tears of happiness glistened on Hades' cheeks, matching my own. At long last, after so many stolen moments and fractured time, Hades and I were as we were meant to be—together, unbroken, ruling side by side in our cherished kingdom.

# PHILLIP

*W*e were free, yet peril still awaited. The air hummed with uncertainty and resolve. The gods caroused heedlessly above, oblivious to the chaos unleashed below. What came next was unknowable.

We stepped into an eerie circular chamber, ringed by obsidian pillars. Their glossy surfaces reflected distorted images of us, rippling strangely. Spellbound, my fingers reached out and grazed one of the mirrors. And at once, mysterious scenes began to take shape in its murky surface...

"Phillip, we must go!" Eloise urged, torch aloft.

I tore my gaze away and joined her swiftly. Unease prickled on my nape as we hurried through the disorienting space. A thousand fractured versions of myself scrutinized our every step.

"It's a labyrinth down here," Eloise said shakily. I could only agree.

At length, we came upon a large chamber. It was shadowy and still, illuminated only by the unsteady flames of wall-mounted torches. The flickering light cast menacing shapes across the cold stone floor as I stepped forward.

In the center of the room stood a pedestal, with two weapons laid reverently upon its surface. My pulse quickened at the sight of our swords. Dawnbreaker, my trusty blade. Moonshadow, Eloise's cherished weapon. Taken when we were captured, I'd feared them lost forever.

Eloise and I exchanged an intense look of recognition. In unison, we stepped forward and reclaimed our blades, hesitation cast aside. Strength surged through me as Dawnbreaker's worn grip welcomed my hand once more.

Eloise caressed Moonshadow, undisguised affection in her voice. "Oh, I've missed you." Whole again with our swords restored, we were ready to face any trial ahead.

"We must be cautious," I warned, scanning for threats. "There may be guards nearby."

Eloise nodded, eyes alert.

We crept onward through narrowing tunnels, guided only by distant flickering torchlight. Our muted steps echoed eerily in the oppressive silence. Damp air chilled our skin—whether portent or warning, I did not know.

The passage opened into a grand courtyard awash in moonglow. As the Netherworld's cool breeze greeted us, I couldn't help but feel a blend of dread and exhilaration. Eloise had thrown caution to the wind, and now we would face the consequences of her boldness.

The gods' raucous feast swelled louder, underscoring the world that awaited beyond this maze.

"We must stay strong and undaunted to make it out of this alive," I murmured as I edged out warily.

Eloise's hand found mine, gripping tightly. "No matter what comes our way, we face it together," she said.

We ventured forth. The cobblestone path beneath our feet crunched with each step—the very sound sending shivers down my spine. We were so close to freedom...

Through a veil of mist, a grand terrace emerged, crafted

of pure white marble pillars and flecked with gold detailing that sparkled even in the dim light. The scent of Bloodmoon Red hung heavy in the air, mixed with something else—fear?

And then it came. A raucous chant, like an anthem of destruction, reverberating through the courtyard. And we stood frozen in the middle of the sacred garden, witnessing as gods and monsters clashed before us.

Harpies descended from the skies with ear-piercing shrieks, centaurs stampeded through the devastation. The elegant banquet lay in ruins, shattered by the rampage.

I turned to Eloise, straining to be heard over the din. "This is our chance, while they're distracted!" At my words, hope flickered in her eyes. Together, we slipped into the seething tumult, liberty so close we could taste it.

# PERSEPHONE

*T*he distant revelry faded as Hades and I strolled the moonlit grounds, stars scattering overhead like diamonds. His hand was warm in mine—in this hushed moment, nothing else existed but our love and the promise of a new beginning.

"You knew," I murmured as my hands trailed up his muscular arms. "You knew who I was all along."

Hades nodded, dark eyes burning into mine. "Yes," he rasped. "At some point, we *all* knew."

The memories of Stonewall and my days as Aurora echoed in my mind. "I summoned you," I uttered softly, "begging you to stop the devastation against my people. But you refused."

"No," he replied to my astonishment. "The truth is, I was not there to refuse you." Remorse edged his words. "I was called away to a council in Elysium, leaving Hypnos in my stead. Not until later did I learn of your plight."

I waited, my heart throbbing, as he continued the story. "The council dragged on for years. And when I returned, Hypnos couldn't stop gloating about the magnificent

Sleeping Beauty that reigned in a human kingdom by the sea..." The corner of his lips curled in a smoldering smirk, his voice thick with desire. "And when I found you, so captivating in your slumber, I knew. You were no ordinary woman, but my Persephone, trapped in mortal flesh by your mother's curse."

I drew a shuddering breath, grappling with this revelation. Sensing my turmoil, Hades framed my face gently. "I longed to tell you," he confessed wretchedly. "But Demeter's curse forbade it. Had any of us spoken, your true name would have become lost forever. You alone could unlock this truth."

I melted into his touch, understanding dawning. We'd both been shackled, but were now finally free.

"Having me so near, knowing there was nothing you could do to restore my name... That must have been—" I managed before words failed me.

"Painfully unbearable," Hades finished for me, his gaze darkening with rekindled anguish.

I pulled him into a fervent kiss, pouring all my longing and devotion into it. When we finally broke apart, gasping, I whispered, "But now, I'm here. Back with my love, in his arms where I belong." I trailed my fingers down his taut abdomen. "My beloved husband."

Hades groaned, crushing me against him. "Say that again," he purred in my ear.

A seductive smile tugged at my lips. I relished having this power over the mighty Lord of the Netherworld. "My handsome and most beloved husband," I repeated throatily, tracing the edges of his ornate armor with a single fingertip.

Abruptly, he grasped my hands, his gaze stern. "Persephone, do you remember our story?"

His fingers brushed my temple tenderly, and with that gentle touch, I saw myself in the fields of the mortal realm, the daughter of Demeter, sheltered and overprotected. I saw the day I first met Hades, the god who captivated my heart with his darkness and hidden vulnerability. I relived the gradual unfolding of our love, the secret meetings in the shadows of the world, the day we decided to defy the gods and marry.

My gaze bore into his. "I remember," I said, my voice barely a whisper.

He smiled enticingly. "And do you regret any of it?" he asked. Something intense flared through his entrancement.

I shook my head, my heart swelling with emotion. "Not a single moment," I replied, and gliding my delicate hand along his strong jaw, I continued, "Even in the darkest of times, you were my light, Hades. You showed me a world beyond the surface, a world filled with beauty and mystery."

He drew me close, our racing hearts beating as one. "You are the one bright thing in my endless twilight," he rasped, voice laden with devotion. "My destiny, found at last."

We leaned in, mere inches apart, the anticipation of a kiss electrifying the air. But just as our lips were about to meet, the sudden wail of a haunting voice ripped through the silence, shattering our moment.

"No! This is impossible!"

Hades and I whirled towards the sound. A figure cloaked in darkness stood at the base of the palace steps, her face veiled in night.

My heart stuttered as a sliver of moonlight struck her features. Demeter. My mother. The one who'd cursed me to life as Aurora, trapping me within the Realm of Man—and here she was before us.

Demeter's voice rose with her rage as she snarled, "Let. My. Daughter. Go."

Hades' face was a mask of granite, its lines and shadows

harsh against the dim light of the Netherworld. "You have no right to be here," he bit out. "Not after what you did!"

Demeter's gaze fell on me, flickering with remorse. "My child," she whispered, her voice breaking. "I never wanted this for you."

I stepped forward. "You never *wanted* me to be happy," I shot back, my heart torn between anger and heartache. "You *wanted* to control me, to mold me into something I'm not."

Hades placed a protective arm around me, glaring at Demeter with bold determination. "Persephone is no longer under your curse," he said firmly. "She is her own person now, and she has chosen to be with me."

Demeter's shoulders slumped with defeat, the weight of her actions finally catching up to her. "I only wanted to protect you," she whispered, her voice laden with regret.

"Protect me?" I asked, my voice trembling with emotion. "From what?"

"From Hades' cruelty!" she exploded, a faint gleam of divine fury pulsing through her weary frame.

I recoiled, crestfallen. "Yet what of your own? You condemned me to another life and realm. Mother, you made me *mortal!*" Hot tears spilled down my cheeks. "I will never be the same!"

"You've caused us endless suffering," Hades snapped bitterly. "Even my kingdom has paid the price for your selfish whims."

"Mother, this was cruelly done," I said, voice steady with conviction. "I love Hades, and always shall."

"I cannot allow it," Demeter replied, resolute yet wavering.

"Come, Demeter. You cannot change your daughter's heart," Hades interjected, his voice calmer, yet firm. He stepped closer to me, his hand gently folding over mine.

The charged air between us swirled with clashing

emotions. But then came Hypnos, bursting into view, his voice summoning us urgently.

"My lord, my lady..." His hazel eyes flickered to my mother, and he flinched. "Demeter?" he asked with a glower that didn't look away. His hands clenched at his sides as he went on, "The prisoners have escaped the dungeon, chaos is bleeding from the courtyard like a festering wound."

"Secure the palace," Hades ordered gruffly. "I will join you shortly."

Hypnos bowed in assent, quickly scurrying away to carry out his orders.

Hades turned a glacial gaze on Demeter, the power of their unresolved emotions lingering in the air.

"You are banished from this realm," he declared coldly. "Never return."

Demeter bowed her head, a deep sadness betraying her expression. "I go with a broken heart," she whispered before fading into shadow.

In the tense silence that followed, I met Hades' eyes. However painful, protecting our kingdom had to take priority now. Shoulder to shoulder, we would face this new crisis—and shape whatever followed.

"I'm ready to defend our realm," I spoke with valor. As I reached for Voidbringer, Hades caught my wrist. "This isn't your fight," he decreed firmly. "Bar yourself in our chambers. I will face this alone."

"You need me beside you," I protested, longing to stand together.

Hades caressed my cheek, his expression softening. "My love," he said, and I heard the reverence in his voice. "You've already endured great hardship today. You must rest and recover your strength." His tone was gentle, but left no room for argument.

I wavered, torn between supporting him and heeding his

judgment. But he was right—I was still shaken from my brush with death. Reluctantly, I nodded, worry sitting heavy in my heart.

"Please be careful," I implored softly.

"I promise I'll return to you, safe and triumphant," Hades vowed, pride and love mingling in his eyes. Then he marched out, sword glinting like his wrath made manifest, and his black cloak billowing behind him like an ominous cloud of wrath and retribution.

Alone in our chambers, helplessness washed over me. I yearned to fight at his side, defend our realm together. But he wished me kept from further danger.

I paced anxiously, each minute apart feeling an eternity. My mind conjured dire visions of the chaos awaiting him. All I could do was wait, praying for his safe return.

# PHILLIP

The courtyard was ablaze with thunder and lightning, mirroring the storm that raged within me. The dazed gods scattered, leaving only Hades' guards and me remaining.

My heart hammered wildly as I fought them off with untapped prowess. Each instinctive strike aimed to save Aurora and protect our realms from the Netherworld's might. My blade danced with theirs, weaving a lethal waltz too swift for their lumbering moves.

I parried a blow from one guard, using his momentum to shove him back. Whirling, I engaged the other, our swords clashing in a flurry of sparks. He was slow, clumsy—no match for my frenzied state.

Sensing an opening, I lunged, my sword biting the air. The guard's eyes widened as my steel found its mark, and he fell heavily at my feet with a gurgled cry. I stood above his prone form, chest heaving, sword dripping red. The remaining guards stared in shock, hesitation holding them at bay.

Then came the ominous footfalls descending the grand

staircase—Hades himself, armored in gleaming black steel, gripping a sword that promised violence.

The moonlight streaming through the canopy of trees glinted off his armor as he strode forth. But more striking were the majestic raven wings protruding from his back. They stretched wide, feathered pinions darker than night, casting swirling shadows across the marble columns.

I had but a moment to process this before Hades attacked in a blur, forcing me to parry his vicious strikes. His wings flared with each savage swing of his blade, their span as impressive as it was lethal.

Steel clanged against steel as we resumed our lethal dance. Primordial power radiated from him, the crushing aura of a deity whose wrath could shatter worlds. Any sane man would have fled before him. But defiantly, I held my ground, breathing hard, as his fathomless eyes seared into mine. I'd ventured into his realm to save Aurora, and no force of man or god would sway me from my purpose.

For a suspended moment, the chaos receded and we two alone existed. I glimpsed curiosity flickering in his predatory gaze, perhaps intrigued by my audacity.

I would not falter before this maleficent deity. With my sword leveled, I faced Hades, unyielding.

He stood imperiously, obsidian sword gripped tightly, thirsty for blood. But as I stared, I noticed something strange.

Hades' prominent raven wings rippled, the dark feathers seeming to shrink and withdraw into his back. Before my astonished eyes, the magnificent pinions disappeared seamlessly into his flesh. Intricate tattoos emerged in their wake, swirling across his broad shoulders in mimicry of the wings that had just vanished.

I watched, dumbfounded, as the last traces of feathers merged into ink. The tattoos remained subtly animated, rippling with lifelike motion, deceptive in their realism. The darkest magic had allowed Hades to conceal his wings within the artwork adorning his skin.

"I'll win this battle on your terms, insufferable mortal," Hades declared, voice tangled with annoyance and grudging respect.

I tightened my grip, undaunted. "If you think you'll win this, you're in for a rude awakening, *insufferable* god."

Our swords screamed as we clashed, steel on steel. Hades moved with elegant precision, each blow carrying titanic force. He fought with mystifying living tattoos writhing upon his flesh, while I relied only on my mortal grit.

"Your arrogance is quite impressive..." Hades sneered, his dark eyes burning with cold fire. "Challenging me *twice*."

I held firm against his needling. "I fight for what I believe in. Nothing will sway me from my purpose."

Hades laughed mirthlessly, his whirling sword barely blocked. "Bold words. But you remain only mortal." His blade sang a lethal hymn, trailing shadows, and the strike jarred my bones. "What hope have you to best a god?"

I shoved back with fueled might. "Where is Aurora?" I demanded. "You've no right to imprison her!"

Surprise flashed across his face before icing over, his eyes hooding mercilessly. *"She's dead,"* he intoned flatly. "There's nothing left to fight for."

Fathomless despair flooded my veins at his cruel words. I dodged a sweeping strike from his blade that nearly kissed my neck, and I lunged, my sword aimed at his heart. "I don't believe you!" I shouted fiercely. "I won't let you shatter her destiny!"

Our blades clashed again and again, burnished steel ringing through the courtyard. Lightning flashed overhead, illuminating our deadly dance. The sizzling air hummed with the weight of history as god and mortal vied for supremacy.

"You think yourself a champion of destiny?" Hades hissed, striking with inhuman strength. "Foolish mortal! You're but a pawn in a game framed by the gods." A sinister smirk curled his lips.

I gritted my teeth against his crushing power. "Even a pawn can change the game!" I shot back through the strain.

As our blades sparked, uncertainty cracked his invincible façade—my words had struck home. But I couldn't get distracted. With a surge of determination, I pressed the attack, channeling all my might against him.

Our swords met in a deafening clash that seemed to shake the heavens. For a suspended moment, the world held its breath.

Just as despair threatened to crush me, I glimpsed Eloise slipping through the chaos, her cunning eyes meeting mine. A silent message sailed between us—she had a plan. With this hope, I redoubled my efforts to hold off Hades, waiting for the right moment...

A bellowing roar suddenly shook the palace to its foundations. Hades and I turned to behold Asterion, the minotaur, freed from his chains—an untamed force unleashed.

Astonishment flickered across Hades' face as the beast rampaged through the gardens. Beside it stood Eloise, bold and defiant.

With daring eyes, she challenged, "Face Asterion's wrath, Lord Hades! Let's see if you can withstand our combined fury!"

The courtyard went still as the last guards watched the scene unfold, stunned. Hades advanced on Eloise, equal parts chagrin and fascination upon his face. I sensed his indecision —deal with me, or confront this unexpected threat?

With swift grace, Eloise attacked Hades, evading his blows. Meanwhile, Asterion charged, horns lowered, roaring rage.

SILVANA G. SÁNCHEZ

As their clash ensued, panicked guards rushed to contain the minotaur's fury. Bedlam erupted as they strived to subdue the creature while Hades battled Eloise's unpredictable onslaught.

It was now or never. I signaled Eloise subtly. "Run! Escape while you can! I'll find you!"

Reluctantly, she nodded, her eyes meeting mine in tacit promise. Then she turned and fled into the chaotic night. I only prayed she made it to safety.

The minotaur wrenched free of the guards with a mighty roar, smashing anything in its path. The earth shuddered beneath its pounding hooves as it disappeared into the darkness.

With Eloise's diversion in full swing, I slipped away through hidden passages, making for the palace's grand staircase. My racing heart swirled with trepidation and resolve. I had to find Aurora—make her remember the burdens and vows awaiting her in her kingdom above.

Memories of our entwined past filled my mind as I ascended, navigating the maze of winding corridors. At last, I reached a pair of gilded doors, their intricate luxury standing out among all others. I paused before them, gathering my courage like a shield. This had to be it—the room where I'd find her.

Drawing a steeling breath, I pushed the doors open.

There, by the window, silhouetted against the moon's radiance stood Aurora, resplendent in black and golden silk. Her beauty surpassed even our first meeting all those years ago.

I took a hesitant step forward, awe and trepidation grappling within me. But before I could slip back into the shadows, she turned... and froze at the sight of me.

Surprise flickered in her eyes as she breathed a heavy

exhale. It was not the greeting of lovers, but the wary distance of strangers.

My racing heart staggered. Of course, she would not recognize me, with her memories sealed away. But I had to try to reach the Aurora I knew, still trapped inside this goddess' shell.

# PERSEPHONE

*P*hillip stood before me, and for a dizzying moment, all I could do was stare. He was just as I remembered—tall and handsome, stubble dusting his strong jaw. His presence filled the room with long-absent warmth.

"Phillip, what are you doing here?" I whispered, shock and joy swirling within me.

He started, eyes widening. "You know me," he murmured in awe.

I nodded slowly.

As Phillip adjusted to this revelation, he drew a steadying breath. "I came here to find you," he said, voice unwavering. Those sky-blue eyes locked onto mine, and I was powerless to look away, drinking in every detail of his face.

Seeing him now, with my full identity restored, felt like a waking dream. As we stood in loaded silence, memories assaulted me—of my mortal life as Aurora, and my time here as Beauty. Past and present collided, threatening to over-whelm me.

I shivered, desperately quieting my chaotic thoughts.

"Hades will return soon," I urged breathlessly. "You must leave quickly!"

But Phillip did not stir, his piercing gaze boring into me. "He's held you under his thrall too long," he said. "I know you don't remember, but you have duties above—a kingdom that needs you." His hand lifted as if to touch my face, then hesitated. "You have to come back with me, Aurora."

I flinched at the name. Tears filled my eyes as we shared a moment freighted with unspoken emotions. "Things are... different now," I faltered, pulse racing.

Moonlight filtered into the bedchamber as Phillip paced before me, brow creased in worry. "Aurora, you must return with me to Stonewall. Your kingdom teeters towards ruin."

I watched him sadly, torn between my duties here and saving my people. "Surely some hope remains?" I murmured, my throat tight with worry.

Phillip grasped my hands urgently. "With each day here, that hope dims further. Crops rot in the fields. The seas yield no fish... Your people cry out for their queen."

I turned away as tears stung my eyes, picturing withered cliffs and orchards.

"And I fear war brews," Phillip continued gravely. "Whitehaven's unholy alliance with the fae has emboldened our enemies. The rumblings of an invasion of Stonewall grow ever louder."

I paled, heart clenching. My neglected kingdom now faced starvation and conquest. Even then, leaving my duties here felt like tearing out my soul.

Sensing my turmoil, Phillip gently turned me to face him. "Come home. Together, we can restore your lands." His earnest eyes bored into mine.

I searched his face, pierced by Stonewall's plight yet bound by oaths in the Netherworld.

My expression softened with sorrowful resolve. "I can't go

back, Phillip. I can't bear to see them suffer." Unbidden tears clouded my vision. "Too much death and pain have already ravaged my kingdom because of me."

Phillip's thumb gently brushed away a falling tear. "The blight was not your doing," he insisted. "We never could have predicted..."

I shook my head bitterly. "I should have been there to lead them. But instead, I abandoned them." My voice broke with shame. "They will never forgive me."

But Phillip was unwavering in his determination to convince me. He moved closer, his strong yet comforting presence reminding me of what we once shared. When he wrapped his fingers around mine, so familiar yet so long forgotten, it stirred turmoil within.

"You are their sovereign," he said softly. "You have a duty to them and yourself. You can't run from who you are."

His words cast dark ripples in my soul. "Who I am..." I whispered, the past rising like shadows.

"You don't have to face this alone," he reassured me, voice smooth yet earnest. "Let me stand by your side through whatever comes."

His words awoke a long-dormant resilience within. Could I truly heal Stonewall's wounds and lead them from darkness? My gaze fell in bittersweet shame. "You've shown me nothing but kindness. Meanwhile I..." My voice wavered under the weight of past mistakes.

"Stop," he gently interrupted, fingertips grazing my jaw. "When you called for aid, I failed to answer. The blame lies with me." Softly lifting my chin, he met my eyes.

I took a trembling breath. "I can never be your queen, Phillip."

A knowing smile softened his features. "You don't have to be my queen," he told me in warm reassurance. "Be the queen Stonewall deserves. Be the queen that follows her heart and forges her own path, not the one tradition dictates you must be."

Relief swept through me at his understanding. I blinked back tears, finally seen for who I was.

Phillip's fingers brushed a stray strand of hair from my face, his expression open and earnest. "I release you from any promise between us," he said in a low but stern voice. "I want you to find the life you choose, one where you can truly be yourself."

His words washed over me, equal parts sorrow and freedom. No more claims or obligations—my future was fully my own.

I heaved a sigh and placed my palm over his on my cheek. "Thank you," I whispered through watery joy.

Phillip's eyes crinkled warmly. "Follow your heart, Aurora. And know you'll always have a friend and ally who once wished to call you his queen."

As we embraced, a chapter closed but new horizons shone bright with possibility. I would follow my true calling, wherever it might lead. And Phillip's faith would strengthen me along the way.

His hand squeezed mine reassuringly before parting. His smile seemed to say he knew my thoughts already. Despite the pain and sorrow we'd shared together in years past—he still believed in me. His unwavering faith might give me the strength to fulfill my duty, protecting my people no matter the personal cost.

But at the thought of leaving Hades after our long estrangement, my certainties crumbled. How could I part from the man I loved?

I met Phillip's gaze, spirit turned. "My heart is torn. I don't know what to do."

He cupped my cheek with his calloused hand, a flicker of empathy in his eyes. "Take some time to consider what's best for you and your kingdom," he murmured. "I sail back to the Realm of Man tomorrow."

As moonlight bathed us in its ethereal glow, we stood in the stillness, two souls bound by old love and the whims of destiny, each searching for the path that would lead them to their rightful place.

The echoes of discord, drifting from the palace walls, served as a reminder of how much more we had to fight— both within our own souls and in the greater world. But for now, there was only us.

All too soon, the moment ended as Hades' thunderous footsteps neared. Knowing I must protect Phillip and myself, I swiftly grasped his arm and urged him towards the window with all my remaining strength.

"Please, go now!" I said, then reached for his arm and urged him towards the window. He met my eyes in silent accord before leaping down below.

I paused as Phillip escaped, overwhelmed yet strengthened by courage within. If found here with him, there'd be no coming back from this. Taking a deep breath, I steeled myself against my apprehension and whirled to confront Hades.

But before I could take another step, Phillip's voice called me from below: "Meet me in the Veiled Forest at twilight!" he stammered, not nearly as fearful as he should have been given the circumstances. "I'll be waiting!"

I watched until he blended into the night shadows, unable to reply before he departed. His invitation echoed in my mind, adding to swirling emotions within. Destiny pulled me this way and that, its currents as turbulent as the Midnight Sea's tides...

Firm hands crept around my waist as Hades approached me from behind, unleashing in me a shiver of wanting. My knees trembled. His shadows beckoned like a drug, and I was powerless to resist. His touch clung to my curves, his cool breath kissing the back of my neck, and in that moment, my whole body ignited with craving.

Without saying a word, he pulled me to him. His dark eyes burned on mine with an intoxicating intensity that shattered all my inhibitions and roused a desperate yearning for something more.

# PERSEPHONE

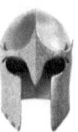

*T*he air was heavy with smoke and desire as Hades' fingertips raked across my skin, leaving trails of exquisite pleasure in their wake. His eyes burned into mine, thunderous and full of longing, like a storm that wanted to consume me whole. I could feel the intensity radiating from his body, an eternity of bliss standing between us that I would selfishly savor.

"How I've ached for this," he rasped, his fingers trailing teasingly along the neckline of my gown, dipping ever lower between the valley of my breasts. "To have you again in my arms, in our bed..."

His words washed over me, stoking the flames of desire that had been suppressed for so long. I gave in to his touch, aware of each point where our bodies connected. "Then ease your suffering, my king," I purred, trailing my nails down the hard muscle of his back and relishing his shudder of delight. "Remind me who I belong to."

Hades accepted my seductive challenge with a ravenous grin, his eyes glowing hotly in the flickering light. "Before this night is through, my queen, you will scream my name so loudly all of Elysium will hear who owns your heart."

With raw passion, he claimed my mouth again in a searing kiss that stole my breath and set me aflame. Every curve in my body molded into his eagerly, ready to relearn every intimate contour of the man I loved.

Piece by piece, our clothes were shed, leaving our bare forms exposed to each other's pleasure. My gaze took in the beauty of his male form, and lingered in his eyes as they darkened with desire.

He snatched me up without a word, carrying me effortlessly across the room and easing me gently onto his sheets.

Hades loomed over me, his breath hot against my ear as he lowered himself, pinning me to his bed. "Every clash of blades, every foe vanquished this evening was done to cease the agonizing hours apart from you," he growled, firm fingers trailing delicately down my neck. "I do not fight for power or glory, but to end my feverish longing when you're not by my side."

My hands clasped behind his nape, drawing him near. "And yet," I murmured against his lips, "it is your pursuit of power and glory that has shown me a burning love that rivals the Netherworld's eternal flames."

His dark, brooding eyes smoldered with unspoken emotion as they searched mine, as if trying to glimpse my very soul. "No vaulted throne or mortal realm could ever mean more to me than the warmth of your embrace," he murmured fiercely. "I would drown the world in blood and darkness if it would bring you back to me."

His words thrummed against my chest and stirred something in my core. I faced him, holding his sultry gaze. "And I've weathered every storm, every trial, to make my way back to you," I whispered fervently.

Feral hunger ignited in his eyes. His firm hand cradled

my jaw, his thumb brushing my bottom lip. "I will never let you go again," he vowed.

"Prove it," I teased, nipping at his thumb temptingly.

A growl rumbled in his chest, and he captured my mouth in a searing kiss that stole my breath and made my toes curl. His kiss then drifted down my neck, over my collarbone, across my breasts and belly until he reached the place of my pleasure. He buried his face in me as I gasped his name, my fingers gripping his hair as holy rapture shuddered through me. His tongue explored me deeply, knowingly. I begged for the ultimate ecstasy as a moan escaped my lips. But abruptly, he pulled away, looking up at me with a devilish smirk.

"Please..." I moaned, my breath quivering in anticipation.

"Not yet," he rasped, his eyes darkening with an other-worldly need.

He climbed back up to me, his hardness rubbing against my core as his lips crashed into mine. His tongue teased apart the slit of my mouth with overwhelming desire, and I surrendered to it, wrapping my arms around his neck and pulling him closer.

His touch explored my curves, tantalizing me with each stroke; it dove lower until it found the place between my legs, shooting sparks of lightning through my veins. I gasped in delight, my back arching as his mouth claimed mine again. His skilled fingers twisted and twirled and, in moments, I was teetering on the brink of ecstasy.

He paused teasingly, leaving kisses along my neck before finally allowing me to release with an earth-shattering cry. My entire body quivered as I clung to him, my whole being shuddering with pleasure.

Again and again, I gasped his name. My eyes creaked open in the midst of our fervor, when a chill snaked down my spine as out of the corner of my eye, I beheld a menacing figure standing on the balcony. His cold gaze pierced through me like an icy blade before I made out the gleam of silver armor and snowy hair in the moonlight—Thanatos, the Lord of Death. My heart plummeted to my toes at the sight of him, as I knew why he'd come.

He was here for me.

"Hades," I panted, gripping his shoulders tight. "We're not alone."

"Aren't we?" His voice was low and commanding.

My throat clenched, trying to find words between the tumult of emotions that rushed through me. "Thanatos—he's outside." My heart twisted, dread and passion intertwining in my veins. "I think he's watching."

"He envies us," Hades drawled, unbothered, as his grazing lips plunged down the taut skin of my belly. "Let him mourn for what will never be his." Pulling back, he drank in the sight of me eagerly, and then devoured me with more sultry kisses that washed away my worries.

"You are mine," he growled against my neck, firm fingers digging into the soft flesh of my hips. "You will *always* be mine."

I couldn't deny it. My body hungered for him, his touch, his love—all of him. Thanatos could watch from the shadows as much as he wanted, but nothing could stand between us now. Hades was my destiny—and I welcomed it with open arms.

A loud cry of pleasure escaped me as he buried himself between my thighs, his length brushing against my throbbing core. With a groan, Hades surged forward, pushing into me with every inch of his length. He moved with intense purpose, his heat brandishing me, until he filled me completely with a throaty moan.

His hips grinded against mine, moving faster and more urgent with each thrust. He was both rough and gentle on me, demanding and tender, caressing yet pushing me to the edge of ecstasy.

My breath hitched as he pulled away, leaving me craving for more. But then he surged into me again, harder this time. I cried out in sweet agony, feeling every inch of him filling me completely. He moved inside me slowly at first, savoring the moment, but then grew more urgent and passionate, and I clung to him, my nails digging into his back as we moved in perfect harmony.

Lost in the haze of endless pleasure, my whole world became consumed by him and his caresses.

Our breaths mingled and our bodies quivered as together we discovered new heights of delight. Then his voice filled my ears, "Eyes on me, my beautiful love," he growled, "and be loud for me. I want to hear your cries when you graze the edge of divine ecstasy."

I did as he commanded, my gaze colliding with the untamed desire and raw love held within his. And as I shattered into a million stars, I sensed him follow me into oblivion. His name ripped from my throat as I sunk into him, our bodies trembling in the aftermath of our fervent passion. Snugly cradled in his embrace, I grasped him firmly, feeling the last shudder pass through me before we lay upon each other in pure contentment.

"Persephone..." he drawled my name like a prayer. "My beloved Persephone..." His scorching intensity branded my soul. "You are mine and I am yours. Forever."

Yes, I was his. I belonged to Hades and no one else.

# PERSEPHONE

The waning moonlight fell across Hades' sleeping form as I slipped silently from our bed. I paused, gazing down at my husband's tranquil features, wishing I could freeze this moment of peace.

I pulled on a gossamer robe and crept onto the balcony overlooking the Fields of Asphodel. The pale blooms seemed to glow in the gloom, and far off, the rivers flowed endlessly through Hades' kingdom. My kingdom.

But my thoughts strayed to the Realm of Man, to the rocky cliffs and the sandy shores of Stonewall. Factions of rebellious fae encroached ever further on my former lands. Without my blessings, the soil grew barren, leaving my people to starve.

I sighed, gripping the balcony rail. I longed to bring light and life back to Stonewall. But to abandon my duties here would bring ruin to the Netherworld. Such a choice should not fall to one soul.

Arms enveloped me from behind. I leaned into Hades' embrace, taking comfort in his strength. He knew the conflict within me, though we'd avoided speaking of it. I sensed he knew this stillness could not endure. A reckoning approached.

The cold night air ruffled my hair. My heart was heavy with the pleas I had to make. "The human kingdom entrusted to my ruling is in ruins," I whispered through quivering lips. A regretful sigh escaped me, my head drooping in disgrace.

Hades' strong hands slid up to grasp my chin. "Stonewall's curse has lingered for many years now." His voice was tender as he spoke, his warm breath gliding along my earlobe, shooting a thrill down my spine. "Why should it cause you any shame?"

A single tear ran down my cheek as I tried to find the words to explain what I had done. "I have failed them," I said, my throat tight with emotion. "Now, they are vulnerable—at the mercy of the fae."

"The fae?" he echoed, unclear.

"The fae pose a great threat to the Realm of Man," I explained urgently, trying to make him see the danger of the situation.

He shifted closer, pulling me to his taut chest and speaking against my hair. "True, but this is not that realm," he murmured dismissively.

I stepped back, astonished at his lack of concern for my people and their plight. "I thought you'd say such prejudice against the fae was foolish," I stammered, eyes wide with shock.

Hades shook his head. "It's not foolish at all—the fae are a ruthless breed, cunning and dangerously skilled in combat. They pose a real threat to humanity." His hungry hands roved over my frame possessively before settling low on my hips.

The words that left his lips were so pointed, so icy, they took my breath away. I stared at him in stunned silence, unable to comprehend the coldness he showed towards the future of my kingdom. All I could do was whisper, "Without me, Stonewall will be conquered or starve. If I cannot find a way to protect my kingdom, darkness will reign." My voice was thin and frail, barely audible in the stillness of the room.

Hades stood motionless before me, his eyes glinting like onyx as he waited for me to continue.

"My people need me," I said softly, with all the conviction I could muster. "Stonewall is powerless without its queen's return."

Hades' jaw tensed and I knew he understood the full meaning of what I'd said. He asked only one question; simple yet loaded with gravity. "You wish to leave?"

My fingertips ghosted over his granite face, aching with the understanding that there was an impossible distance between us now. I let out the breath I'd been holding and whispered, "I have no other option."

For what felt like an eternity, Hades remained unyielding; he could have been a statuesque carving for all the emotion he showed. But then, after an unbearable pause, his lids closed and when they opened again, his gaze held me captive more powerfully than ever before.

When he spoke, his voice held the finality of absolutes. "You are Queen here now, Persephone. Your mortal shadows are the past. Your place is at my side."

Though his words carried truth, they provided little comfort. I feared the choice before me would haunt me either way. But as I turned my eyes to Stonewall's suffering, I knew which path I had to walk, even as my heart splintered.

As I pleaded again for Hades to show mercy to Stonewall, his expression darkened. "These concerns of yours," he purred knowingly, "where do they come from?"

I remained silent, unwilling to voice the truth—that

Phillip had been the one to open my eyes to the mortal realm's plight.

Hades searched my face. "I see," he uttered, a harsh breath leaving his lips as understanding dawned. He stepped away, brooding. After a moment's thought, he lashed out, "Does *he* know your truth?"

I blinked. "Who?"

The corner of his mouth twitched grimly. "Would you have me speak his name?" he muttered in silent fury. "Very well. Does *Phillip* know who you truly are?"

My breath hitched at the harshness of his words. "He does not," I replied, my heart aching. "And he can never know."

"Why?" Hades demanded, his jaw clenched tight.

"Phillip despises the gods as much as he abhors the fae," I explained wearily, turning away. "He believes they abandoned humanity long ago."

Hades scoffed. "I hardly comprehend the ways of mortals. Is *hatred* the cornerstone of love where Phillip comes from?"

I faced him once more, stung. "Please, don't mock him. He cares deeply for his people... and for mine."

His eyes blazed, but he mastered himself. Slowly circling behind me, he murmured, "I speak truths plainly to you, holding nothing back. Can this prince say the same?" His hand gently cupped my cheek. "My love for you is absolute, overflowing with depths of fathomless intensity. My passion for you burns brighter and hotter than his ever could. Don't tell me you can't feel it."

I closed my eyes, tormented by Hades' jealousy. "Do not compare yourself to Phillip," I implored softly.

Hades turned my face towards his, compelling me to meet his burning gaze. "There *is* no comparison. You must see that." His voice softened as he added, "Trust in *us*, Persephone. Give yourself to our love, and only our love. Is that not your deepest desire?"

I stood there, speechless, my heart aching with blazing passion. And as Hades' lips claimed mine, I surrendered to his kiss, letting all else fade away. For better or worse, my fate was bound to his, our souls united beyond all reckoning.

My knees buckled and he caught me, cradling me in his strong arms as he carried me to the bed. He pressed a tender kiss to my neck before whispering huskily against my skin, "I thirst for you, my love. My every sense aches to explore your body and claim all that lies beneath."

His words sent lightning scorching through me. His hands, like fire and ice on my skin, moved with an intensity that both terrified and mesmerized me. I let myself be pulled under the waves of pleasure, losing sight of everything but Hades' seductive touch.

As Hades trailed kisses down my neck and hastily undid the ties of my robe, I shuddered and pressed myself closer. His hand roamed lower, snake-like against my inner thigh before finally finding its destination. My masterful lover knew just how to bring me close to the edge before drawing back tantalizingly, leaving me craving for more.

He whispered my name in a throaty breath that sent tremors down my spine. A gasp broke through me as he caressed me in all the right ways. My hips pushed up to his, seeking touch, until I was writhing beneath him. Until I finally reached the peak, screaming his name in the sweetest release.

A triumphant smile eased on his lips as he looked down at me. Then, with a possessive growl, he slammed our mouths together as waves of pleasure rippled through my core.

"Do you want me?" he murmured against my lips, his

voice a low growl that shot a thrill through my being. "Do you want me to take you?"

"Yes," I breathed, my body still trembling against his.

He smiled darkly, and in one mighty move, he was inside me. His power rippled through me as our bodies connected, and then an exquisite bliss swept over me—filling me, pushing away all doubt until my screams were nothing but his name on my lips.

"Are you mine?" His voice was a harsh whisper, haunting and desperate against the delicate skin of my neck.

I trembled beneath him, but managed to murmur, "Yes." And in that moment, something in his eyes sang to me. As if our souls had woven together in a way that could never be undone—no matter what trials we would face in the times to come.

My breaths came in ragged gasps as his lips trailed down my neck, sending shivers throughout my body and setting my skin ablaze. With daunting hands, he kneaded my breasts and I arched into him, reveling in the sensation.

"You're so beautiful," he whispered hoarsely, his lips finding mine once more. My legs wrapped around his strong hips and I felt myself unraveling, unable to contain the pleasure coursing through me.

The sound of our entwined breaths, whispered moans, and skin slapping together reverberated off the walls like the songs of forbidden gods. Hades claimed me in every possible way, his skilled fingers delving into every secret place, his lips branding me with hot kisses that left me gasping for air.

"Say my name," he growled, his hands gripping my hips tightly as he pounded into me relentlessly. "Say you belong to me."

"Hades..." I moaned and gave him what he wanted. "I'm yours. Yours alone," I rasped, my nails carving half-moon marks on his back as euphoria cloaked me in its embrace.

His roaring cry filled the air as he thrust forward for one final time before passionately kissing me with unchecked fervor. His tongue dueled with mine as pleasure burst within us both, spilling deep inside me in an inferno that kept searing away even after we were both spent.

We lay there for a long moment, my body against his and our arms entwined. His fingertips skittered along the slope of my back before finally lifting himself to look at me.

"Nothing can ever come between us," he said in a low, ardent voice.

My heart thumped heavily in my chest, but I nodded firmly. "Nothing will," I breathed, anticipation building up in my chest. "Not even my journey to save my kingdom."

The fury that flooded his expression sent shockwaves of dread through me. Quickly, I moved away from him and fastened my robe tightly. "I'm leaving for Stonewall tonight," I said, breathless by the strength of my conviction and the embers of our lovemaking.

I stepped back, but he snatched my wrist to stop me. "You are *not* leaving," he growled, so fiercely that I shivered. "I forbid it!"

I stared at him, disbelief and silent fury tangled in my blood. "If that is your command, Your Majesty, then my say on the matter is irrelevant!" I exploded, my voice shaking with pent-up emotion.

He pulled me to him roughly, with such force that the breath was knocked out of me. "I'm more than a king..." he snarled, each word smoldering with rage as his icy gaze pierced me. "I AM A GOD!" His voice thundered, echoing off the walls and shaking the palace to its foundations.

I wrenched my arm away. Tears sprang to my eyes as a discord of emotions overwhelmed me—desire, terror, and sorrow inundated my being like a roaring river.

But I stood firm, although I trembled from head to toe as

I met his gaze head-on. "And how you revel in your divine power, throwing away lives as if they were but specks of dust —playing with my heart..."

"It is *you* who toys with my affections, Persephone!" he snapped, his chest heaving with outrage.

I stumbled back, my mouth agape. "What do you mean?"

Hades clenched his fists at his sides and spun away, yanking on his robe. When he faced me again, a desperate sorrow shadowed his features. "I just got you back," he said softly. "Why must you leave me?"

My heart splintered, but I stayed resolved. "It's my sacred duty, Hades. The lives of my people depend on me."

Silence hung between us like a shroud. Hades turned his back to me, his massive frame coiled tight with tension. At last, he spoke, his voice devoid of any warmth or mercy.

"Then go," he muttered. "Go back to your kingdom."

Tentatively, I stepped towards him. "Hades—"

He held up a hand to stop me. "I have nothing more to say."

Although he kept his tone frigid, I caught the undercurrent of pain. His pride would not allow vulnerability. Not even with me.

"Please, understand," I said, desperately wishing he would look at me. "My duty calls me elsewhere, but my heart will never leave you."

Hades did not utter a single word, his features stony and unreadable.

My chest ached with longing to repair this broken bond between us. But the fate of others was more important than my own happiness; as much as it wrecked me, I knew I had to walk away.

My throat tightened as I barely managed to speak, "I will never stop loving you. Nothing could ever change that."

Desperately, I searched his face for a sign of surrender. But all I saw was an unyielding warrior. Saddened, I bowed my head in acceptance and whispered, "Farewell, my king."

Hope clawed its way through me like a feral beast, but Hades refused to grant me the mercy of his forgiveness. Tears streamed down my face as I turned away, feeling my heart lacerated with every step I took.

Just as I was about to slip out of sight, he glanced over his shoulder, only once alone did he allow his stoic mask to crack, agony and rage warring across his face. He flinched almost imperceptibly but remained unrelenting as I quietly took my leave, tears burning trails down my cheeks.

Darkness grew in his heart, fed by pride and pain in equal measure. And I feared where such darkness unchecked might lead when I was no longer there to be his light.

# PERSEPHONE

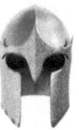

*T*he first glint of twilight filtered into my chamber as I finished strapping on my engraved golden armor, taking care to gently polish each portion until it shone, stalling for time. The familiar weight was both comforting and heartbreaking.

With hesitant hands, I lifted my obsidian blade, Void-bringer, from its stand, trailing my fingers along the leather-wrapped hilt carved with ancient runes before finally cinching it around my waist. The sword's presence at my hip only heightened my sorrow.

After one last survey of my sparse belongings, I breathed deeply, steeling myself. My kit awaited me by the door—saddlebags packed with medicinal herbs, rations, and other necessities for the long journey ahead. All was in order, save the ache in my soul.

A soft knock drew my attention. I turned to find Hypnos leaning against the doorframe, surprise flickering across his gentle features as he took in my battle raiment.

"Going somewhere important?" he asked, eyebrows

raised. But the humor in his voice rang hollow. We both knew the hour was too late for trivial errands.

I managed a faint smile in return, but uncertainty still warred within me. Sensing my turmoil, Hypnos stepped into the room and went to stoke the hearth fire. He busied himself rearranging the ornate iron tools, giving me a moment of quietude I desperately needed.

At last, he came to stand before me, searching my face. I read the question in his eyes, though he already knew the answer.

"You're leaving."

It wasn't a question, merely a statement laced with empathy. I could only nod mutely, not yet trusting my voice. Hypnos let out a soft sigh, gently taking my hands in his.

"Does Hades know?" he said.

Again, I nodded. "We... already said our farewells." I averted my gaze, still raw from that bitter parting.

Hypnos squeezed my hands, understanding written on his features. "I see. Not the most harmonious parting, then."

Despite the melancholy pervading the room, his gift for subtlety brought a wistful smile to my lips. Only Hypnos could find gentle humor even now.

After a long moment, I found my voice. "The mortal realm calls me back for a time. I journey for Stonewall tonight." The admission pained me, even as I knew it for truth. I could not turn my back on the suffering in that distant kingdom. Not when it was in my power to alleviate it.

Hypnos drew me into a warm, comforting embrace without another word, providing the solace I so desperately craved. I clung to him, squeezing my eyes shut against the tears that threatened to spill over.

"I know how your heart is torn," he finally murmured,

still holding me close. "But remember, no matter how far your duties take you, your home is always here, Persephone."

I nodded into his shoulder, moved by his sincerity. He'd always possessed the gift of seeing into my heart and knowing my pain. When at last we pulled apart, Hypnos gifted me with his easy, dimpled grin.

His eyes gleamed roguishly as he said, "And should your brooding husband give you any more trouble over this, simply call on me to put him to sleep for a decade or two."

Despite everything, his gentle teasing brought a watery chuckle to my lips as I pictured Hades' reaction to such an act. Dear Hypnos never failed to lift my spirits with his tranquil wisdom and skillful humor. I would miss his steadying presence.

As if reading my thoughts, Hypnos squeezed my shoulders and said bracingly, "I shall keep watch over these lands until your return. Fear not, my queen, your kingdom will remain safe." He gave a flourishing bow that coaxed forth a teary smile.

I embraced him fiercely once more, wishing I did not have to say goodbye. But the pale moon sinking towards the horizon reminded me the appointed hour approached. Phillip awaited me beyond the Veiled Forest, ready to guide me back to Stonewall. I could tarry no longer.

Hypnos walked me to the servants' stairwell I had chosen for its secluded location. As we descended the winding steps, I committed the craggy palace walls to memory, tracing every familiar crevice and ridge. Who knew when I would walk these stairs again?

Too soon, we reached the concealed side gate near the stables, kept locked save when the king and queen desired privacy. Hypnos unbolted it deftly, the hinges uttering barely a groan as it swung open to reveal my white mare, already saddled and waiting.

I embraced Hypnos one last time, blinking back a fresh wave of tears. "Thank you, my friend," I whispered. "For everything."

He cupped my face in his hands, smiling gently. "May your travels be swift and safe. And know that even when you feel completely lost as you walk among humans and fae alike, I will be with you."

I managed a tremulous smile in return, then pulled my midnight blue cloak tight and swung up into the saddle. With a final look back at my dear companion, I spurred my mare into the creeping mist that shrouded the Veiled Forest.

The shadows seemed to swallow me as I left behind the only home I had known for solitude and uncertainty. I clung to Hypnos' parting words, letting them bolster me. The road unfurling before me was long and fraught with perils, but I did not walk it alone.

As the dark trees enveloped me, I glanced upward through their needled boughs to the velvet sky. The stars of this realm sparkled cold and distant above. I sent a silent prayer to the cosmos—though the heavens rarely heeded such pleas, tonight I hoped with all my weary soul they would listen.

*Watch over him. Do not let his spirit grow too darkened in my absence.*

For I feared what Hades unfettered by love might become. And what havoc he could unleash if that precarious balance tipped.

With grim purpose, I turned my face from those indifferent stars and rode on into the unknown.

## 78
## PHILLIP

*I* paced beneath the shadowed eaves of the Veiled Forest, unable to keep still. Moonlight filtered through the trees, illuminating little. What if she did not come? What if Aurora held no allegiance to me or the mortal realm?

Beside me, Eloise kept her own silent vigil, one hand resting on the pommel of her sword. Always prepared for anything.

"Do you think she'll come?" I finally voiced the fear that plagued me.

Eloise reached out and stilled my restless movements with a gentle hand on my arm. "Trust her judgment," she said simply. "Aurora knows it's her duty."

At that moment, a silhouette emerged from the mist. I froze, scarcely daring to hope. The shape coalesced into a regal woman astride a white mare.

*Aurora.* She had come after all.

Relief nearly buckled my knees as she drew her horse alongside ours—the ones we'd stolen from Hades' own

488

stables the night prior. Her eyes widened slightly at the sight of Eloise, but she greeted us in her usual serene tone.

"Phillip. I'm pleased you did not make this journey alone." Her gaze shifted to Eloise, radiating quiet authority. "And you must be Captain Moorskill. Your reputation as a warrior precedes you. I appreciate you lending Phillip your fine sword arm."

Eloise inclined her head respectfully. "I am at your service, Your Highness. And please, call me Eloise."

Aurora's lips curved into a hint of a smile. She turned her luminous blue eyes back to me. "Shall we depart? Night's cloak will not hide us forever."

I nodded, still somewhat stunned that she had truly come. With Aurora riding beside us, a flicker of hope sparked within me. Perhaps together we could save not only her kingdom, but the entire realm from ruin.

I spurred my horse forward, leading our small company out of the wood's shadow. Twilight's first light awaited us beyond the Veiled Forest, marking a new chapter and all the perils it held. But no longer did we face them alone.

The lingering dark of night slowly surrendered to twilight's first light as we rode, heralding the end of the Veiled Forest's shadowed domain. Shafts of radiance pierced the leafy canopy, illuminating our path ahead. The woods thinned gradually until they gave way completely to rolling hills and sweeping valleys.

I drew my mare to a halt atop a craggy outlook, gazing out at the country unfurling before us. The dying sun cast long shadows behind each hill and tree, elongating their forms into strange shapes like misty giants roused from slumber.

In the distance, the land gradually sloped downward to meet a glimmering expanse—the Midnight Sea, its wind-rippled surface reflecting the pale pinkish light of the newly setting sun.

"We're nearly there," I said over my shoulder to my companions. Aurora's steed drew up beside mine as she peered out at the shimmering waters with an impassive expression. But in her eyes, I glimpsed a twinge of melancholy at this herald of our impending parting.

Eloise trotted up on my other flank, breaking the somber spell. "By nightfall, we shall be aboard the Dragon's Breath and on our way home." Though weariness lined her face, determination blazed in her pale blue eyes.

I nodded, shaking off my heavy thoughts. "Then we'd best make haste. We've lingered here long enough."

Digging my heels into my stallion's flanks, I led the way down the steep, rocky path leading from the overlook to the coast far below. The horses' shod hooves sparked against the loose stones as we picked our way cautiously down the treacherous grade. More than once, my heart seized as my steed skidded on the gravelly slope, but the sure-footed beast maintained his balance.

By the time we reached level ground, a sheen of sweat coated the horses' flanks. Their heads hung low with exhaustion. Poor creatures—after our rapid flight from the Netherworld, they deserved a long rest.

The black sands of the coast cushioned the horses' footfalls as we turned north, following the craggy shoreline. The beach glittered as if dusted with powdered stars—grains of obsidian and crystal worn smooth over eons by the tides. Out at sea, the waves crested liberally with white foam, crashing down on the dark sand with hissing fury.

Rounding a cliff face, we came upon the hidden cove that sheltered our vessel, the Dragon's Breath. The sleek ship floated serenely at anchor, precisely as we'd left her. At the sight of our escape route, relief loosened the knots in my shoulders. This arduous overland journey was nearly at its end.

As we dismounted on wobbly legs and freed the grateful horses to graze, I caught Aurora staring out to sea, her expression unreadable. I wondered if she was having second thoughts about embarking on this dangerous voyage and leaving behind the only world she knew.

I stood at her side, my boots sinking into the ebony sand. Her arms were crossed tightly over her chest, gaze cast on the pitch-black sea.

"What is it that troubles you?" I asked softly. "Do you not wish to leave this place?"

Aurora chewed anxiously on her lip, keeping her troubled eyes on the waves. "My heart will always stay here. But my duty lies in Stonewall."

The question was heavy on my tongue, but I pushed it out all the same. "What ties you to this realm? I must know before we depart."

An emotion flickered across Aurora's fair face—anguish, regret, longing—and then vanished as quickly as it had come. Her voice was weighed down with sorrow when she spoke again. "It matters not now. Stonewall takes precedence over any attachment I might feel here... and there I must go."

My following question died on my lips as a deafening beat rumbled like thunder through the air. I slowly tilted my head up, searching for the source of such an incredible sound. It was then that I saw them— vast dark wings stretched out across the sky like an endless night.

My hand flew to the sword at my belt, before I realized the source of the disturbance was not some vile creature risen from the depths, but rather three winged horses descending from the twilight skies above. Their coat gleamed purest black, though one was distinguished by a collar of braided gold about its neck.

The pegasi flared their graceful wings, landing soundlessly on the obsidian sands. Astride the lead steed sat the striking figure of a woman with fiery hair that seemed to glow with an inner light.

"Hecate..." Aurora said.

The immortal sorceress. Power radiated from her slender frame and piercing amethyst eyes.

To my shock, the goddess inclined her head towards Aurora, gaze full of reverence. "My queen. I have come to bid you farewell."

*Queen?* Aurora stilled beside me but did not correct her. Watching their exchange, I felt understanding creep upon me. There was far more to this woman than I realized.

With a musical laugh, Aurora smiled fondly at the sorceress. "Come now, Hecate. There's no need for such formality when it's only us." She gestured to Eloise and I. "These are my dear friends, Phillip and Eloise."

Amusement flickered in Hecate's eyes as she appraised us. Aurora's smile took on an impish slant. "Though I suppose I haven't been entirely forthcoming with them." She paused, her gaze lingering on mine as she pursed her lips. "I am actually the goddess Persephone, hidden away in the mortal realm for... safekeeping."

Though her admission was delivered lightly, sadness tinged her voice. I stared at her, mind reeling. The woman I had thought a mere princess all this time was in truth a powerful deity. One who had endured much, if her melancholy was any indication.

Hecate gave a knowing smile. "Now we shall see you restored to glory."

The world as I knew it shattered at that very moment.

Aurora, a goddess—Persephone, no less! Her ties to the Netherworld explained, bound by its ruthless sovereign.

I stood frozen, struggling to process this revelation. Beside me, Eloise seemed equally stunned, her eyes wide.

Persephone continued speaking in low tones with Hecate, their conversation unintelligible to my ears. I exchanged a loaded glance with Eloise, seeing my own shock mirrored on her face.

Eloise broke the silence first, her voice hushed as if she had just witnessed something sacred. "It seems Aurora was far more than either of us realized."

I let out a long breath. "A goddess. She's a goddess…" I murmured in wonder. Everything we thought we knew had changed in an instant.

Eloise's face was thoughtful. "One who carries heavy burdens from her long exile." She shook her head. "May she find the strength now to bear them."

"She will," I said with quiet certainty. "If anyone can set things right, it's Persephone." As the words left my mouth, I could scarcely believe them. But I knew in my heart Aurora —or rather, Persephone—possessed an indomitable spirit.

Eloise gave me a small smile. "Onwards then," she said. "Our part in this tale is not yet done."

I nodded resolutely. We would continue aiding Persephone however we could. There was still much uncertainty ahead, but we would stand ready when called upon.

The sorceress soon helped us mount elegant pegasi, their pearl-like wings gleaming in the twilight. As I settled into the saddle, Hecate said, "These steeds will carry you safely over sea and land alike. You shall reach the mortal realm swiftly on their wings."

I glanced at our ship anchored in the cove below, sails furled. "You believe flying is a wiser course than sailing?" I asked, wary at such a daunting endeavor.

"Much swifter, and free of the perilous storms that roil these waters," Hecate confirmed, stroking her pegasus' graceful neck.

Eloise and I exchanged a look. The prospect of crossing the aptly named Midnight Sea had weighed heavily on us both.

Persephone voiced our shared thoughts. "We humbly accept your gift, Hecate." She inclined her head graciously. "May our voyage be swift and safe thanks to your aid."

Hecate smiled. "I shall pray it is so." She bade us a safe journey, then dissolved into the shadows, her work done.

I signaled Persephone and Eloise. As one, we urged our pegasi skyward, leaving the lonely cove and slumbering Dragon's Breath behind. Wings beat steadily beneath us as we gained altitude, ascending into the cloud-strewn firmament.

Though treacherous waters still lay miles below, I already felt safer aloft in open air. We flew towards salvation, leaving the land of death behind. The light of dusk shone on our faces, heralding the promise of home.

# 79

# PERSEPHONE

The first graceful rays of dawn caressed my face as we soared over the cliffs of Stonewall, ushering in a new day. My heart swelled at this precious dawn—the first I had witnessed in what felt like an eternity spent cloaked in endless night.

Far below, the sea shimmered under the rising sun's warmth, the white-capped waves reflecting the light like countless scattered diamonds. Stonewall's towers and parapets emerged from the shadows, the castle awakening with the new day.

We circled lower until the courtyard opened up beneath us, guards and servants gazing skyward in awe as we descended from above. Our mounts swept down with a rush of air, their feathered wings angling to land us smoothly amidst murmurs of shock. The pegasi's hoofs clattered lightly on the stones as they alighted gracefully, their pearl-black pinions folding neatly against their flanks.

For a moment, all was still but for the fountains' song. Then the throng surged forward, joy and relief writ across countless faces. They called my name in disbelief—although not my true name.

I dismounted and stepped into welcoming arms, hands reaching to affirm I was real. Tears flowed freely down my cheeks.

The crowd parted as Lady Rhian and Lord Morgan strode forth, their aged yet proud faces familiar to me. I recognized them as loyal servants to the Steelborn crown. Their deep bows held genuine feeling as Lady Rhian greeted me warmly, "Stonewall welcomes its rightful queen home at last."

Before I could respond, Phillip stepped forward. "Lady Rhian, Lord Morgan," he addressed them respectfully. "In the princess' absence, you've kept her kingdom strong and safe. Steelborn owes you both a great debt."

I nodded in agreement, touched by their steadfast loyalty through the long years, and I embraced each in turn, too overcome for words.

As we moved through the well-wishers, three ladies emerged from the crowd—my dearest friends Alys, Elin, and Ceridwen. Overcome with emotion, I rushed forward and threw my arms around them. They returned my embrace fiercely, the four of us clinging together as joyful sobs shook our frames.

After endless lonely years apart, we finally held each other again. I buried my face in their familiar, sweet-scented hair, tangible proof this was real. Their hands clutched at my back convulsively, as if they too could barely believe I stood before them in the flesh.

We stayed locked in our emotional reunion, uncaring of onlookers. In this moment, all that existed was our sister-hood reunited against all odds. The intervening years fell away, powerless before such friendship. Together once more, it felt as though I had found missing pieces of my heart.

"We prayed this day would come," Alys soothed, brushing my hair affectionately.

I gazed out upon the sea of hopeful faces before me and felt strength fill my spirit. Clearing my throat, I spoke with conviction:

"People of Stonewall. A new dawn rises for our kingdom. For too long have we suffered, but no more. The long night is over—now we walk together into the light of a new day, hand in hand. If we stand united, we will see our beloved home blossom once more."

My words rang clear in the brisk morning air. For a breath, the crowd was silent. Then a cheer swelled across the ramparts and out to sea, rolling like thunder.

Restored to my rightful place among loved ones, with my brave people behind me, I felt whole and hopeful for the first time in forever. The trials ahead no longer seemed insurmountable.

I was home.

*I* trudged into the strategy room, worn from the long journey and filled with dread. The council members who awaited my arrival wore solemn expressions on their faces that confirmed what I already knew—I was home, but danger lingered in our walls. All eyes were fixed on me as I settled at the head of the table, dust still clinging to my clothes.

The Master of Coffers cleared his throat and spoke first, a somber note in his voice. "Your return brings hope to us all," he said, "but Stonewall is not yet safe."

Exhausted loyalty surrounded me—Phillip, Moorskill, and trusted advisors who had served faithfully in my stead.

Lady Rhian spoke, lines deeper from struggles. "The fae warlord Maegon saw your absence as his chance to claim Stonewall."

I leaned forward urgently. "Did your words have no effect? Did you not try to reason with him?"

"Endlessly, Your Majesty," the master replied bleakly, "But Maegon is a loyal subject of the Fallen Fae King

Raathiel and will not be dissuaded from his course of conquest."

Master Morgan's face was grim. "It only gets worse," he murmured, a hand gliding along his chin. "Whitehaven has formed a union with Maegon's rogue cousin, Arthion the One-Eyed King. If Maegon has joined forces with his ruthless cousin Arthion, he'd have enough power to tear this kingdom apart."

I closed my eyes and hung my head, the weight of his words crashing down on me. Our forces were far too few to hold off an attack from both armies. And Stonewall had grown weak in my absence, its coffers almost empty.

Lady Rhian gave voice to our shared fear. "We have no army, no weapons..." She hesitated. "Your Highness, we are defenseless."

Despair filled the room like a tangible fog, when a hurried knock broke the stillness, pounding at the chamber door. The Master of War bid entry, brow furrowed. Inside, a windblown messenger stumbled, grasping a rolled parchment. With a shallow bow, he handed the paper to the Master. The messenger withdrew, yet unease lingered.

Silence fell as we watched the grim tidings unfold on the Master's face. At last, he looked up, catching my eye.

Master Morgan, a stern and formidable figure, rose from his seat with unease. His eyes met mine, the weight of the message he carried etched upon his face.

"Your Majesty, this bears ill news that cannot wait," he said, crushing the scroll in his grip. "A message from Maegon's encampment has arrived. They demand our surrender by dawn or..."

My voice was hollow when I finished the words for him, "Or else they attack."

Confirming nods circled the room like an ominous ripple

in a pond, and Lady Rhian spoke into the silence that followed. "Maegon's patience has finally expired."

I surveyed the circle of grim faces around the council table. "Have we sent urgent pleas for aid from our allies?"

Master Morgan nodded solemnly. "Ravens have flown, Your Grace. But no kingdom wishes to spark Maegon's ire."

Phillip sprung off his seat beside me. "Steelborn will answer Stonewall's call," he ardently declared. "My forces will march here with all haste. If I summon them now, they should arrive come morning." He slammed a curled fist over the table, chin raised in stern determination.

I gazed at him, gratitude and admiration swelling within. Ever fearless, Phillip offered his own army in our time of need.

But the Master of War appeared grave. "A grand gesture, Your Highness, but I fear Maegon's forces far outmatch your infantry."

Phillip's jaw clenched stubbornly. "You underestimate the courage of my people," he protested. "Steelborn does not shrink from a worthy fight."

I touched his arm gently. "Let us pray it does not come to open war. There are still avenues of peace left to explore." I hoped I spoke truth, though doubt gnawed at me.

Phillip covered my hand with his own. "No matter what comes, Steelborn will stand with your kingdom." His eyes blazed with conviction. "You need only ask, and my sword and my soldiers are yours to command."

His steadfast loyalty brought warm tears to my eyes. If words had failed to sway Maegon, many lives would be lost. I had to find another way before the first blood was shed come dawn.

A bleak silence enshrouded the room. I closed my eyes, wrestling down despair. Stonewall was in crisis, its people, dependent on their sovereign for salvation. But was I strong enough to protect them?

I rose slowly from my chair. "Leave me. I must deliberate on this alone."

As the others filed out, I moved to the balcony over-looking the sea. The glittering expanse once brought me peace, but today I found no solace in its familiar beauty. Stonewall's fate rested on my shoulders. And I could not falter.

Somehow, I had to find an answer before the armies marching north reached our unguarded borders. I only prayed the gods granted me enough time to save my kingdom from annihilation.

A soft knock heralded the entry of my ladies-in-waiting. Though over a century old, the three fae women appeared as fresh-faced and lovely as in the early years of my childhood, blessed with everlasting youth.

Ceridwen turned to me, her ageless face grave. "Aurora, our hearts are brimming with joy to have you with us again. But there is something we must reveal, a secret kept for too long."

I gazed at her quizzically. "What is it?"

The three exchanged mournful looks. Alys spoke first, her voice heavy. "We've known the truth since you were but a babe," she began with a tremulous voice. "We know you are Persephone, goddess of spring."

I stilled, stunned. They had known?

Elin nodded sadly, taking my hands. "Queen Leah was barren for many years. In her grief, Demeter offered a bargain—she would gift Leah a child, but that child would be you, placed into mortal flesh to hide you from those who wished you harm."

Tears shone in Ceridwen's eyes. "We were tasked with raising you as Princess Aurora, protecting your true identity."

My mind reeled. All this time, my most trusted confidants had kept this secret from me. Anger and hurt warred within me.

Sensing my turmoil, Alys entreated, "Forgive us, my child." Her hands held mine. "We wished only to keep you safe, as Demeter asked of us."

I searched their faces and saw only love and remorse. At last, I found courage and spoke through the lump in my throat. "You need not apologize," I said, easing my hand along Alys' soft jawline. "You have been as mothers to me all these years. I could ask for no greater devotion."

"Oh, Aurora!" Ceridwen cried, bursting into tears. She cleared her throat. "I mean, Persephone."

A giggle escaped me as I wrapped an arm around her shoulders. "That's perfectly all right, Cee." I sniffed.

My sweet ladies embraced me, weeping in relief. I clung to them, my heart overflowing. We had weathered this revelation together. And with the truth revealed, I felt stronger and more prepared to face the darkness gathering on the horizon.

Ceridwen cleared her tears, garnering her poise once more. "Now about that warlord..."

"Maegon shows no mercy, even to his own kind," Alys said, her voice tremulous with wariness. "If we don't stop him now, his wrath will spread through the realm like wildfire."

I nodded grimly. Tales of this warlord painted him as vicious and unrelenting.

Elin drifted to my side, flawless features etched with worry. "Perhaps we could flee, Your Majesty? Escape his notice until his malice cools?" She nervously fidgeted with her emerald locks, twisting and turning the silky strands between her fingers.

"And leave Stonewall to burn?" I shook my head fiercely. "I will not abandon my kingdom."

Alys touched my shoulder, her ageless face full of compassion. "Do not underestimate this foe, my child. He will show no quarter."

I covered her delicate hand with my own. "While I live, hope endures," I stated firmly, but inwardly I quailed. What chance did I stand against such merciless power? I wasn't a goddess of death and destruction, but one of life and light.

Ceridwen stared out at the darkening sea, her fierce beauty accented by sorrow. "Dawn approaches," she said gravely. "Stonewall will look to its ruler for salvation."

I lowered my eyes, the weight of my people's fate bearing down upon me. Could I alone protect them from the coming darkness? I feared I would not be enough.

As the last light faded beyond the horizon, I watched the moon caress the midnight sea. Somewhere in that vast celestial expanse, an answer waited.

I prayed dawn would reveal it before all was lost.

# 81

# PERSEPHONE

The sky slowly shifted from midnight black to a deep cerulean, overcast and dreary, as though the heavens themselves wept. The sea beneath me churned and swirled in an endless waltz of waves, its constant motion matched by my throbbing heart. Daybreak's soft light illuminated the length and breadth of my despair; with its arrival would come the reckoning my kingdom had been avoiding for so long. Maegon would arrive soon, bringing chaos and ruin.

My anxious ruminations were shattered when alarm bells suddenly clamored through the Stone Keep. Men shouted in unison, darting across the ramparts, their panicked screams filling me with a sense of dread. Sails approached from the north, still hidden in the mist but nearing fast.

Our time had come.

Pulse racing, I bolted to my chamber and hastily donned my engraved golden armor, fingers fumbling in my haste. I seized Voidbringer and raced to the courtyard. If Maegon was early, we would face him head-on.

Phillip and Captain Moorskill joined me as we rushed

through the chaotic halls now swarming with panicked servants and scrambling guards. My heart hammered against my breastplate—in mere moments, we could be battling for the kingdom's very survival.

Phillip's voice rang urgently, a lion's roar. "How far off are they?"

"We have minutes at most!" I gasped breathlessly. "They're nearly at the docks!"

Moorskill's expression was grim but determined beneath her helmet. "We'll make our stand together, come what may," she declared with conviction, her even-keel voice reflecting that of a seasoned warrior.

I gave her shoulder a grateful pat amidst the jostling bodies. In mere moments, we could be battling for the kingdom's very survival.

We burst from the keep onto the harbor just as the first ship emerged from the mist's veil, midnight sails billowing. It glided swiftly towards us, a behemoth on the glittering steel blue sea. But where I expected to see Maegon's blood-red banner, a white skull on black emblazoned the sail instead—*the royal emblem of the Netherworld.*

Shock rooted me in place. What was Hades' fleet doing sailing here unannounced?

When figures came into view aboard the mysterious craft, ice flooded my veins. A solitary form stood tall at the bow, cloaked head to toe in burnished armor that shone remarkably, even at this distance.

The ship sliced smoothly through glistening waters. As it neared the dock, all around fell into hushed anticipation of what may emerge.

With practiced grace, the lead warship eased along the quay. As the plank lowered with a dull thud, revelation came at last. It was Hypnos himself who first strode down, clad in full battle raiment, his gold and sapphire armor resplendent with an otherworldly glow. Two dozen of his fiercest warriors disembarked behind him, armed to the teeth.

Before I could react, Phillip darted past me and stormed up to the war god with a snarl. "Have you come to revel in our misery, vile monster? You are not welcome here!"

Hypnos arched an eyebrow, supremely unconcerned. "Restrain your temper, boy," he said, a commanding hand raised to subdue him. "I come at your queen's pressing need for aid. Nothing more."

Phillip bellowed with untamed fury, and the sound ripped through the air. "You lie!" he growled, venom dripping from his tongue. "Return to the Netherworld and leave this realm alone!"

I stepped forward before swords were drawn, my voice ringing with urgency. "Phillip, wait! Lord Hypnos is on our side!"

Phillip stepped forward, shock clear in his expression. "My lady, you cannot trust him! His kind lives only to bring chaos and suffering."

"His... *kind?*" I echoed, startled and wounded. "May I remind you, I too am a goddess. Am I unworthy of your trust as well?"

He halted, his breath labored and tense. Phillip refused to meet my gaze, instead casting his eyes downward in shame. My fingers cautiously clasped around his arm, pressing gently as I coaxed him towards me. "Right now, we need every ally we can find," I murmured softly, struggling to stifle the anguish in my tone. "Even those who have wronged us in the past. Old hatreds must be set aside, for Stonewall's sake."

Phillip's jaw clenched, but he dipped his head in grudging acceptance. Turning back to Hypnos, I clasped his gauntleted hand in gratitude. "Thank you, old friend. However you learned of our plight, your aid is deeply appreciated."

Hypnos' smile held a cunning edge. "I'm not the *only one* keeping watch over you, my queen," he cryptically said.

I rushed to embrace him as the rest of his fleet disembarked on the docks, countless warriors already fanning out behind him. But my strides faltered when I recognized the imposing figure striding at his side—Ares, the formidable god of war.

Hypnos gave a knowing grin at my surprise. "I took it upon myself to recruit some *additional* aid, my queen."

He stepped aside, allowing Ares to approach and clasp my hand in greeting. I had to crane my neck to meet the fiery green eyes of the muscle-bound god towering over me. His stern face intimidated, but his handshake was gentle.

"Lady Persephone," his rumbling voice greeted me as he clasped my hand. "I could not stand idle while your kingdom faced invasion."

I bowed my head as a sign of respect. "You honor us with your aid, Lord Ares," I replied carefully. His ferocity in battle was legendary, as was the carnage left in his wake.

As if sensing my trepidation, Ares declared, "I shall only unleash enough force to decisively end this conflict. You have my word."

I placed a hand on his vambrace. "I know you wield great power, Ares. But remember—mercy can achieve what violence cannot. Stay your hand when possible."

For a moment, Ares was silent, holding my gaze with an unreadable expression. "As you command, my queen," he sternly said, bowing his head in acquiescence. "There are still some who call me the Curse of Men. But those days have passed, I assure you."

Relieved, I clutched his massive arm in appreciation. Violence breeds more violence, as I knew too well. If Ares could temper his legendary rage, perhaps much bloodshed could be avoided on the coming dawn.

The words trembled from my lips, but I forced them out. "My Lord Ares—Stonewall owes you a debt of gratitude. Thank you for coming to our aid." My chest swelled with sincerity as I spoke.

The Lord of War nodded gravely, hefting his enormous spear and shield. "Now, I suggest we prepare. The enemy marches ever closer as we speak."

As we hastened back to the castle, I shot Hypnos a heartened look. Securing Ares' assistance had been a masterstroke. With these two mighty gods now bolstering our ranks, hope kindled anew.

Perhaps we could win this war without the slaughter Phillip seemed resigned to accept. Ares was matchless in strategy—if anyone could find a path to victory with minimal loss of life, it was he.

The dawn no longer seemed an end, but a beginning. By Ares' skill and our united strength, we could send Maegon's hordes fleeing like whipped dogs. Stonewall's salvation was at hand if we had courage and faith enough to seize it.

I discreetly blinked back relieved tears. Hades had answered my desperate plea—yet his absence wasn't lost on me. My heart ached, a deep chasm of grief engulfing me like never before.

On we marched, Phillip's stare a searing brand upon Hypnos. His hands never strayed far from his sword hilt. Though we were united against Maegon for now, the prince clearly did not trust this frail alliance.

I prayed Phillip's hatred of the gods would not blind him at a critical moment. The coming battle would require level heads and absolute focus if Stonewall hoped to weather this storm. We were forced to unite, the past no longer significant in this battle... or Stonewall would inevitably be doomed.

# 82

# PERSEPHONE

*D*awn's first light oozed over the mountains, staining the eastern sky crimson—an ill omen of the bloodshed this day could bring. I stood atop the battered parapets overlooking the sweeping valley where Maegon's forces gathered, their numbers blotting out the land below. My engraved armor felt cold and heavy upon my shoulders as the fierce cool wind lashed out announcing an inescapable battle.

I spun around to take in the imposing force behind me. The palace guards stood at attention, bronze helms shadowing their faces, swords shimmering in the sunlight as if hoping for a use. Hypnos' elite Netherworld warriors lined up behind him, their fearsome presence sending a shiver down my spine. And there, at the head of them all, was Ares. His chestnut locks gleamed copper as they danced in an unfelt breeze, imposing in his battle raiment and wielding his legendary spear.

Their courage kindled a spark of hope within me, even while staring down the teeming horde arrayed around

Maegon's banner. I offered a silent prayer to the gods for victory on this day.

A howling herald echoed across the valley, announcing Maegon's approach. The masses parted to allow the fae warlord passage astride an ebony destrier. His silver armor bore not a scratch, his handsome face, not a scar—evidence of his fighting prowess. Dark power coiled around him, setting my senses on edge.

Maegon drew his mount before the castle gates and lifted his visor. His lip curled with disdain as he spied me atop the parapets. "Lady Aurora," he called up mockingly. "Does a kingdom hide behind the skirts of its princess?"

I kept my voice calm and clear. "Lord Maegon. Let us settle this without bloodshed. Withdraw your forces, and we may yet find grounds for agreement."

Maegon threw back his head and laughed. "The only agreement you shall have is unconditional surrender! You are outnumbered and outmatched, my lady. Open your gates before this comes to slaughter."

I lifted my chin. "Do you only understand conflict, Maegon? Stonewall seeks harmony between our peoples. But we will defend our home if forced."

"Defend?" Maegon smirked. His angular features were sharp and predatory beneath war-braided locks the color of blood. Pointed ears peeked through the crimson mane, marking his fae lineage. "With what army? That pathetic rabble I see trembling atop your walls?" He sneered. "You are no warrior, only a foolish girl playing at valiance. Now stand aside and let your betters determine your fate."

Fury blazed through me at the contempt in his words. I allowed a hint of my divine aura to shine through as I declared, "You will find Stonewall guarded by forces *more powerful* than you can comprehend. Cross these walls at your peril, Maegon."

The warlord's smile turned sinister, revealing the points of fanged teeth. His skin was pale as bone, made even more striking by the black armor that girded his muscular frame. A flicker of unease crossed the warlord's features, but he quickly masked it with bravado. "Last chance!" he yelled harshly. "Open your gates or taste oblivion!"

I turned my back on him, signaling the herald to sound the horns. Across the valley, Maegon roared his battle cry. As one, his ocean of soldiers surged forward, an unstoppable tide.

My pulse thundered in my ears. All hung in the balance now. I faced the swelling horde without flinching, prepared to unleash my full might. Challenging days lay ahead, but Stonewall would neither yield nor fall. Our destiny was yet unwritten.

A taut silence enshrouded the valley in the wake of Maegon's ultimatum. All eyes were upon me as I stared down at the vast horde thirsting for blood. I had mere heartbeats to decide the kingdom's fate.

At last, I turned to the herald and nodded. As the horn sounded, I called down, "Very well, Maegon. We shall open our gates for parley."

A savage grin split the warlord's face. He turned and roared to his army, "Victory!" They howled for blood and surged forward.

I descended the parapets swiftly to where my ragtag defenders awaited, faces grim. "Courage!" I rallied them. "We will end this threat here and now!"

Though outnumbered, we took heart. The trap was set. Now we needed only spring it.

I hurried to the courtyard where Hypnos and Ares directed their phalanx into positions, their shields and spears at the ready. I braced myself as Maegon's horde battered the gates.

"He comes swiftly, my queen," Hypnos remarked, eerily calm amidst the chaos.

"We are prepared," Ares added, a confident smirk curling the corner of his lips.

I nodded, steeling myself. The clamor of Maegon's horde now shook the very gates as they battered them down. We had only moments before they came pouring through, drunk on promised victory.

With a resounding crack, the reinforced gates finally splintered inwards and the tide of fae warriors flooded the courtyard—then stumbled to a shocked halt. Where they expected to find cowering subjects, a disciplined army awaited them instead, led by the god of war himself.

In the confusion, Hypnos bellowed a war cry. His phalanx sprang forth, spears impaling the stunned invaders. Swords clashed and warriors fell as brutal hand-to-hand combat erupted.

From atop the inner parapets, I unleashed arcs of divine fury that scythed through Maegon's ranks. But still, they kept coming, howling and bloodthirsty. We would not hold forever.

As planned, I raised a flaming arrow, signaling Phillip. With a thunder of hooves, his cavalry charged into the keep through the yawning gates, crashing into the enemy's exposed flank. Trapped on both sides, the unprepared invaders fell in droves.

In the chaos, Phillip cut a swath straight towards Maegon, teeth bared ferociously. Ares intervened, his spear flashing as he cut off the warlord's retreat. But the warlord was no fool. Seeing the trap sprung, he attempted to fight free of the press, bellowing for his honor guard.

In the distance, I spied Captain Moorskill leading a contingency of archers raining arrows on Maegon's position, complicating his escape.

Phillip charged after him, sword swinging in fury as he sought to thwart Maegon's escape. They traded vicious blows amidst the roiling fray. I dared not intervene for fear of distracting Phillip at a fatal moment.

At last, with a bellow of pain and outrage, Maegon wrenched himself onto a riderless horse and galloped for the ruined gates. "Retreat!" he desperately howled. "RETREAT!" A roar heralded his flight—the fae warriors began pouring back out onto the field in disarray.

Sensing victory, our forces pressed forward with renewed vigor. And within moments, the brutal battle was over. Maegon's projected conquest had disintegrated into chaos and bloodshed. Across the valley, the remnants of his host scattered in defeat.

As the city erupted in jubilation, I flew down to the courtyard just as Phillip dragged a battered, seething Maegon from his mount to throw him in chains. The prince's grin was vicious with triumph. We had won the day.

Maegon strained against his shackles, eyes blazing with impotent fury as Phillip forced him to kneel before me. "You will rue this day, wench," he spat. "My armies will raze your kingdom to ashes!"

"Silence!" Phillip cut him off sharply, his own eyes flinty and cold. "You are defeated and in chains. I suggest you learn when to guard that serpent tongue."

I studied the warlord dispassionately. "Your warmongering ends today, Maegon. No longer will Stonewall bow and scrape for peace while you threaten and pillage."

Maegon bared his teeth, exposing keen fae fangs, but said nothing.

"You will remain here in our custody," I continued evenly, "until such time we decide your final fate. I suggest you settle in for a long stay."

At that, Maegon strained furiously against his bonds,

spitting curses. Phillip roughly hauled him back before more harsh words could be exchanged.

"Get him out of my sight," I commanded wearily. I turned away as Maegon was dragged off screaming maledictions at his captors.

I heaved a long sigh. At last, it was over. Against the odds, Stonewall stood strong, thanks to bravery and alliance. Now we could begin the long road towards true peace. Our freedom was won not through base violence, but determination united in the pursuit of freedom.

Pride swelled in my heart as I beheld our courageous fighters. Though the war was far from over, this victory would show the realms that Stonewall yet stood strong. Here was proof that courageousness could prevail over might.

There would be time later to bind wounds, honor the fallen, and tally the immense cost of the battle. But for now, we raised our voices in celebration under the banner of the withdrawn fae army.

Against all odds, our kingdom had endured.

# PERSEPHONE

*T*he Stone Keep's great hall glittered with a thousand golden lights, illuminating the vibrant banners of purple and gold lining the soaring stone walls. Garlands of blossoms decorated every marble column and archway, filling the air with sweet perfume. Below the great arched windows, nobles danced and reveled to soaring music, their jewel-toned finery winking in the candlelight. An atmosphere of joyous celebration filled Stonewall's castle, for this long-awaited occasion marked Princess Aurora's coronation as queen.

I stood surrounded by my ladies, observing it all from a shadowed alcove off the main hall. No one but my closest confidants knew the truth—that I was no mortal princess. Tonight, that would change.

A fanfare of trumpets announced the arrival of Princess Aurora. I watched my ladies arrange my voluminous golden gown before ushering me into the hall.

As one, the crowd knelt in deference. I raised the gathering with a smile and glided through the parted sea of bodies.

Nobles bowed and curtsied, faces beaming with joy to see their princess crowned at last. I greeted each by name, embracing my role one final time. Soon, all pretenses would end.

My procession reached the soaring dais where the High Priest awaited beside the empty throne. The relics of rule—scepter, orb, and crown—had been laid reverently across velvet pillows. The room hushed in anticipation.

"My people," I addressed them. "Before we continue, I must reveal a truth long hidden..."

Murmurs rose, but stilled at my raised hand. "I am *more* than merely your princess," I declared, emboldened by newfound strength. "I am Persephone, goddess of the spring."

Gasps and whispers echoed, but no dissent. I allowed my aura to shine through the mortal façade I had worn since infancy. Divine light rippled through the hall, dispelling all doubt. At last, I was revealed as a goddess in their midst.

When the radiance faded, a shocked silence lingered. Father Emrys spoke first. "My lady, forgive our ignorance." He sank to his knees in supplication. "We're unworthy of your celestial presence."

"No, good father. It is I who was unworthy of you." My voice rang out clearly in the hush. "You who loved and sheltered me, never knowing my true nature. You have proven yourselves the worthy ones. And for that, you have my eternal devotion."

I turned slowly, meeting the eyes of the awestruck crowd. "I was sent to live amongst you for protection, raised as your princess. But don't mistake that for who I truly am—a daughter of Stonewall through and through. I swear to you, I shall defend these blessed lands forevermore as your goddess queen."

Once more the priest spoke, his voice rough with

emotion. "Then by the covenants of old, I now crown you Persephone, Goddess Queen of Stonewall!"

He raised the ancient diadem upon my brow. A resounding cheer shook the hall, the voices imbued with wonder and trust. "All hail Queen Persephone!" The words resonated through my spirit, sealing an unbreakable bond.

The crowd roared wildly, celebrating my long-awaited revelation and ascension. Firemagic filled the night sky in an explosion of dazzling colors, while music blazed loudly around us. As golden confetti rained down on us, I could feel the joy radiating from every corner, tangible and powerful. This was a night to remember.

Love and purpose blazed in my heart as I gazed upon my people. No longer needing to conceal my divine abilities, I could now wield my full might to safeguard Stonewall through the dark days ahead. With its true queen openly on the throne, no enemy could threaten this kingdom again.

I turned to Phillip, my gaze full of admiration. "You gave me the courage to reclaim myself," I said softly.

With a reverent bow, he replied, "My queen, I only wish to serve our kingdoms." Squeezing his hands in gratitude, I allowed myself to believe it. Even when he did not know my divine identity, Phillip had never wavered in his devotion.

"Your loyalty is unyielding, as this kingdom's steel and stone," I said in awe. "Through every changing season, through storm and calm alike, you've stood unshaken as Stonewall's steadfast guardian."

"I was never alone..." Phillip quietly replied, his sharp blue eyes angling towards the crowd.

My gaze followed his, sweeping the gathering masses, and spotted a solitary figure standing amidst the throng. A familiar silhouette, arms crossed proudly over its chest. The sharp features of the warrior woman gleamed beneath the light—Captain Moorskill, who'd fought beside Prince Phillip to defend my kingdom.

When our eyes met, I beckoned her forth. The revelers cleared a path for the captain as she approached and knelt before the dais.

Tonight she wore no armor, but an exquisite gown of sapphire silk embroidered with golden thread. It draped elegantly over her strong frame. Both armor and finery equally suited her beauty.

Her long, pale blonde hair cascaded freely down her back, no longer constrained beneath a helmet. The golden tresses shone like silk in the torchlight, complementing the rich blue of her dress. I was struck by how the severe warrior I knew transformed into a vision of elegance, yet her keen gaze remained unchanged.

"Rise, brave Captain," I bade her. "You have done Stonewall a great service beyond measure. It shall not be forgotten."

I unpinned an amethyst brooch from my robe—a royal jewel gifted only to those of the highest distinction. Fixing it to Moorskill's gown, I proclaimed, "For your courage and dedication, I name you Hero of the Realm. Stonewall will ever owe you its gratitude."

Moorskill bowed low. "I pledge my sword and my life to you, Your Divine Majesty." As she turned to humbly withdraw, the crowd erupted into deafening cheers of honor and praise for their newest champion.

I smiled as she took her place once more amongst the worthy heroes of this kingdom. Stonewall was blessed to have such noble souls defending its lands. With Moorskill standing guard, the future looked bright indeed.

As the ceremony concluded, I felt peace settle over my heart. After so many years of struggle, my kingdom was healing. My people were safe and hopeful, their lives restored.

I took my leave of the great hall with measured steps, emotions swelling within me. Emerging onto the moonlit balcony, I gazed out over the sleeping city and shimmering sea. A new era dawned with the sunrise, one of hope and light unending. While I reigned over Stonewall, my people would forever know prosperity.

I sighed contentedly. The lonely years of hiding were behind me. I was finally free to be my true self, serving my kingdom openly as goddess and queen.

As the first rays of dawn crested the horizon, I sent a prayer of thanks to the stars for guiding me to this sacred purpose. My reign would not be untroubled—dark forces stirred and many trials still lay ahead. But united with my people through bonds of trust, we had nothing to fear from the gathering shadows.

Stonewall's Golden Age had begun.

# PHILLIP

The night unfolded, and the grand ballroom came alive with laughter and celebration. My heart raced, a tangle of nerves and anticipation. Eloise looked resplendent in her silken sapphire gown, and every time her ice-blue eyes met mine, a rush of warmth and delight washed over me.

As we swayed to the music, lost in each other's arms, I gazed at Eloise with pride and affection.

"You look like a goddess," I breathed, my smoldering gaze roving over her sensuous frame. "No doubt, Ceridwen is pleased with the beauty you embody."

Eloise rolled her eyes. "She's been grinning at me from ear to ear every time we pass each other. It's almost nauseating."

I snickered, relishing in the sight of Eloise in all her glory. Everything about her sparkled brighter than the stars above us—from the way her dress cascaded down her body, to the razor-sharp wit that lingered beneath it all.

"You have fulfilled your dream, my love. At last, you've

carved your name in legend," I purred against her ear. "Not only that, but you've been appointed Hero of the Realm."

"What does that even mean?" she uttered with a small laugh.

I smiled gently. "It means that you must give up your duty as Captain of my Guard..." I said sadly. "The role suited you so." Unease filled my heart as I thought of her facing whatever dangers came her way without me.

A smirk tugged at the corner of her lips as she regarded me fondly. "Dearest Phillip," she murmured reverently, her words carrying a strong weight. "Wherever fate leads, I shall ever guard you. And though this role grants a new destiny, you remain the sovereign of my heart, to protect and love."

Her promise dispelled all doubts in my mind. She should not have to face the unknown alone—although it was true that her courage and sagacity far surpassed mine.

"The gods be praised," I growled, a hand cupping the back of her head fondly. Whichever path destiny chose for us, no force would ever break our everlasting bond.

Eloise flinched. "Don't tell me you're a believer now?" she teased.

I snickered and shook my head. "No—not in the gods," I replied softly, and my gaze bore into hers. "I'm a believer in *you*, Eloise. In your strength, your courage, and your unwavering love."

She blushed at my words, leaning up to press a tender kiss to my lips. "As I am in you," she murmured against my mouth, her fingers tangling in my hair.

The music swelled, entwining us into one as we swayed in each other's arms. In this moment, the truth of my heart burned deep inside me.

"Eloise," I whispered, fearing that if I spoke louder I'd shatter the spell that enclosed us. "Ever since I met you, you ignited a flame inside me that could never be extinguished.

You've been my courage, my strength, my longing... I can't imagine a future without you."

Her eyes widened with surprise, and in their depths, I glimpsed a glimmer of hope.

"I love you," I said, my grip on her hand tightening. "I want to spend the rest of my life with you." I paused, steadying my breath. "Eloise, would you marry me and *not* live happily ever after by my side?"

The corner of her lips quirked up, intrigued by my odd phrasing.

"Forget the obligations and expectations—of ceremonies and crowds, of protocol and duty," I fervently said, taking her hands to my chest. "Let's build a *real future* together, of shared joys and conquered challenges. Let's cast aside fate and forge our own destiny—a strong, unyielding love that will never fade away. With you by my side, I know anything is possible."

Tears shimmered in her eyes as she nodded, a radiant smile spreading across her face. "Where you go, I follow," she whispered. "That has and will always be my choice. Weaver of destiny or soldier in the field, nothing can sever what love has carefully connected."

With those simple words, my heart soared, and I couldn't help but pull her close, holding her tight as we continued to dance. The music swirled around us, the rest of the world fading into the background as we lost ourselves in each other's embrace.

Here she stood before me—my love, my soulmate, and my partner for life. True love was not written in the stars or preordained by fate. It had walked beside me through storm and calm, hand in hand, since we were children. I'd only needed the courage to see it.

Eloise was not assigned to me by some grand design. She chose me, despite my flaws. And I chose her in return. That gift was worth more than any cosmic fortune. Our love was not dictated by powers on high, but built through shared struggles and trust.

As we swayed together now, I knew our future held endless possibilities. Not bestowed by fate, but shaped by our own hands.

# PERSEPHONE

*A*s dawn's first light etched the horizon, I slipped away from the tumultuous ballroom into the silent courtyard. Despite my triumph, melancholy crept at the edges of my weary spirit. My heart ached for the one soul missing in this victory.

I slowly paced the flagstone path, my fingers all but whittling the opal locket pending from my neck. How I missed him, my dark lord of the Netherworld. His imposing figure, his broad shoulders that sheltered me, his piercing eyes that saw through to my very soul. Had regret now softened that intense gaze? Did his strong hands still clench in stubborn anger or reach for me in sorrow?

I stared down at the locket. The bony skull etched in its glimmering pearly surface suddenly glinted alive in the soft torchlight. Lost in bittersweet memory, my thumb ran reverently over the pendant. With a soft click, it opened before me with magical ease.

Nestled inside was a single, glossy crimson pomegranate seed like a drop of his heart's blood given to me. I plucked it out with trembling fingers and marveled at its delicate texture, rolling the ruby orb between my fingertips.

Despite our rift, Hades remembered me with this intimate token. I clutched the seed tightly, before raising it to my lips and drinking down its tart sweetness. My eyes closed as blissful memories flooded my mind—languid days spent feeding each other the ruby arils, juice staining our fingers and mouths as we laughed. A simpler time, full of passion and promise.

The seed's nectar tasted of melancholy and desire. My body ached for his touch, to be enveloped in his strength again. I prayed this offering meant he felt the same longing across the divide separating us.

"Persephone..."

I started, pulse leaping at that beloved baritone. And he was there, materializing from the shadows—so much more real than any dream.

"Hades..." I breathed.

His striking features were broken with pained regret, his midnight tresses tossing in the breeze as if he'd traversed through seas and skies to find me. Slowly, he advanced closer.

"Forgive me," he pleaded, graveled tone filled with anguish. "I've been an imbecile blinded by arrogance and the fear of being without you. But never again. Your path is mine now, wherever it leads."

My eyes welled up with tears of joy and relief. Before I could stop myself, I thrashed the space between us and clung to him tightly, half-laughing and half-sobbing into his tunic. Marveling, his strong arm curled around me protectively, his free hand cradling my head against his chest.

When I pulled away, an air of playfulness had taken over me. "Does this mean you're staying?" I asked with a mischievous smile. "The people of Stonewall would be delighted to have the Lord of the Netherworld as our guest."

Hades arched one dark brow, his mouth quirking wryly. "I may not remain permanently in the lands above, my queen. But," he added quickly at my crestfallen look, "I swear to you, we will share our days between both realms. I wish only to be at your side."

I rose on tiptoe to press fervent kisses to his jaw, his neck, any patch of skin I could reach, as happiness overwhelmed me. Hades rumbled a satisfied laugh, smoothing back my windswept hair.

"However brief our stolen moments together," I told him earnestly, "we will cherish them. For you are my home, Hades, in any world."

Tenderly cradling my face in his broad hands, Hades replied, "And you are all the home I require, Persephone. In your arms, I am complete."

No further words were needed. We came together in a kiss that bridged the bitter separation of past days, replacing it with passion's sweetness. The future now stretched ahead brightly, full of promise and new beginnings.

Arm in arm, we lingered in the moonlit courtyard until the hour grew late and the feasting died down. And I nestled contentedly against Hades' side, unwilling to let this blissful reunion end.

Our love had weathered countless tempests, yet emerged unscathed. And even when untold trials lay ahead, together we would face them without fear.

# A NOTE FROM THE AUTHOR

Dear Reader,

*Write what you know,* they say. Well, if there's something I know about, it's death and dying.

In my new fantasy romance, *Steel and Stone,* we follow the hazardous journey of Aurora and Phillip through the mystical Netherworld. While fantastical in nature, this setting was inspired by my own brief yet profound encounter with the afterlife a few years ago.

When I was 37, an unexpected pregnancy complication brought me to the brink of death. As my body failed, I felt my consciousness plunge into an endless void. Suddenly, I found myself walking through a landscape of indescribable beauty. Lush gardens in full bloom stretched as far as the eye could see under azure skies. Every flower and tree radiated with ethereal light. I felt warm, loved, at peace—senses that exist beyond words.

In this moment, I knew I was crossing into whatever lay beyond our earthly realm. Though part of me missed the life and people I'd left behind, for the first time, I felt I was exactly where I was meant to be.

But my journey was not over. As swiftly as I arrived in this idyllic place, I was pulled back—reawakened by doctors as my loved ones silently grieved over me.

In the days spent between life and death that followed, I discovered untapped depths within myself. Emerging from the void at last, I gained a fresh perspective which has shaped me ever since.

Though fictional, the Realm of Death depicted in Steel and Stone echoes the peaceful beauty I was blessed to experience.

I was initially hesitant about openly discussing my near-death experience. After all, many dismiss these accounts, reducing them to hallucinations or chemical reactions in a dying brain. But the more I reflected, the more I found insights from my own brief glimpse of the beyond weaving themselves into this novel.

This book also explores the bonds of our souls that persist beyond earthly life. Aurora and Phillip's journey teaches that while death may separate us for a time, our connections with loved ones remain stronger than the veil between worlds. Love reaches across any divide. This truth resonates in my heart with each word written.

The mysticism of ancient cultures has always fascinated me as well. Like early societies, we cling to superstitions and rituals to feel some control over forces larger than ourselves. Aurora and Phillip encounter many mysteries as they navigate between fantastical realms. But their faith in one another is the greatest magic—there *is* true love in friendship.

In the end, I want readers to close this book with fresh inspiration—a renewed curiosity about life's greatest mysteries. Our existence may be short, yet it is incredibly meaningful. Make the most of your time here, and appreciate each breath as the gift it is.

*Steel and Stone* is a product of my own unexpected brush

with mortality. I hope my characters' courage in confronting death will uplift you. May their tale inspire you to embrace every moment.

So often we feel powerless before the unspeakable. But we have more strength than we know. The bonds of love light our way, even in the darkest hours. Hold onto hope, keep faith in your heart, and pursue joy. We are forever bound by the human experience we share.

With love and gratitude,
    Silvana.

# ACKNOWLEDGMENTS

As I reflect on the journey of writing *Steel and Stone*, I am filled with immense gratitude for the many people who helped bring this book to life.

First and foremost, I want to thank my incredible husband *Eric*. You have been my rock at every step of this writing process. From late-night brainstorming sessions to emergency coffee runs when I was on a deadline, you supported me with unwavering love and patience. Thank you for believing in me even when I doubted myself. Having you by my side makes everything possible.

To my sweet son *David*—you are my daily inspiration. Your boundless creativity, innocence, and capacity for joy motivate me to imagine beautiful worlds. When the writing got difficult, your smiles kept me going. One day, when you're *much older*, I hope you'll read my books and feel proud of what your mama created.

I'm eternally grateful to my mother, *Conchita*, for nurturing my passion for literature from my earliest days. You taught me how to find magic in stories and instilled confidence that I could craft my own someday.

I owe immense thanks to my cherished friend and editor, *Julie Cocaigne*. You pushed me to make this book the absolute best it could be. Your keen eye for pacing, voice and emotion always brings out depths I never knew were possible. Thank you for being my sounding board, voice of reason, and partner on this journey. I couldn't have done it without you.

I want to especially thank my high school best friend, *Miroslava Villegas*. You were my first reader and editor and encouraged me to pursue a career in writing. I'm grateful for your friendship and support.

Special thanks to my wonderful therapist, *Norma Sanz,* for her invaluable support through the emotional ups and downs of the writing process of this book. Our sessions provided me grounding, insight, and encouragement that was vital in keeping me motivated. I appreciate you more than words can express.

To the many loyal readers who have accompanied me through my writing career thus far—thank you hardly seems enough. Your constant encouragement and hunger for new worlds inspired me daily. Knowing you awaited this book kept me dedicated to crafting a novel that would move you. I write for you and because of you.

To the many book bloggers who previewed Steel and Stone and helped spread the word—I'm appreciative beyond measure. Know that your voice makes all the difference in introducing new books to eager readers. Thank you for taking a chance on my fantasy romance and sharing your honest thoughts.

I'm grateful to the bookstagrammers who created gorgeous visuals capturing the essence of my tale. Your artistry brought the book to life in stunning ways.

I'm thankful to the baristas at my local Starbucks. You fueled me through many long days of writing with perfectly crafted dairy-free frappuccinos.

And to all the authors who inspired me—your works nurtured my creativity. I stand on your shoulders. *I'm looking at you, Mss. Rice.*

Lastly, I want to thank YOU, the reader, for giving this

book a chance. I hope it transports you to fantastical realms and makes your heart swell. Thank you for coming along on Aurora and Phillip's journey. May their tale inspire you to have courage and hold onto hope. *Steel and courage to the end!*

With overflowing gratitude,
    Silvana.

# ABOUT THE AUTHOR

Silvana G. Sánchez is the USA TODAY bestselling author of sinfully addictive dark fantasy new adult novels *Ash and Snow, Steel and Stone, Written in Blood,* and more paranormal and fantasy romance stories, including the *Vesely Academy* series. She lives in Mexico with her husband Eric, her spirited son David, and two adorable Shih-Tzu pups she calls her dragons. When not plotting away in her writing den, she's known to poke eyes in her practice as an ophthalmologist.

*For more information:*
silvanagsanchez.com
sgs.author@gmail.com

www.ingramcontent.com/pod-product-compliance
Lightning Source LLC
Chambersburg PA
CBHW051306190726
48290CB00001B/28